ANNA'S
DANCE

A BALKAN ODYSSEY

MICHELE LEVY

Black Rose Writing | Texas

First printing

This is a work of fiction. Names, characters, businesses, places, events, and
incidents are either the products of the author's imagination or used in a
fictitious manner. Any resemblance to actual persons, living or dead, or
actual events is purely coincidental.

ISBN: 978-1-68433-486-5
PUBLISHED BY BLACK ROSE WRITING
www.blackrosewriting.com

Printed in the United States of America
Suggested Retail Price (SRP) $20.95

Anna's Dance is printed in Calluna

*As a planet-friendly publisher, Black Rose Writing does its best to eliminate
unnecessary waste to reduce paper usage and energy costs, while never compromising
the reading experience. As a result, the final word count vs. page count may not meet
common expectations.

Praise for

ANNA'S DANCE

"The year: 1968. On her odyssey: Anna, nearly done with college. One thing leads to another as she makes her way from Trieste, Italy, through Yugoslavia and Bulgaria to Istanbul, dipping in and out of danger, beauty, history, gracious hospitality, brutal politics, love, turmoil, music and dance."
— Ellen Elias-Bursać, President, American Literary Translators Association

"Prepare yourself to be swept away with Anna, a young American alone and adrift in the Balkans during the tumultuous year of 1968. As she strives to comprehend her own complex ethnic heritage, she finds herself woven into the yet more intricate tapestry of Macedonia, a palimpsest through which the region's bloody history can always be seen, faintly or with a stark violence that makes participants, and readers, catch their breath. Author Michele Levy's deep knowledge of this region and its many cultures is expressed through lovingly described food and music, architecture and landscape. This is a Romantic tale of passion, commitment, and danger, a thriller that you will not want to put down."
— Valerie Nieman, author of *To the Bones* and *Blood Clay*

"With a firm control of time, landscape, and geopolitical tension, Michele Levy has crafted a thoughtful, nuanced coming of age story about a sensitive woman in search of herself. A young American who longs to make sense of her Eastern European religious and familial past, Anna Rossi opens herself to adventures that bring profound changes to her life. Men whom Anna meets both protect and endanger her, while a fragile, beautiful relationship forms in a tiny Bulgarian mountain village not isolated enough from regional insurgency and national repression. Set in the turbulent late '60's when civil rights issues burned in America and national identities clashed in the Balkans, *Anna's Dance* gives us a memorable protagonist whose strength of character will be tested with every step she takes deeper into the living history of ethnic and ideological conflict."
— Thomas Phillips, Interdisciplinary Humanities, Wake Forest University

"This well-crafted, lyrical novel takes us straight into the fascinating world of Anna's heart. Exotic locales, enriched by history through the author's genius, function almost as characters within Anna's haunting love story."
— Sandra Sider, author of *Exploring Your Artistic Voice* and *Handbook to Life in Renaissance Europe*

"In this beautifully written novel, a young woman finds her own identity through a poignant love that reflects the history of the Macedonian people— their struggle for a land, a name, and human rights."
— Dragi Spasovski, renowned Macedonian singer-dancer

"*Anna's Dance* moves compellingly, hypnotically, through time and space, linking disparate histories of suffering— both individual and collective— uniting, perhaps healing, them through thoughtful, informed compassion. As Anna journeys toward self-acceptance and love, the reader is carefully led in a complex dance of knowledge and forgiveness, a dance whose steps bring us deep into the past and present of Europe and the United States. Exquisitely written and memorably shaped, Michele Levy's subtle, bold novel takes us to places known and unknown, helping us to find ourselves."
— Joyce Zonana, prize-winning literary translator and author of *Dream Homes: from Cairo to Katrina, an Exile's Journey*

To Mel, Marc, Jennifer, and Michael

ACKNOWLEDGMENTS

Throughout this long journey, I have had generous readers. My New Orleans writing group was with me at the start, while those in Greensboro saw me to the finish. Beta Readers from the Women's Fiction Writers Association raised vital questions for me to ponder and helped me hone the novel. Several good friends and my sister offered valuable encouragement and meticulous critiques. And, of course, my family gave me the time to write and think and dream. Finally, I thank Black Rose Writing for working with me to put together the final product, this book.

HOW TO PRONOUNCE SOUTH SLAVIC AND TURKISH WORDS AND NAMES

South Slavic

Vowels are short

	As in
a	ah
e	fed
i	bit
o	hot
u	bull

Letters that sound different from English or that have diacritical markings

	Sounds like	As in	Example
c	ts	cats	Divaca
č	ch	chin	čoček
ć	softer ch, like "ty"	picture	Petrić
đ	soft dy	judge	Doviđenja
j	y	yam	Jane*
š	sh	shell	Niš
ž	zh	pleasure	Živkov

*Each vowel is pronounced, so "Jane" is pronounced "Ya-ne."
If a male name ends in a consonant (like Trifon), an "e" is added when you address the person directly. So in dialogue, Trifon and Trifone refer to the same person.

Turkish

Vowels are also short except for "o," which is long as in "note."

Letters that have diacritical markings

	Sounds like	As in	Example
ç	ch	church	Dolmabahçe
ğ	soft g that lengthens the preceding vowel		Beyoğlu
ş	sh	shell	kuruş
ü	between a short and a long u	German *führer*	teşekkür

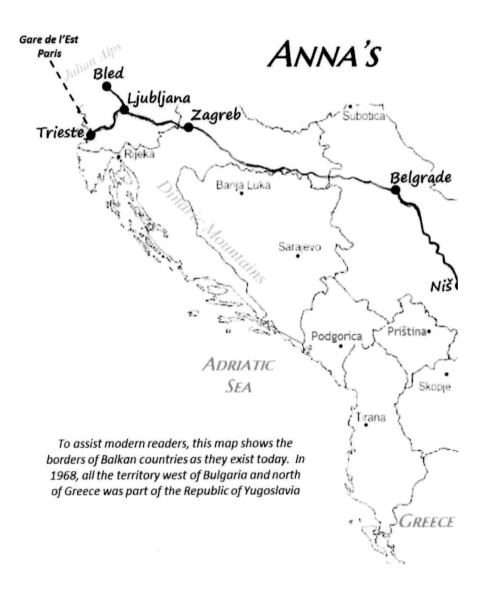

ANNA'S

Gare de l'Est
Paris

Julian Alps

Bled

Ljubljana

Zagreb

Trieste

Rijeka

Subotica

Banja Luka

Dinaric Mountains

Belgrade

Sarajevo

Niš

Podgorica

Priština

ADRIATIC
SEA

Skopje

Tirana

To assist modern readers, this map shows the
borders of Balkan countries as they exist today. In
1968, all the territory west of Bulgaria and north
of Greece was part of the Republic of Yugoslavia

GREECE

JOURNEY

ANNA'S DANCE

DANCE

A BALKAN ODYSSEY

TABLE OF CONTENTS

O body swayed to music, O brightening glance,
How can we know the dancer from the dance?

~William Butler Yeats, "Among School Children"

PRELUDE

ALONG THE HIGHWAY
SOMEWHERE EAST OF ZAGREB

June 23, 1968

Heat and dirt. The whir of tires against concrete. Sun waves scorch the shimmering surface of the autoroute. Beneath the huge sky only stunted bushes, hard-baked earth, and highway. Tiny cars like dolmas, stuffed with families and picnic gear, trail clouds of dust that choke Anna and Peter where they stand hugging the shoulder of the road.

Anna sighs. A bead of moisture trickles down between her breasts. The cotton blouse sticks to her skin. Beside her, Peter stoops beneath the weight of his backpack and sleeping bag, his blond-red beard shiny with sweat.

An almost empty car draws near. "Anna," Peter barks, "this one." But the ancient Peugeot darts past her out-stretched thumb. Peter scowls and makes a fist. He jerks back from the road and motions her to join him. "C'mon. We haven't got all day."

They'd spent two hours already. And though there was a Zagreb-Belgrade bus, Peter's hard stare told her he would keep on till they found a ride. She muttered, "I'm coming," and lurched along on swollen feet. This fourth day of their venture out from Trieste, the ease of their first meeting seemed a memory from long ago.

Peter pointed to a tall bush recessed from the road. "You stay here. I'll wait down there."

"Whatever you say, Master." She glared as he drew his long, powerful body up to its full height and stalked off toward the bush. Something inside her went hard. She hadn't crossed the Atlantic to play these games. But all-out war would be a risk right here, in the middle of nowhere. So she took up her position in the spot he'd designated.

The afternoon wore on. The cars rolled past. The riders' smiles and waves made Anna try to see herself as they would. A young woman alone. Dark hair Medusan. Body bent. Clothes dirt-streaked, sweat-soaked. Arm locked into hitchhiker position. Smile affixed with clothes pins. Hardly an alluring sight. So much for Peter's logic.

The steady hum of traffic lulled. The sun-inscribed white circles dimmed her vision. Anna lapsed out, thoughtless, until a huge Mercedes zoomed past, haloed by the rays that struck its shiny black and chrome veneer. Metallic edges sharply defined space, then vanished into sun-fog once again.

Brakes screeched. A car backed up. A door opened, then shut.

Damn Peter. They'd returned for her. A clear breech of road etiquette. That summer's rule for drivers, at least according to the hitchhikers she'd met, was a gradual stop, a pulled-down window, and an amiable inquiry as to destination. Her neck went cold beneath the sweaty knot of long, thick hair. But she would enter the car; she had reached her limit.

Lowering her gaze, she sniffed the air. No alcohol, at least. Then she straightened up and dared to look, which didn't help at all. Had she gone stupid from the sun?

The car was empty. Before her stood its occupant. Arms crossed, head cocked, he flashed an imperious smile. The man was slim and little more than average in height, but his clothes drew her attention, defying both the intense heat and the spartan South Slav dress code. A loose-fitting but well-cut navy linen jacket. A crisp white linen shirt, open at the throat. Knife-creased ecru linen slacks. Italian-cut black loafers, elegant against the dusty road. A Greek fisherman's cap thrust rakishly back on the head. He looked like an ad for single malt in a glossy magazine.

Anna caught a whiff of lime and musk. Her cheeks grew hot, then hotter still when she saw him record the blush. She wanted him to speak, but he said nothing. Just nodded, on his lips a cool, sardonic smile that seemed to acknowledge her unspoken thoughts. Unwrinkled, well-groomed, the man exuded an impossible freshness. Apparition? Mirage? Clearly a miracle, given the conditions everyone else was subject to this Sunday on the autoroute to Belgrade.

She studied his face. Dark. Smooth-shaven. Slavic? Features precisely balanced, as if Europe had softened its eastern angles. High cheekbones, but not too prominent. Dark eyes with a hint of slant. Jawline well defined but rather narrow. Something in the look evoked medieval knights and poets, Byzantines and Ottomans. She—

"Anna." Peter's voice was cold. He'd wandered up from his bush and stood beside her.

The stranger watched in silence. Anna thought she caught a flicker of disappointment as he rubbed his chin and volunteered, "*Une jeune couple.*" Sweeping off his black cap to reveal a head of dark, luxuriant hair, he bowed first to her, then to Peter, whose rigid mouth and squinting eyes condemned them both. "*Vous êtes très fatigués?*" His wry smile mocked his halting French.

"*Nous ne sommes pas français,*" she retorted, brushing aside a piece of hair that had flopped into her eye. "*Je suis américaine*—Anna Rossi."

Peter's blue eyes seethed. He stood rigid and silent.

"American?" The stranger's eyebrows arched. "Rossi?"

Anna's body stiffened. His accent sounded German. And why was he so puzzled?

Observing Peter's red face, he asked, still smiling, "And your friend?"

"He's Danish. Peter Hansen." Why had he chosen French? Her sun-bronzed skin? Her blue eyes, black-lined, thick-lashed? The narrow oval face? The nose some called "exotic"? People would refer to Cleopatra or Durrell's Justine, then ask where she came from.

"Ah, myself I am a German. Max Heidl, at your service." He gave a little bow.

German? Anna stiffened. But the man shook hands with both of them, and his rogue's grin beguiled even Peter, who smiled back. She let herself relax, her mind shift gears, her body loosen.

"And now," Max Heidl asked, "where do you go?"

"Belgrade." Peter had finally found his voice.

The German shrugged as if there were no other answer. "So we must put the bags away, isn't it?" Picking up her canvas satchel from Trieste, he headed toward the car.

The pristine trunk was empty save for one leather suitcase. "Brand new," Peter whispered, sniffing the inside. She wasn't sure whether he meant the suitcase or the car.

Heidl stowed her dusty bag alongside his fine black one, then let Peter fling his heavy roll and backpack in on top. Helping her into the plush back seat, he motioned Peter to the front. Before he put the key in the ignition, the man turned around to her. Bright-eyed, he doffed his cap and flashed that impish grin. "Your chauffeur, Mademoiselle."

In the speeding Mercedes Anna felt light. Peter and the driver—Max, she reminded herself—bantered back and forth in Germanic English, trying to include her. But she began to disengage, yearning to be still and float.

Now and then a phrase of theirs broke through her mental screen. "In Trieste . . . to Skopje . . . from Munich . . ." She wondered vaguely about the dashing German but didn't have the energy to follow these unfolding plots. Instead, she let the talk bounce off her while she savored being quiet and alone.

As she burrowed into the soft leather seat, she caught the rush of air through the open window, the rhythmic throb of rubber against the road. With growing lethargy, she fielded questions from the front. These two might pass the time telling their pilgrims' tales; she would free her mind to drift . . .

PART I: BEFORE

WASHINGTON, DC

Spring, 1968

Anna flinched as Sari poked her shoulder.

"Over there," her friend whispered, "that's him."

"Who?" Anna was snapping her fingers to the rhythm of the music, a song she liked, a dance she wished she were doing. But they hadn't ordered yet and she was hungry.

"The man from your doodle. Your dreams."

"Huh? Where?"

"The guy you always draw. You know. The cheekbones, the chin—"

Sari stopped speaking as the man she'd pointed out moved toward their table, his muscular body constrained by the red-sashed pseudo-sailor's uniform. The regulation polyester bell-bottoms stretched tight across muscular thighs. His broad chest and shoulders rose from a narrow waist.

Sari was right. For years Anna had drawn him, the handsome but dangerous creature that stalked her dreams. Eyes hungry. Two slashes of protruding bone over hollow cheeks. Full lips pulled tight in a sneer. The cleft chin a call to arms. Hands like the giant paws of a nightmare cat, with thick, brutal fingers that didn't come naturally to holding a tray.

"I take your order?" Heavy Greek accent. Low voice like coarse sand. The brash stare framed by thick black curls.

Anna cleared her throat. "Two glasses of retsina and an order of calamari." Jotting down his hieroglyphs, he stared at her. Trying for a casual tone, she added, "Thanks." With a quick smile he left for the kitchen.

Soon he appeared with their orders, setting down beside the squid a plate of fried *kasseri*.

"This must belong to someone else," she said.

The waiter shook his head and kept his eyes on her. "For you."

"Thanks." She wondered who'd sent it. Likely Nico, the maître d' of the Athens West, the Astor's small upstairs music venue. He sometimes made such gestures to the regulars.

They'd never had a more attentive waiter. But every time he checked on them, he treated her as if she were alone.

Already the band was playing good *zembeikiko*. Below the stage, on the wooden dance floor circled by small tables, a wiry-haired man rolled his belly like a woman. The diners whistled, clapping out the rhythm. Someone yelled, "*Opa*!" It would be a lively night. But Sari's ashtray was almost full and Anna felt the squid and cheese making hard lumps in her stomach.

When the waiter returned, she traded nods with Sari. "Check, please."

Once he brought the bill, they cleared out quickly, leaving a decent tip beside their half-empty plates and glasses.

He headed them off at the stairs and took her arm just hard enough to show he meant business. Sari stared as Anna shuddered at his sudden touch.

"I Mikis." He jerked his chin in her direction. "You?"

When she mumbled, "Anna," she saw Sari shake her head.

"Oikay, Anna. You give me your number." He held out a pen and napkin.

She wrote it down and handed it back without meeting his eyes.

Despite all logic, she'd obliged, curious to peer into the psyche of a man like this. Raw energy and power, he aroused less her desire than a certain envy. How must it feel to own this massive body? Its arrogant swagger? Its unselfconscious physicality? The look that simultaneously sized her up, ingested, and expelled her? What did this body know that hers could not? Still, she wondered why this mattered to her.

Outside the Astor, Sari gave a little laugh. "I feel rather left out. I guess he prefers blue eyes and long, dark hair."

Anna recalled that, a few weeks before, a tourist had made moves on Sari. "My turn tonight." Then they set out for the Atherton, their Foggy Bottom walkup.

* * *

The following Friday evening Mikis filled her narrow hallway, dwarfing the upright piano. He held his upper body like a dancer. Taut, but not rigid. Moving from the hips, he trailed her into the room that held her private universe. He said nothing, but his eyes never left her as she sat down in the wicker rocker, clutching the afghan like a talisman. She rocked slowly and waited.

His movements meticulous, Mikis undressed in the dim light from the lamp on the bedside table. He kept staring at her. She rocked and rocked, a metronome marking out the rhythm, to resist the force of those opaque brown eyes. He took his time folding his clothes—jacket, jeans, blue shirt, white briefs—and placed them on the table, depositing his shoes and socks beneath. In the half-light, a gold cross glittered on his strangely hairless chest. Eyes cold and distant under heavy lids, he resembled a column of sculpted bronze. She held the afghan close.

Then he thrust back the cover on the bed and stretched out on its narrow length, transforming her room with a blatant sexuality that oozed beyond the confines of the flat. Still she rocked as he consumed her space.

At last he rose, came to the chair, and stopped her motion with his arm. He lifted her onto the bed and took off her clothes with far less regard than he'd given his own.

They spoke no words, the only sounds sharp thrusts and grunts. She felt him hot and hard inside her, pounding, stirring, crushing her will with the force of that strong body that was finally everywhere. But she willed herself to drift away, to move beyond sensation, brought back to the bed only by a gut-wrenching groan that sounded like some force were squeezing the life from her lover.

A quick glance at Mikis confirmed a different story. Face against the pillow, left arm flung across her, he was breathing hard. His eyes were closed, lips parted in a smile, as if after a fierce combat he'd slain the dragon and claimed the princess as his prize. He turned to kiss her neck and stroke her sweaty hair, then finally broke the silence, whispering, "*Koritsi mou.*"

His little girl, indeed.

The next Friday he came again. Entering her room, its window fan humming noisily, he sang dark, broken tones that merged into a plaintive melody filled with *mavra matia*—black eyes—and a sorrow that rose from some empty space inside him. He seemed almost to chant the words as he undressed, until at last he stood silhouetted in the light beyond the window. She blocked the images of love and loss his song evoked. They made her want to look for explanations. Had she only dreamed last Friday night?

"Anna, Anna." He lifted her from the rocker like a doll, placed her on the bed, and undressed her with great care. As his huge hands caressed her body, he mumbled to himself. Then he cupped her chin and, looking straight into her eyes, asked a question she couldn't decipher, in the softest Greek she'd ever heard.

His eyes implored. "*Agapi mou. Agapi mou.*" My love, my love. Over and over he murmured her name, stroking her as he might a child.

She lay still, barely breathing, not wanting to interrupt whatever he was going through. And when he entered, it was softly, like a breeze rustling the curtains. His body touched hers with tenderness.

She didn't want him like this, offering more than she needed. She fought to keep a distance. "Anna, Anna," he whispered, moving above her with a gentle force that should have carried her away. But the harder he thrust, the farther she withdrew. At last he came with a short cry and a great heave. Then he lay back on the bed, exhausted. A thousand miles away from him, her head on his chest, Anna ached for them both.

Night closed in around them. Lying sleepless by his sleeping body, she wondered what his dreams might be. Or hers. She tried to fathom what had happened here, what might come next, and whether such encounters could help her uncover her soul or find her a place in the world.

The Astor crowd all knew they were an item. Especially Panos Kotsis, who would needle her for stooping to the level of a Mikis. "Guys like him could never get near a girl like you back home." A wealthy lawyer's son from Patras, sometime bartender, and eternal graduate student in economics, Panos scorned "Greece jocks," his name for those poor Greeks who made it to America, worked the restaurants, and maneuvered short-lived marriages to well-heeled local women. Still, Panos allowed, "Mikis has a good heart. Just doesn't know a thing. No education. Comes from some drab village where they have only tradition." He winked at her. "You're too much for him, Anna."

One Tuesday at the Astor, Panos asked, "So, Anna. Want to know why Mikis takes his Tuesdays off?"

"It's not my business, is it?"

Panos took a long drag on his Chesterfield. "Maybe not. But maybe you should know. He studies English at the Y." He paused. Looked straight into her eyes. "For you."

All that spring semester, Mikis was her Friday night. He would come after the Astor closed at two. After an official date would bring her home. But never in the daylight.

Late one evening, as they lay quiet in her bed, Mikis turned to her and said, "Anna." He spoke her name like an incantation, his fine teeth gleaming in a radiant smile. "*Kukla mou.*" My little doll.

She saw him as a shark. But if *she* were a shark, she would devour the doll.

He reached out to caress her arm. The moonlight showed his smiling eyes, in which she glimpsed the two of them long married, raising curly-headed moppets, working hard at life together. The vision terrified her. How had she let him into her bed in the first place, with his animal eyes and his hard, hungry stare that hid such desperate longings for love and possession?

Lurking in the background, more threatening than the savage power that still excited her, was the story she read in that look—of his nightly returns from a tedious job to their neat suburban cottage, where he swept her into his arms, hugged and kissed their children, and sat at the cozy dinner table to eat the meal she'd made with love, happy to be home at last. She might have dreams like his sometimes, but she couldn't pay the price, couldn't forge a bond with him, couldn't lose a self she hadn't found. With all those stares, had he missed this?

How could she, mere flotsam in a swirling sea, become his sanctuary? She had no goals, no visions of a future for herself. Once, she'd planned to be either a pianist or a PhD. But her first college semester revealed these as her parents' dreams for her. Yes, she loved the piano. By fifteen a local prodigy, she'd performed in benefit concerts with members of the National Symphony. But she'd never be a Rubenstein. There was no point.

And yes, she read with passion, especially literature and history, which honed her perceptions and stirred her imagination as they let her enter other lives. But Bryn Mawr's ivied walls had stifled her. Each Monday on her trek to Manhattan for piano lessons, she'd welcomed the bustle of Grand Central Station and Times Square. Yet the Paoli Local would carry her back to empty midnight streets, and the Lantern Man, like Diogenes, would escort her across the silent campus to her tiny, distant cloister. By spring semester she'd come to see herself as a set of random chromosomes adrift in a meaningless life. Before the end of that first year, she'd fled college and family. Later, she'd found a way to balance work and school, fully committing to neither.

Useless, weak, a creature of clashing impulses, she didn't trust human connection. She was good at flirtation, and sexual games promised power. To outwit an opponent, to upstage an arrogant man, gave her a rush, a validation, even at the sacrifice of pleasure. But now Mikis demanded more than sex. She'd have to step away. And yet . . . and yet . . . something lay beneath these thoughts. But she couldn't find it, couldn't name what haunted her.

One Sunday afternoon she was spring-cleaning. She'd put a record on to energize her, a long-ignored LP of Greek island music. The chorus of young girls was pure, but the songs did nothing for her. They had no sensuality or heartache. She was about to change to some *zembeikiko* when Mikis showed up at the door, something he'd never done before in daylight.

Reluctant to admit him, she watched his lips part in a smile so innocent that she could see the child he once had been. His eyes softened. His face relaxed. Was it memory that filled him with such peace? Searching for the right word, he found, "Pretty." Then he added, "Very nice, this music." He moved toward the stereo.

Eyes nearly closed, he raised his cleft chin toward her. "You like, Anna?" She said nothing but sent a look that showed her scorn.

He winced, swallowed, then asked, reduced, "I borrow?"

"Sure." She handed him the record as if it were a filthy diaper.

Mikis demanded too much of her now. He had to go. But how and when she wasn't sure.

It happened in her bedroom at the end of March, when he said, "I care for you, Anna. I want to see you more."

Her fears fulfilled, she spoke the words she'd practiced. "Mikis, this must stop. I've met someone else." That line usually worked.

His eyes grew wide. Then he stared straight at her, lips together in a sneer she knew by now was pure defense. "You full of shit, bitch lady."

Ashamed, she said, "I'm sorry," and she was.

She hung up when he called and boycotted the Astor.

* * *

One April evening heavy with the fragrance of new growth, a fine, crisp breeze floated the last of the cherry blossoms up from the Ellipse. She couldn't bear to sit at home and study. She phoned Sari, and off they went to the Astor, where Mikis never worked on Tuesdays. They walked; the night was lovely. But by the time they hit Pennsylvania Avenue, she was seeing Mikis behind every tree.

The Astor had a good crowd for a weeknight. The few tourists were gone by twelve. Then the Greeks showed up, the belly dancer disappeared, and the band grew livelier. She and Sari joined a coed *tsamiko* and never sat again. Lots of *tsiftitelli* and *syrto*. Dancing straight till two.

They left the club elated. But after several blocks she felt on edge. Only street lamps lit the dark. Their footsteps echoed on deserted sidewalks. All the way home the trees seemed to have eyes.

When they reached the Atherton, she stopped for a nightcap at Sari's, where drinks and gossip calmed her. Then she tiptoed to her third-floor corner flat in a fairly tranquil state. Once inside her doorway, she chided herself for her fears.

The air was close. She opened the windows wide to catch what remained of the night. After a quick shower, she burrowed into the crisp cotton sheets and let her body relax.

A knock. A hoarse whisper. "*Agapi mou. Agapi mou.*" Another knock.

She lay still as the door began to vibrate on its hinges. The thick lock rattled. The whispers continued. Urgent. Electric.

"Anna. Anna."

She trembled in the bed grown cold. How had her name become a lover's chant? Love was the end of a journey she hadn't begun. Marriage meant four walls. But he defined those words so differently.

Knocks became hard thuds. The floor began to shake. How much could the door withstand? Lucky her only next-door neighbor was almost perpetually stoned.

She lay rigid and shivered. Held her breath. Her body ached from trying to keep still, from fighting off the part of her that longed to let him in—to be the one who gave him what he yearned for. She could never tell him why it had to end, why she couldn't unlock the door. She didn't know herself. Those lessons he was taking wouldn't help. Even in English they spoke two different languages.

At last the whispers ceased. The banging stopped. The door became itself. She felt her muscles loosen, took a deep breath, and wiped tears from her cheeks. In the night silence, she heard a muffled groan and the sound of footsteps in retreat.

She woke at eight o'clock the next morning. She'd have to call; she'd never make the Institute by nine. The sun streamed through her rough blue burlap curtains, promising another day of work and school. She ate two spoons of oatmeal, then set the bowl aside. It wouldn't fill her hunger.

Opening the door to get the paper, she found the borrowed record on the mat.

THE ORIENT EXPRESS

June 18, 1968
Gare de l'Est, Paris
Excitement kept Anna awake while Claudia slept. Leaving their *couchette*, she tiptoed to the next car and found an empty compartment. Dim light from the hallway seeped through the thick glass window in the door. Alone in the dark, she stared out at the Alps. Even in this velvet black studded with stars, the peaks were monumental.

Footsteps stopped outside. The door creaked open. Anna cringed.

A head thrust in—the young man with the tickets from the station. His eyes wide under thick eyebrows, he gestured in a way she couldn't read. Of course, she shouldn't have been here. Afraid to speak, she found a grin she hoped looked innocent. His face, so un-French in its width, seemed somehow sympathetic. She half feared, even so, that he would force her from the seat. But he vanished down the corridor without a word.

Several minutes later he returned. He opened the door with care, a finger to his lips, and signaled his desire to join her. She nodded, hoping she'd concealed her shiver. Once he sat down facing her, they studied each other for a moment.

"So, Miss, you cannot sleep?"

Thank God he'd begun, and in English. "I should. I'm really tired." She chose her words with care, enunciating clearly so he could understand. "But I just can't let go. I've dreamed of riding the Orient Express since I was small, and it doesn't look like there'll be many more chances."

The boy nodded. "They say it will not last much longer. Even now, they chop the schedule. Mostly it is for tourists." His tone seemed to exclude her from that group.

"It must have been quite something once."

"Many years ago, I think." He grinned. "Before the war. At least that is what I have heard."

Given his comfort with English, Anna dropped the care she used in cross-cultural exchanges, speaking instead as she would to some acquaintance in DC. "For me, the name is magic, like a spell. And I may never get nearer the Alps—"

"Why? I do not understand."

His question disturbed her. She and Claudia could have stopped in Austria and Germany on the way to Italy. Why had she ruled out the northern route? She didn't have an answer. Perhaps sensing her unease, he didn't press her further.

"We are near the last car here. So when we reach the next station, there will be dim light and you will see something of the mountains." Then he smiled. "Maybe you are hungry?"

For hours she'd fought the gnawing in her stomach. Neither she nor Claudia had thought to buy food at the station, and the dining car was overpriced. "A little. Isn't it too late?"

"The dining car is closed, but if you would accept to share my loaf and ham. I have a bit of bad wine, too."

"That's kind of you. I . . . I don't even know your name."

"Daniel." He rose and extended his hand. "Daniel Iliev. And you are Anna Rossi."

Before she could ask, he said, "I saw your papers."

Now she remembered. She kept the Eurail Pass inside her passport. He'd held it no more than an instant.

Daniel left to fetch their midnight snack. He was back in a flash and they feasted on crusty bread and slabs of ham, washed down with gulps of not-so-rotten wine in paper cups. By the time they shared the bar of Belgian chocolate, they were friends.

Afterward he lowered his voice, speaking fast, as if time were running out. "Until last year I studied at the Sorbonne. Philosophy and Art." His voice faltered a bit. "Then my father died." He shook his head, as if to dispel an unwelcome vision.

"Oh, no. Had he been sick?"

"He had a weak heart, a hard life. He left Bulgaria at fifteen, joined the Resistance in the war, and stayed in Paris after. He married, had his family, and watched his homeland trade fascists for communists. He said it made no difference. People suffered under both. But he hated Živkov for his cruelty, his prison camps and torture. Said the guy took orders from Moscow."

"It must be hard when politics destroys your home country—though maybe now it's happening in mine. But, honestly, I don't know much about Bulgaria."

"Like most people." He smiled.

"I'm sorry about your father."

"We were lucky. Their marriage was happy. We loved each other. Still, to watch life wear him down, to see him grow so tired. One day he never woke up. He was only forty-seven." Daniel sighed. "My mother and my sisters needed help, so I work on this train."

"I know it's not the same," she hoped her words wouldn't seem frivolous, "but my mother's father died at forty-nine. Cancer. When my mother turned fifty last fall, she said that for the first time, she realized how much he'd lost, how much he hadn't lived."

"Maybe I will, too, when I have those years. But now I wonder what he would think about the world today."

Daniel's words kept coming at her as if the spies were out in force and he had only moments to impart some secret code. At first, he'd mourned his rotten luck, his dead father, the studies put aside. But now, the Sorbonne closed, the students emptied out, he felt ambivalent.

"You cannot imagine it, Anna." He gestured vaguely into space, his eyes inviting her to share his vision.

And so she did—the lines of French police with tear gas bayonets pointed at students in sweaters and jackets, their faces angry masks, teeth bared, fists raised—exactly like the Vietnam protest on the Mall last October. The same rage and frustration brimming over. Impotence on both sides. She'd been eating leftover Chinese one night in early May when the radio announced, "They've shut down the Sorbonne."

"Police, students, the craziness and screaming." Daniel's head turned suddenly. He was staring at the windowpane as if it showed his past. "Exciting, you know. But ugly, too, like a bad movie, too much pleased with itself, too much enjoying to break the rules. And so now what will happen?" He stopped to take a breath. "I do not see really what we want. Perhaps that is the problem. We do not know what we need. Only that there must be something else. But how are we to find it?"

A pause. He shook his head and gazed out at the mountains rushing by. "To look for God in mushrooms, along the road to Kathmandu? Merde." He pressed his forehead against the glass, as if he required its cold to soothe his skin.

His words evoked Berkeley, San Francisco, LSD-laced parties at the Atherton. "I know exactly what you mean. I saw it in Haight Ashbury last summer. All the kids wanting escape, release, some sort of answer. Me, too, I guess, though not with drugs—they make me too depressed."

He nodded. "And even with this noise we make, this craziness for travel, maybe, after all, we go nowhere." His hands worked at the braiding on his cap. "Even the two of us. This train. For you, maybe, it is still adventure. For me, only routine. Back and forth, moving in circles, never getting anywhere. I wish I can read the future. To know if there is really a place in it for me." Resting against the wall, he shut his eyes. At last he rose. Excused himself. The station was near. He had duties. "I will come back later," he whispered, shutting the door behind him quietly.

The compartment felt so empty now. His words trailed down the tracks, leaving behind a palpable dread that conjured up the bloody spring in Washington. On the fire escape outside her living room, she'd stared out at the smoke from burning buildings, a mad tribute to Martin Luther King, Jr. First his death, then My Lai, and only days ago she'd learned that Bobby Kennedy had been murdered in some LA hotel. She felt what Daniel had described. An emptiness. The sense of a world spinning out of control. Events had blurred, merged. Which had come first? All of them linked to the horror she and her classmates had witnessed in the Bryn Mawr smoker. Students gathered there, to study, relax, or watch TV, had looked up from their notebooks just in time to catch the end of Camelot.

A whistle pierced the night. The train slowed to a stop. From within the warm drowse of the wine, Anna looked out on another world. Silent and still in the deep night, medieval chalets stood watch over mountains still white-topped in June, outlined by the moon, the stars, and the dim light from the distant station lamps. A place of perfect beauty. She opened the window. Inhaled the cold night air. Her mind flooded with images from Christmas cards and Advent calendars. Of sleeping, snowed-in hamlets that beckoned a cozy warmth. Inside her head, soprano voices sang pure melodies.

From the earthy medieval ballads to the spiritual eroticism of Bach's eternal ebbs and flows and the richly sensual textures of the Brahms quartets, the glorious strains of Germanic music had resonated throughout her youth—which she'd brought to passionate life with a string of Johanneses and Ernsts. Weaving the crystalline patterns of the music, one with her piano and the players, she would herself become a crystal, perfect and lustrous, at once ice and heat. Why had she bypassed the North?

The question edged its way under her skin and made the scenes she'd never lived grow darker; their picture-postcard perfection summoned images of the Holocaust and fragments from her past. Sudden random shards of memory hurtled into one another. Vied for her attention—

The tales her mother, Ruth, told her, of poverty and exclusion. When the Minneapolis Symphony had laid off players during the Depression, Ruth's violinist father had become a Willy Loman—a traveling soap salesman who died at forty-nine.

The Indiana years of being bullied. The shame of being called "those Jews."

Despite Ruth's mathematics scholarship for anywhere she chose, the interviewer at Purdue's engineering school said, "We can't admit you. You're a woman and a Jew."

A Chicago cinema late in the war. Many cheered when the newsreel spoke of Hitler's killing Jews. In her naval ensign's uniform, Ruth rose and shouted, "I'm a Jew." Then she left the silent theater.

After Anna's birth, Ruth's widowed mother took the train from Indianapolis to Providence to see her first-born grandchild. But Anna's mother and father were living in the carriage house of her paternal grandparents: her Irish-American grandmother, Fiona, and her Lower East Side Jewish grandfather, Asher. Fiona refused to admit "that filthy immigrant Jew" until Ruth threatened to leave and take Anna with her. No wonder Anna's father, Connor, had broken down at Harvard, torn between his mother and his wife, angry at his parents' attitudes.

The visit of three unimposing strangers to the law office of Connor's father, Asher. A well-known patent attorney, Asher had cast off his Lower East Side origins by marrying Fiona. His family ties severed, he'd let her raise his son Catholic. Asher asked Ruth, who was helping out that day, to bring coffee and shut the door. Entering with a tray, she caught the four speaking Yiddish, her stern, reserved father-in-law guffawing and making hand gestures—unable to reclaim his heritage except behind closed doors.

Then images stamped from her own life. Belle Terre, the DC suburb where she'd grown up. A fifties wave of Eastern intellectuals, many of them Jews, had bought its glass and aluminum split-levels, strewn far apart among tree-lined hills. Despite its award for excellent design, indignant locals and their children labeled it "The Ghetto."

The country club a short drive from her family's home, a white-columned icon of Virginia's antebellum past, the collective myth of those nearby who dressed their brick traditionals in bronze-eagle doorknockers, Confederate flags, and backyard bomb shelters. Its restricted membership allowed no Jews.

A nondescript commercial street in Arlington, where Connor slowed the car and pointed out a dull storefront only a half hour from their home. "George Lincoln Rockwell's headquarters." At twelve, she hadn't recognized the name. "The Nazi party, Anna. Right here in our backyard." That hate, so close, scared her.

In ninth grade, Robby Beckman, a hell-raiser from the trailer court on Route #1 by the drive-in, had tagged her "Miss Israel." Then sophomore year and Mr. Denby, her algebra teacher—the principal made him change her grade from C to A. Ignoring her presence in the room and his own grade book that clearly showed her As, the skinny aging man in thick glasses and poorly tailored suit asked, "Why do this? They're not like us." Under the principal's glare, he added, like a child whose world had come undone, ". . . are they?"

The news last year of Rockwell's death, murdered by one of his own. The casserole dish flew from Anna's hands. She clutched the sink amid slivers of glass, her fingers bright with blood, afraid despite the presumed safety of her flat, reminded once again how this hate lived.

An April lecture at Georgetown on rising anti-Semitism in Europe. The catalogue of horrors over, she said to the boy who'd taken her, "It's almost as if the Holocaust never happened. As if it's fallen out of history." He nodded, "Right. Only its victims have the bad grace to remember."

Last summer over marinated lamb at Mama Ayesha's, her Palestinian friend Mahmoud criticized Israel's response to a Syrian attack from the Golan Heights. "The whole world," she was moved to say, "would have let the Germans rid it of its Jews. Don't Jews have the right to defend themselves, like everyone else? Must they only passively absorb this hate?"

Mahmoud stared into his demitasse. "Perhaps you're right, Anna. But understand the cost. My own countrymen," he whispered, "murder innocents. Can this be justified? Can any of us escape the circle?"

As Anna stared out at the mountains now, she pondered Mahmoud's question. Could she ever escape the circle, make peace with her identity? She lived in the gap between feeling and reason, yearning to belong but fearing others' labels. To her friends, she was the "exception Jew." But she remembered pointed fingers, sly nods, winks that said, "Ah, yes. A good disguise, but now we see the truth. You're one of them." Would she always dread exposure?

Safe was separate. Good was free of guilt. Love thy neighbor as thyself, though he might long to murder thee. But Israel had won October's Six Day War. Etched upon the psyche of that state, like the numbers in the flesh of the survivors who'd helped to build it, she read the bitter truth that Might makes Right. Perhaps the world had changed since her parents were young. But it seemed to her that anti-Semitism had only moved underground. Like her mother, Ruth, she felt isolated, insecure, and vulnerable.

By the time Daniel returned, Anna was sweating despite the cold that came through the closed window. How could she explain herself to him? The North was too complex for her, its depths incomprehensible, merging "Silent Night" and Schubert lieder with lampshades of skin and soap from Jewish bones. This place seemed utterly pure. Like Keats' unravished bride, it rose up cold and perfect and unfathomable. Yet its serene exteriors hid a world of charm and danger that seduced her with its beauty and froze her with its power. She wasn't quite sure where these mountains were—Switzerland, Germany, Austria? She hadn't paid attention to the route. But here, despite their beauty, she felt herself an outsider. And that, she guessed, explained why she'd chosen the southern route.

She and Daniel exchanged addresses and assurances that each would write. When Anna's eyes began to close, he produced a heavy blanket. Wrapping it around her, he gave his warmest smile and hearty Gallic kisses on both cheeks.

She fell asleep, and when the Italian sun woke her in the morning, her newest friend was gone and she had to look for Claudia.

TRIESTE

June 20, 1968

Alone on her high rock, Anna watched the boats float idly on the Adriatic, as if like her they had no place to go. The sun whitened the sky. Behind the cliffs, just up the beach of grainy sand, stood the youth hostel. Beside her lay the sequined Indian bag, a relic from Haight Ashbury last summer that held her wallet, documents, and daily needs. Near it stood a small white Samsonite suitcase, packed with what she'd chosen for this trip.

Her lap cradled the crumpled note she'd found on Claudia's empty cot after breakfast. Her friend's unease aboard the ship had lessened in England but worsened in France. She'd said her stomach couldn't take French food, too rich, had begged Anna to make all the decisions and connections. Claudia's sudden departure had shocked Anna and made her feel guilty, as if she'd caused the break—although she'd always done what Claudia asked.

Again she forced herself to read the blue ink marks, in case they'd somehow changed since she last looked:

Anna,

I'm not like you. It's too much stress. I need routine. I can't communicate or eat the food. I've had enough of chaos and imposed rusticity. I'm flying back to London for a while, then home. You're better off without me.

Sorry,
Claudia

Shutting her eyes against the light, Anna heard the surf pummel the rock, the distant buzz of human speech, the soft breeze stirring papers, sails, and beach gear. Claudia's note seemed to close the path that had opened on Christmas morning.

She could still see that tree, so regal standing next to the piano. Each year Connor would search until he found the perfect evergreen, tall, straight, branches full, symmetrical. Sometimes they would visit several tree lots. Three days earlier they'd held the trimming party. Her friend Claudia, home for the week, had sacrificed an Early Music program at the Cathedral to come and help. Glühwein. Christmas pastries. Caroling. Anna had played the piano. Her younger sister, Miriam, had sung with great enthusiasm, her fourteen-year-old's reedy voice off pitch.

First the lights, set in with extravagant care. Then the ornaments, each with its own history. This little clown from the Donovans, Fiona's New York family. That sad angel from the summer house of her parents' artist friend in Ogunquit, Maine. Last, they'd hung the tinsel, strand by strand. Lit up, the tree shimmered in pagan beauty.

The ritual. The ornaments. Relics of Connor's bitterly rejected Catholic upbringing. With just a passing nod to Hanukkah, her secular Jewish parents made Christmas the highpoint of their year—rounds of parties, the ideal tree, the gifting ceremony. All this from intellectuals who professed a clear-eyed atheism.

She'd never understood it. Unless it was that they embraced the bright-lit Christian holiday to escape, as Asher had, the dark spirituality of their East European forebears. In her favorite family myth, the priest warned Connor, an altar boy, that Asher would burn in hellfire for having gone unbaptized. That news had prompted serious reflection, and by the time Connor joined the Navy to fight Hitler (though they'd sent him to the Philippines), the former altar boy had disavowed his Catholic roots, denounced the clergy, and become an atheist. But when the Great Lakes Naval Base had forced him to declare a religion, he'd named himself a Jew. By Jewish law, of course, Connor didn't qualify—his mother was a Donovan.

This history still confused her, as did its undercurrents. When she was young, they'd spent most Christmases with Asher and Fiona in their antebellum mansion close to Brown. Fiona, whom Ruth had said often denigrated Jews although she'd married one, would take Anna to Midnight

Mass and ply her with lavish gifts. A somber disciplinarian, Asher remained in the shadows and followed his passion, Asian art. Connor, a product of Catholic schools until he went to Brown, had angered Fiona, whom Anna adored, when he'd become a Jew. And then he'd had the nerve to wed the daughter of impoverished Eastern European Jewish immigrants.

Yet despite Connor's breakdown at Harvard when Anna was three, Ruth's recurrent bouts of deep depression, and their often spiteful skirmishes, they adored each other and maintained this family tradition. Every year at Christmas, Anna returned for a short stay but always left before their sniping resumed. At least for a few days, peace reigned in the Rossi household.

Exquisite packages lay beneath the tree on Christmas morning. Miriam laughed as Connor, ruddy-faced, his thick hair mussed, snapped posed pictures. Ruth, still lovely, served coffee and fresh-baked stollen in her long, pink-velvet hostess gown. They opened the presents one by one, smiling for the camera.

"Anna, Mimi, careful with the wrapping," Ruth admonished, her tone at once loving and serious. "I've saved it all these years. Let's try to make it last." Anna wondered if other families kept wrapping paper as heirlooms.

All the gifts opened, Anna headed toward the stairs; dirty dishes waited in the kitchen. But Connor took her arm and said with unexpected tenderness, "There's one more left. For you."

She glanced back at the living room. The white sheet underneath the tree was empty, but Ruth and Connor hovered nearby, all fond looks and gentle eyes, and Miriam wore a broad grin.

Anna inched closer to the tree. Scrutinized the branches one by one. There, behind a haughty angel dangling from a tinsel-laden bough, hung a slim white envelope marked "Anna" in Connor's chicken-scrawl. She almost feared to open it.

"Come on," Miriam said.

Anna dislodged it from the branch and broke its seal while her family waited, silent.

A paper lay inside. She took it out. It read: "*With love from Mom and Dad. For a wonderful summer.*" Digesting this, not yet quite comprehending, she saw a second paper, thin and pale green, folded small inside the envelope—a thousand-dollar check made out to her, on the bottom line, "*For Europe.*" Frozen on the threadbare Persian rug, she clutched it in her right hand.

Connor's smile was childlike. "You've worked so hard, Anna. All the other kids your age have gone. We decided you deserved it."

She examined his face, so full of pleasure at this gesture he could make. "I never imagined something like this." Then she glanced at Ruth, to be sure this wasn't one more of her loving but volatile father's whims, his moods that came and went without warning. Ruth's warm smile convinced her it was genuine. On the couch, Miriam beamed, her braces sparkling.

"Thank you so much," Anna managed, stifling tears. Then she kissed her parents, hugged her sister, and retreated to her room to store the check.

For a while she sat still on her bed, peering through the glass wall of her room to the hill beyond, its bare trees stark against the snowy background. The first thrill gone, a creeping cold sensation had replaced it. Europe had always drawn her. As a child, she'd loved Connor's bedtime tales of French resistance fighters and RAF men downed over the Pyrénées. Later she'd devoured Greek myths and adventure tales with European settings. *The Count of Monte Cristo, The Scarlet Pimpernel, The Man in the Iron Mask.* Ambler, Fleming, le Carré. She'd longed to visit this Europe. But then came Hesse and Mann, Durrell and Kazantsakis, and most recently Bowles, whose *Sheltering Sky* gave form to her own deepest fears. As the Sahara had consumed Kit whole, effacing her essential self, Anna feared that, given her love of risk and taste in men, the Europe to which she felt promised might destroy her.

At an open-house later that day, Claudia petitioned her. "Hey, Anna, look. Now you've got the money, let's do Europe."

Anna hesitated. She wondered what kind of team they'd make. Both twenty-three, they'd grown up in Belle Terre and attended the same high school. But Claudia was a graduate student in English at Columbia, while Anna was working her way toward the end of a History BA at George Washington. And Claudia's family was wealthy. She'd gone with her parents to Europe several times and spoke of first-class flights, Hilton hotels, and five-star restaurants. Though Connor, an economist, had traveled abroad with his job, Anna had never left the US, except for an hour on Canada's side of Niagara Falls.

But now Claudia pleaded, "I can't bear another season of those aging *haut-bourgeois*. I want to meet some European kids, you know?"

At last Anna said yes. But as an inexperienced traveler, she handed Claudia the reins, insisting only that they go by ship. She feared flying. To crash, to lose oneself in a charred mass of flesh and body parts—an isolated death seemed preferable. At least one kept autonomy.

They'd sailed on the *Aurelia*, a small Italian freighter that carried professors and students across to Europe. A boy from Ankara had taught her baby Turkish. She'd swapped addresses with a visiting Smith professor going home to Dubček's Prague. Days were filled with madrigals, folk dance, and good art films. She rose early to watch the sun come up over the horizon, to see the dolphins dance through white-tipped waves. She was almost sorry when the ship reached Southampton. But even on the *Aurelia*, Claudia seemed passive, withdrawn. Anna did the planning, asked the questions—

An ern's shrill cry aroused her from her reverie. She reminded herself that Claudia had deserted her. With each loud slap of the sea against the stony shore, she weighed her choices—fly home or travel on alone. The stench of brine and garbage heating up under the morning sun oppressed her. Like Claudia, she lacked the strength to seize her freedom. Despite her fear of flying, she would leave Europe behind.

Shouldering her Indian bag, she stumbled down the rocks with her suitcase. But before she reached the hostel up the beach, an arm grabbed hers.

"Hey!"

The voice, more than the arm, stopped her. It belonged to a tall, bearded blond boy in worn blue jeans and a madras shirt. She found his open expression reassuring.

"Don't go yet," he said, eyeing her suitcase. Beneath his tousled hair gleamed periwinkle eyes. His full lips smiled above his copper beard, dimpling each cheek. "And where's your friend?"

She marveled at his flawless English—the slightest lilt, the accent almost imperceptible. She thought he must be Scandinavian. "I, I . . . Claudia left this morning."

"Left? Then you're alone?" His eyes lit up. "What will you do?"

"I'm going home." She hadn't meant to snap, angry only with herself. The boy dropped her arm and took a few steps back. His recoil made her add, "Sorry."

"Calm down, Miss America, okay?"

She started to retort, then stopped in mid-thought, ashamed to be so sensitive, to waver so predictably between self-love and self-loathing. He'd struck a nerve. Till now, the Europeans had assumed she was a native of wherever she'd last been, so she'd traveled identity-free. His labeling put her on guard.

"In case you're interested," he said, his tone so sure and affable she had to stop pouting, "I'm off to Yugoslavia. Ljubljana to Zagreb to Belgrade. Then Macedonia and—"

She felt the power of those names. Their complex past and blend of East and West had long enchanted her. A land alive with history, some of which she'd absorbed from school or on her own, and through her passion for Balkan dance and music. "Sounds exciting."

He shrugged and drew a cigarette pack from his shirt pocket. "Have one?"

She nodded, always glad to bum a smoke. She never bought her own; then she would feel she needed them.

"So, look," he said, handing her one. He struck a match and, with his hand, shielded its flickering flame from the breeze blowing off the water. "Success. Now may I light up from yours?"

She held it out for him.

After puffing hard to start the flame, he said, "You know, I'd like some company. You really don't want to leave, do you?

He was right, of course. What would her friends, her family, say if she showed up now? And what of her yearning to see more? She asked, "How are you traveling?"

He held out his thumb.

"Makes sense," she said. "My friend and I hitched a ride to Paris from Le Havre. A college kid in an old Renault. It was fun. I practiced French with him and got some tips on where to eat and what to see."

"That was the only time?"

"My friend didn't approve. We took the Orient Express to Trieste."

"Too bad." He took a drag.

Head cocked, the boy stood watching her. She felt him sizing up her road potential.

As she puffed her cigarette, Anna weighed the route her new acquaintance had suggested. Serbia, Macedonia, Greece. She thought of Alexander, ancient armies, craggy peaks. Byzantine cathedrals, Turkish minarets. A club in Philadelphia a week before she left Bryn Mawr had sparked her love of Balkan dance, and back in DC four years ago, her Institute position had connected her to people from the Yugoslav embassy, including the ambassador's son. Introduced to those complex, interwoven ethnic histories, she'd begun to study Yugoslavia, first on her own, then through courses at GW and Georgetown. The stories had felt familiar, almost as if they were hers.

He was waiting for her answer, so she had to stop daydreaming. She should have taken more time to reflect. But she didn't dare go home or carry on alone. Besides, the East excited her, and this fellow seemed trustworthy. "I'll go . . . but won't I slow you down?"

He shook his head. "It's better with a girl." He squinted at her suitcase, took the handle, hefted it. "Get a canvas bag. This one' s too heavy. You'll have to ship it home."

"I'll need my stuff in Athens." Had she agreed too readily? But she felt he'd make a good traveling companion—sturdy and dependable.

"Then send it there." With a loose-limbed shrug, he eyed the eggshell Samsonite. "If it's heavy now, it'll weigh more when you're tired."

"True. After Paris, I wanted to ditch it." She didn't add that it held good clothes for dinners and receptions pledged by all her contacts from her previous job, helping arrange the official visits of southern European diplomats. The suitcase was her anchor. But the route and conditions had changed. She said, "Okay."

She trusted his full-lipped, dimpled smile. His rangy body, shaggy locks, and scruffy beard reminded her of the guide from her family's Sierra Club trip last summer. She'd visited him later in Berkeley, gone with him to Haight-Ashbury—her brief exposure to the Summer of Love. Like him, this boy seemed steady even in his wanderlust.

He extended a large golden hand. "I'm Peter Hansen."

She offered hers. He gave it a firm shake.

"I'm Danish. Been studying awhile, languages mostly." He took a last drag and flipped the cigarette into the sand. "Right now I prefer to travel. I know Yugoslavia pretty well. Been through it before, then down to Greece. Sold blood in Saloniki." His blue eyes gleamed. "I'll take good care of you, don't worry. But . . . what's your name?"

"Anna Rossi," she blurted out, embarrassed at her lapse in etiquette. The change in plans had excited and distracted her.

As she finished the cigarette, she felt relief. Traveling on with Peter meant she didn't have to deal with flying home.

He moved fast up the beach, unbowed by his huge backpack, her suitcase in his hand. Pleased with her decision, she trudged along behind. He could plan, take care of things. She would enjoy the ride. Too bad Claudia would miss the tables turned, the leader following.

KARST COUNTRY

June 20, 1968
Southwestern Slovenia

They left beach and hostel behind and followed the sidewalk into the town center. She chose a canvas satchel and stuffed it with her lightest clothes. Then she shipped the suitcase to American Express in Athens and sent her family a postcard with an update.

Bound for the eastern outskirts of Trieste, they wandered narrow streets that smelled of lemon, garlic, and olive oil. They must have walked two miles before they hit the road to Slovenia. Soon, they caught an ancient cart-like vehicle that carried them across the border into Yugoslavia.

Here the countryside grew wilder, mountainous and stony—the northern edge of the karst. Beneath the land, she'd read, ran labyrinths of underground rivers and limestone caves. She recognized their traces. Water rising from the ground, forming rivulets and pools, then vanishing. Sinkholes. Trees, flowers, and grass growing among the whitened stones.

The driver set them down on the eastern side of Divaca. As he honked farewell, they moved to where the road curved, by a well-trimmed hedge that bordered a stone cottage. A few small cars passed by without stopping, but an old Peugeot rounded the bend and pulled over for them. The man was jolly and fortyish. After they'd introduced themselves, he announced in strong Slav-English, "I—Goran." His plump cheeks swelled as he beamed in pleasure at his unexpected haul.

Goran's meaty hands kneaded the wheel while he boasted of Slovenia's ties to Germany and Austria, its difference from the rest of Yugoslavia. He turned his head to Anna, who was sitting in the back. "Not like East here. We Catholics!"

She couldn't help but like his hearty smile, his lively eyes. Yet she hadn't missed his certainty that West was best or the pride with which he'd called Slovenia Catholic. And that right here in Tito's communist garden, where religion was supposed to be the opiate of the masses.

Between Divaca and Postojna the landscape greened and softened. "Anna. Peter. Look." Goran gestured toward some trees. "Strange thing happen during war."

All the Yugoslavs she'd ever met in Washington, mostly Serbian diplomatic families, told stories of the war. It seemed to have defined them.

"Close by, in small village, they murder German general. It's 1943, maybe."

As she recalled, Slovenia had tried to resist both Germans and Italians. Theirs had been a bloody occupation. She gazed at the forested hills to which he'd pointed.

"See, there. Germans shoot all men. Make women watch. Then burn down everything. Take away women." Goran stared out at the hills like it was happening now. "After war, women come back. Build town again. Wear always black. They never let no man come in that town no more."

Peter said, "Quite a story."

Thinking of those black-clad widows, Anna shivered.

"Those years," Goran continued, "Germans keep petrol in caves. One day partisans light it. Big boom! Everything blow up!" He stared at the sky. "Fire last long time."

Anna was trying to picture the scene when he added in a neutral tone, "Nazis, Partisans, king-lovers—they throw prisoners down pits."

Invaders, resisters, fratricidal foes—she was glad to miss the caves. She would have looked too closely. There seemed a tragic irony in how the hidden cracks in this landscape mirrored its ethnic history.

"So to save on funeral expense," Goran sniggered.

Before they parted company, he invited them to Rijeka. "You come with me. Is good. Coast beautiful."

Anna thought Goran would make a good guide. Old enough to recall the war—perhaps he'd even taken part. A stock of tales to pass the time. But she couldn't read his sympathies. Collaborator or partisan? And she wondered what he thought of Jews. Slovenia, too, had nurtured anti-Semitism.

Peter said, "So kind of you. But people are expecting us."

Anna was grateful for Peter's polite refusal. She'd begun to wonder about him. He'd barely spoken during the ride. Was he naturally phlegmatic, or had he seen it all on other trips, or been preoccupied or bored?

When Goran let them out beside the road to Ljubljana, she and Peter waved until his Peugeot disappeared. The sun was gentler now; the afternoon was wearing down. Soon a heap of rusted metal picked them up and drove them toward the capital. Peter and the burly driver exchanged a few words in pidgin-German. Then the radio began to blare and Anna concentrated on the view. So close to Trieste, yet so many changes. The land began to unfold in a sea of undulating hills. Green fields edged the road, marked off by stone partitions. An occasional stone cottage. Here and there a cobbled village embroidered with bright flowers.

Bouncing over bumps and potholes, the car hurled Yugo-jazz into the air that was cool and bracing, redolent with the tart-sweet smell of mountain herbs. Dark spots dotted green meadows in the distance. Soon they passed a group of women all in black bent to their tasks. They reminded her of Goran's tragic widows.

Then the field was gone, as if she'd dreamt it. They were in the foothills of the Julian Alps, not far from Austria. But with each kilometer she seemed to journey not only farther east, but deeper into the past.

LJUBLJANA

June 20, 1968
Anna loved the faded pastels of Ljubljana's Baroque and Renaissance facades. Beyond the narrow buildings, a clock tower crowned the old Town Hall. Horse hooves clopped against the ancient cobbles. A carriage-load of tourists—the driver tipped his fedora as he passed. Hapsburgian, she thought. This had been an outpost of the Austro-Hungarian Empire. Yet modern buildings ringed the old town, celebrating energy and order. The people here walked fast, as if time mattered and they had things to do and destinations.

At a sparkling outdoor café, they ordered coffee. Peter shrugged as he eyed the prosperous street. "Pretty town. But the countryside is beautiful." He sipped his steaming cappuccino. "There's a campsite not far out. Shall we find another hitch?"

"Yes, let's. These old districts are lovely, but the urban centers seem so much the same. Businesses and banks. Hotels and parking lots. I want to see what makes each place unique."

She couldn't tell Peter, who only now expressed interest in where they were, that she longed to know the people and their lives. She'd felt this need since visiting an over-stuffed Bronx flat four years ago. Orthodox Easter with her Bryn Mawr soul sister, Mariam, a high-strung member of the Crikorian clan. Black-haired, dark-eyed Armenian youths and octogenarians, all with the same strong-featured, handsome faces, had roamed among antiques and oriental rugs. A huge brass samovar in the center of a dark buffet, the air was thick with the scents of herbed roast lamb, garlicky yoghurt dips, and cognacs made from berries, cloves, and cardamom.

When a whiny clarinet, high-pitched and sinuous, started playing, drums pulsing beneath its line, many rose, linked fingers, and began to dance. She couldn't catch the undulating rhythm. But one of Mariam's great-aunts led her to a far bedroom and taught her how to recognize the off-beats, to move with grace and subtle sensuality. "That's good, my dear," she ventured after Anna had tried it several times. "Remember. Just a little movement is enough, if it is right."

Rejoining the line, Anna swayed with it. The music entered her; her body answered. The living chain snaked in and out among brocaded chairs and brass-nailed leather hassocks, then wound on through the kitchen, where Mariam, dicing eggplants, gasped, "My God, you're more Armenian than me."

Anna kept dancing. Exultant in her union with the line, she dreamed she'd grown up under the shadow of Mt. Ararat. On and on they danced, with a brief pause for lamb and kvass, fuel for the dancing yet to come. Having fled Turkish swords and Stalinist Tbilisi, these new New Yorkers joyously affirmed their ancient heritage. It made Anna ponder the distance she felt from her own.

Back at Bryn Mawr, among so many high-achievers driven by the distant goal of intellectual conquest, she'd grieved for those like Mariam and her, whose comfortable lives had detached them from their complex histories—the genocides, oppression, and the pain of relocation. Connor and Ruth seemed to crave that separation, to deny their connection to that suffering. But Anna yearned for some link to her past.

Two weeks before the term ended, she and Mariam dropped out. The letters she wrote her New York friend came back marked "Return to Sender." Later she learned that Mariam had broken down and been hospitalized. But the seed had taken root. From then on Anna required the wholeness dancing brought—mind and body fused in primal rhythm, transported from a sterile present to an elemental past. At ethnic clubs and parties in DC, mostly Greek and Yugoslav, she began to feel how different cultures moved. Through research, she learned how the styling of a simple dance might exhibit subtle changes from one place to the next, embodying one's point of origin, and began to understand the discrete genetic and cultural codes that rendered each ethnicity and area distinct.

"Anna?" Peter said.

"Sorry, I got sidetracked. I'm ready now. Let's go."

Soon after, they slid from a rickety truck into a picturesque valley strewn with tents, cars, trailers, and kids with bulging backpacks. The campers came from everywhere, a Tower of Babel with license plates to match.

Some boisterous Aussies invited them to join their potluck supper. Anna and Peter added their bottle of a local white wine, *radgona*, to the bread and cheese, sausage and fruits. They ate, drank, sang, and told stories beneath a dying orange sun that stained the clouds kiwi and mauve. A couple of French kids appeared and passed around some joints, though she didn't indulge. The pastel sky and mountains further mellowed them.

By the time the group dispersed, the sky had turned an opaque black, lit by a pregnant moon and stars. Peter threw his backpack down beneath a nearby chestnut tree and spread his sleeping bag on the ground. Anna felt a moment of regret. A city bed would have brought warmth. Here, she had only the thin sleep-sac the youth hostels required.

Then Peter came to her and took her hand. His face drew near her, calf-like. He whispered, "Anya," pushing the hair from her eyes, "my little Gypsy girl."

She flinched. Till now, only her favorite uncle, Matt, had called her Anya. And why his little Gypsy girl?

"I spotted you outside the hostel last night. Thought you might be Arab or Greek. You had a certain look, and then your smile . . . Your friend said something and you spoke. American. Those eyes. That look. American?"

His look matched his soft tone, but his words brought back a story her mother Ruth had shared about her younger days. The photographer she'd modeled for had sent her photos to Hollywood, where they hoped to cast an unknown as Scarlett O'Hara. She made it to the interview, where she was told that she was "beautiful, but too ethnic-looking for the part." Anna seemed to have inherited that trait.

Before, she'd admired Peter's competence on the road, even if sometimes he seemed insulated from the people and the places. But this romantic streak was unexpected. Of course, they should commemorate the day. He was kind, attractive in his way. And she didn't want to hurt him, couldn't say no just because . . . because he was too placid? Too stolid? Too bland? What exactly did she want?

When she was ten she'd wept for Heathcliff, destroyed by a girl who cared too little to save him and too much to save herself. Later, like Cathy, she'd learned the danger of dark men, whose liquid brown eyes and smooth olive skin made her tremble. Marvelous snakes, they would slither away, leading her to a world where she became strange to herself. But somehow, as with Bowles' Kit, this was what she craved.

Still, her irrational quirk was no reason to dismiss him. Funny that her first lover in Europe would be a fair-haired Dane with light blue eyes whose English was almost as good as hers. To Peter, hovering close to her, she said, "Wait. I'll be right back."

Anna wove past sleeping bodies to the women's WC to put in the diaphragm she always carried with her now. She envied the girls who popped their daily pills, but wanted that control, to make a conscious choice before yielding to men. As she began to prepare it, the process brought to mind an incident that seemed related in a way she didn't fully understand—Halloran last fall.

Working full-time, self-directed, she hadn't been fully plugged into the academic pipeline; she rarely consulted an advisor. She'd called Professor Halloran on a mid-October Monday during morning office hours, hoping for some guidelines on the Honors Comprehensive. His Russian History course among the toughest in the school, she'd earned an A, which made him a logical choice. In early middle-age, tall with broad shoulders, a freckled Irish face, and a head of thick red curls, he excited the female students. Yet she found him slightly repellent, like a chocolate éclair whose icing covered up a tainted filling.

He suggested an appointment. "I'm terribly busy this week. Shall we say Friday?" The barest hint of Irish lilt came through the black receiver.

"That's fine. What time should I stop by?" So much for an early start on her study plan.

"Perhaps you could come to the boat . . . around six?"

The boat? At six? The rumor was he had a bachelor's pad on the waterfront.

"I won't be in on Friday. A chapter's due Monday . . . goddamn deadlines. Can you get here on your own?" He named the slip number and pier.

That left four days to wonder why she would visit a professor's home at six on a Friday evening.

She dressed with care. Sleek jeans not too tight, mauve silk shirt, soft but tailored, good black leather flats. She combed her hair until it gleamed, cascading fine and heavy down her back. Applied light lipstick. Mascara. The barest hint of color. And the diaphragm, in case . . . in case what? she asked herself.

The taxi dropped her off at the marina a little past six. Elegant boats bobbed in the water under a dazzling copper-rose sky. Halloran stood on the pier in khakis and an eggshell chamois shirt. "Hallo! Any trouble getting here?"

"No problem."

He led her toward a graceful boat at the end of the pier, its deck a forest of ferns. Jumping aboard, he extended his hand. "Let me help you up."

Incense swirled around her as they stepped into the cabin, where Halloran's smile took on a different texture. But she wouldn't make assumptions.

As the sun dimmed, Anna studied the interior. Bargeboard walls, thick wooden planks, a plush white bearskin rug, hammered-brass-tray coffee table, over-stuffed black leather couch with mirrored Indian pillows, embossed red leather hassock on carved Moroccan wood. Like the setting for a *Playboy* spread.

Halloran beckoned her to the couch and handed her a champagne flute. "Let's toast, then, Anna. To you." They sipped and watched the last rays fade away over the water. Then he ushered her behind an oriental screen, sat her in one of two black chairs before a matching table, and left through a beaded curtain.

Anna sniffed the air that smelled of bread and herbs. On the table, four tall, slim mauve candles, in its center a bowl of salad greens and vegetables. Sleek china shone mauve and gray against the glossed black wood, and the silver lay on cloth napkins of damask rose. She matched the decor perfectly.

From the rear came galley noises. Soon, Halloran appeared with a tureen. "Lobster bisque. Eat while it's warm."

She tried a spoonful—rich and smooth, delicious. Then salad, quiche, and more champagne—small sips chased down with swigs of mineral water.

Halloran kept the conversation neutral. Her plans after college? Her job? She answered with care. Still no word on the exam. She only wanted a sense of what it would cover, how best to prepare—information full-time students would glean from their trusted advisors.

After perfect coffee and a fresh-baked raspberry torte, she asked, "Were you a chef in another life?"

He threw her a dark-edged smile. "My ex taught me."

At last he rose and pulled her into the sitting area, down on the couch and under him. No preamble. A long, hard kiss. Huge hands, clumsy, struggled with the tiny buttons on her shirt. Fingers, tongue, and the weight of legs and torso pinned her down. Her jeans unzipped. A massive hand inside.

Suddenly he pulled away and stood upright, his khakis deformed by the great bulge in their center. He said, "I'll be right back. I've got something to keep you safe." His tone affirmed his prowess and his sacrifice.

"You needn't bother. I came prepared." She watched his smug smile slip away in stages.

They finished the sex. Too late to stop. But like an amateur boxing match, it was energetic and not much good. After, he announced, "Now you'll get what you came for." She begged him to stop, but he spat out questions like a drunken Greek at the Astor smashing plates.

Later, he called a cab and thrust a too-large wad of bills into her hand. "For the fare." As he helped her into the taxi, he shook his head and tossed her a rueful smile. "You remind me of my ex. Another Jewish bitch." All the way home, Anna wondered how he'd known she was Jewish and how his wife had hurt him.

Given what happened, she hadn't prepped for the exam. But she'd passed anyway, and now she needed only one more course for her degree.

She sighed as she inserted the diaphragm.

By the time she returned to Peter, the campsite had grown quiet. The nomads lay in pairs. The acrid smell of hash and marijuana filled the night and stung her throat. She shivered in the mountain air. Peter's eyes implored. She craved his warmth. The night was chilly, the sky vast, reminding her again of how small humans were, how tenuous the bonds they formed while trying to find their way in this chaotic world.

They climbed inside the bag, she first. She stroked his arms and back, buttocks and thighs, glad for firm muscles and smooth, taut skin. He kissed and touched. Caressed and licked. Fondled her breasts. Yet despite his skill, she felt nothing. And his penis, long and stiff against her belly, made her somehow sad, like an empty offering. Once he entered her, she wrapped him in her arms. But she might as well have been on the peaks above them, or on one of the distant stars that sparkled in the moonlit night. After all the pants and moans, the small spasm of ending, he fell into a deep sleep.

She lay tense in the tiny space his body left her, reflecting on her empty liaisons. Would the walls she'd built ever come down? Curled beside him in the too-warm sleeping bag, she felt the weight of her parents' damaged and damaging love, the pressure of their dreams for her. Four years since Bryn Mawr and still she had no goal beyond these paltry sexual skirmishes.

They woke to a cold sun. The pairs gathered around another fire and shared leftovers. The campsite came alive. Washing, clearing, cleaning, loud leave-taking. A couple bound for Holland drove them out and left them on the road to Zagreb. Peter seemed a little shy. Anna kept her distance.

BLED

June 21, 1968
Northwestern Slovenia

A ride turned up within the first half hour. After some time, the driver asked, "You see Bled?" Anna didn't recognize the name, and Peter's blank stare told her it was news to him as well. "So, I take you." They lurched up twisting mountain roads that corkscrewed ever higher till their nameless mentor stopped the car and said, "Here Bled." Staring out the window, they approved it.

"Amphitheatrical mountains," Anna whispered to herself as she left the car. *A Hero of Our Time.* The cynical Pechorin in the Caucasus somewhere. Nabokov had translated it. She'd faulted the master for his hyperbole, had even checked his version against Lermontov's Russian text. Reflecting on it here, she wondered why she'd had to prove herself so precisely smart, as if it mattered in the least. Yet it had mattered. She'd felt somehow redeemed by this trivial triumph, this trumping of the Culture Gods. But why? What had it gained her? How petty she could be.

Yet these mountains were amphitheatrical, grand and still as they circled a green-blue crystal lake that sparkled jewel-like in the morning sun. On it lay a small green island from which rose a fairy-tale church. Behind it, straddling a lesser peak, at the precise angle required to balance the tableau, an enchanted castle out of some Austro-Hungarian dream. She absolved Nabokov.

Their blustery benefactor gunned his motor. Having set them down in fairyland, he would go about his business. "*Hvala! Nasvidenje!* Thanks. Goodbye." They waved until the car vanished, then sat down cross-legged beside the road, marveling at the view until their empty stomachs urged them to explore the charming town etched into the mountainside. A tiny grocery provided bread and cheese, a hunk of sausage, several beers. They left their bags with the storekeeper and headed up a trail into dense forest, hiking in silence, letting the scent of wild herbs and pine refresh them. Deep in nature, lost to time, Anna welcomed her distance from the human world, and Peter.

As the afternoon wore on, they wandered back, reclaimed their bags, and found an office that matched tourists with host families. A pale blond man with thin lips and a sharp nose helped them find a place and told them how to go. Soon they stood on a sloping street before a two-floor wood chalet like the ones in the illustrated *Grimm's*.

An old man greeted them in halting English. He showed them upstairs "to your room." Smiling at them both, he said, with no hint of disapproval, "Now you wash for dinner."

In the center of the high-ceilinged chamber was a tall canopy bed. Anna touched its pristine white duvet. Reveled in its almost silken texture. The simple wooden sideboard held a porcelain bowl and jug, despite the water closet on the landing. Out the windows, open on their hinges, the sun was just slipping behind the castle.

"Anna, Peter. Remember. I *Hausvater.* You need, I get. Enjoy your stay."

Mr. and Mrs. Skertić, Karol and Olga, proved engaging hosts. Their children grown and living on the coast, the old couple missed young people and loved to share their home. "Come. We walk around lake," Mr. Skertić said, after roasted pork and sauerkraut, potatoes and plum dumplings.

They followed the chestnut-lined promenade. The moon, grown even larger since last night, illumined the castle. Anna said, "It's beautiful."

As Mr. Skertić spoke of Bled's past—its Celtic and Roman roots, the vassals to the German emperors who'd hidden in it nearly a millennium ago, the sixteenth-century discovery of its healing thermal springs, how its temple to *Živa,* the pre-Slavonic life goddess, became a Catholic shrine for Western pilgrims—Anna pondered this history that countered the relative youth of even the oldest American towns. Like the petroglyphs and burial mounds she'd seen in the Southwest, Bled touched her with its hidden mysteries.

At last the handsome old man said, "Today, still, Bled famous. Tito have his villa here."

Back at the house, Olga Skertić plied them with pastries and cordials in the sitting room. The rich dinner, the vigorous walk, the alpine air . . . Anna yearned to plunge beneath the quilt, to let the cool air bring her sleep. But now there was Peter.

Those high ceilings. That magnificent bed. Beyond the windows, an ebony sky lit by the glow of stars and moon. A sharp sweetness that entered on the mountain breeze. Anna had often imagined herself in a room like this, a princess wakened out of some dull dream of life into the fond embrace of a perfect prince. But Peter wasn't the actor she would have cast, though he was young and handsome and would have served for many damsels in distress.

He stood there, naked, by the bed, rapt with a dream that mirrored hers—except that he'd chosen her as his princess. She would give the role her best. Etched in moonlight, he had a kind of silvery aura, a heroic silhouette. Yet she dreaded the sharp pricks of his beard, the clumsy exuberance of his well-meaning fingers.

He performed like an athlete focused on his goal. She tried to stop thinking and willed her body to respond. His breath skimmed the soft flesh on her nape. His skin was supple. Her hands and fingertips enjoyed the contours of his wiry shoulders, traced the indentations in his muscled back. Then he sighed and the moonlight showed his eyes shut tight. His earnest "Annas" made her wince, pleased to take his fantasy of love and make it real. But she never left the room, the boat-like rocking of the bed. Never joined him in his dream.

When at last he gasped and eased his body down on hers, the warmth and pressure made her long for someone she could really want. Stroking her face with his palms, he whispered, breathless, "Anna, you're so good."

Here she was again, shipwrecked, alone. As Peter turned to give a final awkward kiss, his whiskers tickled her. The laugh she couldn't stop, a simple reflex, brought her close to tears.

While Peter slumbered instantly, she tried to grasp why she had to refuse what he offered. Why this distance, punishing them both? But no answer materialized beyond fear of commitment and self-loathing. At last she fell into a sleep disturbed by intermittent hoots and barks and distant forest yelps and moans—she'd heard some tales of bears—and the soft, even breathing of the Dane.

Next morning, as the sun streamed through the still wide-open window, Peter took her in his arms and bent to kiss her neck. She couldn't help the way her head shrank from his lips, her body went rigid. A quick glance at his face told her the limits of her acting had been reached. In his eyes she read the end of the myth he'd woven in the night.

After breakfast, they traded addresses with the old people, collected those of their children ("Maybe after you visit Korčula."), and headed toward the roadway out of town. Peter brooded under the bright sun, while Anna drank in one last time the splendor of the place. Bled seemed to wink at her, as if recognizing the gap between the poetry it invoked and the prose of real life.

ZAGREB

June 22, 1968

Plunging descents from tall mountains. Dusty rural roads. Miles of highway edged in fields or thickly wooded hills. And so, at last, to Zagreb, capital of Croatia, cultural showcase of Yugoslavia, remote outpost of the Austro-Hungarian Empire.

The driver dropped them in a drab square ringed by low buildings and narrow streets. Peter said, "I think I recognize this place. The hostel isn't near."

Anna's legs felt shaky; she wasn't up to walking much. They'd hiked for hours between rides, spent time cramped in small cars. She pointed to a stubby man with a food stand on the corner. "Maybe you could ask him how to get there." Shoulders hunched, Peter slunk off like a scolded dog.

She turned from Peter to the square. If only she could press a button, find herself lying on something soft. A few men scuttled past in ill-fitting dark suits or polyester pants and shiny shirts. Their glazed eyes made her think of how it felt to work all day in a windowless office with lousy light— her first job after leaving school, processing receipts for a jewelry company.

Something caught her eye, across the street, beneath a round blue sign. She blinked, but they were still there—three women in multi-tiered skirts, bright with yellow, pink, and purple flowers against reds, greens, and mauves. Large breasts under billowing, bell-sleeved blouses. Thick black wavy hair cascaded out from under flowered scarves on heads held high, atop each one a woven basket full of fruits—melons, apricots, and plums. Balancing their loads, they looked like statues.

A bus pulled up. The Gypsies with their baskets disappeared. The scene returned to gray.

A voice said, "After all, it's close."

She hadn't seen Peter return.

"Let's go." He pointed the way.

Leaving the square, they followed a street of one-room offices and dark warehouses. Several long blocks later, they arrived at the hostel entrance. Inside, they showed their papers and registered. Before leaving the lobby for the men's and women's dorms, they arranged to meet in the entrance hall at seven.

Alone at last, Anna savored her two hours of solitude, thankful that this evening she would lie among young women who would let her sleep in peace. The cold spray of the shower washed away fatigue, frustration, and what remained of Peter.

* * *

Seven o'clock. With clean hair, in a white blouse, khaki skirt, and black sandals, the Indian bag on her shoulder, Anna strode into the lobby, walking as tall as she could. She saw Peter with two boys who resembled him. The same rangy bodies, the same blond hair. Excited, he introduced them. Thorvald and Jørgen, from Copenhagen. "They want us to join them for dinner, and dancing afterwards."

Her nod was less than vigorous. She didn't object, having nothing else in mind. But left to herself she might have explored the knot of dark-haired young people in the corner who were speaking something Slavic.

The two boys led them out the door and down the street. Anna wasn't paying much attention. Yet after rows of nondescript buildings, she said, "But I heard Zagreb was lovely."

The boys stopped short and circled her. In a nearly flawless English like Peter's, Thorvald said, "The center is splendid. Tomorrow we sightsee. But here it is only the city spreading out. It has to go somewhere."

She recalled those trips from Bryn Mawr to Manhattan for her piano lessons, how the ugly tenements outside the train window would yield at last to the pulsing urban center. "I understand."

Just then she caught the tiniest quiver of wailing Balkan brass as it slid out onto the street through a crack in a battered storefront. Not the light, quick beats of a Croatian *dermiš*, but a twisted, haunting eastern blues that invoked those Gypsy women, in their vivid splendor far from the banalities of city life. Wanting to hear more, she moved toward the building. But Peter pulled her back, as if the music were a call to some dark quest.

The dining hall was one huge room, every table filled, too many people. Speech and sounds swirling together made it hard to hear. Tobacco smoke hung thick about them, annihilating other smells. Tough gray mounds filled dirty plates, but they ate it anyway. The price was right.

Afterward, they headed to the club, a purple-black facade that hid a neon inner-space. The cave-like disco blared a tinny local rock'n'roll. A crush of bodies—students, workers, tourist kids—gyrated and jerked, the strobe lights turning them into frenetic ghosts. Even in Washington's trendy clubs, Anna found this scene unbearable, loathed the frantic striving after some kind of electronic release. She missed that realm of pure color and strangled pain the Gypsy music had evoked.

The boys claimed an empty back table and cluttered it with beer bottles and ashtrays. When Thorvald asked her to dance, she said, "Sorry. I've got a headache." He and Jørgen wandered off, but Peter stayed to keep her company. He wasn't saying much. As they nursed their beers, the silence grew between them.

Finally, she stood and Peter followed. She ventured into the center of the throbbing chartreuse light, pinned herself to a small square of space, and began making the crude motions the music seemed to call for. Bump and grind, hip and shoulder, bump and grind. A coarse and strident imitation of sensuality. Like mechanical sex, without heart. But who was she to judge?

Across from her, Peter shook his head from side to side. He'd found his own rhythms. Time passed. He seemed happy enough.

They returned before the hostel closed for the night. The boys basked in the evening's light flirtations. Even Peter joked. She was glad that now he had less need of her. And once inside the women's dorm, in her narrow lower bunk, she hugged the thin sheet to her body, savoring the soft sighs and snores of the other sleeping beauties.

* * *

Light streamed through the window Sunday morning, waking her and promising a fine day. Bells pealed in the distance, recalling Goran's voice, his Catholic Slovenes. According to her DC friends, Zagreb was a city of cathedrals. Evidently Croats, too, prized their Catholicism, their link to Austria and the West.

Anna hit the lobby early. The Indian bag on her shoulder, the canvas satchel in her hand, she looked for a comfortable place to wait. By the window sat a boy she'd spotted the previous evening. She took a chair across from him and set down her belongings.

"You're with the Danes, aren't you?" he said. His hazel eyes slanted upward in his long, thin face.

"Yes."

"Dušan." He held out his hand.

"Anna," she said as she took it. Elegant fingers, long and dark. "Dušan. Isn't that a Serbian name?"

"It is." He smiled. "They've made you wait? They said today they'd take you around the Old Town."

Despite his heavy accent, the words came out perfectly. "Your English is awfully good."

"I lived in Oxford for a while. My father taught economics there."

Those aquiline features, the fine, light eyes. She could see him as the bright child of a visiting professor. She didn't volunteer that her father, too, was an economist. "Are you from Zagreb, then?" He seemed about her age. She liked his face, a narrow oval ruled by probing eyes.

"Dubrovnik, not Zagreb."

"They say Dubrovnik's beautiful."

"They're right." Eyebrows arched, he rummaged through his pocket. "Care for a smoke?" He held out the pack.

She nodded, took one, and let him light it for her.

"What brought you here, if I can ask? I mean, Zagreb isn't Mecca."

"Well . . ." She took a drag. "I'm interested in Yugoslav history. But I didn't really plan this. I met Peter in Trieste, and, you know . . ."

"Sure." He chuckled as he ran a hand through his black hair. "I know."

She liked the wry curve of his lips.

"You've studied the place?" he asked.

"A bit. I've focused farther east."

His eyes flickered. "Like where?"

"Serbia. Old Macedonia."

"My father's from outside Skopje. I've been there twice, to visit relatives. He came to study here. My mother's village is a bit southeast. Anyway, it's good you'll see Zagreb. It really tells the story of Croatia."

"The medieval stuff, you mean? I know it was divided once, the classes separated—like Dante's Florence."

"More than that." His face hardened. He took a drag and stared at her from under eyes grown serious. "It's how they idolize the West."

"The Austro-Hungarian link?"

"Yes, that, but also after." His lips twisted into a strange half-smile. His eyes gazed through, not at, her. "Croats are masters of divided loyalties. For almost a thousand years, Croat kings ruled here. But they bowed to Hapsburg emperors . . ." He inhaled deeply. Blew out a column of smoke. ". . . and scorned the Serbs." An angry spasm flashed across his face. Then his features realigned themselves into their scholarly mask.

He'd spoken with such bitterness. Was he, like her, ethnically mixed?

"So, Anna, where do you come from? Before America, I mean. Your family."

A warning bell. Her back stiffened. And even if she'd wanted to, she couldn't give a good answer. The truth lay buried with Asher, who'd never spoken of his origins. "Rossi" came from an Ellis Island customs inspector, likely an Italian, given how he'd 'Anglicized' her great-grandfather's name. From what? Rosenberger, Rusinov, Russinsky? She would never know. The names of Ruth's parents were also changed. Ruth hadn't pursued it, and they were both dead now.

"Why do you ask?" She hoped he would be honest.

"Your coloring. Your tragic eyes." He shrugged. "Just curious."

The eyes again. She sighed.

She watched Dušan's face muscles tighten. He wasn't being straight. But she'd feed him the truth to check his response. Bessarabia's history confused her—once Ottoman, then Wallachian, Russian, Romanian, Moldavian, and today, she thought, part of the USSR. But when Ruth's parents had fled Kishinev as young teens nine years past the pogrom in 1903, it had been the capital of Bessarabia.

She needn't share Fiona's roots, though they were more clear-cut. Her great-great-grandmother had come from Ireland during the Famine. According to family lore, her father had sold her for a cow at the Dublin docks to a man bound for America. He'd married her, at least. She said, "My mother's parents came from Bessarabia."

He nodded. "I knew it had to be from somewhere near. And you must be a Jew."

Anna fought the urge to bow her head and apologize, as if he'd caught her in some ugly act. "Yes," she said, her voice a little shaky, wondering what had given her away.

"If you'd lived here, you likely wouldn't have survived the war."

"The Ustaša?"

"Too right. That bloody gang of Nazi-loving murderers."

His vitriol surprised her. "Zagreb was their center, wasn't it?"

"Yes, and Jasenovac is close."

She shuddered at the mention of the infamous concentration camp.

"So, you know about it. The commandants—the Catholic priests were the worst—slaughtered maybe a hundred thousand, maybe more. Mostly Serbs and Jews, but Gypsies, too, and Partisans. They didn't need mass gassings. Preferred to kill one at a time, with mallets, axes, knives."

"I guess I'm confused. I've seen no vestiges of war in Yugoslavia, except the stories of a guy who drove us in Slovenia. The fighting was so bitter— some here must have been directly involved, or at least complicit. But everyone seems placid, focused on the moment."

"Anna, look." Dušan took a drag, exhaled. "Life is better than it was. People appreciate that. And Tito preaches "Brotherhood and Unity" to eliminate ethnic divisions."

Like the Holocaust. Trying to bury an ugly past.

"But you must understand—Croats are nationalists. They cherished the NDH, their so-called "Independent State of Croatia"—even though the Nazis gave it to them and the Ustaša controlled it. Now Croats feel bold again; they want more power. Like last year, when they tried to make Croatian the official language here, not Serbo-Croat. And a few months earlier, the consulate bombings in Canada and the US."

"I remember those. The one in DC got hit, too. They still don't know who did it. You think they're linked?"

He nodded as he ground his cigarette into the ashtray on the table. "Likely both the work of right-wing Croats. Here, intellectuals are often fascists."

He bent his head closer. "If we had time, I could tell you stories—"

"Dušan! Anna!" The Danes hailed them. "You'll come with us, Dušan?" Thorvald asked.

"No, sorry. I'm meeting friends."

Anna and Dušan rose to greet the boys. As she gathered her belongings, he scribbled something on a scrap of paper, folded it, and placed it in her hand with a light squeeze. "In case you come through Dubrovnik between next week and August."

She saw Peter throw her a sidelong glance.

Several hours later, Anna rested on a bench near St. Mark's Church and its famous square. They'd visited the Stone Gate and the Bloody Bridge, relics of Zagreb's embattled medieval past. At each stop she'd heard Dušan's voice, "Masters of divided loyalties." Now she wondered how their chat had become so intense, so nearly intimate. Why did strangers often speak so readily to her? Because she was receptive, keen to understand how others lived, unafraid to stumble over language?

All through France, she'd entered conversations while Claudia sat silent, afraid of misspeaking in French. Claudia couldn't comprehend why ticket takers automatically spoke to her in English, their faces cold, while Anna collected smiles and *bonjours*. And once at a student eatery, when Anna joked in French to the proprietor, he asked where she came from. Incredulous at her reply, "the US," he called his wife from the kitchen to meet this young American 'with whom one could talk.' While they spoke of students, war, and cultural change, Claudia waited, rigid, at a table.

Since Ljubliana, Peter's apparent indifference to others, or at least to people here, had reminded her of Claudia. He and his friends now huddled beneath a nearby chestnut tree. She caught the rhythms of their Danish, robust *ja's* and *du's* freely exchanged. She could picture Peter in Denmark. He would lead there, as he'd first led her, his seeming certainties charming, persuasive. She could even imagine his women. Tall, slim, reddish-blond. Athletic bodies, long straight legs. Attracted to his affability, which she now sensed hid jealousy and suspicion.

Red-tiled roofs and lovely trees, museums, shops, and churches unfolded below her with the slow grace of an era lost to time. Sunday-clad Slavs in Western dress. Here and there a splash of color, a villager or Gypsy. The gothic spires of Saint Mark's sparkled in the sun. But its sculpted cornerstone had made her cringe—the head of Matija Gubec, leader of a sixteenth-century peasant revolt.

She had little interest in Papal Bulls or military treaties, but stories like Gubec's fascinated her. From various sources she'd shaped a narrative. Desperate peasants sought a government with Gubec at their head. Croat overlords vanquished the serfs, captured their leader, and marched him to St. Mark's at Carnival.

On the square she'd closed her eyes. Could see them drag Gubec in chains. Set him on a mock throne in its center. Lay upon his head an iron crown. The urban crowd awaits the spectacle. Black-clad men remove the crown, thrust it into leaping flames until it glows red-hot, then place it back on the unbowed head. The stench and pop of sizzling flesh. Smiles of wily overlords. Frenzied cries of pleasure from the crowd that mask his howls of pain. After, they had torn apart his body. Becoming a folk hero wasn't easy.

She thought somehow of Nick, the gentle Cretan uncle of a former lover, Christos. Horrified, she'd stared at the ear that floated in a jar on Nick's mantel in College Park. The sickly old man explained it as a relic from his youth fighting the Turks. "I was a boy. What did I know? He was the enemy." The shame he radiated made her feel he'd come to see the trophy as a symbol of his youthful ignorance, of the way old scripts dehumanized.

Gubec's murder and Nick's Turkish ear were real. But what about those tales of Ustaša violence? Victims' eyes popped out, amassed, displayed in barrels. Jewish villagers forced onto conveyor belts, their bodies left to dangle from meat hooks. Were they history or myth? Were these among the stories Dušan knew? His voice had held such fervor. Had someone close to him died in Jasenovac, or someone in his mother's family worked there?

Peter and his friends still chatted in their happier universe. But Anna shivered, as if adrift in an underground river of hate. Despite Tito's efforts, she wondered how long this country could unite its disparate cultures.

At last the boys collected her and they hiked down to a trolley stop. After they'd said their goodbyes, she and Peter caught an ancient tram that wound past towering trees, arrogant baroque façades, green squares, and stately homes until it moved beyond the dreary fringes of the city. In a treeless realm of dust and dirt, the tram stopped and expelled its sweltering riders.

They'd reached some kind of lake or swimming hole, a spot they'd thought would freshen them. At first, grateful, she and Peter gulped *kokta*, a local cola, and wolfed down slabs of juicy watermelon. But now, as nearly naked bodies splashed and bobbed while others displayed their flesh on rocks, their preening like a mating dance, the sexually heated atmosphere made Anna feel self-conscious. Her eyes lowered, she said, "Let's get the hell away from here."

Sometime later, they found themselves on the autoroute to Belgrade. Sweltering in the sun's glare, they stood along its shoulder with their thumbs out-stretched, hoping for a ride . . .

PART II: HEADING EAST

OF APRICOTS AND TURKEYS

June 23, 1968

Rocking . . . Rocking . . .

Anna raised her head from where it rested against the window sill. She must have fallen asleep while Max and Peter were chatting. Unrelated memories still clung to her like a silken shawl—the Astor, Trieste, Bled, Zagreb . . .

The air was warm and heavy with a sweet smell, and she was by herself in the Mercedes.

From the window she saw a tiny roadside stand displaying baskets of apricots. Behind it, a stout figure gestured to two men, one muscular and tall, rumpled, with dirty jeans, loose tee-shirt, and a lion's mane of hair, the other elegantly slim, pristine, the dark folds of his jacket graceful over linen trousers. Peter and Max. She recalled her first glimpse of Max—the impeccable clothes, the fisherman's cap, the wry smile on his handsome face. A fascinating puzzle.

A breath of cool air swirled in through the window now. The sun was lower in the sky. Gentle hills rolled off toward the horizon. Toting small bags, Max and Peter returned to the car. "Anna," Peter said, "You are back with us again."

In his low-pitched, grainy voice, Max laughed. "It is hard work, the hitchhike." Opening her door, he added, "Here, Anna. Walk a bit. Good for the legs. After, you come in front. Let Peter have some rest." She and Max watched Peter stretch his long frame over the back seat. She was happy to stand up and stretch her body.

Then Max walked her to the stand. The round-bellied proprietor repeated several times, "Very nice—Amereeka," his smile full of yellow-stained teeth. By the time they reached the Mercedes, Peter was making noises in his sleep. Before Max put the key in the ignition, he offered her his black cap full of apricots. She reached for one, then hesitated.

"Not to worry, Anna. They are clean."

Snatching it before she lost her courage, she savored that first bite of cool sweetness even as the burst skin squirted pulp and juice down Max's jacket. His dark eyes flashed. His body tensed as she blotted the sticky ooze with a crumpled tissue from her shoulder bag. She said, "I'm sorry, Max."

Eyebrows arched, a wry smile on his lips, he reached under the seat and extracted a small thermos. "Water . . . maybe it can help."

She saw him watch her while she worked, let her rub the spot until all traces of the fruit were gone.

"Thank you," he said. "Now I think it will survive."

On the road again, the Mercedes flew. Anna gripped the door handle, beginning to regret she'd given up her seat to Peter, snoring in the back. "These Turkies," Max sneered.

"Turkeys?" She looked for large birds on the road.

"They do not know how to drive. See?" He gestured out his window.

Her eyes followed his hand. Off the highway lay two twisted metal heaps. Skeletons of an old car wreck. Seeing them, she could almost hear the splintering glass, the screams of shattered bodies.

"Amazing. Do they leave them as a warning?"

"Maybe. Or maybe just they do not have money to remove them."

"Max," she began uneasily, edging toward the question that she really wanted answered, "Why do you call them turkeys?"

He gazed straight out the windshield, shaking his head as he searched for words. "Once they are all Turkies, yes?"

She was thinking there might be a Turk in his own family tree, when Max said with his short, dry laugh, "Me, too, maybe. My family, some of them come west to Slovakia, then to the Erzgebirge."

She could only stare.

"So. This name you do not recognize." His eyes narrowed as if he were debating something with himself. "It is the southern hills, in the East, near the Czech border. Once they are big coal mines there. Now," he shrugged, "not so much. My father and my uncle, they are miners. Also . . . me."

A coal miner? She found no useful response.

They disengaged. Preserved an edgy silence. In the space that followed, Anna tried to reconcile this past with the man who claimed it. She sat still but alert, tracking the driver and the road.

Suddenly two cars loomed out of nowhere, bodies hard and rounded like the crusty shells of huge roaches. One careened into their path. The second hurtled by them on the left. Burning rubber. Screeching brakes. Doors flew open. Men burst out like soldiers primed for an assault. Anna held her breath and closed her eyes. The Mercedes shook hard. Wobbled.

In the time it took her heart to start beating again, they had come to a stop on the right side, well away from the warring cars and men. A glance at Peter in the back revealed that he was still asleep.

Both hands on the wheel, Max shook his head. He breathed deeply and let the air out slowly. Then he said, with a tight smile, "You see, Anna?" He pointed first to the angry knot of men, fists clenched, exchanging hard, guttural shouts, then to the broad gray stripe that met the horizon. "They cannot wait to leave, make lots of money. Always they take this road north. The cars, maybe, are on the *autoput*. But the drivers are in Germany already, getting rich."

The corners of his mouth and eyes curved up. The fine lines around them crinkled irresistibly. Anna longed to stroke his smoothly pleated cheek. She thought he must be in his early thirties, but the smile made him seem younger.

Back on the highway, Max steered with the light touch of his right hand, his car among the fastest on the road. With a teasing grin, he asked, "Another apricot?"

"Oh, no. Too big a risk." She thought she'd hit the right tone.

They kept up a barrage of quips, volleying back and forth about the place, the day, the weather. From time to time he would take his eyes off the road long enough to shoot her a darting glance that didn't translate. As if he weren't quite sure why she was there or what to do with her. She'd thought she might relax within the cloak of his indifference. But now she named what she'd begun to feel from Max and in herself—excitement.

"Anna," Max said, "We are close now to the city. Look."

They hit the outskirts of Belgrade under a deep mauve sky. Warehouses, boxy steel high-rises—colorless, not old or new. No character. No soul. Then Max asked, "Where do you go next?"

Inside the casual tone, the simple words, she detected something murky.

"Down through Skopje into Salonika. And you?" She hoped he heard no more than courtesy.

For some reason Max drove with great care on these streets, obeying the posted limits. He seemed preoccupied. Had he even listened? All at once she heard him say, "To Istanbul." She caught him as he watched her from the corner of his eye, gauging her response as if he knew that name would tease out the thousand images she'd stored over the years.

"You," he paused a millisecond, stressing the separation, "and Peter, can ride with me, if you like."

Istanbul. Stamboul. Constantinople. The names evoked a world of dreams. Intricate shapes in creative geometries. The burnt smell of hashish. The slow shimmy of heavy-muscled shoulders to a shrill, arrhythmic beat.

"Oh, I don't think so, Max." She aimed for polite disinterest. "Peter's set on Salonika. But thank you anyway."

They were headed toward the center of the city under flickering tendrils of rose and persimmon that trailed from the setting sun. Max turned his head toward her. "You have a place to stay?"

Her body stiffened. "Peter and I will find a host family, like we did in Bled. A great old guy. Called himself the *Hausvater.*"

"*Hausvater?*" He chuckled. "Yes, sure. Slovenians, they speak a good German." His brows knit for a moment. "Why don't you two stay at my hotel?"

"We're trying to save money." He was homing in. On what?

"Ah," Max parried. "I have plenty money. A room, maybe some meals, for me it is nothing. Belgrade is . . . not Western Europe. Even good places, they are quite cheap." This time he let her see the pause. "Then we go to Sofia together. To find a ride south into Greece is easy, and you will see a bit Bulgaria."

Sitting at an intersection lined with ugly shops, Max seemed to ponder the Cyrillic print on a drab storefront until he turned his face to her and almost sotto voce said, "Too much travel, you get lonely, isn't it?"

Despite his smile, the tone was serious, the words some kind of plea, which made it harder to figure him out.

From the back came grunts and groans. The snapping of stiff joints. Peter returning to the world. "Where are we? Is it already evening?"

"You rest good, Peter?"

Max had become a *Hausvater*.

"My God, what time is it? This looks like Belgrade," Peter said.

Exhausted from the verbal sparring, Anna let Max do the talking. "Yes. You know Belgrade?"

"I've been here twice this year."

"Twice? Why? For me it is a need. But Belgrade . . . it is not so interesting, so, how do you say, picturesque . . ." He pursed his lips. "Not like Mostar. Dubrovnik."

He turned onto a narrow street lined with drab barrack-like buildings, ugly oblongs in gray cement. She'd almost forgotten. Bombs had damaged Belgrade—first the Germans, then the Allies.

Max said, "Even Sofia, I think, is more exciting. You visit there?"

"Not yet. I've heard it's nothing special. Not like Budapest or Prague."

"I am not expert. But for me it is more—uh—eastern."

"Maybe someday. Now Anna and I have plans to visit Greece."

"So Anna is telling me."

Max braked suddenly. An ancient truck had nearly sideswiped them. He honked his horn and snarled, "Turkies."

"Peter," he continued once he'd settled down again, "maybe you two come with me into Bulgaria. From there you can find a ride along the southern highway into Greece. You see some different country, a little change. The mountains, they are wild, rugged. The villages, like a hundred years ago."

She had to give him credit. He'd figured out how to entice her. Now he was pushing Peter's buttons too.

"With you?"

"Why not? You are good company. Too much travel, it is boring. You understand, I think. You are almost a countryman. And Anna, well, she is the American you can laugh with, isn't it?"

Anna listened from a distance, resolved to let Peter carry the rest. The men could work it out. Do what they pleased. She was tired. She wanted only a bite of food, a bathroom, and a bed.

"I guess Anna and I will talk this over. Maybe we could visit Sofia. Aren't they hosting something big this summer?"

Max nodded. "They call it the World Youth Festival. It is in late July, but now they make things ready."

"Might be fun to see what that's about."

"Kiosks everywhere. Everything sparkles—" Max slammed the brakes and muttered to himself. The city seemed no safer than the highway.

She closed her eyes as Peter grabbed the bait. Like her, he was stupid, or greedy, or both—drawn by the lure of adventures for which somebody else would be paying. She refused to exert herself further as siren or salvation.

A BELGRADE *KAFANA*

June 24, 1968

From the Bulgarian Consulate, where she'd gone to get her visa, Anna headed back toward the Majestic. Belgrade sweltered in the heat. Compared to Zagreb's rich textures—its handsome trees, red roofs, and Central European architecture, the bright fabrics of its burdened Gypsy women— this capital seemed gray and bureaucratic. Older buildings vied with nondescript high-rises. At one end of Republik Square, the graceful lines of the State Theater and the National Museum, two massive steel rectangles at the other.

Anna reached the café off Republik Square at 4:00, half an hour early. She took an outside seat and savored the afternoon quiet. Ordered soda water. Scanned the sidewalk, nearly empty in the lull before the evening rush. Every time the door opened, she caught the blare of taped Serbian rock.

At a nearby table, a beautiful boy of about sixteen sat hunched over a book. Drinking something tall and dark. Smoking a cigarette. Expressive lashes framed dark eyes that studied her with feigned dispassion. She checked her blouse. Was glad to find it buttoned. She could see him trying to label her. Another Western whore or some lost girl? She couldn't help him.

The boy sat up. Thrust out his narrow chest. Put his shoulders on display. He tossed her a hard stare. A cool half-smile. His need to be a man, to take what would come too easily before he understood the cost, gave her an almost maternal pang. Something in the dark grace of his fine slim beauty summoned Reza's image, that night at the Yugoslav Consulate three years earlier. His small but strong, smooth hands. Those long-lashed, deep-brown eyes—

She'd met him through Ali, a former student from Iran, whose unfocused left eye and twisted right leg affirmed the pleasantries bestowed by SAVAK, the Shah's secret police. He'd introduced her to a man no taller than she, with the delicate features of a Persian miniature.

"It is my pleasure." He had a soft voice, a steady grip, and a dark, unwavering gaze. An idea seemed to burn in his almond eyes.

She'd become his oasis, he her dream of old Shiraz. He seldom spoke. Never told his story. But his lovemaking was gentle and serene, like the music of a cool, clear mountain stream, or the soft wing-beats of a dove. They fit each other perfectly. His SAVAK-damaged penis evoked sweet rippling waves that took her far from the world of crude sensation. No grand finale—neither coda nor cadenza. Not Beethoven, but the delicate *ghazals* of a Persian troubadour.

Their idyll ended barely two months later. Ali spirited Reza away to Canada's cold north, the latest haven for lost souls and lost causes. Unsure whether Marx or Allah drove him, Anna feared that one day she would read his name in *The Washington Post.* Some failed coup against the Shah—

"*Izvinite,* g*ospodice.*"

This "please, Miss" from the balding waiter, eager for her order, snapped her back to the present. She'd been a waitress once; she understood. "*Molim tursku kafu.*" A coffee would ward off the headache she felt coming on. Now and then the young man darted a glance at her. His tentative posturings, Reza's torture and uncertain fate, Belgrade's rising from its rubble—they made her feel what strength survival took.

These disconnected battles brought an image of her once-robust and handsome Uncle Matt. Soccer player, ladies' man, teller of tales, he'd succumbed to cancer in the summer of 1958. She'd begged Ruth to let her visit him. Had combed her hair into a ponytail. Worn her nicest skirt set— Matt liked his women pretty. Driving along the Potomac in the pastel August twilight, she and Ruth had listened to the ball game. Over the car radio, the Senators' announcer said that Albie Pearson had slid in safe at second. She could see the boyish smile that fit the tiny center fielder's frame.

The red brick hospital had been so cold. Her mom stayed in the waiting room, as Anna had requested. Walking down the long gray hall, Anna smelled a strong odor that made her feel like gagging. The door to Room 220 stood ajar. She slipped inside. The person in the bed gave a wan smile, too gone from the mundane world to see that his naked skull and maze of tubes would frighten her. That huge head on its frail torso with toothpick arms—was that really her Uncle Matt? She would have bolted from the room, but his wasted arm beckoned her closer.

"Aa-nn-aa." As his voice wheezed in and out, she forced herself to listen for the words they formed. "One day—" He gasped for air and coughed. "You—" He seemed almost to choke. But his once-blue eyes, red-veined and watery now, looked at her with such kindness, even as he tried to catch his breath. "Find what you—" He sputtered. Gasped. "Looking—" Something else got swallowed up. She took his withered hand in hers. Kissed its ugly purple veins until it freed itself to rise and stroke her lowered head. Her tears fell on the yellowed sheet.

Their silence and the soft whirr of machines produced a quiet that was comforting. She stayed by his bed, enjoyed the light weight of his hand, until a nurse arrived to warn that visiting hours were over. Then she saw that night had entered through the drawn venetian blinds. Careful not to jostle him, she rose and helped him move his arm away. He started making sounds again. She leaned her head toward him, prepared to strain. But it came out in one piece. "Never forget, Anya. Life is a gift." Or at least that was how she remembered it.

Two weeks later, sitting in the over-air-conditioned funeral chapel, she'd fought back tears that came despite her rage. Comfortless eulogies clotted the air. Though meant to soothe, the rabbi's prayers seemed to mock Matt's brave last days.

In the material universe it was after 4:30. At last Peter appeared. "Success?" he asked.

"Yes, but the line was very long." From the corner of her eye she saw the Serbian boy retract his gaze. Retreat behind his heavy lids.

"And I suppose you think I had an easy time."

"I didn't mean a thing, Peter." She picked up his resentment. "Hey, wasn't Max with you?"

"And so?" His smile mocked her.

"I guess I thought you'd show up here together."

Peter shrugged. "Excused himself. Said he had some business. Had to meet some friends." He smirked at his poor joke. "He'll be along. Doesn't seem to want to lose us yet."

"So, Peter. Did you find out what he does?"

He shook his head. "Maybe you'll do better." His full lips curled. "Runs a clothes shop, by the look of him. Whatever it is, he's never short of money."

Before she found a comeback, Max strode up and draped his arm across her chair back. "Good to see you, my friends."

Speak of the devil, resplendent in a linen suit. The fitting end to their verbal thrusts and parries.

"If you excuse me one moment, I get drinks."

Max's appearance bullied them into an uneasy silence that lasted until he returned. Wearing his latest version of the hero's smile, he carried three glasses of swirling whitish liquid.

"Ouzo?" Anna asked. She'd caught the heavy sweetish scent that permeated the Astor.

"Here they call it *mastika*." Max raised his glass. "To Sofia."

"*Prosit*," Peter said, subdued.

Anna murmured, "*Živeli*," hoping the local touch would bring good luck.

"No problems with the visa, Anna?" Max exuded a paternal interest.

"Easy as pie." She left out the burly middle-aged Bulgarian who'd snarled as he'd filled her request. "Passport," he'd demanded in a brusque voice, flipping through her papers. "American." A judgment. Stamping the paper hard. Stapling it to the inside of the passport. Exacting payment in a sneering monotone.

But was she being fair? Maybe this was how he stood the long hours, the dull work, the stale odor of Gitanes, Gauloises, and Balkan Sobranje smoked by all those shaggy youths who sought admission to his homeland, only to pass through it on their way to India or Kathmandu. Maybe she'd deserved his scorn. No different from the rest. All seeking sanctuary from adulthood. By the time he'd slapped her passport down onto the wooden desktop, she'd been happy to retreat once more into Max's protective custody.

"Tonight we celebrate," Max said. "We eat. We drink. We dance."

She didn't want to ask Max for a favor, but to herself she whispered, "We visit Kalemegdan," the ancient fortress that symbolized for her the Balkan past.

Peter frowned. She could see him itemizing—drinks, dinner, a night on the town, the hotel room with its private bath, tomorrow's trip to Sofia. It added up. To what?

"So, Max, we're off to do Belgrade. How charming!" Peter's drink went bottoms-up. He spread his arms wide, signaling submission. But his smile had sharp edges.

As she rose and pulled her bag off the chair, Anna saw the young Serb track her with his eyes, on his lips a half-smile. He seemed to be shaking his head.

NIGHT IN BELGRADE

June 24, 1968

Quaint cafés and restaurants lining cobbled streets. Wood and stone. Wide shuttered doors and windows. Old street lamps. Flowered, tabled patios. Strains of music, old and new. Heavy scents from every doorway swirling down the sidewalks. People strolling, sitting, talking, many of them young and casually dressed.

"Skadarlija," Max said. "You're here before, Peter?"

Peter gave a nod.

Anna knew the name from books. For over a hundred years, the hub of Belgrade culture—first the Gypsy, then the Artist Quarter. "It's wonderful," she said.

They passed a one-story café behind a low, wrought-iron fence. Max pointed to its sign. "This place goes back, maybe, a century. Before then, it is the shop of a hatmaker."

That explained the caps on pegs above the entryway. She loved the feel here. Like the Left Bank, but Eastern. People passed by munching *pljeskavice*, spicy hamburgers sold from sidewalk stands. From somewhere came the rustic tones of a *kaval*, a shepherd's pipe.

Max led them to a table on the patio of a white stone house with slanted roof and tall brown-shuttered windows. He ordered for them all—steak tartare, cucumber, tomatoes, round loaves of heavy bread still steaming from the oven, and *vinjak*, Yugoslav cognac, 'to bring out all the flavors.'

Her tongue relished the tomatoes, juicy, tart but sweet. "Fantastic."

Peter stared at her like she was mad, but Max's dark eyes sparkled. "Anna, you know how Serbs call them?"

"No."

"*Paradajz.*"

"Paradise. A perfect choice."

Anna savored everything but sipped her cognac slowly. She intended to stay sober. Saying little, Peter concentrated on his plate. Max toyed with his food as if he had no appetite. Nibbling at a cucumber, he studied them. "Such trouble with the students, isn't it? Coming and going, all of them. Riots everywhere." He gave a little shrug and shook his head. "And what about you two?"

His smile made those creases she found so attractive.

Peter said, "School began to bore me."

"Anna?"

"Me?" What could she say? That she was floating through her life? That her parents had funded this aimless adventure? That American unrest had sickened her? "I'm taking a short break. America's so crazy now." Reminded of Daniel on the train, she told them how he'd described the Paris riots, the fleeing students. "He didn't seem to grasp why it had happened, what it meant. I guess I don't, either . . ." She looked for words. ". . . except, maybe, we're fed up with corrupt systems and wars."

Eyebrows knit, Max seemed to shake away some thought. Then he said, "In early June they riot here."

Anna stared at him. "I never read about it." Her tone hinted a challenge, though she might have been on the *Aurelia* then, or sightseeing in London, and so perhaps had missed this news.

"Not much in the papers. Tito makes it go away." His eyes narrowed as he ground pepper over his meat. "Police use tear gas. Beat kids with batons."

His words evoked the demonstration she'd gone to in DC. But riots in Belgrade, a few weeks ago? "Everything seems peaceful now."

"Sure." Max wiped his mouth with the cloth napkin and watched Peter chew his last few bites of meat. "Tito takes good care. He makes some empty promises."

"But aren't things pretty open here?"

"Better than Bulgaria, the Red bloc. But still, you know, not like the West." Max shrugged, ate a bite of steak, and sipped his cognac. "The Yugoslavs, they do not like each other much. The Slovenes and the Croats think, you know, they are best." He gave a mocking laugh. "For them Serbs are just Turkies. Tito keeps things—how do you say—" A grin at his verbal helplessness. "Together."

But yesterday he'd called Yugoslavs "Turkies."

Over *palačinke sa orasima*, crepes with ground walnuts, and coffee, Max told stories from his Serbian travels, advising at last, with a snort, "Always, they are Serbs first. Not Yugoslavs."

He seemed to scorn the Yugoslavs in general, but now had singled out the Serbs. Was this a German bias, or his own? Yet he mingled with Serbs so well, his Serbo-Croat halting, like his English, but evidently adequate. They all gave him those hearty laughs, their eyes aglow with pleasure. Something didn't add up.

Peter hadn't said a word in ages. Anna studied him as he sat rigid, focused on his crepe, and saw Max watching too.

"So, Peter," Max said, loud enough to grab the Dane's attention. "More *vinjak*?"

Peter flushed. "Sure. Good stuff." The right words but no spirit.

One last round of drinks. A genial "*Hvala puno.*" A slap on the back to the moon-faced waiter who'd anticipated Max's every whim as if he were a regular. Then off they went, arms linked, the men on either side of her. Roaming from bar to bar. Drinking too much *šljivovica*. Soaking up the Serbs' robust intensity. Anna was deep into the evening now, though working to stay vigilant. She didn't want to lose herself completely, to upset the equilibrium the three of them maintained.

They left Skadarska Street and headed down a narrow lane along an empty sidewalk. From far away they heard strange, muffled sounds that grew louder as they walked on. A kind of low-pitched groan. The clank of metal. The noises lured them to a dark, stinking alley that turned into a narrow cul-de-sac. In the circle at the dead-end, people clustered near a lone street lamp that cast eerie shadows.

A finger on his lips, Max inched them forward. Anna followed, though with some reluctance. Beneath the smells of rotting food and urine, she'd caught an ancient odor from a different sort of place she couldn't pinpoint. As they edged closer, groans and mutters merged with a cat's shrill screech. When they reached the small group gathered there, everyone was staring at the lamppost. Taking Anna's arm, Max signaled Peter and worked them to the front.

Her senses vindicated, Anna gasped. A large brown bear was tethered to the post, his muzzle elongated, his teeth and gums exposed. His chain allowed some movement; he stood on his hind legs, prodded by a small, dark man with pockmarked skin and deep lines in his face.

"*Cigani*—Gypsies," Max whispered. "Sometimes still they come with bears. Make some money from the crowd. The Slavs, they always like the bears."

Anna wondered what the Gypsies called themselves as she watched the man with the stick size up the bear, the crowd, his eyes steady. His dull brown trousers sagged and a white shirttail had found its way out over them. But his smile held an alien knowledge and his compact body moved with fine economy. Off to his side, a woman in a tattered skirt and red stiletto heels clutched the hand of a curly-haired toddler. Her husky voice intoned a melancholy song. Her head shook to the rhythm, making gold-coin earrings chime. Dancing on his stubby legs, the little boy mimicked the bear while mirroring the crooked smile the Gypsy man had sent him.

Suddenly the man looked straight at Anna, with a grin that showed some missing teeth and one of gold. He poked the bear again. The creature danced. The Gypsy bowed to her.

Why had he singled her out—or had she imagined it? But she hadn't missed his tender glance at the woman and the child. Or the way he moved, as if anchored in himself, his life—so comfortable in his body. Had he sensed how far she was from that?

The Gypsy woman's hand, shiny with bracelets, pointed to a basket on the ground.

Max left Anna's side. He eyed the bear, walked to the basket, and dropped in a hatful of *paras*. The coins jangled together as they fell, making metallic music. Anna saw the Gypsy woman, her face impassive, study Max. When she nodded toward her mate, the look in her eyes made Anna feel lonely.

The bear began to bellow. She bristled as Peter put his arm around her waist. The bear reared on its hind legs. Pawed the air. The crowd let loose excited "Ah's" and "*Ajde's*" as Max reclaimed his spot. Then the furry creature lunged at them. Forgetting his chains, some women shrieked. The crowd fell back. So did Anna. But Max touched her shoulder. "No worry," he said. "It is just for fun."

Anna inspected the couples in their light summer garb. Flushed, excited faces. Broad smiles all around. Max was right. They'd savored this thrill, the Gypsies' parting gift. Even Peter smiled. "Never saw a thing like that outside a circus." Hand in hand, the couples inched away.

Then Max led them through a maze of streets to a *kafana* with a heavy door, above which hung a large red shield, a gold *C* in each corner. It looked like one she'd glimpsed in a book on medieval Balkan heraldry. Beneath it, blue Cyrillic letters spelled out *Kosovo Polje*.

That name—she'd seen it first in a leather-bound book in the Library of Congress stacks. The yellowed papers came slowly into focus; she could often see whole pages and their contents—not quite photographic memory, but close. The Field of Blackbirds, 1389. Serb-held Kosovo. Turks repelled a pan-Balkan force. The battle claimed most fighters on both sides and the leaders of both armies—Serbia's Prince Lazar captured and beheaded, Sultan Murad stabbed by a Serb or poisoned by a rival.

The victory had cost Serbia its empire, ushered in five hundred years of Ottoman rule, and spawned Serbia's great heroic epics, nostalgia for its lost kingdom, and centuries of pain and dark lust for revenge. She knew that each June 28 Serbs celebrated *Vidovdan,* St. Vitus' Day, to honor Prince Lazar and the Kosovo martyrs. And every spring when poppies turned the plain bright red, folk wisdom traced it to that Serb blood shed so long ago. Why had Max brought them here?

"We will go in?" Max asked.

His tone made her smile, inviting them to ponder his suggestion. As if she and Peter might have some other plan.

A young waiter, his thatch of black hair rising from a pronounced widow's peak, sat them in a corner. Brandy-heavy smoke layered the air. Max coughed.

On a stage against the far wall, a folk band in black vests and red sashes performed a twisting tune. No brass, accordion, or high-pitched *frula*. Nothing like a Serbian group. Excited, Anna recognized the instruments as Macedonian—*kaval, gajda, tapan, zurla, tambura*—like the ones she'd seen at an ethnic club in Philadelphia. The pregnant bag of the *gajda* moaned, the player's cheeks puffed fat with air. Applause greeted the Balkan bagpipe's fading drone.

A man rose from the table next to theirs and limped toward the stage. He whispered to the *kaval* player, who gave the sideways head-shake that meant yes here. The band members exchanged nods. The *tapan* beat a syncopated measure, the *kaval* gave a low whistle, and the oboe-like *zurla* began to wail. The man's gaunt face grew somber as he sang in a gruff bass, "*More sokol pie/ voda na Vardarot.*"

"I love this song," she said. A popular tune among American Balkan dance aficianados, its slow, dark rhythms always made her neck grow cold.

Peter asked, "What does it say?"

"A falcon drinks water from the Vardar."

As Peter knit his brows, Max said, "It is old?"

"More than a century." She translated the next verse: "Oh falcon, hero's bird, has a hero passed with nine hideous bullet wounds and another from a knife?"

"Typical Balkan violence," Peter said, shaking his head.

Max shot him a look she couldn't read, then gazed at her.

Those nine wounds made her think of Jug Bogdan and his nine sons, the Jugovići, mythic figures in the Kosovo cycle. On the Field of Blackbirds, Jug's wife found her husband and their nine sons lying dead. Anna wouldn't share this now; the images would validate Peter's remark.

The room chanted the chorus: "*Jane, Jane le belo grlo/ Jane, Jane, le krotko jagne.*"

"'Jane, Jane, the white throat, the gentle lamb.' One of Macedonia's hero-songs," she said. But the words recalled a newer hero, Jane Sandanski, and a story she found intriguing. A founder of the Internal Macedonian Revolutionary Organization, IMRO, in 1901 Sandanski kidnapped an American missionary, Ellen Stone, in the century's first hostage crisis. The US paid for Stone's release, Americans briefly noted Macedonia's bondage to the Turks, and once back home, Miss Stone strongly supported the rebels' plight until her death. Anna often wondered how Sandanski had won her over to his cause.

The men's discordant harmonies began to swell. Raw emotion filled the space—longing, despair, homesickness, love of country—intoning the pain of those who lived far from their homelands. Enslaved, transported Africans stolen from families and cultures. Her own forefathers and mothers, who'd fled famine and violence to arrive alone, unwelcome, in the new world.

Voices trembled on the edge of sobs. A man two tables over, hollow-cheeked, face tight with rage, stared into the space beyond his raised glass, as if the song had brought its bloody battle scene right here, into the heart of modern Serbia. At last the sounds receded. The singer stood silent, head bowed. Then he left the stage.

Across the table Max was studying her, his eyes opaque, his smile a screen. "You are too quiet, Anna."

She couldn't tell if he was moved, or bored, or puzzled by her absorption in the music. "It was so beautiful." She couldn't explain how lucky she felt to be among these men for whom the song seemed almost sacred.

The room stayed still for a few minutes. *Šlivovica* and slow talk. Peter sat silent. Max turned his head away as she smoked one of Peter's cigarettes. Until the *zurla* buzzed, the *gajda* wailed, and the band began a rousing Gypsy *ćoček*. Rhythms swirled, insistent, as the music speeded up. Anna couldn't keep her shoulders still. They started twitching, one first, then the other, shimmying to the drumbeat. Beneath the sandal straps, her toes were moving up and down, marking out the tempo with the *tapan*. At last she rose without a word to Peter or Max, wove her way onto the floor, and joined the line in the center of the small wood square. Others followed. The steps came easily. The music told the pattern of the changes. The band played with controlled abandon, especially the double-sided *tapan* and the *gajda*. Under dim lights, in the smoky haze, the dancers, mostly tall and male, took on an eerie cast.

Merged with the line, Anna let her body move to the syncopated rhythms. The drumbeat echoed in her chest. The *gajda* drilled into her. Sharp. Deep. Low. Until she felt an almost sexual heat. Step behind, step behind. Right-left-right. Left-right-left. The slower back steps the most essential part. Like the point in Bach when the rising tide of voices halts before the absolute, subsiding into a quiet undulation of sub-dominants and tonics. Her shoulders shook without her will. The hawk-faced, gray-haired fellow on her right inclined his head and beamed approval. "*Bravo, devojče. Ajde.*" Despite herself, she blushed, glad it was too dark to see.

Then Max and Peter burst into the dance on either side of her. They fought to catch the rhythm, to find the proper foot. Their stumbles upset the balance of the dancers nearest them. Positioned between her and her new admirer, Max soon found the beat. But Peter floundered. Anna tried to help, half-heartedly; they'd spoiled her union with the line.

At last the dance absorbed them all. As one, they pulsed with the music, mostly Macedonian. Long *lesnotos* built from slow to fast. Something frenzied with a mad rhythm she didn't recognize. A few south Serbian dances. A ballad, slow and sinuous. The line snaked round and round in tight concentric circles of concentrated energy until the band declared a break. Taped pop began to play. Flushed, exhilarated, the dancers reclaimed their seats.

After one last drink, Max paid the bill and left a tip that made the waiter happy. As they wound through the crowded room toward the exit, their fellow dancers hailed them.

Outside, Max rasped, "Now we see Kalemegdan."

Anna took a deep breath. He'd answered her unspoken prayers.

Beyond exhaustion, buoyed by the night, they wandered through Republik Square. A torn, weathered poster read "*Slobòd*—" *Slobòda*— freedom. A vestige of the June riots? It hung from a tree-trunk near where Prince Mihailov rode his great stone horse.

They followed the lovely old street that bore his name, Knez Mihailov, to the foot of Kalemegdan Park. A cooling breeze refreshed them as they hiked up to the summit, past fragments of old walls, a zoo, a war museum, gates and statues, stone terraces, and a clock tower. Soft green grass and trees filled empty spaces, then stone steps, an ancient church, and at the top a statue.

Below, they saw the Sava meet the Danube. On the Sava's far bank winked the lights of Novi Beograd. At the bottom of the terraced hill, the old city spread out against the star-filled sky. Above its roofs, the moon hung like the Gypsy woman's earring.

While Max led Peter off, apparently to show him something, Anna rested on a stone bench, spellbound by this vast but battered shrine to the human condition. Here was the core of the city, its ancient embattled heart—Kalemegdan. The standing walls were Austrian, but before them Turks, Hungarians, Byzantines, Slavs, Romans, and Celts had built their fortresses on the bluffs above the joining of the rivers. These stones, like the bagpipe and the drum, embodied the fate of the Balkans, telling her their stories in the language of the soul.

But even as she watched the Sava flow serene below her, she knew that to the west lay Zemun, where Nazis had murdered eight thousand Jews in 1942. Was that total right? She didn't like the trick some played, bloating or shrinking numbers to suit their ends. The SS had disguised mobile gas units as Red Cross vans—a dress rehearsal for the gas chambers.

She heard the men approach. She would have shared this story but didn't want to reveal herself as a Jew. She couldn't predict their responses.

PAS DE TROIS

June 25, 1968

Max tapped her shoulder. "It is already tomorrow, Anna. We must sleep some, yes?"

All the way back to the hotel, the three of them walked silent and apart. Anna suspected that Max and Peter, too, were adding up the night's dead spaces, hidden glances, vacant looks. What she saw was anything but pretty—thrown together randomly, each struggled to control the complex dance their alliance had become. A graduate student in physics had once tried to help her understand Uncertainty. Then, she could see it only as metaphor. Now she, Max, and Peter seemed to mimic Heisenberg's model. Trying to grasp what governed the phenomenon they shaped, they changed its very nature.

The short ride to the third floor took too long. They had the elevator to themselves, but no one spoke. The presence of both men tormented Anna, like an accusation or a threat. She'd welcomed Peter's southern route through Macedonia. So why had she encouraged him to travel east with Max? Sensing the answer, she thrust it away. No time now for self-recrimination.

The silence grew as they neared the room Max had booked for them last night; his own lay down the hall. Outside their door, she and Peter found no exit line. Max reached for Peter's hand, gave it a firm shake, and offered her a crisp salute. "Ten o'clock. The lobby, yes? Sleep well."

"Thanks, Max." Anna tried to smile.

Peter only nodded.

She watched Max walk away, his bearing less erect than usual, as if pursued by the echoes of unspoken words.

Peter unlocked the door and stormed inside, his face bright red.

From alcohol or anger? She couldn't tell. The brandy was making her temples throb.

"That bastard," he spat out through clenched teeth. "Does he want to come and watch?"

She'd seen him track her exchanges with Max, had sensed a storm brewing, but hadn't known how to prevent it. "I thought you liked him, Peter."

"I want to know why he treats us so very nicely."

"Last night you didn't seem to have a problem."

"You weren't with him all day. He knows the place too well. His bloody clothes. The car. The money. All those damn phone calls. Don't you find it strange?" He pulled off his watch and held it like a string of worry beads.

Even without the quick looks Max had sent her, Peter's list made her uncomfortable. "Why should he lie to us?"

He let the watch drop on the nightstand and began to unbutton his shirt. "It has to be a setup."

If he'd had suspicions all along, why choose now to pull up short? "Funny how last night you called it good luck. You're not jealous, are you?"

She saw him wince.

When the silence got too heavy, she recalibrated. "You could be right. What sort of setup do you mean?"

"Drugs, the white slave trade."

She laughed. "I should have guessed. As powerful as he is, he can take us both."

Peter sucked air through his teeth. His jaw muscles tightened.

As her body inched away from his, she heard him sigh. He stared at her, squinting, his brows wrinkled—the way Connor looked at Ruth when they fought.

"He's not working alone. You weren't with him, Anna. He doesn't even hide the fact that he's got 'friends' out there."

She squirmed beneath his gaze that almost begged for her acceptance.

"You're such a fool, Anna. Turkey's close. Anything can happen."

His look, so full of hurt, made her regret her subtle treasons. She stared at the floor. The time had come to take some blame. Facing him again, she said, "Maybe I've been wrong."

"Always in your own world." He pulled off his shirt, balled it up, and threw it on the floor. "Never pay attention. Make me watch out for us both."

"I know." Her stomach churned—the brandy or the truth? "I'm really sorry."

Then she found the germ of an idea. "I keep thinking he's a decent guy. Like Goran, or the man who took us up to Bled, or Mr. Skertić. Bored driving the same route. Finds us entertaining. Glad to have the time go faster. Makes sense, right?" Feeble logic. Unresolved questions. Phone calls, stray glances, money—all unaccounted for. But if it fed his ego, maybe it would buy some time, reassert the status quo.

Peter stared hard at the pastel still life on the papered wall. Was he measuring the journey east from Zagreb? She watched him stoop, undo his sandals, and stretch out on the bed like a Manet odalisque—arms behind his head, legs crossed, torso and underarm hairs on display. But his eyes were closed and his bare feet hung off the mattress.

At last he made a sound like a balloon whose air is leaking out. "All right. We'll stick to the plan. But I've got a lousy feeling."

His words struck her hard in the stomach. They promised an unquiet night.

After lukewarm showers, they burrowed into soft, clean sheets, so different from the ragged coverlets of Zagreb's hostel. Then they made a cursory love devoid of warmth, Max Heidl's spirit crowding them in the bed. Having paid for the room, he seemed to have authored their intimacies.

NIŠ

June 25, 1968

Lucky Peter, slumbering there, turned on his side. He looked so innocent, while she felt hard, empty, like death. Replaying their time together, she'd found it difficult to sleep. The images had coalesced into a rancid stew of stifled hopes. His quiet, even breathing and his clean, well-shaped blond head seemed to deny her darkest thoughts. Yet she was finally ready to cut loose. This era of careless love made endings easy.

She shivered at what she'd become—a wasted mind inside a useless shell driven by hunger. But what could fill it? Not her sexual games, with their brief moments of triumph. Not the orgasms she didn't let them bring. Not the storm of love portrayed in films and romance novels. Digging deep, she found the word passion, a commitment that gave life meaning. Dostoevsky's Father Zosima had taught that active loving made life good. But what was that, exactly?

She left the bed and tiptoed to the window, then drew the heavy drapes against the sun. She didn't want the light to kindle sparks of fury in the room. Retrieving one of last night's towels from the floor, she pulled it around her and dropped into the chair beside the window.

From there she watched the bed, saw Peter stir, take in the empty spot beside him, sit upright. She heard him groan and crack his bones. His eyes met hers and lingered for a moment. His lips made a thin line. Silent, he rose and started sorting through his backpack near the bed. Armed with clothes, he stumbled toward the bathroom.

The door slammed shut. A storm of bangs and clatters burst, protests against the promise of the morning. Anna closed her ears, became a little child again, cowering in a corner of the dining room from the thunder of parental duels. Connor's urgent curses. Ruth's serrated retorts. Random bits of dinnerware whizzing by her head to shatter, indifferent, against the wall, or bouncing on the ancient Persian rug. Ruth would ask her each time, "Shall we leave him today?" Peter stomped out dressed and somehow smaller, as if his combat with the soap and shower stall had sapped his strength.

Side by side they packed their few belongings, forming neat stacks on the unmade bed. Smoothing and folding in silence, they worked in the same slow rhythms of dejection. Anna felt the rumpled sheets accusing them. They couldn't leave the room quickly enough. Locking the door behind them, Peter might have been an ancient palace guard sealing a secret tomb.

Half an hour later, they faced off in the hotel dining room. The dregs of Anna's Turkish coffee foretold change. Licking crumbs of good bread from her mouth, she braced for action. Max had gone to make a call. Peter sipped his coffee with studied decorum. She was planning her lines when he said, "I've changed my mind. We'll do what we first planned—head south into Salonika." He wiped his lips with care.

The bright white of the napkin matched his arctic smile. His tone shocked her. Strong and measured, dispassionate yet venom-edged, it made her cringe. Searching for the right comeback, she gave him one of her slow stares. But his scornful gaze forced her at last to stammer out, "I really want to see Turkey. If you'd rather go south, I'd just as soon head east with Max."

Peter sat unblinking, that frigid smile glued to his face. Anna examined her plate. Propelled her fork around it. While Peter glared at her, she pushed crumbs into mounds. She felt as if her brain were on display, revealed in all its mess of tangled motives. Fighting the comfort of the well-upholstered chair, she smoothed her blue skirt and managed a half-hearted feint. "Come with us, Peter. Salonika can wait."

"A nice gesture, Anna."

His smile skewered her like a piece of lamb for shish kabob.

"But no thanks. Maybe Max can drop me off near Niš, if that's the route he takes."

The knowing parent humoring his child. He was all ice now and miles away, savoring his triumph. Always the gentleman, Max would honor his request. Let Peter have his medal for good conduct. A small price for her freedom.

When Max came back, she sensed something amiss—a slight but perceptible pallor to the cheeks, a bit of hesitation in the stride. Had he caught the tension in their silence? As she struggled to puzzle it out, Peter jerked his head toward her. "Max," he said, "I'm going to Salonika. But Anna . . ."

Peter's wink made her back go rigid.

". . . she will travel on to Istanbul, if that's okay with you." He seemed pleased to have thrown the first dart.

But Anna was too preoccupied with Max to vent her fury. His eyes seemed elsewhere. His brow was creased. Then in a flash he was himself again, attentive and intact behind his charming grin. The shrug of linen shoulders. The nod of his fisherman's cap. Max's eyes and mouth turned up. "As you wish. That's fine with me." And as if he'd read their script, he asked, "You want to ride to Niš with us?"

An hour later the sumptuous black Mercedes was tearing southeast along the Morava, Peter in front with Max, Anna tacked on behind like an afterthought. The highway hugged the river valley that wound its way south toward the mountains of Macedonia beneath a cloudless, bright-blue sky, craggy hills on either side. Lush meadows and green-shagged slopes enfolded her, gathered her in among cornfields and plum orchards, mountain laurel and clumped rockrose. But as the Mercedes traced the zigzags of the tranquil valley, the river flowing swiftly northward in its bed recalled the distant rumble of ancient wars. The green of grass and hills took on a dull red cast. The bouquet of plum and wild lavender masked a musty memory of dried blood and death.

Markers to places she had read about dotted the way. Ancient monasteries hung from rocky peaks, unreachable except by foot, beyond the grasp of worldly power—though not the Ottoman Turks—within a wildness that increasingly enveloped them. Far up along the rough dirt roads at which Max only shook his head lay towns and villages that gave their names to dances she had danced. From time to time she glimpsed an oxcart round a bend, churning up a cloud of dust as it lurched toward some destination high in the thickly wooded hills. Scattered ruins whispered to her of the hordes that had wandered through this land on their odyssey to empire or redemption.

On the right, a large breach in the hillside created a natural arch crowned by fir and beech and outcroppings of rock. In the speeding

Mercedes, Anna strained to fix the blurred image she caught—a past and present linked in stone. She tried to blink away the Turks who seemed to surge out, en masse, from the gap, astride their splendid steeds, flamboyant in billows of bright cloth, scimitars held high, hurling blood-bespattered pleas to Allah along with dreadful shrieks against the infidel, prepared to slit throats, sever heads, hack off limbs and breasts and genitals, pluck out eyes and cut off ears to fulfill the Sultan's yearning for this wild, bewitching land.

Then somehow space and time collapsed. Faces from so many pasts stampeded into Anna's skull, each with a voice. Bandits, soldiers, farmers, lovers, parents, infants, dry old men, all jumbled together, clamoring their stories till her head reeled from the flood of sounds. Curses, howls of pain, a newborn's cry, a vow of loyalty squeezed out through a dying boy's chattering teeth, bitter tears of loved ones left behind—the manifold phases of mortal being. In that moment, she allowed them to possess her, to shrink her till she became a cosmic speck.

The instant passed. The hills slid by. Drained of all that life, Anna sat quiet. Now she understood. The three of them were the latest to pursue illusions here, their own desires paltry against the epic scale of their predecessors' dreams. Yet she felt joy and awe. For the place had welcomed her, had trusted her as a channel for its sacred spirits, weaving her into its complex tapestry.

At last a sign appeared for Niš—crossroads of migrations, birthplace of Constantine, home to Justinian, way station for Frederick Barbarossa on his Third Crusade, reluctant host to conquering Turks. Last night at *Kosovo Polje* had brought back bits and pieces of stories and epics she'd hastily skimmed and casually stored. For Lazar had faced the Turks in Kosovo partly to retake Niš.

The ancient town had long held a spot on the mental chart she'd hoped would clarify the scheme of things for her—the grand plan, or whatever cliché one chose to suggest that life might not be totally absurd. Her plan had once been to study the tribes that had wandered Central Asia and the Balkans for millennia. It seemed a sort of key—to what she wasn't sure. But she didn't intend to search for a lifetime only to die without answers, leaving a file drawer filled with useless facts that formed no pattern.

Suddenly her feet and shoulders began to move within themselves to the swirling rhythms of a stray tune that had drifted into her head right out of the rocks. She didn't know its name, but it had some Albanian flavor, a low-to-the-ground heaviness, those off-beat halts and quick step-steps with the most subtle of sways. From Macedonia or the Kosmet. Then it whirled into *Niška banja*, the Baths at Niš, both a spa near Niš and a brisk Serbian couple dance she'd last done in a sweaty gym somewhere in College Park, a motley crew of males looking on, assessing her charms and weighing their opening lines. But even then the dance had brought her nearly to this place, as if the body's motion could reconfigure space, transport itself to some other domain. She felt she was coming home.

At the highway's edge Anna spotted a tall, narrow stone obelisk, behind it several more. They had a special name . . . what were they called? *Kraj—krajputaši*. Memorials to the dead—the essence of a life carved into stone. She pleaded from the back, "Hey, Max! Can we please stop?"

The Mercedes screeched to a halt along the shoulder. They all got out and walked back to the first stone. Into it was carved a proud young man wearing a fez-like cap, his martyrdom affirmed by the silent slopes and the river that would flow past his lonely shrine for eternity, renewing the earth with its annual floods. Or at least until the sun grew cold or a vagrant meteor destroyed the planet.

It was hard to decode the ornate Cyrillic script on the weathered stone; Serbo-Croat wasn't Russian, and even there she was shaky. But she got the name and date—Marko Stepanić, 1855-1878, and a sense of the inscription, something like "here lies a Serb hero, slain by Turks in the name of our fatherland and the freedom of our people."

The men talked in low voices by the car. But Anna found a sunny spot near the river, by a patch of wild flowers she didn't recognize, their odor sweet. She sat down with her legs out straight for the cool grass blades to soothe. The boy, Marko, had been her age, only twenty-three when he was killed—on the threshold of real life. Gone in an instant, as if he'd never existed. Had his love of country sustained him to the end? Or had he known the agony of second thoughts?

She felt tears form. She didn't want to cry. It made her feel like Hopkins' Margaret, grieving for herself. But she recalled the voices she'd so recently sheltered and their pain washed over her again. As she surveyed the river and the solemn slopes, she traced the long line of humanity back to its origins and tried to imagine the future. At last she reached the certainty that all who lived were doomed to Marko's end, a few years more or less between, a difference in the method. Then she let the dammed tears flow, careful to make no sound and keep her head turned toward the water, away from Max and Peter. She felt a cleansing peace.

Soon Max came to her. He shook his head, the indulgent scout master rounding up his troop. "A pretty place. But we must get back on the road, yes?" Walking her to the car, he gave a low snigger. "Another hero, isn't it? The same old story, after all."

Why had he mocked this boy? How did he know his story? He irritated her just now, tossing out those easy ironies.

In the car she thought of Matt. Her uncle should have been a Serb. This lonely shrine surrounded by the raw and ancient landscape would have suited him far better than the cold marble in his neat suburban graveyard. They traveled on in silence. The brave boy on the stone had cast his spell.

More signs appeared for Niš. Then Max veered left and followed the Nišava east. The land flattened. The outskirts of the city reminded her of those half dead New Mexican towns her family had passed through on their road trip west. Decrepit, single-story shacks. Pools of filthy ooze. Skeletal, flea-bitten dogs, their fur matted and filthy, scavenging for garbage. A stench of decay and a passive gloom rose from the dust. Like those old shots of Baku, where refinery smoke stacks expelled their toxic fumes into the ancient air of Azerbaijan—a huge chemistry set that nullified the power of place.

Anna stared at a three-legged dog with a rat's tail and a missing eye that yelped at the car in impotent hostility. Some small, dark boys chased after them, their high-pitched voices yelling words she couldn't understand. Were they Gypsies?

"We will eat something before we drop you, Peter," Max announced. Peter nodded. Though not hungry, Anna didn't protest. She knew he meant the meal as a peace gesture.

Once they hit the city, Max steered the Mercedes toward the central square. Along the north bank of the Nišava stretched a fortress so well preserved that Anna felt some Turks must lie within its walls, waiting to attack the puny shell of their proud but defenseless car. As if in response to her fantasies, Max drove the Mercedes like a battering ram straight across the bridge toward the citadel. No Turkish missiles issued from inside its massive walls. But even in the bright light of the early afternoon sun, Anna heard the grave silence of secrets sealed in stone.

The black-muzzled Mercedes burrowed deep into the old city. Narrow streets became tight, winding passageways scarcely wide enough to fit the car. Two-story row houses of white stone lined steep lanes. Red-tiled roofs and overhanging eaves shone in the sunlight. Oriels and second-floor verandas, flower-draped, extended out over the road. From somewhere came the scent of rose and oleander.

Max parked the Mercedes on a cobbled lane and walked them toward a patio above which spread a wooden trellis draped with purple bougainvillea and pink and yellow roses. Clematis wound around the posts, turning them green and purple. A large clay pot of rosemary gave off an aromatic scent. Anna shot a quick glance at the street. The shiny black Mercedes threw into relief the timeless eastern beauty of the scene.

A few wood chairs and tables rested on stone tiles. An old woman in a shapeless dress and flowered apron burst through the door, her movements brisk despite her age and bulk. A warm smile lit her deeply-wrinkled face. Large brown eyes undimmed by time beamed out at Max, who swept off his cap and bowed to her as he once had to them. They hugged and spoke in Serbo-Croat until the old lady called, "Stojane!"

A gaunt elderly man came through the doorway. Tall and straight, he strode with energy to where they stood and clapped Max on the back. He spoke a rustic German with Max, who gestured to the two of them. "Mila, Stojan, my—friends, Anna—and—Peter." Anna saw Max check the old faces to make sure they understood. "Anna—is—American. Peter—from Denmark."

The old man shook Peter's hand with great vigor. Then Anna watched his eyes run up and down her. "Nice, very nice," he said to Max, a gold tooth glinting in the sun. "Pretty girl." Smiling, Stojan nodded to his wife. "Look little bit like Eva." His heavy accent had followed him from German into English.

Max's face paled. Then he laughed and threw himself into a chair. "We're—hungry—and thirsty. Bring us . . ." His hands made a broad gesture. ". . . everything."

For once he seemed spontaneous as a child, wholly immersed in the moment. She was glad he'd dropped his mask of genial irony, attractive though it was.

The two old people heaped before them plates of cheese and bread, of cucumbers in yogurt sauce with garlic, mint, and lemon, of *gibanica*, a tart cheese pie, and thin-sliced lamb so savory and tender that Anna went beyond the point at which her stomach warned, "Enough." All this washed down with cooling mugs of local beer. They ate as if they were starving, whether from hunger or nerves. At one point Peter paused to say, "You seem to know all the right places, Max."

"They keep a good kitchen, Mila and Stojan," Max replied, his wry grin back in place.

"Funny," Anna ventured, flushed with beer. Only now she realized there were no other diners. "It's almost like you're family."

Max squinted, as if reflecting hard on this. "You think so?" He said no more, returning to his food, content to let the sentence lie there on the table with the dirty plates and the beer mugs. But the words seemed to reverberate among the forks and knives like the drone of a Balkan bagpipe, with nuances and signs she couldn't decipher.

Then Mila set down bowls of apricot compote, and Stojan brought a huge brass tray that bore a long-handled pot of Turkish coffee, a bowl with lumps of sugar, and five small cups and saucers. Their hosts joined them for dessert, posing harmless questions in zesty but faltering English. When Max stood up and went inside—to relieve himself, Anna assumed, of his several beers and coffees—Mila implored them, "You take good care Max. He drive always alone. No good."

Shortly after Max returned, he gave a sign. They rose to leave. No bill was presented; no money changed hands. Instead came vigorous hand-clasping, exuberant Slavic kissing of cheeks, and goodbyes in three languages. As Max ushered her into the Mercedes' front seat, Anna yelled back one last ardent, "*Dovidenja!*" Huddled together under their trellis, next to the table stacked with empty dishes, the two old people waved the Mercedes on its way. In the distance, they looked like brave abandoned children.

The car retraced its course west, to where the road forked off toward Skopje and the south. Max pulled onto the shoulder. He left the car, walked to the rear, and opened the trunk. Peter, too, stepped out and headed to the back, his movements sluggish, as if the meal had weighed him down. Or was it the finality with which Max had called his bluff?

Max had to pry Anna loose from where she sat glued to the passenger's seat, her head turned toward the rear. She didn't have a clue how she should act, what words to speak.

He brought her to Peter with a look that said, "We must do this right." Then he pumped Peter's hand. "A pleasure, my friend. Good luck for the road. I wish you well!"

Peter's instant smile wore sullen edges.

At Anna's approach, Peter withdrew. But she took her cue from Max, who was watching like a parent from the wings. Standing on tiptoe, she grabbed Peter's shoulders and kissed his cheeks, with as much warmth as she could manage and he would allow. "Thanks, Peter." She gazed for what seemed a long time into the strong planes of his bearded face. "If not for you, I'd have flown straight back to London or DC."

His snigger left them nothing more to say.

Undaunted by the failure of his would-be happy ending, Max resettled Anna in the front, spun the Mercedes around, and headed back toward Niš. She took a final peek at Peter's solitary silhouette beside the empty highway, framed by jagged ridges running straight across the sky. Sagging a little, the Dane was staring down the long gray road to Macedonia, as if the Mercedes had never existed at all.

ĆELE KULA

June 25, 1968

As they left the tiny gas station, a rush of hot air swept through the open windows. The pavement hissed beneath the Mercedes' wheels. Max kept silent. Beside him, Anna waited for some clue about the proper tone for this leg of the journey. That little half-smile played on his lips as he watched her from the corner of his eye. Like the trip to Belgrade . . . or did she only imagine it?

They'd lost time dropping Peter off, so Anna assumed Max would stick to the highway. But outside Niš he turned onto a rutted road that ran southeast. Anna's stomach churned. "This isn't the road to Dimitrovgrad."

"I want to show you something first."

The slight *v* to his *w*, the way *thing* became *zink*—sounded both funny and sinister. Zsa Zsa meets Dracula. What did he have in mind? She'd buried her doubts for two days, but with Peter gone, she'd lost her shield and saw nothing but question marks.

Max gave his rogue's smile. "Do not worry, Anna. It will please you."

Minutes later they parked on a crust of rising land beside a battered Fiat. A small man in an ill-fitting gray suit emerged and motioned them to follow as he marched off to the right. Though Anna felt slightly queasy, she did her best to keep pace with the men.

Flushed from the climb, her cheap Italian sandals filled with dust, she surveyed a flat expanse of grass extending to the line of hills that bordered the horizon. There she saw stone blocks, some broken slabs, a headless, tilted pillar, another with its capital intact, the ornate swirls still well-defined. At the far end of the large rectangular site, a massive arch framed grass, dirt, hills, and clumps of wildflower and weed.

The man led them to the arch and down a narrow stone staircase into a cramped, dark space, its walls adorned with stone ivy and Byzantine crosses. The vault contained four crypts. Anna reached out, touched the grainy marble surfaces. Gingerly, fearfully, under the vigilant eye of the rumpled gray suit, she felt the stony skins of splendid lions, bears, and wolves, the profiled human shapes like Hittite bas-reliefs. Their rough beauty made her feel so small. Then the power in the stone surged out, connecting her to the martyrs of a vanished world and time. The tombs began to spin, the ground to shake—

Max caught her as she fell. The two men helped her up the stairs and into the Mercedes. Max retrieved his mineral water and had her take some sips. As he wet a cloth and held it to her forehead, he said, "They build it before even the Slavs come."

Back on the road, she wondered why she'd fainted. The heat, the meal, the beer, the lurking spirits? When she felt herself again, she asked, "Who was that guy?" The man and his gray Fiat had vanished by the time she'd come to herself in the car.

"A government tour guide. I call from the . . ." He paused. Cleared his throat. ". . . the café. You need an appointment. I worry it is too late."

She'd caught his hesitation. As she searched his face for something she couldn't name, she gave him a tentative smile and whispered, "It was special. Thank you, Max."

"Maybe you sleep a bit, Anna. We see another place. I wake you."

His gallantry unnerved her.

The Mercedes pitched and rolled along the grooves and potholes. Its motion lulled Anna into a stupor. She shuddered awake when Max gave her a soft tap on the arm. In his low Germanic rasp he said, "Come, Anna. We are here."

For a moment she mistook him for the last monstrous figure in a reverie from which she wasn't quite yet free. It lingered as a sense of dread, the impression of a handsome face behind which leered a death's head that pursued her to the brink of a high cliff. Anna rubbed her eyes and stared at Max, who was scrutinizing her. She managed to ask, "Where?"

The nasty borders of the daydream curled around her, cold, almost palpable. She didn't need a Gypsy fortune-teller to interpret it. With his Slavic features, German accent, steady flow of dinars, and unflagging chivalry, Max Heidl was a fascinating puzzle. He'd dangled 'Istanbul' like a brass ring, as if certain she'd snatch it. In heading east with Max instead of hitching south with Peter, she'd chosen risk. Now these unplanned stops made her uneasy, reminding her that Peter might have been right, and she might have to pay a price for staying on with Max, whose smooth dark features suddenly oppressed her.

"*Ćele kula.*" He squinted to screen out the sun.

Ćele. Tower. Tower of, of . . . oh, God. The Tower of Skulls.

"You are okay?"

Specters from Byzantium and Rome had stalked the ruined sepulchers to which he'd brought her earlier. Fragments of dead cultures. She wanted to tell Max she'd had enough of ghosts today. Yet wasn't this why Yugoslavia had first attracted her? To confront those ghosts and through them grasp . . . what? History? Humanity? What crap! She couldn't even grasp herself. "Yes, thank you, Max."

Though he'd opened the car door to let in air, they smothered beneath the stagnant heat that settled over them like a woolen afghan. As she worked to collect herself, she saw Max studying her again, his fine brows knit. At last she said, "I'm ready."

She grabbed her Indian bag and forced her sluggish feet to move. Max gave her his arm for support, but she recoiled from his light touch. "No, really. I'm . . . I'm fine now."

They entered a small chapel. Inside, she stared at the column in its center—some twelve feet tall, composed of even rows of sandy clay and—

Her stomach heaved. She blinked, then forced herself to look. Everything she'd read came flooding back to her. Among the empty indentations were the last few dozen skulls from the Battle of Čegar. Whitened. Hollow sockets. Halloween grins. Proof that might makes right, that justice lies in the eye of the beholder.

Though she knew the tower from photos and research, seeing it was different. Before it now, she wasn't prepared for its power.

Briefly rendered speechless, Max said, "You know its history?"

"A bit. They're Serbian skulls from 1809. The first revolt against the Turks since *Kosovo Polje*."

He sniggered. "Not a good outcome, to look at it."

"At least three thousand Serb deaths."

"And the tower?"

"Well, if I remember right, the Turkish pasha forced Serbs here to fill the victims' scalps and skins with something . . . cotton? sawdust? Anyway, he shipped a thousand stuffed heads to Constantinople, but the Sultan had them emptied and returned to Niš. To build this tower, a warning for Serbs not to mess with Turks."

"Just so. Those Turkies miss nothing."

As they circled the eerie shrine, Max asked, "But where are the rest?"

"The skulls, you mean?"

He nodded.

"The Turks never covered the tower. Weather hurt it . . . looters, trophy-seekers, Serbs wanting to bury their dead."

"Hard to tell from only skulls."

"One would think. Then some pasha had more removed. He thought they made Serbs angry. After Turkey had to withdraw, Serbs began protecting it."

"Of course. They love their martyrs."

Anna stepped back for a different view. The few skulls left stared out unseeing at the walls, evoking ghostly images. She turned to Max. "You know, this place intrigued Lamartine."

"Who?"

"A French Romantic poet." Max's knit brows made her feel ashamed. He'd told her he lacked formal education. But he seemed so worldly, knew a lot about so much. Sometimes she forgot.

"Ah." A sheepish grin. "He puts it in a poem?"

"No, but he described it well." She closed her eyes to find some of those images. "'The tower rises from the plain, gleaming like white marble . . . the skulls' remaining wisps of hair flutter in the mountain breeze . . . the wind makes them all moan.'"

Max was staring at a bony cranium, its mouth a scream. Without a trace of irony, he said, "I see it, what he tells."

So Max had felt the poet's power. But maybe it was more than words. Anna could almost hear the skulls cry out. Memorializing victim and victimizer, the lust for power and the brave but futile gestures of resisters, *Ćele kula* countered the romance of battle with the naked face of death. It embodied McLuhan's thesis—the medium was the message.

"We go now?" Max said. Restrained, opaque, he had whispered, as if he didn't want the skulls, their only company, to hear.

"Yes, Max. Please."

As she shivered in the heat, he gave her his arm for support. Close to the exit, Anna turned to see the tower one last time and seemed to catch the death's head of her dream.

NEAR THE BULGARIAN BORDER

June 25, 1968

The land began to rise and green. The outer edge of the *Stara Planina* pushed up in rugged folds and lofty peaks studded with oak and beech. A breeze came through the windows. A fading sun painted the sky in soft pastels and bathed the earth in soothing light. Anna welcomed the muted rays, the cool edge to the air. His right hand on the steering wheel, Max sat back in his seat, elegant, unreadable. "So, Anna, you feel better now?" The voice was low, the sideways glance solicitous.

"Much better, thanks. It's lovely here."

A sign appeared for Dmitrovgrad and Sofia. "The border, Anna." Max snagged her with his eyes, his forehead creased. "We're close." He began to hum under his breath. A melody in a twisted minor key.

"What're you humming?" For a moment Max seemed someone else.

"Humming?" His jaw tightened. The furrow in his brow deepened as he began to search, to track himself. "Oh, that. About Jug Bogdan. You know the name?"

She nodded yes. Recalled last night in the Belgrade *kafana,* how the song had evoked for her that hero's tragic end. Why had Max brought them there? And how did he know Jug Bogdan? In his eyes, weren't they all Turkies?

In a mountain valley, with twilight coming on, Max pulled off the road beside a lovely meadow. "Let's walk a bit," he said.

Though it wasn't quite an order, Anna shrank back a little, into the corner by the door. But Max helped her out, his right hand smooth and skilled, infallible. She felt herself Persephone, about to be abducted to the underworld. But she didn't push the hand away.

Max drew her slowly through the weeds and lovely mountain flowers that carpeted the lea. He walked slightly ahead of her; she couldn't see his face. Laurel, basil, rosemary—the place smelled like a Balkan peasant feast. Her legs were jelly. Where would he throw her down? Nothing he did here would break the surface of the world.

But Max made no strange moves.

When they reached a large boulder whose flat gray top invited rest, he motioned her to sit and stood before her, hands on hips, shaking his head. "So, Anna. We are close here to the border."

She caught his pause. He didn't usually repeat himself. He seemed uncertain now, fumbling toward the next thicket of words.

"The Serbs, they don't give trouble. The Bulgars, though, you cannot tell. And Turkies, they make trouble when they can." He let her chew that bite before continuing.

"And one thing more I must tell you." His feet shifted. His head cocked to the left, as if to catch a distant sound. His hands slid into pockets. But his eyes stared straight at her.

Anna couldn't fake a smile. A chill worked its way along her spine. "I'm listening." She concentrated on a furry bug that inched across the stone as she waited for the punch line.

"I am, you see . . ." Max squinted at the purpled mountains and swallowed hard. ". . . a smuggler."

She heard as if from miles away. The rolled *r* gave the word a comic twist. Oh, it was lovely here. The birds. The flowers. The patch of lavender at her feet. The soft gold of the sun tinting the blue. Quiet. Serene—shit! Peter had been right. She studied Max. Why had he held this back, beneath the chivalry, the charm, but always there? Why had he drawn her away from Peter and safety?

He sat down silent next to her. On the narrow rock his thigh brushed hers. The pressure made her body tense. She shut him out. Looked inward, backward, all the way to Sunday. Checked out the Mercedes' trunk, back seat, front seat, roof. Found nothing but the steady flow of dinars and the phone calls. Straightening her back, she turned to Max. His face seemed a text in some strange tongue, its letters mystic in their beauty but quite incomprehensible. "So tell me, then." It came out harsh and bitter. "What are you smuggling?"

He'd stretched out on the rock, leaning back on linen elbows, casual and cool. A nod. A wry grin. But the eyes weren't smiling. With a little laugh, he answered, "The Mercedes."

She exhaled slowly. There it was. The stillness suffocated her.

She rose. Blinked. Felt her heart race. Fought for air. Clogged lungs. A flooded brain. Her lungs filled up with air. Something—fear? excitement?—was bubbling up inside her, swelling, not to be contained.

"Anna." Two gentle arms restrained her. "You are okay?" The arms moved to encircle her, then fell against his body, tight, as if he'd tied them up.

Those damned folds at the edges of his smile. She almost reached to touch them. The eyes bored through her. Made her wonder what he saw.

"So, Anna, if you want to leave, I understand."

And now she reminded herself of the truth. The choice had been all hers. Max bore no blame. She started laughing. At herself. At him.

His eyes were burning holes in her.

"Hey, Max. I'm fine. Do we make Sofia tonight?"

She saw him nod. His eyes relaxed. She'd passed the test.

"Tonight Sofia, yes. But first we make a plan, in case they bother us. You will ride in back. Yes?" He stooped to pick a wild flower and held it out for her. "They stop. They look. Maybe make us step outside. Then I tell them just I pick you up. You're making auto-stop. The Bulgars, they don't like the hitchhike much. In case they make you pay some fine, I give you *leva* now, before we cross. After, they will put you on a bus to Sofia. It's good?"

She nodded. *Leva?* He must have changed the *dinars* yesterday. A world ago. Before she'd decided to leave Peter.

The mountains followed them into Bulgaria, ghost-like in the gathering dark. As Max had instructed, Anna rode in back. At the makeshift border checkpoint, a single-story hut of weathered boards, a roly-poly guard, his uniform too tight, beamed at her through a comic movie villain's black mustache while a younger, sleeker model flipped through Max's passport, silent. His thin lips pursed, he sent them through. The heavy one gave Max a wink. Watching from the back, she saw Max hand him something else—was it *leva?*

A mile or so beyond the spot, around the rugged body of another great stone giant, Max stopped the car and Anna got into the front. The clear cold tingled. She wore his jacket now. The darkness seethed with potent truths and possibilities. Max's sculpted profile seemed a guard against danger, a watch in the night.

SOFIA

June 25, 1968

Spiraling down from the mountains, the Mercedes floated Anna through a hushed domain of black shapes and layered space. The charged air and the heavy silence lulled her, while darkness wrapped around her like the soft folds of a silken cape.

Ahead, shimmering threads of gold lit up the sky. From the gilt-edged black emerged the outlines of a city, mute and still, caught in the spell of the night. Haloed beneath the pale beam of an ancient streetlight, Max leaned toward her. "Sofia. We go right to the center. The Grand Balkan." He gave a little laugh, it wasn't clear at whose expense. "It's not so grand, maybe. But good enough."

Anna didn't want to stir the quiet needlessly. But he seemed to await a response. So she said, "I'm glad we're here," which was, at least, the truth.

Max parked the Mercedes and squired Anna to the registration desk. The crone at the counter eyed them both with wariness and spat out broken German as if it were a fruit gone bad. Anna thought she'd asked how many rooms they'd need. Max smiled and stood quite still, his body somehow lithe and loose despite the long hours on the road. Then he turned to Anna. For an uneasy moment his eyes, lit with a dark intensity, swept her up and carried her into a thirties thriller filled with Balkan spies. At last he nodded to himself and answered, "*Zwei, danke.*"

Two. He'd chosen separate rooms.

Outside Anna's door, he set down her satchel and tapped her on the shoulder. The light touch made her shiver. "Till eight. Breakfast. Sleep well, Anna." Before walking away, he tossed her one last rueful smile.

Inside she hurled her satchel into a corner and sprawled across the bed. Her body tensed; a wall of questions stopped her cold, questions she should have asked before. Who was Max? What was his game? And what about her? What had made her go with him, embrace that risk? The afternoon's truth-telling seemed too pat. She ought to march straight down the hall and hammer on his door. Break through that cool veneer. Dislodge the mask. Uncover his true face, his plan for her. But she wouldn't. Couldn't let her own mask slip.

She fought back the sharp pang in the core of her that felt like death. The lacerating throb of an old hunger that ambushed her when she thought she'd broken free. This morning she had longed for change, for a purpose that would fill her life. Ridiculous. She lacked the strength, the confidence.

Arms pressed tight across her chest to lock in pain, she rocked as if the rhythm might enable her to shed this skin that pulsed with need, this mass of fevered nerve-ends like hot mouths. She rocked and rocked, the urge to scream held in, until at last a flood of longing pummeled her into a tight ball on the narrow bed, where she waited like a fugitive for sleep to come and take her far from anger and desire.

Max entered her dreams, surrounded by the close-pressed giant trunks of ancient trees, a vital presence in a shaggy mountain glen. Baggy peasant pants. Wide purple cumberbund. Feet in leather *opanci,* those Serbian shoes with toes like curved boat prows. He snapped out orders in a gruff, staccato German to a band of bearded ruffians with rifles in their hands. A blend of Balkan-Turkish brigand and high-ranked SS officer, he was sending thugs to ambush lost merchants and wandering Jews. Along with her dream-self, Anna trembled as she cowered behind a rock. Shared her alter-ego's fierce desire to run her fingers through the thick tousle of hair, to feel those lips, grown cruel, on hers.

The morning shower was cold. She didn't feel quite clean. Hard bed. Stale sheets. Bad dream. A long night. But the show had to go on, the role she'd shaped for Max. For everyone. She intended to experience this fascinating world, and Max was her guide, for good or ill.

She chose her only dress, a blue sheath that made her eyes shine "like pools," at least according to one former authority. The black sandals with the little heels. Her favorite earrings, courtesy of Christos—their shiny silver set off the tanned glow of the face that stared back at her in the tiny bathroom mirror. Their triple dangles delivered a challenge. Then mauve lipstick and a trace of black eye liner. Good she hadn't shipped these to Athens.

Bright sun invaded the elegant murk of the Balkan's dining room. Cool in his seersucker suit, Max waved a paper from a white-clothed table in the back. His smile seemed forced. "You sleep okay, Anna?" Puffy circles edged his eyes, as if he'd had a rough night too. He handed her a tourist map. Attached to it with a large black clip were several sheets of paper. "I make today some errands. Here. A sightsee plan."

She took it, careful not to touch his fingers, as his glance moved from her eyes down to the scoop neck of her dress.

"We check out after breakfast, then meet at 5:00 in front of the hotel. It's good?" The little smile. The tilted head.

She gave him a reluctant nod.

Yesterday Max had said they'd start for Istanbul this morning. Why had he made the change? While Turkey receded in the distance, Anna rummaged for a knowing look. Wasted effort. Max had turned from her, his knit brow focused on the distant reaches of the vast white room. Seconds later he turned around once more. Delivered himself to her, all chivalry and smiles. "I tell you after all these things."

After? She cursed herself for not mounting a challenge. But she didn't want to break their rhythm now and lose the chance to penetrate his mysteries.

An hour later, Max escorted her to the hotel entrance. The yellow cobblestones of Lenin Square gleamed in the sun. He set down the bags and pulled a pouch from an inner pocket. Her eyebrows moved together; her mouth became a scowl. But Max grinned back at her.

"Only more *leva*. To eat. To pay some fees. Okay?"

He touched his right hand to her face, as Connor used to do when she was younger and at home, to push away the stubborn lock of hair through which she saw him now.

"Enjoy your day, Anna."

She managed a small nod. Then he marched off, back straight, armed with their luggage.

Anna tracked his progress till he faded around the corner like the last ambiguous chord of a Bach prelude. Only for an instant did she wonder if she'd ever see her bag again. Her watch read 9:45, though what that meant she no longer was sure. She'd lost all sense of time, couldn't even say what day it was, her Timex rendered obsolete by a subtle shift in the physical laws that governed this new world. Here, Balkan time held sway. Yesterday and Tomorrow converged in a Now that jerked along in fits and starts, lulling her, then abruptly lurching forward.

She studied Max's papers. On the map, the Grand Balkan lay on the western edge of Sofia's center, home to three sites Max had circled in red. She needn't take his route, of course. But she should orient herself.

Now she surveyed the broad prospect. Across the square, Lenin on his pedestal reviewed traffic. To the south, a green-cragged peak with tiny white patches—Mt. Vitoša, the notes said—towered above the city. Then it struck her—maybe she should follow Max's plan, to see if reading it she might begin to read its author too.

The first stop on his map took her south to Sveta Nedelja, an enchanting little church. Glossy notes clipped to the map, ripped from some English-language source, described it as the last of many sanctuaries built atop the ancient fortress of Serdica, a Roman trading hub. On the bottom sheet of rough, lined paper, next to #1, Max had scrawled in red, "*Secret Police spy from the cupola. So church is useful after all.*" She could almost see his sneer, which made her laugh.

Next came a site behind the Grand Balkan—Sveti Georgi, the Rotunda of St. George, the dragon-slayer. Built on the ruins of a pagan temple, the tiny church contrasted in its round grace with the huge hotel that virtually surrounded it. The Turks had made it a mosque; Max's scribble read: "*The Gül Camii welcomes you.*"

Many red dots clustered to the east, so Anna followed the yellow-cobbled Boulevard of the Liberator Tsar—Russia's Alexander II. According to the notes, he oversaw the fight to free Bulgaria from the Turks. The broad street ran from Lenin Square to the Alexander Nevski Cathedral, whose domes gleamed green and golden in the distance. With stops marked all along the way, she wondered how long the walk would take. But somehow she had energy despite the night, and the morning air was pleasant.

She bypassed the dull but massive Party House with its huge red star but stopped before the National Museum. The red scrawl said, "*The ones at Niš are better,*" but Anna entered anyway. She paused before a large engraved gray slab from the sixth millennium BC, its strange markings, faint squiggles, all but wiped away, some deep linear cuts still sharp and clear. Within its sterile glass, the carved stone whispered from a distant world. What did it say, and what could she reply?

Along the chestnut-bordered sweep of Alexander Battenberg Square, Anna spotted young people from everywhere. The university was close; perhaps they studied there, or would attend the Youth Festival. In one corner, somber guards in uniforms and weird plumed hats goose-stepped before the entrance to the Georgi Dimitrov Mausoleum, "the preserved corpse of Bulgaria's first communist prime minister." Max's red words clucked, "*Another hero to adore.*" So many forms of madness.

Near the cathedral, Anna passed Sveta Sofia, another small but lovely Byzantine church from which, apparently, Sofia took its name. Turks had made this, too, a mosque, as Max had underscored: "*Also Turkies remodel here.*" *Sofia,* Orthodox Wisdom, lighting Muslim souls. Maybe now was worst of all, reduced to pleasing sightseers and fledgling history buffs like her. Her feet throbbed. She'd been treading hard pavement for over two hours.

Finally she reached Nevski Square. The cathedral swelled in pompous majesty, splendidly self-satisfied, a neo-Byzantine fantasia of swirling, gilt-edged shapes. According to the notes, it was begun in 1904 to honor the two-hundred thousand Russian soldiers sacrificed to wrest Bulgaria from the Turks. So this shrine embodied Bulgaria's debt to its spiritual Mother. As if reading her mind, the red script teased, "*In Sofia, the biggest church is Russian.*"

Inside, a white-haired God stared down at her from the huge central cupola. She exited the main entrance past *The Last Judgment* and took an outside door into the crypt, which housed a vast collection of icons. Elongated faces filled the dark internal space, haunted features twisted in appalling torment of spirit. As if they detected the sweet stink of evil in its countless forms and despaired for those, like her, who saw only an absence at the heart of things. Their eastern eyes viewed her with distant pity, as if saddened by her failure to embrace their truth. Like her Staten Island relatives at Fiona's funeral, anguished that Anna's unbaptized soul would writhe in the fires of hell.

All these saints and martyrs trapped on wood, metal, and canvas, forever caught in the horror of vision. Anna all but ran from the cathedral. Eastern icons worked on her this way; their keen eyes seemed to understand what Dostoevsky's Myshkin and Conrad's Marlow didn't dare confront. But these would accept the abyss and say, like Zosima, "Love God. Do good."

Three dots remained to the northwest. Anna hurried back toward Lenin Square. She needed food and rest. At 2:00 she found a small café near the hotel and ordered bread and yogurt, with a strong, sweet Turkish coffee. Max's *leva* lay untouched inside their envelope. She would have liked to linger at her table, to see if some among the passing faces bore the icons' olive ovals, high cheekbones, and brooding eyes tinged with a hint of spiritual distress. But little time remained to complete Max's script.

Revitalized, she headed north, past the Banja Baši Mosque, a vision from the Arabian Nights. But she couldn't enter if she hoped to rendezvous with Max at 5:00. Instead, she hustled toward the stalls the notes labeled "the women's market." Noisy, dirty, swarming with life. A buzz of flies. Produce on the verge of going bad. Stands of aprons, vests, and belts—a dance of shape and color. Anna pondered buying her family keepsakes but decided to wait till Istanbul.

Recalling the red directive, "*Buy a vest,*" she roamed from stall to stall. So many choices. At last she thrust into her bag a fitted vest of teal wool worked with mauve and crimson flowers. She opened the pouch of *leva*. Max had told her to buy it; let him pay.

A cool breeze from the mountains showed the afternoon was ebbing. One last stop remained. Several blocks later, she stood across the street from a building no less fanciful than many she'd seen today. Filigree and Moorish domes, it might have been a mosque minus the minaret—the Synagogue of Sofia.

An image flashed—her last time in a temple, after which she'd cut her tie to Judaism. Her family had moved to Virginia when she was ten, but she had treasured her dim memories of the tiny congregation in their Wisconsin college town. At fifteen, yearning for the warmth of that community, so small it had to import student rabbis and cantors for its special rituals, she'd found a congregation in Alexandria and told her parents she wanted to attend a service there. Surprised by her resolve, they'd let her take the bus alone.

She'd entered with respect, ready to be carried toward some cosmic truth, her soul naked and open to the transcendence for which she longed. The service itself was splendid, perhaps even too grand—gorgeous music, soft light streaming through the stained-glass windows, a magnificent ark. Yet as the many congregants greeted one another and recited countless prayers she didn't know, she felt herself recoil. Invisible within that well-dressed throng, she'd fled. No marvel had occurred, no sacred vision—only a greater sense of isolation. On the bus ride back, she'd recognized her own naïveté. As if one visit to a large and well-entrenched community could make her feel at home. But she'd never returned to the religion or the culture.

Now she brooded, yearning to escape, afraid that entering here would somehow force her to renew that bond. And something else disturbed her. She'd followed Max's map all day and felt his presence in his caustic words. But for this stop he'd filled three lines with red, then inked them out. Seeking clues to why he'd sent her here, she scrutinized the paper from all angles but could decipher nothing. With a strange presentiment, she crossed the street and opened the heavy arched door.

IN THE SYNAGOGUE

June 26, 1968

A musty odor ambushed her in the semi-darkness. On both sides of the entrance hall a dim light cast shadows. An ornate chandelier hung from the ceiling of the inner gallery, but few of its bulbs gave off light. As her vision adjusted, she made out dust, disorder, and an old man with a trim gray beard and penetrating eyes beneath thick brows. He was sitting on a hard-backed chair beside a battered table.

As Anna moved into the gallery, she tried to recall what she knew of Bulgaria's Jews. Hadn't most come from Spain in 1492, expelled by the Inquisition? And Turkey, needing a merchant class, had welcomed them. But one story she'd never understood. Bulgaria had made Jews citizens and saved them from her German allies during World War II. But she'd sent those Jews in her occupied Macedonian territory to die in Hitler's camps. The sources didn't explain this paradox.

Anna felt the old man's eyes on her. So she stepped with care around the inner space that seemed in disrepair, its shrine cluttered with scaffolding and ladders, a lovely ark with pews in disarray. Still, her neck grew hot beneath his glare.

As she worked her way back toward the entrance, she heard a raspy whisper like a ghost's and a string of words that sounded somehow Spanish. She wheeled around. He hadn't used Bulgarian. Then she understood. He'd spoken Ladino, the language of the Spanish Jews, the Sephardim. She wasn't sure how to respond.

She saw him frown, his eyes narrow.

He said, "*Russkaya devushka?*"

Why had he thought her Russian? She decided to try her Spanish. "*Pues no. Americana.*"

He shook his head in disbelief and said in English with a heavy accent, "American, they never come."

Fierce eyes awaited an answer to the question he hadn't asked. But how could she tell this patriarch that an East German smuggler with whom she shared a dubious connection had simply put the synagogue on his list of spots not to be missed? She didn't understand either. Who would make this place a red dot on the map of musts?

The old man snapped, "No matter. Here come only old ones." His rounded shoulders shrugged. His tone dismissed her. But then he added, "Young ones gone to Israel, or just they stop to be a Jew."

"To Israel?" The Iron Curtain countries weren't exactly known to let their Jews escape, especially not to Israel.

"Most of them, they . . . gone."

"I thought Bulgaria saved its Jews."

"So. You know that story." His tone was short, icy; his eyes pierced hers. "Is true. But what it means? For what they did it? Not for love. What else I don't know how to say."

She had so many questions. But studying that old face, worn, wrinkled, almost abandoned—as if he'd locked his soul away in some far safer place— she couldn't find the words.

His eyes like sharp skewers, he gestured to the gallery. "See this? We try to fix." He paused. "We keep now only Hanukkah and Purim. You know why?"

Anna winced, embarrassed at her ignorance. She tried to think . . . both holidays were child-oriented. Parties, special sweets, costumes, and games. And both honored military victories. "Not so very godly?"

His lips curled in a frosty smile that validated her response. But then he asked, "And how to celebrate?"

She really didn't follow, wasn't sure exactly what he meant.

"So, we must make dance. For all Bulgarian people. To make only for Jews is crime against Bulgaria."

A crime against Bulgaria? It made no sense. Watching his face, his angry, grieving eyes, the deep lines in his forehead, she sighed but found no comeback. The silence grew until she asked, "Are you here to take donations?" On the table she'd noticed a small black box.

"Yes. And to watch—if someone take things, write on walls. Police never find who. We try to see."

Putting some of Max's *leva* in the box, Anna recalled the random violence of the young neo-Nazis near her parents' home. Wondered how this old man, or any of his ancient group, could stop a band of kids or ruffians from making mayhem. She swallowed hard.

"So, young lady." Eyes grown somehow softer, he offered her a slow, sad smile, seeming at last to inhabit his face. "Maybe now you see what happen here. Is left no heart. True, not only Jews. But now we are so few, with no ties no more. To be Bulgarian patriot, not can be Jew."

Anna wished she could put her arms around him, to show with an embrace that she'd begun to understand and, more, that she cared. But she could only listen.

"Someday they make big display." The old man raised his right arm and pointed toward the east wing of the synagogue. "Fix building. Show tourist. State pay. How Bulgaria save her Jews." He gave a dry, cracked laugh. "Maybe then they watch."

Anna longed to hear about his family, his history, but the words died in her throat.

"Since war last year, Jewish paper here make only bad for Israel. Council tell us proper citizen hate Zionist fascist."

"The Party council?"

"Not. The Jewish."

"I don't understand. The Jewish council?"

"Yes."

"But . . . if so many went to Israel?" She couldn't clarify her thought. Yet given Bulgaria's anti-Zionism, she wondered how its Jews could stay connected to family there. She caught the pain that cracked his face—as if his world had ended and he was its lone survivor.

The old man turned away. She began to leave. Almost to the door, she heard him summon her.

"Please to wait one moment, young lady." He approached her, in his wrinkled hand a small black book. "Take."

She did.

"Open."

Inside she saw the Hebrew letters she'd tried to master when she was eight. Her mother, Ruth, who'd never wanted to learn Hebrew, had volunteered to teach the third graders, including Anna, its letters and some simple words each Sunday in the office of their physician, a congregant. On Saturdays, Anna, even then gifted at languages, would read over the material and offer Ruth some strategies. The plan had failed, of course, and her Hebrew study had ended. She could feel her eyes about to tear. "I . . . I can't accept this. I can't even read the words. It would be a waste."

She tried to give him back the book, but the old man shook his head. He took her arm and walked her to the door. "One more, one less." His shoulders shrugged. "Maybe, even, Party bosses buy new one when tourist come to see our ghost. When no Jews no more live here." At the entrance he placed his hands on her shoulders. "I wish for you . . ." he said, fixing her with bleared but piercing eyes, ". . . a good life."

She darted from the synagogue, clutching the book that smelled of black-clad men and short, round, scarfed women, of prayer shawls and phylacteries, of candle-lit small kitchens and fresh-baked loaves of challah, but also of the poverty and prejudice her Jewish ancestors had fled, the murderous pogroms of Eastern Europe. And all that Ruth had suffered in Indiana—the hate-filled rhetoric of Father Coughlin, the violent antics of the KKK, the daily scorn. No wonder she had sought to shed her identity, had married an Ivy Leaguer whose Italian last name hid his Jewish father's origins. Breathless, unnerved, Anna ran southward to the Grand Balkan. Her watch said 5:30. Half an hour late. Could Max have left without her?

It was nearly six when she reached the square. Her sandals clicked against the tiles as she ran to where she saw the Mercedes outside the Grand Balkan. Cool and handsome, Max lolled against its hood, deep in conversation with a short, dark man in a shiny white shirt open to the third button, his hairy chest on prominent display. A heavy-featured peasant face beneath a wide forehead and spiky mop of coarse black hair. Thick lips pursed in a permanent leer. The compact body, lean and muscular, seemed poised to spring, recalling the Belgrade Gypsy's bear. She recoiled before his animal energy.

"Anna," Max exclaimed, pulling himself upright, bestowing a broad smile. He offered her his hand and pointed to the stranger. "My comrade, Kosta Stojkov."

"A pleasure, Mees Anna," the stranger offered in a voice like rich, dark beer. "Forgeeve, please." He took her hand between his own warm, hairy paws. "My Englees only leetle." His flashing gold-toothed smile wrapped itself around her, brown eyes beaming under heavy brows. Anna smiled back, cautious, a warning signal buzzing in her brain.

"Come," Max ordered. "We go to Vitoša to eat." He opened the front door for her, while Kosta Stojkov burrowed into the back seat as if it were a woman.

MOUNT VITOŠA

June 26, 1968

Night wrapped the world in sequined black. The air was bracing, pungent with the scent of mountain growth. Noises filled the stillness—branches rustling in the breeze, fluttering of insect wings, unseen creatures calling one another in the dark. Nothing seemed itself as Anna looked down from Mt. Vitoša. So much she didn't understand. So hard to stay afloat.

At last she made her way back from the carved-wood terrace railing to the table. Everyone had gone inside but Max, his fingers curled around another glass of *rakija*. Kosta's chair was empty, too. An acrid odor rose from the mound of close-smoked butts in the large ceramic ashtray near his plate; more than a few bore mauve half-moons. Below, the many lights of Sofia flickered.

"You are too quiet, Anna," Max chided.

Damn him. As if she were a stewardess, her job to maintain charm whatever happened.

She cleared her throat. "It's been rather a long day, Max." Ice-dipped, the words earned her a puzzled look. She nodded toward Kosta's ashtray. "Why is it, Max, that all of Europe chain-smokes foul, unfiltered cigarettes?"

"Ah, yes. The ones you like to—how do you say—'bum'?"

Bastard. "Everyone but you."

Behind his grin, Max studied her. "Why do you ask me first now?" He nodded toward the fresh brandies he'd ordered. They clinked glasses. Then she began to sip the fiery stuff.

Why, indeed? She mulled over the hours in the chaste Mercedes, the leather plush, pristine, reeking of money. Peter had only smoked outside, at stops. Had Max said something to him? Kosta, on the other hand—but even he had waited till they'd reached the lodge and found an outside table.

At that moment she looked at Max. The veil that hid his eyes had disappeared. Two points of dark light smoldered at their centers, snared her, drew her toward them. She couldn't pull her gaze from his. Helpless, she could feel him reeling her in closer and closer.

Suddenly he shut his eyes and let her go. Anna neither moved nor spoke, just watched him lean back in his chair, exhausted, like an angler she'd once spotted on a boat in Narragansett Bay. Having battled hard against his prey and won, he'd sighed and cast his worthy prize back into the ocean.

Max shot her a look she couldn't read. Then his eyes moved off, took in the black beyond the railing. "My father," he wrestled with each word, "he smokes too much. Coughs too much. Dead before he has fifty years."

"Hard for you." She tried to find those dark points in his eyes, but they were once more veiled.

He sniggered. Shrugged. Let his smile deflect potential drama. "Hard for everyone. The war. The Reds. Not a good time."

"You remember?" She worked to hide her excitement. He'd chosen now to let her in a crack. She mustn't push. Max shook his head, his little grin making those teasing creases at the corners of his mouth and eyes.

"I am born in 1935. So then I am just a kid."

She'd gotten his age about right.

"But some things I remember clear, like yesterday. Always hungry. Bad food. Cold nights. My mother, grandparents, always whispering. My father gone."

"Gone?"

"In '38. Before even the war."

"The army?" Had his father been a Nazi?

"No. Jail." Max's smile went hard. "He stays away till after. When he comes back, Czechs send us to Germany."

She scrutinized his face. "You told me you were German." She saw his fingers tighten around the brandy glass. "You said you came from somewhere near the Czech border."

His jaw clamped down. "Yes, sure. But I come first in '45." He paused to sniff his brandy. "'The Ore Mountains,' they call that place. My family is coal miners."

Now she remembered. He'd told her that their first day out, but she'd long since forgotten. It hadn't fit his image. "Not good for coughs," she quipped, aping his dark humor.

He grinned. "Not good for nothing . . ."

The words trailed off into some thought he didn't share. Her eyes stayed glued to the mask behind which Max concealed himself. He sat graceful in the chair, an elegant mannequin. But his fingers tapped the glass.

"Why, Max?"

"Why what?"

"You said your father went to jail."

"Ah, yes. First jail. Then later, I don't know, moving around, here, there. He ends up in some camp in the east . . ."

Her mouth snapped shut. She couldn't stop a shiver.

"You okay, Anna?"

"I'm fine." She pressed the rough cloth napkin to her lips, as if to wipe off brandy.

Max swirled the liquid in his glass, peering deep into it as if the ripples might explain his fate. "*Sudetendeutsch*. It means something to you?"

Lederhosen. *Oktoberfest*. No. The wrong track. Pages far back in the brain. Something. What?

"You're not quite sure? Maybe this time you need some help?" Eyebrows raised, he smiled at her confusion. "Germans live a long time in the northwest of the Hapsburg lands."

His mordant grin and arched eyebrows compounded the shame she felt for this gap in her knowledge.

"Allies give those German towns to Czechs after the first war. Always there is tension. All those Germans, but Czechs want their own place. When Henlein makes a party only for Germans, things get worse." Max took another sip. His nostrils flared to catch the smell. His tongue traced the sticky sweetness on his lips. "My father is a Social Democrat."

"They were leftists, weren't they?" Had she at least gotten this right? And what label might fit his son?

He nodded. "When Allies give Sudetenland to Germany in '38, Hitler's men hunt down the ones who don't join Henlein. Others leave, but my father stays, for the family. Of course, the Nazis take him."

"And your mother?"

"Some days pass. Then they come for her." He scrutinized the well-kept nails of his right hand. "Three days, then she is home. Bruises everywhere. Clothes rags. Even now I can hear my grandfather screaming, cursing Nazis. Then we go to live with Uncle Rade."

"The Germans let her go?" Rade? A Serbian name.

"She is pretty then. Long, dark hair. Blue eyes. A bit like you. So maybe they rape her." His seeming nonchalance made Anna shudder. "For them she is only . . ." Another sip of brandy. ". . . some kind of whore."

"I'm confused."

"Papa works the mines with Rade. From Rade, Papa meets her. Their family comes from the east. Papa's parents never like her. For them, for many Germans . . ." He stared into his *rakija* and sighed. ". . . Slavs are Turkies. Backward. Low. But even if she is some kind of misplaced Serb, he wants her. Before my older brother, Ernst, comes, they get a priest and go to live with her parents."

The heavy-lidded waiter, flaccid paunch hung out over his belt, handed Max the check and hovered near the table. While Max settled the bill and left some *leva* beside his glass, Anna digested his stories. Born in Czechoslovakia. His German father jailed for not supporting Hitler. His Serbian mother, despised by his father's family, detained, maybe raped, by the Nazis, then released. If all this was true, then she and Max, Irish-Romanian and Germano-Serb, were matching specimens of . . . of what? Could she dub them Euro-trash—ethnic hybrids shaped by the quirks of history and the defiant logic of the human heart?

They left after midnight. Despite the well-padded Mercedes, Max and Anna bounced along with every rut on the narrow road. Scraps of identity lay on the seat between them. From time to time she caught him in a corner glance that mirrored hers.

No highway. No city lights to help them navigate. Just mountains and more mountains, lit only by the moon, the stars, and the beams of the Mercedes. The way wound in and out among sharp curves. On either side rose natural obstructions to clear vision. Overhangs threatened to fall upon the car. For once, Max held the Mercedes to a crawl. At least the night was clear and no one else was on the road. They seemed to have the mountains to themselves.

Anna sensed that they were traveling southwest. Istanbul was east. Kosta had vanished. But to ask something would cost her now. She'd likely find out soon enough.

"You don't ask where we go," Max said, as if he'd read her thoughts.

Suddenly a huge shape leapt in front of them. Max hit the brakes. Anna grabbed the dashboard. As the creature lumbered off into the darkness, Max exhaled.

"What was that?" she asked when she'd found her voice.

"A bear? Or maybe buffalo. Up here they have still Asian buffalo."

Once again they snaked along the mountain's edge in silence. She meant to keep an eye on Max, but all her bones told her that sleep was good. She fought to keep from dozing off until at some point he instructed her, "Sleep. It is late. You walk too much today."

The first reference to her Sofia trek, so far away it seemed a part of someone else's ancient history.

"Kosta we will see again. He goes to Goce Delčev."

Goce Delčev? The name struck some dim chord. Another Macedonian nationalist? A school teacher? Yes, now she recalled. Like Sandanski, another IMRO leader. Dead, she thought, in some doomed uprising against the Turks. *Ilinden*, 1903? Not sure. So sleepy now that nothing mattered much.

Arms clutching her shoulders. Legs pulled up. Rocking like the motion of the tiny student ship on which she'd crossed the sea. A sudden warmth enclosing her. Drifting. Sinking beneath the gentle waves. Letting go . . .

PART III: IN THE MOUNTAINS

SINA GORA

June 27, 1968

Shrill screams. Behind, a moving horde of dark bodies. Ahead, a towering waterfall. She plunged into the rippling curtain. Twisted round and round in the foam-edged swirl. Stone-battered, she let the river carry her away. But still the ghostly shapes pursued, their war-shrieks shattering hope.

Why? What had she done? She was so cold.

And where was he . . . the shadow-man who'd sheltered her, wrapped his jacket around her shivering arms, assured her they would break free?

No rest. No companion. No time to breathe. To scream—

A rush of garlic. Floating up through space. A warming weight and hands not hers.

"Mees Anna." A coarse, deep voice. "The brandy was too much?"

She rose through cloudy layers of shredded dreams. Found herself beneath a quilt, atop it Max's jacket. A tiny whitewashed room, low-ceilinged and windowless. She lay on a pillowed banquette that ran along low walls hung with tapestries and rugs. Light streamed from a narrow archway screened with flowered cloth. Beside her on a stool beamed Kosta, his gold-toothed grin still like a leer. "Where's M-m . . ." Her dry mouth locked up. Couldn't speak. She had to will it. "Max?"

"He gone." Kosta's glance seemed gentler than before. "I take care you teel he come back." A thick-bodied woman in clogs entered the room. Kosta turned to Anna. "Ljuba seester." She caught the fond glance they exchanged.

Ljuba's face was broad like his, but the smile she gave them both showed dimpled cheeks. Her sloe eyes beamed beneath thick brows that matched the mass of heavy hair escaping from her scarf. Hard to tell her age. She might not even be thirty.

A nearly adolescent girl came in bearing a tray with Turkish coffee, bread slices, and a honey-pot.

"Good bees," Kosta said. "Ljuba's honey best!"

Then a boy of eight or nine burst in with plum jam in a jar like those Ruth used when putting up preserves during those long Maine summers back when Anna was five and six. Picking chokecherries and blueberries. Braving burrs and bug bites, scratched limbs, spiders, sticky hands. How good that jam had tasted even slathered on store-bought bread. But this hot loaf came straight from Ljuba's oven.

* * *

A sparkling web of light shone through the canopy of branches. Beneath its tree umbrella, this place was dark and still. Legs out straight on pine needles, back against a boulder, Anna listened to the forest breathe. The sound of distant water. The smell of wild herbs, puddled moisture, rot, new growth. Above her something rustled leaves.

Exhausted after Sofia and Vitoša, she'd slept through most of yesterday. Once she'd awakened, Ljuba had tended to her like a mother, urging her at last into the cramped but homey kitchen, with its rough wood table and massive fireplace. Though tiny, Ljuba's whitewashed stone cottage felt welcoming to her, filled with its occupants' warmth.

How good to sit at last, to rest before the next segment of climb. She'd planned to help Ljuba today, but Kosta had said he wanted to show her something. Though she liked to hike, this was far more grueling than the high Sierras last July. There, trails had been well marked, while here she'd stumbled after Kosta into barely trodden wilds slippery with undergrowth. Had scaled white scarps with tough footholds—like crawling along the surface of a giant geode.

A twig snapped. Kosta entered the thicket, two sheepskin pouches slung around his neck. He'd gone to fetch more water. Despite the sulfuric under-taste—the village had mineral springs—she'd drained the contents of her water bottle, drawn from Ljuba's backyard well.

"Hey, Anna, you was sleeping?"

"Daydreaming, I guess." She saw his brows wrinkle. As he struggled with the word, she realized how Max and Peter had spoiled her. Kosta's English had big gaps. "I was looking at the place. Smelling. Listening . . . it's very beautiful here."

"Pirin—God mountain." He smiled.

She waited, not sure what he meant.

"Old God. Perun—thunder." Unknotting the cotton cloth around his neck, he blotted his face with the red square and eased himself to the ground across from her.

Kosta lit them both a Lucky Strike, apparently a gift from Max before he'd left two nights before. The smell of burnt tobacco screened out forest scents. Kosta seemed relaxed, his legs crossed Indian-style, his back against a tree trunk. No better time to break the peace they'd shaped. In a tone she hoped sounded casual, she asked, "Where's Max?"

He sucked in deeply, savoring his drag, and blew out the smoke. At last he threw a sidelong glance her way. "Sandanski. He come back soon."

She'd glimpsed the Mercedes inside Ljuba's barn, half covered by a sheet. Though Kosta's eyes called for a change of subject, she asked, "How?" stopping short of "Why?"

"Ah, Mees." He tilted back his head, eyes laughing, mouth turned up in a gentle grin. "You like always to know. But maybe not to know good now. Maybe just you enjoy mountain."

He rose and led her from the grove. They stepped into harsh sun. Purple ridges rippled the horizon. More white tors, between them patches of low brush. Despite the knapsack on his back and the sheepskins, Kosta kept his compact form balanced above his feet, while her hands grabbed at sharp branches to keep from hurtling downward.

A fierce gust chilled her sweat. She felt goose bumps beneath the baggy long-sleeved overblouse. Kosta had refused to let her wear her single pair of shorts. Now she was glad. Ljuba's pants, thick cotton shirt, and handmade boots gave some protection from rocks, wind, and sun. But when he'd first seen her in these clothes, Kosta had said with a laugh, "You not so beeg like Ljuba."

Hard to measure time, but the sun was higher in the sky. They'd wound along the rim of one arête and were descending into forest once again. The way was easier. A grassy slope. That woodsy smell. Then a constant roar and there, below, a dark patchwork of blues and greens—the cold, deep waters of a mountain tarn. Ahead she saw the rising banks converge to form a cliff from which tumbled a sheet of foam.

She followed Kosta down the slope and out along the smooth rocks at the lake's edge toward the falls. She could feel light drops of spray. They climbed the bank until he seized her hand, pointed, and whispered, "Look."

Within a stand of pine and beech on another gentle rise, she made out crumbling gray walls.

They hiked up to the ruins. Sides and roof mostly caved in. Bits of rounded archway and old tiles. Carved above the doorframe, an Eastern cross. Fern and trailing plants covered the stones. Ignoring ants, spiders, and grubs, she drew her hand along their cracked surface. Touching the encrusted stone, she wondered what its history might be, tried to picture those first few holy men who'd fled a violent world to grow old here. Had they found God in nature, or loneliness and death?

Too long a pause. Kosta asked, "You like?"

She shook her head sideways, to let him see her gratitude and understand her silence came from awe. "What is its name?"

"I find thees place. Tell only friends. We call eet . . . *Sina gora.*"

Did that mean blue mountain? "It does look blue from far away." The building was so small—a miniature. How many had lived there? She couldn't tell its age, but it had an ancient aura. And how had it been built?

In the Grand Balkan, she'd seen a flyer for the Rila Monastery—"In the heart of Pirin. Elaborate. Well-maintained. A living history! Call for information and bus tours." But she thought she'd read somewhere that the last monks had left in the early sixties. A 'living history'? She could understand why Kosta and his friends had kept this secret. Roads, tourists, bus fumes would kill the spirit of this tiny, hidden place that felt holy.

Kosta spread a rough cloth on the clearing near the ruin. From his bag he took some bread, a hunk of whitish cheese, sausage, a few plums, and a flask of amber liquid. "Eat, Mees Anna. After walk so much, you need."

She was hungry, and this simple fare was perfect here. She wasn't sure about the drink, but Kosta poured some into a mug and handed it to her. "From our grapes."

She shut her eyes, savored the tang, aware that too much of the stuff would make her want to sleep again. Kosta soon refilled his mug. Crumbs adorned his shirt. His mouth worked at a piece of cheese. She took a bite of bread and sausage, sipped the wine, and savored the tastes that blended on her tongue.

Time passed. Eating, drinking, they spoke little. But as she sucked the juices from the last plum, she saw that lunch and wine had done their work. Kosta, yawning, heavy-eyed, sprawled out beside the picnic, his knapsack for a pillow. She asked, "How do you know Max?"

"From München. Many years now—in feefty-eight."

"Munich? How?"

He turned his head and spat into the grass. "I go for work. Bad papers. Must to leave."

So he'd been an illegal. Wandering back through what Max had said, she couldn't find a thing to tell her when or how he'd crossed into the West. Whether it had happened before or after the Wall. Now she had more pieces to process.

"And Max came here?" She didn't like the rising voice that signaled her suspicion.

"Yes. Max know people."

She tried to keep her eyes steady, to show no special interest.

"From before. When . . ." He stared into blue sky, the sun already softening. "We rest before go back." His eyes full of strange hints, he added with a smile, "Tomorrow *Panair.*"

"I don't know that word."

"Our . . . village fair."

THE SQUARE IN MIHAJLOV

Pirin

June 29, 1968

Boom of *tapan*. Drone of *gajda*. Richly costumed dancers at the center of the square circle the band. Arms linked at the shoulders, men step high. Their leader twirls a bright red cloth. Behind them women move with more restraint.

Beneath the afternoon sun, families with children and couples of all ages fill the chairs and tables. Others sample food and drink along the perimeter, and some join in the dance lines.

Ljuba had insisted Anna dress for the occasion. "A special day, Anna." In her trunk she'd found a pretty cotton blouse with purple-smocked white bodice and a mid-length skirt in blue and green, both, she said, from "when I small, before babies."

Glad she'd listened to Ljuba, comfortable despite the heat, Anna sat next to Kosta.

When they'd first arrived, three men had come to their table, set somewhat apart from the rest. Kosta had spoken, something she hadn't understood. They'd nodded and walked away, and no one had disturbed them since.

Anna was asking Kosta about Max.

"Magdeburg," he said. "You know thees name?"

"I don't."

"Beeg strike. Beeg violence. Feefty-two, maybe. Max brother, Ernst, bring heem. Poleece come. Many hurt. After, Max leave mines. Make new friends. Take reesk. Ernst try keep heem safe."

With a sigh, he retrieved some Maricas from a shirt pocket and lit one for each of them. They'd finished off the Luckies. "One night, more poleece. Max run. But they shoot Ernst. Then Max go west—"

As Kosta's glance shifted, she tracked it. Saw a tall man striding across the square, his head above the crowd, a grayish jacket loose around his shoulders. Nods acknowledged him as he passed by.

He came to their table. "Mees Anna," Kosta said, "Thees Max friend, Spiro."

She sensed that Kosta had expected him.

Spiro said, "Welcome to Mihajlov." His voice was deep and low, as if he'd pulled the words right from his chest.

As his piercing gaze appraised her, she felt a sudden frisson of excitement. She was glad she'd worn Ljuba's blouse and put on lipstick.

The men signaled each other. Kosta stood. "I get food."

Headed across the square, he turned back for a moment. Looked in their direction, as if to scan the tables nearest them. Then she lost him in the crowd.

Spiro eased himself into Kosta's chair.

Anna studied him—well-proportioned frame, olive skin stretched taut across strong features, straight black hair pulled back at the nape into a ponytail that sharpened all the angles of the oval face. She acknowledged his charisma. But his forceful, deep-set brown eyes belied his air of nonchalance, and while he conveyed a natural power—a lithe body, a self-contained expression on his face—something in his bearing made her feel that he was wound up tight. As if the slightest jar could detonate him. And even as she put herself on guard, this hidden vulnerability drew her to him.

"So," he gave a half-smile, "Kosta had good things to say about you, pretty lady. How do you find our village?"

"It's—"

A burst of bagpipe filled the square. "The *gajda,*" he said. "Special *Makedonski* style."

Makedonski? The word seemed strange embedded in his idiomatic English, and he lacked the heavy accent of the Eastern Europeans she'd met in Washington, even the professors and interpreters.

He pulled out a pack of Balkan Sobranje. "Have one?"

"Not now, thanks." She'd just survived Kosta's Marica. Though filtered, it had burned her throat.

Across the square four wrinkled *babas* danced, their arms outstretched to make a basket-hold. Undeterred by age, coined vests, or heavy skirts, they still swayed with such grace. Would she ever become a grandmother? It seemed so distant now, yet time moved in strange ways. If she should live that long, she hoped to duplicate these *babas'* pleasure in the body's movement to a strong drumbeat.

"Kosta tells me," Spiro's low voice demanded her attention, "he took you up the mountain yesterday."

"Yes. It was very special. May I ask where you learned your English?" She squirmed a little in the chair. The heat had stuck her legs to one another.

"*Gimnazia,* our high school. Then Pittsburgh."

"Pittsburgh?"

"Duquesne. I had a . . ." He studied his cigarette as if its burning end contained some message. ". . . a scholarship."

"I lived there once, in '48. My father taught at Carnegie Tech. But I was only three. I don't remember much.

"I imagine not." He laughed. "A few more years, we might have overlapped. I came in '52."

Something didn't add up. He was clearly over thirty. In those years, Bulgaria was isolated from the West. How had he entered America, received a scholarship? But to ask might raise sensitive issues, at least given what Daniel's father had said about Bulgaria—too risky with a stranger, especially someone this intense.

They sat quiet until he said, "Max tells me you know something of our history."

"Only bits and pieces, mostly old stuff. Nothing about modern Bulgaria." What had Max told him?

"You know *Kosovo Polje?* When Serbia fell? And after, when the Turks took Macedonia?"

"Of course. That shaped Balkan history." She could still see the Belgrade club—its Macedonian band, the men singing, the fellow at the next table, remembering.

"Yesterday Serbs celebrated *Vidovdan.* To honor their martyrs. But here we are not Serbs, Miss." He flicked his ash to the ground. "This is Pirin.

Today we honor our culture—the music, dances, ours—and remember this land once belonged to us. You are in Makedonija here." His body tensed like a coiled spring, he reached out for her hand.

His touch—rough fingers, damaged skin. It jolted her.

As the *zurla* made its double-reeded madness on the square—swirls of shrill, pulsating sounds like Mongol hordes invading—Makedonija echoed in her head. More than a century ago, the French had named one of her favorite salads after Alexander's multi-ethnic empire—the *macédoine*. But what did that name mean now? For him?

Spiro scanned the square, then pulled his chair closer to hers. He whispered, "Our language, as you may know, is quite old. Two monks from Macedonia created the Cyrillic alphabet."

She saw him register her frown, her pause. But what she'd heard here didn't sound much different from how people spoke in Sofia. The way an Appalachian dialect was still English. And he'd implied the monks were Slavs, though what she'd read linked them to Thessaloniki. Greek Macedonia.

And what about that name game—Makedonija, Macedonia? Was he a nationalist, expecting her to smile and nod and feed him back exactly what he wanted? To sidestep mines she wasn't trained to sense? To give up history for myth? She was glad when Kosta reappeared with a tray that held a plate of *ajvar*—that spicy roasted pepper dip she loved—some bread slices and cheese, three glasses, and a bottle of *rakija*. He set it down and sat across from them.

She turned from Kosta to Spiro. "Your language? I've read that it's a Bulgarian dialect."

Spiro's lips shaped a half-smile. "That depends on who wrote what you read. Politics determines what is language, what is dialect." Nodding to Kosta, he filled their glasses. "But even if it is only a dialect, it is how we speak." He took a sip of brandy. "Bulgaria changed our names. Denied our roots. Suppressed our culture."

In his tone, earnest, not stagy, she heard the pain that led to *Ćele kula*, Zionism, the Irish Revolution, the civil rights movement . . . to all the groups this century who were fighting for their freedom. Strange. In traveling from DC to Mihajlov, it seemed she'd moved from one conflict zone to another.

Spiro gestured toward the peaks beyond the square. "Macedonians battled for this land." Then he pointed to Kosta. "Last year, he spent four months in jail. They did not treat him well."

She pondered his implication, while Kosta muttered to himself.

Spiro seemed far off, lost in some distant memory, until he raised his eyes and looked straight at her. "His crime? Speaking our language—our dialect, if you prefer—" He flashed a sardonic smile.

She winced. His barb had stung.

"How much longer must we live like this?"

"But are there many—?"

"For you only numbers matter?"

His dry laugh made her wary. Beneath his unrelenting gaze, she felt dirty and small. He'd echoed her response to those who claimed that Jews inflated the Holocaust death count.

"Two years ago, a boy wrote 'Long Live Makedonija' on a wall in the next town." His voice dropped so low the noise on the square nearly drowned it. "He is in a camp somewhere. When he comes out, we will see if he has balls."

She cringed. Kosta busied himself with his brandy.

"Once Bulgaria called us Macedonians." Spiro's long, discolored fingers gripped his glass. "Now we are Bulgarians. No more minorities, except the special ones—Armenians and Jews."

Kosta glared at him.

Jews? She longed to challenge him, but swallowed her words from habit. For years she'd backed away, ashamed, from instances of latent anti-Semitism. She hadn't dared to risk being detected.

The men traded sharp glances.

"I'm lost," she said. "I know 'the Macedonian question' played a role early this century. But I didn't realize it still existed."

If only she could figure out his subtext. But he was staring at her as if he thought maybe she had one too.

MORE THAN A HISTORY LESSON

June 29, 1968

Spiro drew his chair so close their knees were almost touching. She felt her body tremble.

"Maybe I can help you understand. You know VMRO?"

"In English it's IMRO, the Internal Macedonian Revolutionary Organization." She tried to calm herself, control her breath, as his eyes moved from her neckline to her face. "It began near the end of the last century, to free Macedonia from the Turks."

He tipped her his glass and took a swig.

Before she could decide if he were mocking her, the square resounded in a haunting ballad. Many voices joined the band. The beauty of the melody and the unity of the communal chorus moved her.

Once the music ended, Spiro said, "You liked that song? It honors Jane Sandanski and *Ilinden*."

"That failed revolt against the Turks?"

"Touché." He shooed away a fly that hovered overhead. "Already in 1903, the rebels were divided. Delčev opposed it; Sandanski helped lead it."

His statement jogged her memory. Kosta had left Mt. Vitoša for Goce Delčev; Max had gone from Mihajlov to Sandanski. Two towns named for Macedonian heroes. Coincidence?

A sudden mountain gust swooped down along the square. Anna shivered visibly. In a flash Spiro jumped up, removed his jacket, and draped it over her shoulders. His swift action surprised her, and the brief weight of his hands gave her what felt like an electric shock. She said, "Thank you. Sudden temperature change does that to me," and pulled the jacket closer.

"Anyway, didn't VMRO strengthen between the wars?" Why had she invited him to dredge up more history?

"Yes. Under the army hero Aleksandrov. But someone in his group killed him in '24, maybe because he would not join the Communists. Then Mihajlov took over."

"The guy who planned the death of Yugoslavia's king?"

Eyebrows raised, head cocked, he gave her a smile that softened his sculpted features. "Were you always the smartest student in the class?"

She blushed. He had really seen her.

"Yes, that one. Under Mihajlov, Pirin became almost independent. Bulgaria helped VMRO because Mihajlov raided Vardar and Aegean. But this angered Yugoslavia and Greece, and Bulgaria could not afford the costs of further local conflicts. So it suppressed VMRO."

"And that's why Mihajlov fled to Turkey?"

"Exactly."

"By the way, I know the Vardar river, the Aegean Sea, but not the way you used them here."

He gave that little half-smile. "You do not recognize these terms?"

"Sorry." She'd tried to sound flippant.

"They are from the Balkan Wars."

"Oh, God, not those! I'd need a graduate course to sort them out."

He laughed. "At least you are honest." Then he continued, "The 1913 treaty that ended the Second Balkan War split Macedonia between Serbia, Greece, and Bulgaria and called the new territories Vardar, Aegean, and Pirin. After World War I, the West endorsed those divisions."

He stretched out his long legs and shook his head. "I do not wish to offend you, Miss, but the West thinks it knows best how to run the world."

She considered his words for a moment, reviewed the global hot spots. "I see your point. Most trouble spots today are areas we've colonized, where we've created artificial borders. I didn't know that list included Macedonia."

"So maybe now you see Mihajlov's role? Bulgaria hoped to reclaim through him the missing parts of Macedonia. In fact, this village honored him. In '28 it took his name."

"Speaking of this place, maybe you can tell me why Max brought me here." A huge non sequitur. But given the past few days, Max's absence, all this history—she felt on edge.

Spiro watched the dancers on the square and poured them all more brandy.

He'd chosen to ignore her. Maybe more questions would lead somewhere. "Did VMRO weaken after Mihajlov left?"

"Officially. To save his followers, Mihajlov advised them to disarm and swear they were loyal Bulgarians." He wiped his lips with a white handkerchief from his pocket. "But World War II gave VMRO another chance. In 1941, its right wing helped Bulgaria occupy Vardar, while the leftists joined Yugoslav and Macedonian communists and nationalists. The two sides fought each other until '44. Then Tito won and purged them both, Mihajlov's men as fascists, the leftists for trying to take Vardar from Yugoslavia." He sniggered.

"This sounds like all the Balkan history I've read—a labyrinth."

She saw Spiro study her, a question in his eyes. Then he drifted off again, as if seized by an unrelated thought. A moment later, with a somehow bashful smile, he passed her the plate of bread and cheese Kosta had brought. "You must eat more," he said. "You are a bird."

"A bird?" She felt her cheeks grow hot and noticed that, improbably, his olive skin had changed color.

"A pretty bird. But too thin." His smile became a charming grin. "You will not survive the winter."

They shared a quiet laugh. But the impromptu exchange had disconcerted her, and Spiro seemed uneasy too. Kosta observed them both in stony silence.

She saw Spiro watch as she ate the sandwich she'd made. She washed it down with brandy, then asked, "Where did that leave Macedonians after the war?"

He shook his head, his look incredulous. "I thought you might have heard enough."

"Too much." She smiled. "But I want to understand how this leads to what you say is happening now."

"I will try to make it clearer. To strengthen his bloc, Stalin pressured Yugoslavia and Bulgaria to heal their differences. In '47, Dimitrov and Tito signed the Bled Agreement, uniting Vardar and Pirin."

Bled, where Mr. Skertić had said Tito kept a villa.

"After, Bulgaria named us an official minority. The State supported our culture, subsidized our schools and churches, designated Macedonian Pirin's official language."

"Interesting what politics decrees." She realized he'd long since dropped the hard *k* version of that name. He must have thought he'd made his point.

"But a year later, when Tito broke with Stalin, Bulgaria stopped pacifying Yugoslavia and began to build a homogenous state. Then, Macedonians became "Bulgarian," and protestors were sent to prison camps."

Prison camps—was that why Daniel's father had hated Živkov? She felt unsteady, overwhelmed. From Spiro's searching gaze and furrowed brow, she knew he'd grasped her confusion. But that question in his eyes—was it doubt . . . or something else?

She felt almost as if she were auditioning for a play, like the Living Theater's avant-garde productions on the *Aurelia*, with Spiro as producer and the scarred but handsome hero—though he seemed to keep changing the script. But she couldn't figure out her role. She had no script at all.

"So, Miss, like VMRO, we in Pirin are divided now."

He was staring hard at Ljuba's blouse. She could barely breathe.

Suddenly he rose and walked toward two tots playing near them on the grass. A woman approached, nodded to Spiro, and carted them off.

When he returned to his chair, he paused, as if to form his thoughts. "The Bled Agreement labeled everyone in Pirin Macedonian. That angered ethnic Bulgarians here. Now, today, many, maybe most, Macedonians identify as Bulgarian, like Goce Delčev, Mihajlov, even Jane Sandanski, whose allegiance remains uncertain. They embrace Bulgarian culture and dream of a Greater Macedonia annexed to Bulgaria. But Mihajlov, despite its name, supports a separate Macedonian nation, its three parts reunited."

Anna swallowed hard. "And what about the other groups in your utopia—Serbs, Greeks, Albanians, Gypsies, Turks?" She didn't mention Jews.

"*Ilinden's* leaders envisioned a nation with equal rights for all—the Kruševo Republic. It lasted ten days; then the Turks destroyed it." Spiro nodded to Kosta. "He is one of us."

"And Max?" Us? What could that mean? A matter of identity, or something else?

"Max too."

"But Max told me his mother was a Serb."

Kosta stared into the middle distance. Spiro shrugged and nodded. "A common Balkan story. Her grandparents came from Vardar. Moved to Belgrade first, then Czechoslovakia, for work."

He took another cigarette and offered her one from the pack. When she declined, he lit his. "Max has family in Niš, Skopje, and Petrič."

Petrič—a name she remembered. A border town alleged to have more Macedonians than any other city in Bulgaria. An infamous history—assassinations, plots and counter-plots. A nest of mixed allegiances. Skopje was the capital of what Spiro called Vardar. And Niš? The old people had been family. "Then is he a Serb or a Macedonian?"

A mirthless laugh. Spiro sat back in his chair, the cigarette between his mottled fingers. "This is complicated. Each nation imposes its culture on those who live within its Macedonian lands. It is safest to assimilate, but some in all three parts choose to retain their heritage. A mad idea, maybe, given reality. But still . . ."

As he paused and seemed to look inward, she searched his face. Saw anger, despair, and something else—was it desire?—though maybe this was only wishful thinking. "How did Max and Kosta meet? Kosta said it was '58, in Munich."

Spiro glanced at Kosta, whose nod confirmed he'd told her this. "Max hated Germans." Anna recalled how Max had introduced himself five days ago—"I am a German."

"Nazis? Reds? No difference. Germans raped his mother, jailed his father, killed his brother, and made his life a hell."

His tone more personal now, he spoke as if she knew all this. But Max and Kosta had left huge gaps in their backstories.

"They clashed with police. Kosta was deported; Max was jailed." Another fly was circling Spiro, buzzing like a miniature *zurla*. As it darted in and out, he batted it away. "This is when he first contacted us. Inside, someone had links . . ."

That "us" revealed the existence of a group, whatever its purpose. But why tell her, a stranger? Wasn't it too risky? He'd scanned the square repeatedly and made sure no one came near them. Then what did he want with her? She felt pinpricks of fear.

Kosta's fingers tapped his glass. Blank-faced, he seemed to check each word she and Spiro exchanged.

Spiro said, "Max found an uncle, Ljuben, in Dobarsko, near here. Ljuben came from Vardar between the wars."

Spiro swigged his brandy. Though the men seemed untouched by the alcohol, she was careful, barely sipping hers.

"Ljuben said in Vardar you had to become a Serb or run."

Like the Inquisition. The Marranos had stayed, converted, and kept their culture in secret. Others had fled to places like Amsterdam and the Ottoman Empire in order to remain Jews.

"Ljuben's home was Štip, where Goce Delčev worked with VMRO."

Anna nodded. Mad histories kept circling back to her.

"His father was a Serb. But his mother was Macedonian, and that is how she raised him. Many came from Vardar to Pirin in those years, hoping . . ." Spiro's broad shoulders rose as he breathed in deep, fell again as he heaved a great sigh. ". . . they could be themselves."

"Please. I can't keep all these stories straight—different ones for Serbs, Greeks, and Macedonians, who seem to have at least two or three."

"Yes, it is hard when each group has its own history. But is that not also true for America —Indians, slaves, immigrants, ethnic mixing?"

She couldn't disagree. This was her story, too.

For a moment there was no sound. She and Spiro were sitting almost motionless. She saw his dark eyes watching her. Then suddenly the square vanished. The air grew thick and hushed, as if before a storm. Electrons swirled around them in a space they seemed to occupy alone. Her breathing slowed. She felt so light . . .

"Time to go." Kosta's low voice broke the spell.

Spiro looked, as she must, too, as if he'd traveled back from somewhere far away. She was trembling. So was he. They said nothing until he bent so close she caught a whiff of soap and sweat, of apricot and garlic. Then he whispered, "Ljuben has a son, Slavko, of Max's age. In Razlog."

Cousins—Slavko, Max. What had made Max bring her here and leave? She gazed past Spiro to the peaks beyond the square. A thick web was entangling her. A moment flashed—on *Sina gora* yesterday. After lunch she'd risen, intending to explore inside the ruined walls. She'd thought Kosta was sleeping. But he'd shouted, "Mees Anna, we go now. To have sun for the way back." Then, she hadn't given it much thought. But now she wondered why he'd stopped her. Maybe tourists weren't their main concern. She'd read about the mountain men who'd fought the Turks so long ago. Maybe new despots meant new resisters.

Her gaze returned to the table. Spiro was studying her, his face naked, unmasked. He said at last, "I want to take you somewhere. Will you come?"

Despite his proud demeanor, she felt his need, as if a "no" from her would cause him pain. Traveling with Max had been a risk, but this seemed far more dangerous. Yet she longed to return to that charged space they'd shared. Something more than history had brought them there. She wanted to pursue it. "Yes."

Spiro rose. His hand shook as he helped her from her chair. Kosta stood, too, but his chin jerked up to signal "no." The men moved off to trade words Anna couldn't hear.

When they returned, Kosta seemed resigned. Spiro took her arm again and addressed them both. "Do not worry. It will be okay."

NIGHT IN PIRIN

June 29, 1968

Silent, pensive, Spiro led her from the square, down winding cobbled streets, past two-story houses with slanted red-tiled roofs, along unpaved lanes strewn with huts. Kosta's willingness to let her go had reassured her, but now she felt on edge.

Soon they were in open meadow, mountain peaks outlining the horizon. The air was crisp. The setting sun had turned the sky lavender-mauve. Ahead, Anna heard noise. "A soccer game," Spiro said, using the American term.

Now she could make out the field. Poles and nets. Men scrambling toward the ball. "Do you play?" She thought that might explain his powerful body.

"I did." He filled his lungs with clean air. "No time anymore."

They came at last to a gentle rise. On the crest, between two plum trees, a single-story, whitewashed brick cottage, its roof tiles glowing in the soft rays of the dying sun. "My home," he said, turning them down the stone walkway, lined with red rose bushes. Then three stone steps. A narrow stoop. A battered wooden door. Two large windows, beneath each one an empty window box. A gentle downward slope in back.

Spiro opened the door and held it for her. Ignoring a ripple of fear, the inner voice that whispered, "don't," she entered.

A narrow hall, on either side two doors. He guided her through the right-hand one, to a throw-covered couch in a cozy room. "I have to find a few things. Care for tea?"

"Sounds good. The brandy and the walk have made me thirsty."

He left through a curtained opening that must have led to the kitchen. As she waited, she studied the room. One front window, another on the side wall; muted light filtered through both. A scarred wood floor, a threadbare floral rug, a lamp beside the sofa, its red shade edged in silky fringe. And on the wall behind her, a flower-embroidered purple shawl.

She rose and walked to the bookshelf on the far wall. Glimpsed Cyrillic titles, some unfamiliar, Bulgarian, others Russian—Gogol, Dostoevsky, Pushkin, Tolstoy, Turgenev. Spines with Latin letters stood among them, including Shakespeare, Byron, Conrad, Eliot, and Yeats.

Spiro entered with a wooden tray from which he served her tea. Then he placed it on a low table and left the room again.

He came back with a large red woolen shawl over his left arm and some papers in his hands. "Shall we go out in back? The view is pleasant there."

They sat in weathered rocking chairs as the sun slid behind the mountains, the sky like moistened tie-dyed silk. Spiro drew his jacket from her shoulders, placed it on his chair arm, and wrapped her in the heavy shawl. Insect noises filled the air until Anna broke the silence. "You act as if you trust me. Why?"

His eyebrows arched. His lips curled up. He looked as if he'd waited for that question. "Max brought you and he does not make mistakes. At least, not anymore."

She might have pondered this, but asked, instead, "What you said earlier . . ." She thought about the boy in jail. Kosta. The history lesson. "You kept watching the square. Was it for agents?"

Another half-smile. "No. For members of our group."

"Why?

"In case they had questions about you."

"So you didn't worry about being watched?"

"I will explain. Near here, they stopped a band from playing Macedonian songs. But that was a mixed town. Many Bulgarians."

She remembered the old man in Sofia, telling her how Jews had to hold dances for "all Bulgarians."

"In Mihajlov, since we identify as Macedonian, on a few special occasions, they let us sing and dance our way. Leave us alone." He rocked slowly and scanned the darkening sky above the cliffs. "But you, Anna."

He hadn't used her name till now. She wondered what that signified.

"I knew you would challenge me."

"I . . . why?"

"From Max. Our little chat about language. And when I spoke of the monks. Your face shows what you feel." His eyes were on her now, intense, unblinking.

"Those monks were Greek, my sources said." What about his mention of the Jews? He must have seen her frown. And what had Max told him?

He flashed a playful grin. "But sources often claim what suits their cause, like me."

"Then you were only testing me?"

"Not only."

"But why, if you trusted Max?"

"You came here by chance, or so it seems. But what if . . .?" He paused. Deliberated. Shifted his body and seemed to redirect himself. "I had to find out what you know. Who you are."

"And did you?" He'd evaded the core of her question.

"Enough." He cleared his throat. "I may be wrong, but I do not think so."

Wrong? She wouldn't press him now. "You saw my limits on display."

"But surely you know, Anna, that ignorance can sometimes be a useful mask."

"The real question is . . ." She paused. ". . . why should I trust you? You took me on a crazy ride through Macedonian history, and I still don't know why." The air had cooled. She huddled in the warmth of Spiro's shawl. But his last words had implied something that made her even colder.

He pulled himself up in the chair and leaned his body toward her. "Shall I tell you a story?"

"Will it help me see better?"

"I hope so. My father came from Vardar, too, like Max's uncle Ljuben. In 1930, from Strumica. Did not want to be only a Serb. In Vardar they changed his last name from Svetkovski to Svetković. Here they made him Svetkov." Steadying his chair, he bent over to pluck a wild flower.

She thought then of her family's own renamings.

The air had grown heavy and hushed, like the eerie calm before Hurricane Carol had struck Providence when she was young. The light had turned a misty gray, with ghostly fingers of purple and rose, as if a storm threatened.

"Anna, we are split so many ways. For us, essence counts more than truth."

The lavender flower looked fragile in his large, rough hand.

"Slav or Greek, who knows about those monks? But they were Macedonian." He lifted the flower to his nose. Sniffed it. "My mother came from Melnik, in the south, near the Greek border. Her father was Aegean Macedonian. My father's family lived in Vardar. And I was born in Pirin, in this house my father built. All of us Macedonians."

His lips twisted again; his voice grew bitter. "Now Bulgaria tells us Macedonia does not exist. Only Bulgaria, Bulgarians."

He handed her the papers he had taken from inside—identity cards from 1952 and 1958.

She studied the earlier picture, noting his birth date. 1934. The slanted eyes above those cheekbones held a youthful arrogance. The smile carried a naïve self-importance. Its beauty compelling, that smooth young surface lacked the force she saw in his face now. "Where should I be looking?"

He pointed to a line that read *Graždanstvo.* Nationality. The card from 1952 labeled him *Makedonec,* the other *Bulgarin.* "Now," he waved the newer card, "I am Bulgarian. Without this, I can go to jail."

For an instant she recalled the Southern voting laws. The ways of separating black from white, of keeping Blacks from active roles in American life. At her Virginia high school, she'd worked with DC ministers to organize forums on civil rights. She'd marched with all those solemn men and women, arms linked, candles lit, to hear King on the Mall. As blatantly unjust as the Bulgarian regime appeared, was her country much better? Both oppressed their minorities, if in different ways.

"In Petrić," he said, rocking slowly, gazing out toward the mountains, "they gave my father poison."

A breeze swept through the meadow, swaying plants and branches.

"You mean he was . . . murdered?" Anna heard her voice, frightened and small. As if a dark abyss had opened up and she was falling in. "Do you know who?"

"The DS—the *Državna sigurnost.* Bulgarian security police. Of course, they told us 'Serb agents.' They wanted me to help fight what they called 'our enemies.' But now I know it was their work, doubtless with KGB guidance. The Soviets want to keep Bulgaria close." His laugh was full of undertones.

"I was still in Pittsburgh. My mother had to bury him alone." He sighed and kept rocking.

"But why?"

The flower had wilted in his hand.

"My father was a Communist. He wanted better lives for us, and once the Party gave our culture support. When Bulgaria entered Vardar in '41, they sent him back to Strumica to work with locals in the NLF, the National Liberation Front—to help organize the anti-fascist resistance. Three years later, after the Communists took Bulgaria, he helped secure their power in Vardar." Spiro paused briefly. Pulled out, then put away, another cigarette.

"I'm guessing this project didn't end well."

A nod. A hollow laugh. "At first Vardar was hopeful. But soon they saw that nothing changed. Tito named Vardar the People's Republic of Macedonia and tried to turn them into Yugoslavs."

Spiro coughed, then whispered in a hoarse voice, "*Makedonsko ime nema da zagine.*"

It sounded like a warning, or a threat. She shook her head. "And that means what?"

"'The Macedonian name will never perish.'"

It reminded her of "Remember the Alamo," or "The South Shall Rise Again"—words some still held sacred.

"When he came home after the war, my father swore to us that he would live by that slogan. He had lost faith in the Communists. Called them Moscow's puppets. Said they cared only about themselves. But he could not defy them openly. Purges had begun. He had to protect his family. And the Party needed him, his links in Vardar, to . . ." Spiro set the flower on the armrest and pulled the cigarette pack from a shirt pocket. "You know, Anna," he mumbled, patting pockets to find matches, "Živkov's government has passed new laws. Now they can arrest and sentence without trial anyone they label dissident." His right hand made a tight ball. "Easier to handle our extremists."

He said this in a smug voice that belonged to someone else. Now she could see why Daniel's father had loathed Živkov.

Spiro offered her a cigarette. This time she accepted. Her lips and fingers held it while he cupped his hand and struck the match he'd found. Then he lit one from hers, his head bent close.

"And your mother?"

"My mother . . ." He took a drag. Exhaled a stream of smoke. "She died in '59, a year after I came back here, to Mihajlov. Cancer."

As his eyes wandered the valley, Anna felt him travel far from her.

"And what about you, Spiro? What do you do here?" She was thinking of his cottage, all the books, his roughened hands

His eyes met hers. Clear. Intense. "I teach school. Like my father did, before . . ."

"Like Goce Delčev and the early VMRO members."

That little smile, self-deprecating somehow.

"It is good work for those who think they can help people see better."

She winced at his ironic tone. "What subjects?"

"History, math." He gave a low snigger. "A little science."

A self-effacing laugh laid bare his sense of desperation and futility, its edge so sharp it almost made her cry.

"Sometimes English, if they need. And most Sundays I work with local kids. To pass on our language and culture."

That still didn't explain his hands.

As if reading her thoughts, he added, "Here we are collectivized. But they gave me a small plot."

She wondered who this 'they' was, who could mete out land. The village council? The district authorities? 'We,' 'they,' 'us.' So many ambiguous pronouns.

"I grow potatoes, peppers, other vegetables. I like to work the soil. It makes me feel . . ." His voice trailed off. His face and body relaxed. "Anna, we are not all quite mad yet."

The *are* and *not* ran together, almost like one word, *arnut*, yet not quite *aren't*, either. She'd only now begun to discern this pattern.

"For me, it was not just my father's murder. My pupils, their families, have suffered." His voice, still low and deep, was gentler now. "People here lack education, Anna. They seldom finish high school, even with my pleading. They are simple in their views."

She stood up. Started walking toward the meadow. Her world had grown so strange, shifted so suddenly. She had to move, to feel her body as a real thing. What had made him bring her here? Open himself? And what of all his stares and heavy silences?

"Please forgive me, Anna."

The words came from a distance. He hadn't followed her.

"I know this is too much to hear at once." A pause. "But I have had no one to speak with for so long. Kosta and Max, they are a part of this. They . . . we do not . . . I cannot explain. But you . . . you make me feel less . . . alone." His voice caught at the end.

It seemed almost a plea. But really, what could she, so lost, so unformed, give him? And what of all he'd kept from her?

He rose abruptly. Came to her. As he took her arm and gently turned her to him, she felt heat from his body and recognized a deep need in his eyes.

"It is hard to understand," he said. "And once you do . . . harder to live." He bowed his head, took a deep breath, and let it out slowly. "If you are willing, I would like to show you one more place before I take you home."

Home. The word resounded in her head like a melancholy tune. He couldn't know the power it held for her. When . . . where . . . was the last time she had ever truly felt at home?

IN A *KAFEANA*

June 29, 1968

Rough-hewn tables. Wood-plank floor. Fumes of alcohol and cigarettes filling the air. He sat her at a table in the center of the room. Ordered *kevapćinja* and *rakija*. "Anna, I will not be long." He'd said he had to meet some men and settle a few issues. As he left, he added, "If you need more, you can ask the waiter. He speaks a little English."

Spiro's tall form wove among the tables toward four men in the far corner. They were huddled over something. Hard to make them out. Poor light. The distance. She barely sipped the brandy, but nibbled on the sausage, though she had no appetite.

Soon she heard the ping of metal strings, a thump that made a drum-like beat. A well-played *tambura*. Then a male voice joined in, chant-like, wandering up and down the scale in Phrygian mode. Exhausted, she heard without seeking the source.

The song ended. The *kafeana* was quiet. The *tambura* began what sounded like a tragic love song. She looked over at Spiro, in the corner with his men, their earnestness so different from Christos' affectations. Eyes closed, she let the haunting sounds transport her back to winter, to that night in College Park when he'd told her he would leave for Canada.

In his tiny but well-furbished flat, Christos had turned to her, his thin face mimicking the martyred look of an El Greco saint. "I have to go, Anna. I have no choice. They say I'm needed there."

She'd bit her lip to keep from laughing. What use could "they" have for this posturing boy whose greatest passion was himself? And what good timing. After a semester that had not gone well for him. "Don't worry. I'll contact everyone."

His look said he didn't trust her.

"I'll speak to the landlord too." She tried to sound convincing, though she wasn't quite sure why. It wasn't like she owed him this performance. "You've paid up, haven't you?" She wouldn't mend that loose end. His father sent a fat check every month.

When they'd first met at the Astor the previous December, she'd thought him marvelous. Tall and gaunt, he'd acted the tragic émigré, down to the black mustache that proved him Greek. He knew that national pride could be a potent aphrodisiac. His *zembeikiko,* the eagle's dance, would replicate the flight of that proud bird, his long, lean form extended out, leaping, down onto the floor, upturned. This was how he won the hearts of girls, including her, who spent their idle moments at the club.

At first, she'd felt lucky he'd chosen her from all the rest. But soon she learned that he enjoyed foreplay far less than playing at revolution. Wrapped in the glamour of his role, the wealthy lawyer's son would twirl his sleek mustache and swagger off to late-night meetings with his fellow would-be freedom fighters.

Last fall he'd driven her to the antiwar protest on the Mall. He planned to meet his cohort, so he dropped her off in a crowd of student radicals and shouting hippie kids. She'd spotted him in his khaki uniform and high jackboots, strutting as he led what he called the Greek Revolutionary Army-in-Exile. But Christos liked French cognac, fine Italian shoes, and German radios. Since he managed this without apparent guilt, she wondered how prepared he would be to give up la dolce vita for the sake of Papandreou's Socialists.

In the end, like Reza, he'd run to Canada. But she was sure he'd gone for motives other than the needs of some string-pulling strategists. He was smart enough to see that flight would free him from his books and raise his stock among those left behind. A week before she sailed on the *Aurelia,* she learned he'd wed a pizza heiress in Quebec.

Anna looked again at the table in the corner. This man in baggy trousers. That one in a sort of overall. Spiro in his old jacket, generic pants, and frayed white shirt. Christos would have called them *vlachi*—peasants.

When the *tambura* began a *ručenica,* Spiro crossed the room to her. "Anna, we must dance."

He thrust his shoulders back, his broad chest out. Stretching his arms wide, he began to move in quick threes to the music. His whole being exuded a tough pride, like the best male dancers at the Astor. Facing him close-in, she raised her arms and started swaying in that little three-step. She moved her hands up and down to the beat, swiveling them from the wrists and curling in her fingers as the dancing grannies had.

"Bravo," he said. "Yes."

In his smile, no longer tight, she caught a trace of innocence.

"*Ajde,* Anna." He began to circle her.

Her eyes gazed into his. Lifting Ljuba's skirt a little at the hem, she followed it around him. The swaying triplets speeded up, then slowed, became more sinuous, then rose again. Close but never touching. Never dropping eye contact, except to turn. The dance held them together in its rhythm.

The music stopped abruptly. They stood breathless. Spiro's hand was resting on his hip, in his eyes that question. And she could feel her cheeks begin to flush.

At that moment the outer door opened. Max and Kosta entered, together with a bottle blonde whose teased hair and stiletto heels made her taller than both men. Anna's cheeks grew hotter when she caught Max's startled look. She wondered who the woman was.

"Anna. Spiro. *Zdravo.*" Kosta's smile was tentative. "Thees Donka, Jordan friend."

Jordan? She supposed he was another of their cohort.

A wry smile clamped to his lips, Max watched her out of almond eyes, a tamer version of Spiro's. But there was something dark behind them now. "Come. Sit." Max pulled up several chairs. "We will have something to drink."

Donka's red lips parted to show white teeth. Her hands ended in long red nails. Anna studied Spiro, to learn what red-nailed bottle blondes might mean to him. But he was staring deep into his glass at something only he could see.

"I do not think to find you here, Anna," Max said. His low rasp held an edge. He turned his head to Spiro, who raised his brows, as if to ask why that should be a problem. "Kosta tells me you are gone a long time." His smile darkened.

"And you, my friend," Spiro replied, straight-faced, flat-voiced. "You were gone for longer than we planned."

"But I am here now. Do you want my news?" That mocking grin. "Or maybe I leave you two by yourselves?" He looked straight at Anna.

Ignoring Max's last comment, Spiro said, "The men are here. You must tell them everything."

Anna noticed Spiro working hard to concentrate on Max. But his glance kept darting back to her. Kosta watched in silence. Donka stayed imperious behind her icy smile.

Max leaned close to Anna. "I stay here a while. Kosta takes you back to Ljuba's place now. In the morning I pick you up. We drive to Istanbul."

Spiro said nothing. She saw him let Max take control.

Wordless, without warning, Donka rose and wandered off toward the tall, wild-haired man framed by the inner doorway. "Poor Jordan." Kosta shrugged. "He crazy from her."

The four of them made their good-byes, kissing on alternate cheeks three times all around. When Spiro touched her shoulder, Anna felt her breath stop in her chest. His hand rested there longer than was needed. All the while his head tilted a little, as if he still pondered whatever question he'd asked himself. As Kosta escorted her out, she saw Max put his arm around Spiro's shoulder.

By the time Kosta and Anna reached the hut, Ljuba and the children had gone to bed. Kosta tiptoed in and walked her to her soft-flowered door. "Now you sleep," he whispered.

But he lingered there, wanting what? Surely not to join her.

"Mees Anna," he murmured at last, "Spiro, he tell you theengs?"

"No, Kosta. He saw those men. We danced. That's all."

"Dance?"

When they'd first met, Kosta's eyes had sparkled with an almost sexual gleam. Now they looked forlorn. She wished she could hug him, thank him for his worrying about her. She could count on no one else. Not even Max, whose desires seemed increasingly unclear.

Inside the womb-like bedroom, Anna couldn't sleep, despite the steady cadence of the rain that fell at last against the outside wall. In the dark she saw the far-off look in Spiro's eyes, his hair after the dance, shiny with sweat, like a seal's coat. She felt a deep ache. Not the sexual tingling she was used to—especially the past few days with Max. Something very different. Hard to put in words.

She willed her mind to flow until it led her to the box marked "Home." Now she knew the feeling . . .

But she and Max were leaving in the morning.

A RED EASTER EGG

June 30, 1968
Pirin, Bulgaria
Anna wiped away the crumbs from breakfast, grateful that Ljuba let her help today. Mountains filled the window. A mist was on them now.

She heard a car approach. A knock. Her bag was packed, ready. But she was not. Kosta let Max in. And Max seemed upset, too. His eyes looked tired.

They said their quiet thank-yous and good-byes. Kosta's brow was furrowed, Max's hidden by the brim of his Greek cap. Then Ljuba clattered up holding a lovely red-flowered scarf. "For—you." She placed it over Anna's hair and fastened it, Pirin-style, in back. "To—remember. Kosta. Me." Ljuba's dimpled smile and halting pidgin English saved the scene. Anna had to work to keep from crying. This place, these people, had grown dear to her.

As Anna and Max drove off, Kosta, Ljuba, and the children stood outside the cottage waving heartily. But soon Max pulled over and stopped. He left the car and walked around to her side. "Anna, please come with me."

Once outside the Mercedes, she felt a wave of déjà vu.

Max's face was blank; he made no eye contact. "I have something for you." From his jacket pocket he produced a small, misshapen envelope that reminded her of *The Little Prince*—the boa that ate the elephant.

Before she could respond, he was striding down the road. She followed him a moment with her eyes, then broke the seal on the rough paper. Into her hand fell a wooden Easter egg. She wondered at it, nestling in her palm, dark red, painted with tiny flowers, its light weight somehow solid. One end was slightly cracked. From whom? What did this mean?

As she replaced the egg inside the envelope, she found a note, extracted it, and smoothed it out:

Anna,
I have trusted Max with this. He has feelings for you. But he is my friend.
Stay here with me.

She caught her breath, reread the line once, then again.

I know that you cannot. So take this egg, my grandmother's. My parents gave it to me when I was a boy. For us it is a sign of hope, of new life. Perhaps it will remind you of me sometimes.
Spiro

A rush of tears. An ache. Her lips began to quiver as she stared down at the carefully curved letters.

She worked to calm herself. She didn't want to show Max all her pain, or add to his. But as she held the note, a strange vibration made her tremble.

Max was coming back. He stood before her, feet slightly apart, hands on his hips. "Stay or go, Anna?" He wore his trademark smile, but his eyes shifted uncertainly. "You tell me now. I do not have more time."

Though it might hurt him, she needed something more. "Help me, Max. You know what Spiro wants?"

Swallowing, he nodded.

"Tell me what you think."

"Why do you ask me?" His eyes studied a pothole.

"You know him."

"Yes," he said in his low rasp. He gave a forlorn laugh, his linen jacket hanging loose from lowered shoulders. "I know him." Looking out toward where the mountains met the sky, he crossed his arms over his chest and shook his head. "Anna, they are all blind."

"But still you help them, don't you?"

"Spiro too." He managed a weary smile. "He sees. But he stays with them." Max had taken off his hat, was fingering the brim. "He . . . loves them."

The power in those words. She thought about that love. How Spiro cared for these people, their lives constrained within such narrow limits. His own, too, now, apparently—though why she didn't understand.

"And aren't there other women?"

"When we first meet . . ."

Max gave a slow smile whose corners spread, lifting the tight-drawn skin around his mouth and eyes, making those creases she'd found so attractive.

"Then he has many. But now . . ."

He seemed lost in his memories. She waited, said nothing.

"Anna, these women are not for him." He examined his Italian shoes. "He reads. And . . ." Suddenly his narrowed eyes stared straight at her. "He thinks too much."

She watched him smooth his wrinkled linen jacket. Straighten the lapels.

"I don't ask what goes on between you yesterday. Spiro does not say. But I see how he cares, and . . ."

The shutters on his eyes were gone. They looked tender and young.

"He is a good man, Anna." Max's face was absolutely without guile. "A real friend. That is all what I can say." He cocked his head upward. "If you stay more in these mountains . . ." His voice began to rise. "With these, these shepherds and—" He stopped himself. Gave a loose shrug. "Spiro will be good to you."

Of course, she would go with Max to Istanbul. He was her friend, her guide. That was the plan.

The envelope began to pulsate in her hand, summoning the square in Mihajlov, Spiro's face after they'd visited that other realm, his eyes during their couple dance, so full of what she now could call longing. But how absurd that she should even dream of doing this—to enter the unknown with an enigmatic stranger, to abandon her family, to delay whatever future she might have. Even he'd acknowledged that. And yet . . .

She had Max drop her off at Spiro's cottage.

PART IV: PIRINSKA PESNA

THE FIRST NIGHT

She heard the front door open, the thud of boots removed, placed on the little rug. Then Spiro entered the living room, humming softly to himself some melancholy melody. But once he saw her sitting on the couch, he stopped short. His eyes stared in confusion as he set his bundle down. Then he whispered, "An—na?"

"I've been here since this morning. After Max left." Anna tried to keep her voice neutral. "I found the door unlocked. I let myself in."

Except to shake his head, he hadn't moved. A stone pillar. So, after all, he'd just played games with a stupid tourist girl. Now she was really stranded. Her watch read almost eight. Max must be close to Istanbul.

"I . . ." He inched toward her, his body stiff, awkward, his face frozen. "I never . . ."

She tried to read the pause, his startled eyes.

". . . you . . ." his voice an organ point, lower than ever, ". . . I did not think to find you here, Anna."

"Not to worry, Spiro. I'll leave as soon as . . ." Damn him! ". . . I can figure out just how." She rose to her feet.

"*Prokleto!*" He grasped the arm that dangled limp down her right side. "Do not say more, Anna." His eyes met hers, but they were beaming now. "Funny how it is." His hands tilted her face toward his. Fingers touched her hair. Lips kissed her neck. Then he pulled away. Held her at arm's length. "You are always ready for a duel." He added with a gentle smile, "But we are on the same side."

His words were a preemptive strike. The show closed down. Her scripts tossed out. She'd have to throw her mask away, reveal the self it hid—to both of them.

She let him lead her to the sofa, ease her down beside him. Then she laid her head against his shoulder.

"I did not dream to find you here," he whispered through her hair. "It needed so much trust."

"And you," she said. "You trusted Max." Her body registered his quiet laugh.

"Anna, you miss nothing."

Her head rocked on his shoulder to the rhythm of his breathing. Cradled in the rough cotton of his white shirt, she caught his scent. A mix of soap and sweat. Of apricot and garlic. No cover-up, like Max's musk. Drinking in the sweet-sour smell, she closed her eyes and let it enter her.

"Max and I, you know," his hand moved lightly up and down her arm, "we share something."

A pause. As if he'd entered some dark space of memory.

He cleared his throat and shook his head. "This I will tell you later."

They sat a while in silence, the fingers of their right hands intertwined, letting that "something" stay in the past. For now. At last he said, "You must be very hungry."

"I found some bread and yogurt in the kitchen. Helped myself."

"And that is enough for you, my little bird?" He laughed, twisting her hair around his fingers. "We can go to the village."

"No." She raised her head, turned it, and looked into his eyes. "Not now." She felt his chest tighten, his shoulders stiffen.

His hands pushed back rebellious strands of hair, clearing her face. He kissed her eyelids. "You are ready, then?"

Completely sure for once, she answered, "Yes."

* * *

Exposed beams. Hardwood floor. A high, quilt-covered bed, red flowers painted on its wooden headboard. Windows on the outer walls, unlatched, stand open to the night. On a trunk beside the bed, a water jug, two glasses, and a bottle of *rakija.*

White lace curtains swell with mountain currents. Like sails, they billow out, lose wind, fall straight, then billow out again. Dim light from ancient suns colors the darkness.

His hair is loose, a wild, thick mass her hands explore with caution. He cups her chin in his large hand. "What's wrong, Anna?"

"I wish . . ." She hesitates. ". . . I were a virgin for you." These words astonish her. But she means them. If only she could wash away her history, all those hollow couplings. Begin now, when she feels so full.

A hand touches her cheek. Begins to stroke her thigh. "I would not change a thing. Would you?"

His legs are tree trunks. Strong arms clasp her to his chest. She barely reaches his breastbone.

He asks, "Shall I get something—to be safe?"

She shakes her head. "I'm okay." Condoms in the mountains. Did Max keep him supplied? As he lays her gently on the quilt, his hand brushes her breast. She cannot help the tightening of her body, the way her muscles tense.

Even in the star-lit room, his face appears to darken.

"Anna?" He draws back slightly. "Is it . . .?" He clears his throat. "Are you afraid?"

How can she explain? For years she's ruled her flesh, controlled all feeling. This fire is new, intense, and, yes, she fears it. Wonders what will happen when she stops thinking.

His face draws close to hers. His fingers coast along her cheek. His clear eyes look at her as if, without her speaking, he has glimpsed the truth. "We are together here. You want this, don't you, *sakano moja?*"

She likes how those words sound. *My love.* Her answer is a smile. Her hand moves up to touch his chest.

He lets himself down on her with care. The bed sails them along on waves of air. Tongues taste flesh. Skin touches skin. Anised lips trade kisses. Swirls of heat from fingers, mouths. From the curled hairs of his chest. His weight on her. His feet caressing hers.

Riding surges, swept by waves, she throbs and pants, yet feels oddly secure.

He stops. Laughs softly. Rests a finger on her mouth. Whispers, "It is good we have no neighbors."

The rapids grow more powerful. She gasps, "Not yet?"

"A little more," he says. "Hold on."

"I . . ." She can barely breathe. "I'm dying."

"I know," he says, laughing. In the dark her fingers trace his up-curved lips. He bends his head. Kisses her breast. Mumbles, "Only a bit longer."

Her hands caress the strange coarse grooves below his shoulder blades. Her mind begins to question what they are, but feeling sweeps her far away.

Descent into dark magic.

When she can bear no more, he rears up, arches back, then plunges deep inside her with a soft cry, washing up against her breasts. Spinning in the vortex, she dissolves. Clutches his wrists. Swirling. Drowning. Her ears catch gasps and moans . . .

* * *

His lips brush her forehead. He murmurs, "You were sleeping so deeply . . ."

She finds herself inside the hollow where his shoulder meets his chest.

". . . I wondered if . . ." Smiling, he traces circles on her breasts. ". . . you were alive."

She sees the first dim rose and saffron rays come through the windows. Feels his hands begin to move again, his body tense . . .

SCARS

Sunlight filtered softly through the curtains, now at rest. The morning was no longer new. The room contained the scents of their lovemaking. Lying on her side, Anna felt the warmth of Spiro's body next to hers, his arm across her breasts. They'd slept like nested spoons.

Now he stirred, stretched out his legs. His fingers cupped her breast. He kissed her shoulder, whispered in her ear, "I'll find us food."

She turned to him. His hair was wild, his eyelids still heavy from sleep. His right cheek bore a red mark where it had pressed against the pillow. A smile spread across his face. He looked like a little boy at a birthday magic show. She felt so full she didn't need breakfast.

In one fluid motion he rose from the bed, his back to her. She gasped. Ridges of discolored flesh scored his back, buttocks, and thighs. Some thick, others narrow, the welts zigzagged across and down his back. Old scars, not red but whitened.

He turned around, still smiling like a boy, but when he saw her face, his eyes darkened. "I am sorry," he said, almost in a whisper. "I forgot."

By this time she was staring at his penis, pointed straight at her.

"I . . ." His dark cheeks had turned ruddy. "I did not think to warn you."

A memory of indentations, pebbled seams. "That's what I felt last night." Her fingers hadn't named the roughness then. "I thought they were . . ." Why was this so hard to speak about? Just a body, after all. Some marks on skin. Pure surface. It shouldn't matter. ". . . like your hands."

He lifted his right palm and seemed to study it.

"I'd sort of . . . gotten used to them. Your hands, I mean." She could feel her face change color. He said nothing, but his eyes signaled compassion. He must have moved past his anxiety to sense her own.

"The way the skin is rough, speckled. I thought . . ." She had to clear her throat. "Maybe it was some . . ." She looked out at the mountains, as if they might give her more space to breathe. "Some skin condition. I didn't think gardening could do all that."

His lips parted in a half-smile. "Cigarette?"

"Uh-huh."

She forced herself to watch his back as he headed toward the kitchen. She would have liked to keep this room a site of wonder. But the scars could not be blotted out. Ugly, deeply private, and a vital part of him. A symbol of his history, if she could only decode it.

He returned subdued, smoking. Instead of food, he held a pack of Maricas in his right hand. Once he'd set it on the wood block bedtable, he climbed back in beside her and rolled his pillow into a support. "It is twelve years since Belene."

The name meant nothing to her.

He squirmed his back and shoulders till he found a good position. "On an island in the Danube, near the Romanian border . . ." She inched closer to him. ". . . there is a labor camp."

She could only imagine the Holocaust. Walking skeletons that worked and starved until they metamorphosed into lifeless bags of bones. The stories she had read, had heard. "Here too?"

"Why not? A cheap way to get work done and keep order."

He passed her his cigarette. She drew hard on the end. Filled her lungs, then held the smoke until she felt her insides burn. As she exhaled, he said, "Some stayed a while; some won't come back." He gave a dry laugh. "For me it was a year."

"And what . . .?" She stopped herself. He'd tell her in his own time.

He reached down toward the foot of the bed, grabbed the faded quilt, and pulled it up over his lap, as if to make sure nothing could distract either of them. "Every morning, I washed down the latrines."

His tone had been neutral, stripped of all emotion. The flattened syllables floated in the air, signs for something words could not convey, something she could not yet comprehend.

"What I used came from a local factory. It was mostly lye." His cracked and mottled fingers touched her hand as he retrieved the cigarette. "I had no gloves. It . . ." Puffing hard, he stared out toward the sunlit window on the wall across the room. ". . . burned my skin."

Too bad he'd taken back the Marica. The rhythm of the smoking might have masked the chill she felt, imagining the lye that ate his hands day after day. And he only a kid. How old? He'd said twelve years. Just twenty-two. "Why you?" What could he have done, so young?

He answered with a crooked smile.

"Spiro, please." Something hard had slipped into his eyes. She shrank from him a little.

"When I was thirteen, the Party sent me to study in Sofia. There was a guard in my section." He scrutinized the cigarette in his left hand, like a scientist checking out its composition. "The brother of a kid from Sofia who had gone to *gimnazia* with me." His right hand rested lightly on her belly. "We both took the exam for university." He raised himself up on the pillow. "I passed. He did not."

Was that the punch line? "I guess I missed the point."

"You are not thinking Bulgarian." He ground his cigarette into a jar top on the table. "I could continue my studies." His left hand groped for the Maricas, pulled another from the pack. Then his right let hers go long enough to light the cigarette. "He could not." His head rested against the flowered, pillow-softened headboard. "Of course he hated me." He took a drag, exhaled. "To him I was a speck. Some Macedonian peasant from the mountains."

She moved closer, curled up against his chest.

"This guy, he had the chance to pay me back. That's all."

The same old story. How had Shakespeare put it? Man a bare, forked animal, a plaything of the gods? She hadn't thought of it for years. "But what about the scars?"

"Will we share another cigarette?" He bent his head toward hers and kissed her hair. "Or will you have your own this time?"

The way he said it made her laugh. He knew she didn't need to smoke the way he did.

"I'll take a drag or two of yours."

"I do not know where to begin, Anna. The secret police . . . no . . . well . . ."

Did he censor himself from habit or lack of trust? Or was it to protect her? She felt a sudden chill. Shivering, she pulled the quilt tighter around her.

His low voice said, "Živkov and the Party do whatever they want." His gaze was cold. His upper lip curled at the right corner. "They answer only to the KGB." A hush. The only sound the birds making their high-pitched trills outside the open windows. "Some men came to me there. They wanted me to do something for them. If I agreed, they said I would be freed."

Something?

He rubbed his back against the headboard. Took another long drag. Closed his eyes. "That is all I can say now."

Maybe he knew his words threatened to distance her.

He moved his body closer, till his leg touched hers. "Be patient with me, Anna." His fingers felt her hair. The smooth sole of his foot massaged the top of hers.

She nodded, though his holding back scared her. "Can you tell me what you said to them, at least?"

He puffed, drew in the smoke, and let it out. "I told them no."

"You had that choice?"

"Of course not." A self-mocking smile. "I was a stubborn kid."

She could almost see him then, defiant, sure of what was right.

"My mother was already sick, my father dead." He sucked in on the cigarette and blew out a huge smoke ring. "They could not use my parents as a weapon. Those guys . . ." His eyes were squinting at the Marica. ". . . they did not appreciate my attitude."

"You thought they would?"

He laughed. "I did not think at all."

"So then—"

"One pretended he was on my side. Pretended he would help me. "

"And?" She ran her fingers through the fine curls on his chest.

"I still refused."

"There was nothing else you could do?"

His head moved up and down. "One day I will tell you." A puff. A slow exhale. "So then he came with others, and a . . . a horsewhip."

Remembering the one time her father's belt had almost grazed her adolescent skin—before he'd drawn it back, ashamed at how he'd let his anger take control—she shuddered.

"The beating made me . . ." His brows still knit, he seemed to search for something. "Mad. They came again. And then again. For days . . ." He spoke in a low monotone. "They tried out other ways . . ."

She watched him concentrate on some blank space before his eyes. Like he was trying to get somewhere.

". . . to persuade me. The wounds . . ." His voice flattened the words. ". . . became infected. I—"

His eyes stared into nothing. The lines in his forehead and around his mouth grew more pronounced. Then he must have found his way back. She saw him struggle to translate whatever truth he'd reached into shorthand for her.

". . . was gone, out of my head."

Before he could catch it with the tin, the long ash of his Marica had fallen on the sheet. "*Sranje,*" he said. His fingers flicked the ashes, tried to clean the spot. "And then they stopped."

The beatings or the visits? "But . . . how did you recover from all that?"

He looked directly into her eyes. "This place . . . these people . . . they needed me. I had no time to dwell on my own problems."

For now she would have to accept this answer. Later she would press for more.

He was just about to light another cigarette. But she grabbed his arm and motioned him to lie flat on his stomach. She couldn't read the look he gave as he stretched his body out, his face turned on its side against the pillow, his eyes both fond and curious, his lips slightly apart, not quite a smile. She drew herself up next to him and rested on her side. Her hands began to touch his scars, gently, slowly—first the shoulder blades, then down both sides of the strong back, across the tight buttocks, the muscled thighs. He lay still, like a helpless child, and let her trace each one.

He asked, "Why do you do this?"

What could she say? To transcend time? To soothe the boy he'd been? To let him know he was no longer alone? "Your scars scare me. I have to make my peace with them, so they can't shut me out."

His lips brushed the inside of the arm that propped her up. She kissed each of his healed wounds. Softly. One by one. To suck away the old pain. To let herself know them.

After, in the hot silence of late morning, he turned over and reached for her, pulling her toward him beneath the quilt, enfolding her in the circle of his arms . . .

RED POPPIES. GREEN PEPPERS

A rosy-fingered dawn right out of Homer. Spiro had gone to tend his vegetables on the small plot near the cottage. Anna lingered in bed. She felt groggy, as if she'd taken a sleeping pill the night before. A deep fatigue washed over her in waves. Forced her eyes to shut. She slid her body back under the quilt.

The night before she'd made a plan to check out the empty wooden boxes outside the front windows. She'd asked about them as she'd cleared the dinner plates.

"Those?" Spiro's brows had knit as he was sweeping breadcrumbs off the floor. "My mother tended them." He'd shrugged as if he hadn't thought of them for years. Then he'd come to her and let his hand rest on her neck. "Maybe you can make them bloom again." He'd looked off toward the open door and the looming peaks beyond. "She would grow poppies. Bright red. Beautiful. When I was young, I used to love those poppies in our windows."

For a moment he'd stood still, his arms outstretched before him, both hands on the broom handle. His sweet smile told her he held treasured memories from his childhood.

Alone now, she refused to leave the bed. Her mind continued floating, back to their third day together. He'd found her in the back, scrubbing his white shirt in the washtub. "You are not my maid. Okay?"

She'd felt such peace till then. He'd broken the spell, forced her to see her otherness. Furious, she ran into the meadow. But he chased her, grabbed her in his arms, kissed her. "Anna," he said, "It is only . . . I want you to do things if you want, not out of . . ."

As he groped for words, she searched his eyes and found only concern for her.

"Not because you feel you should."

That caring in his face. After all, it wasn't that he labeled her "American." He only wanted her to be herself. She said, "It felt right, Spiro," and it had.

"Remember, Anna." He tilted her chin with his fingers, his dark eyes full of light. "I lived without you once."

Now, nearly a month later, she could laugh about the chaos of his armoire, the heaps of dirty clothes. But his broom kept the floors clean, and his bookshelf was always neat.

Earlier that morning, in the shadows of first light, he'd kissed her breasts. His side had brushed against her thigh. But even as she'd seen him grow aroused, he'd pulled away. "I want to stay," he'd said. "A lovely morning . . ." He'd walked to the window, parted the curtains. "But I must work the plot or winter will be hard. After, I have errands and a meeting. I may be late." He'd dressed in haste—a pair of pants, a baggy shirt, his gray jacket, and boots. "Eat if you feel hungry." Then he'd turned around, come back, sat on the bed, and swept her into his arms, his hard kiss on her lips almost too much for both of them. But he'd pried himself away and stood, his parting words, "Do not work too hard, Anna."

Savoring those recent scenes, she found the strength to leave the bed. She walked to the armoire, drew his peasant shirt over her head, pulled on Ljuba's heavy cotton pants, and slipped into his mother's too-large boots. Time for a stroll to the garden.

Everything smelled fresh and dewy. Morning birds were calling, whitethroats, warblers, tits. In the distance stood a wild horse, framed by blue sky and high peaks. Suddenly she longed for her piano, to express these new feelings of joy and awe.

The day might bring high heat, but mountain cold still clung to the outdoors. Anna set her feet down carefully, wanting to avoid the snakes Spiro had warned her of, mountain adders that sometimes slithered into the human world in the early morning. But she encountered nothing as she headed to the tall wood box that was the Svetkov outhouse, what he called the *polski toilet*.

Back inside the cottage, she went to each front window, one in the living room, one across the narrow hall in what had once been his room, before he'd moved into his parents' larger chamber. Leaning out, she pulled each box onto its sill. Their plain dark wood, weathered and cracked, was half-full of dry dirt. She knew little of gardening but sensed that this old soil would need renewal. Drawing Ljuba's loose pants tighter, still in the cumbersome boots—she didn't want to meet some snake taking his morning nap—she carried the boxes one by one to the back.

Where the shaggy lea met Spiro's sloping yard, she emptied them and dumped the dirt into a heap. With her fingers she felt the ground for pebbles and layered them into the bottoms. Then she returned to the kitchen for the trowel she'd glimpsed on a low shelf in the cupboard. With it she dug up nearby clumps of weeds, still moist with dew, and added their earth to the mound. Kneading the mixture, her hands remembered helping Ruth make pie dough so many years ago. She filled the boxes two-thirds full of this soil.

Ready now to seek the flowers, she left the boxes where the yard ended and wandered out into the field, closer to the purpling peaks. At last she found what she was looking for—a bed of bright red poppies. The patch was large, but not a whole field full. Not Flanders or *Kosovo Polje*, whose green expanses cradled all their dead. Though their leaves were coarse and hairy, the plants' stems looked too fragile to support their open flowers. When she pulled the first, she saw its long, thin taproot and wondered if it could survive transplanting. She attended to their root systems patiently, disinterring the poppies with her fingers.

Alone in all that wild beauty, she fell into a kind of trance. She found herself humming the jagged melody Spiro would often whistle, some old song he liked about the freedom fighters, what they called the *ajduks* here. She loosened the dirt, shook each flower gently, then eased each from its bed, her movements smooth and rhythmic, like a dance. She began to feel as if she were a midwife, lifting the blooms from their mother, opening them to a new world. She hoped that some would live to sow their seed and add their scarlet to the cottage walls.

When the flowers had turned the ground around her red, she knew that something more than arms would have to carry them. She retrieved the large basket beside their armoire and with it moved the poppies to the boxes at the meadow's edge.

Closer to the kitchen now, she fetched the *stomna*, the large, pear-shaped earthenware jug, and filled it with well water. The sun was climbing higher in the sky and she was hungry. But she didn't want to stop until she'd finished. So she watered the dirt in the boxes, made deep holes, and with great care set the poppies into them.

Last, she searched the area for green creepers to protect the fragile transplants, their leaves and blooms now wilted. She considered moving the boxes closer to the house, but decided to leave them where they were until the plants grew acclimated to their new environment. Or died.

Her task completed, short of breath, she sank into one of the rocking chairs near the back door. The poppies drooped their red heads, but the vines looked comfortable. Soon she would make breakfast.

* * *

She heard noise at the front door. Spiro had been gone all day.

He burst into the living room and lifted her by the waist, as if she weighed nothing. "You see, Anna." He laughed. "You are a feather. I must feed you better."

She loved the smile he gave her. His slanted eyes sparkled. In the soft light of late afternoon he looked unburdened, buoyant . . . free.

"We will go to Mihajlov tonight!"

"I'm too tired, Spiro." She didn't want to spoil things or complain, but the morning's work had drained her. She could barely lift her legs. The thought of walking in, or even bicycling—he had his mother's bike as well as his—was just too much. "What do we have here?"

"Peppers, some rice . . ."

"We can stuff them."

"Yes."

She caught the approval in his eyes.

She loved this kitchen, which she thought of now as theirs. White and old, but clean, it occupied the back end of the house, behind what she called the living room. Its window framed the mountains. Beneath it, herbs grew in two wooden tubs. The kitchen smelled of basil, mint, oregano, and thyme. At least Spiro had nurtured those.

A brick fireplace with open hearth took up much of the inner wall. Above it hung iron pots and utensils, beside it a wood- and coal-burning iron stove. A small white square, an old icebox like the one in their Cambridge flat when she was little, stood flush against the back wall at the end of the stone counter, next to it a hot plate. Their cords plugged into a grimy wall socket. Spiro had sent them to his mother from Pittsburgh. With their buzzing and coils, these strange metallic creatures had seemed at first all wrong here, but she'd grown used to this odd mixture of old and new.

"Rice." He handed her the heavy sack, then left by the back door.

Down to the cellar, she presumed, where he'd asked her not to go for now. He'd said, "It is too dirty. I will clean it for you soon."

Minutes later he returned with a bag of green peppers. She placed them on the table in the center of the room. "Shall we make them all?"

"Why not? Maybe we will ask Ljuba and her kids to come and share with us tomorrow."

Interesting he hadn't mentioned Kosta. Was he gone again? She liked the thought of making dinner for her friends. "Any meat?"

"No, sorry. But let me see what I can find."

After searching the cupboard, he added a bag of onions, some slices of old bread, a garlic bulb, and a hunk of hard white cheese to the workspace she'd cleared on the table.

"Olive oil? Vinegar?"

"Calm down, Anna. I will find them. Vinegar?"

"A secret recipe." A trick she'd learned from Christos' Uncle Nick. Nodding absent-mindedly, she crumbed the bread. "Is there water?"

Over the metal basin in the middle of the counter hung a large, heavy stoneware container, the *češma*. Spiro turned its spigot. "Empty. I will go to the well."

With the knife he'd handed her on his way out, Anna scraped the peppers clean inside and placed the tops on the table. Then she cut some herbs and started chopping leaves. Soon she heard water filling the *češma*.

Then she felt him next to her. Lifting her head, she caught his smile as he set down several lemons and a string of small red peppers.

"Where did you find those?"

"My secret. Careful. They are very hot, those peppers."

As she crumbed the bread and cheese, the scent of olive oil and garlic filled the room. A splat, a sizzle—Spiro was bent over a pan on the hot plate, stirring and whistling that *ajduk* song.

Sauteed rice, garlic, and onions in hot oil. Her stomach started talking.

He emptied the pan onto her chopping board, and together they mixed its contents with the breadcrumbs, cheese, onions, and herbs.

She mused as she kneaded the mixture. So far they'd shared only bits of their pasts. Maybe, like her, he felt they'd shed their old selves on entering this new world that daily brightened their senses and their spirits. But couldn't she approach him now? "Tell me, Spiro. What did you think of America?" She saw his eyes darken.

"America . . ." A pause. "At first I was on guard. It was unreal, like a movie. Everything too big, too fast. Too much freedom. Then I began to enjoy it."

"Did you stay in Pittsburgh?"

"I made a few trips . . ." His hands stopped working, lifted, as he stared into the corner of the room. "New York, Boston, Philadelphia." A slow smile spread across his face. "I learned to like baseball."

"Baseball?" Later she would tell him how she'd loved the sport when she was young. Now she needed something else from him.

"Saw some Pirate games. A friend could get tickets. And I went to Fenway Park."

Fenway Park, where her father used to bring her as a break from dissertating.

She hoped for more but he stopped there, his smile fading as he chopped the red peppers and mixed them in.

They stuffed the shells, replaced their tops, sprinkled the crumbs, and crowned them with lemon slices. Then Spiro pulled the Dutch oven from an iron hook above the fireplace. He laid the peppers inside, added water, lemon juice, and vinegar, set it on the hotplate, and covered it.

"It will take some time," he said, wiping his hands on his shirttail. "Let us eat something and have a drink."

He fixed a tray. *Rakija*. Glasses. Cheese. A half-loaf of dark bread. She followed him outside. They rocked and watched the sun slide down behind the mountains. Sipped and smoked. Spoke little.

"Anna, what are those?" He pointed to the window boxes, all but a few red blossoms hidden by the creepers' leaves.

"My morning's work. An experiment. I'm not sure they'll survive."

He rose from the chair and came to her. Bent down, buried his fingers in her hair, and kissed her. Then he drew his chair closer, sat down, and took her hand. "Funny. When Mihajlov led VMRO, they grew poppies for crops."

"Poppies?"

"They traded opium for guns."

Anna sighed. She didn't want to think about this business now. Her legs were stiff. Her head felt heavy on her neck. Fighting to stay open under drooping lids, her eyes rested a moment on those few small red spots at the yard's edge. From the back door came delicious smells.

"You know, Anna, we have become a *Pirinska pesna.*"

"A Pirin song?

"*Pesna* means 'poem,' too. In our case, a beautiful poem of love." He touched her cheek.

The reassuring roughness of his palm. The tangy kitchen odors. Her eyelids fluttered, drifted shut. She felt somehow complete, as if they were a family, the flowers their fragile children.

A STONE IN A STREAM

From the bedroom Anna heard a bell. She ran to the front and opened the door. A young man in a cap stood by a bicycle, a letter in his hand. She thanked him and laid the envelope on the sofa table. The Cyrillic on the postmark read *Melnik*.

She went back to the bedroom to fold more laundry, Spiro's and some clothes borrowed from Ljuba and her friends. She didn't miss what she'd sent back to Athens in her suitcase, chosen for a different kind of trip. But besides her underwear, the contents of her satchel weren't useful here. Like the Sierra trip last summer, when she'd had to leave her city gear at base camp. Normally impeccably groomed and dressed, she'd cherished the title they gave her: "Most Unkempt Girl in Camp."

The rhythm of her hands smoothing the fabric freed her mind to think. If Spiro could get letters, she could write one. Before she'd reached Bulgaria, she'd sent her family updates on her wanderings. Though isolated here, immersed in this new life, she longed to share her happiness. But how could she write that she was in a tiny Bulgarian village with a man? How could she explain Spiro and how much she loved him? How could they accept it, given her history with men?

Her fingers made perfect creases in Spiro's best white shirt. She could smell the sun-dried cotton. But her mind kept wandering. Her visa had expired the first week in July. If that were discovered, could she be deported? Imprisoned? She'd said nothing to Spiro and he'd never asked. Their perfect inner world had kept them far from this reality.

Maybe their love was only a fantasy. They'd begun to share more of their pasts. She'd told him bits about her family, her work with civil rights leaders in DC, her anger at the war and America's treatment of Blacks. But still he kept so much from her—as if their love existed outside time. Yet she'd seen recent signs that troubled her. Random absences from home—he'd tell her he had "meetings." Moments when he'd look distant, preoccupied, and if she asked, he'd always flash that smile she loved and say, "Anna, do not worry."

But she'd held back as well, hadn't ever told him she was a Jew. Now she wondered. Though she'd never felt so whole and so at home, she couldn't erase her history, how others had perceived her. High school—Robby Beckman and Mr. Denby. Those for whom she was "Miss Israel," "not like the rest of them," "exotic." Halloran, with his ex-wife. Christos, Mikis, Reza, Dušan in Zagreb, and the rest, for whom she'd played a role. Only the old man in Sofia had seen through to her core.

She thought of Olga Ćerenek, whose rosy cheeks and dark, cropped hair imaged her deepest fears. A first-generation Czech, Olga was working to support herself through Georgetown. Despite their busy schedules, they'd had great fun together in their several months as roommates. Lectures, movies, symphonies. Until it came out casually that Anna was a Jew.

Olga's lovely hazel eyes widened. She backed away from Anna. Her small voice said, "You should have told me that before I moved in." Anna would have talked things through, but Olga couldn't get beyond the word itself. What pain to see three English letters undermine a friendship.

The next day she helped carry Olga's trunk downstairs. Walking toward the cab, Olga was silent, her head bowed. But as the cab pulled off, she strained to catch Anna. Beneath her furrowed brows her eyes questioned, as if at last she wondered why this rupture had occurred.

The few times Anna dared to tell non-Jewish friends her tales, she found them skeptical. "Oh, come on," they'd say. "That doesn't happen here. Not now." But anti-Semitism seemed to thrive. With or without Jews. Despite the Holocaust. And Eastern Europe offered fertile soil. She remembered Spiro's words about Armenians and Jews. Uneasy as she stacked his clothes in the armoire, she hoped he wouldn't prove to be like Olga.

* * *

Later, all her self-imposed tasks finished, she wrote her parents a letter filled with her new life. Spiro would see to its mailing. As she rested in the rocking chair, noises from the front room told her Spiro had come home.

"Anna!"

"I'm in back."

He burst through the kitchen door, took the stairs two at a time, and pulled her from her seat. But as his lips neared hers, she moved her head. Eyebrows knit, he held her at arm's length.

"I'm sorry, Spiro." She hadn't planned to stop him, but the time had come for honesty, no matter the result. He had to see who she was, even if that knowledge made him spurn her. She'd left so much behind for him. Put herself at risk. She had to know if he could really love her. "Can we speak seriously?"

"We always do." His lips curved in that charming smile that made him seem a boy sometimes.

"Yes, but . . . not like this."

His eyes darkened. "Something is wrong?"

"I . . ."

"You look so sad, Anna. Is it something I have done?"

"No, no. It's—"

"Shall we talk there?" He gestured toward the peaks. "It is lovely now. The sun is soft. The mountains look like curtains on the sky."

Hands joined, silent, they left the yard and moved into the meadow. The mountains edged closer, their rugged slopes and peaks shadowed beneath the fading sun. A soft trickle of water ribboned down the stone flanks nearest them.

"Anna, look!" Spiro pointed upward. A spread of blue-black wings against the sky. A falcon swooping down. A shriek. The hero bird rising again, something in its talons.

They reached a stream. Near it lay a large flat-topped boulder. "You like this place? Sit down. Breathe in this air." His jaw set, his mouth stern, he hunted through his pockets. Found the Maricas. Lit them each one. "Okay, Anna. I am ready now."

Picking at the torn flesh on the corner of her thumbnail, she asked, "Remember the square that first day?" She couldn't help the harshness in her voice. "The *panair?*"

He nodded, his eyes widening. "Anna, you are white! Please, sit."

"You mentioned Jews, Armenians . . ." She followed his advice and sat. Her legs couldn't support her weight.

"*Ljubov moja,* you are not well! Maybe this was not a good idea."

"Oh, no. It's . . . it's lovely here. It's just . . . we have to get this straight before . . ." She wouldn't cry, damn it. ". . . before we can go on." She shook off the arm he tried to place around her.

"Anna, I am listening."

"It's that . . ." The surface of the rock was hard and cold. She dared herself to say the word. ". . . Spiro . . ." She took a long puff on the cigarette, exhaled, and stamped it out. "I'm a Jew."

His face muscles were still. No visible recoil. But his features sagged, as if he'd grown suddenly old. "This is what upsets you? What we have to talk about?"

She heard shock in his voice, but not like Olga's. He sounded saddened, lost. Still, she needed to be sure. "I shouldn't worry?"

"My God, Anna. Your eyes!" He dropped his cigarette. Ground it in the dirt.

She noted the vertical lines in his face as he squinted into the sun. "According to my sources, Bulgaria sent Vardar's Jews to Hitler's camps. Delivered many thousands to the Nazis." She studied her feet in his mother's old boots. Recalled the Sofia synagogue, the old man's mistrust of Bulgaria's motivations, shielding its Jews from Germans while rounding up and handing over those in its occupied Macedonian territory.

"Shit, Anna." His smile long gone, Spiro hung his head. His shoulders drooped. "You think . . ." He swallowed so hard she could hear it. ". . . a word can change the way I feel?"

She searched his eyes, straining for clarity, and deep inside she saw what looked like pain.

He turned away. Paced to the stream, then back again. His face was tight, its lines severe. "Why did you think this word would make a difference?"

"My life."

His hair had worked loose from its band, become a wild black tangle. Almost to himself, he muttered, "Even in America. But Anna, only now I realize how much you are like Max." He shut his eyes against the dying sun, then opened them and stared out at the mountains.

"What do you mean?"

"His German part fights always with his Slav." A long ash floated on the breeze. He grabbed her right hand and held her gaze with his. "You must not let anyone do this to you."

"Do what, Spiro?"

"You see, Anna, what happens here, how they, Bulgarians, treat us. But we will not hate ourselves for them."

"Spiro, I—"

"I will tell you. Even before we met, I knew you were a Jew. From Max."

His casual words undid her. She felt naked, her inner scar exposed. Max? How had he known? Her looks? Her name? What made him an expert on Jews?

Oh, God. She flashed back to the Jewish surgeon in that trendy club three years ago. He'd asked her to marry him—"You'd be great to take to meetings." But first he'd arranged for her nose to be "fixed" so she would be "perfect." She'd stormed off in a taxi, disgusted by the self-hatred that made him want to change her so the world wouldn't detect their tainted origins. But now she saw that she, too, wore a yellow star inside, shared with him a sense of shame nothing had ever wiped away. No wonder she'd identified with Larsen's Claire Kendry, who'd fled her culture to enter the white world and paid the ultimate price.

Spiro was right. Others shouldn't determine her self-worth. But how—?

"Did Max tell you . . .?" he said, taking her hand in his rough palm.

"What?"

His right eye blinked something away. ". . . about his one great love?"

Silent, she tried to grasp this new image of Max.

"Six years ago. A Jewish girl. Eva Goldstein." He pressed her knuckles to his cheek. "Her mother fled with her from Munich just before the war. Raised her in England."

"He never mentioned her to me."

Spiro let her hand go. Faced the mountains. "After her mother died, Eva returned to Munich. To study, trace lost family . . ." He sighed. "To see if she could understand what happened. To find herself, maybe."

A bolt of cold air sluiced down the meadow, stirring grass and flowers. Anna felt the hair rise on her arms.

"I have seen pictures. She looked a bit like you. Dark hair. Haunted blue eyes."

She remembered now. The old man in Niš had noted her resemblance to some Eva. "Haunted?"

"Yes," he said as he traced her lips with his finger. "What you are is in your eyes. I should have read them better." His hands circled her waist. "Eva also had—at least to hear Max speak—your anger at injustice . . ."

His stare was too intense. She had to blink.

As he went on, his face began to relax. "And the way you love when things are mixed. Not plain, but full of layers." He raised his head. Surveyed the watercolor sky, its pastel clouds bleeding into one another.

Well, no sign of Eva now. So much for inter-ethnic harmony. "I guess it didn't last?"

"She died. An accident."

Some moments passed before she dared to look at him. When she did, she detected something in his eyes, like the black veil of a widow. Was it guilt for stealing Max's second Jew?

He offered her a cigarette. When she refused, he put away the pack. "Maybe because you are a Jew . . ."

She hunched her shoulders against another cool gust.

"Anna . . .," he was still lost in his thoughts, ". . . you understand me."

She inched closer, until they touched. "Spiro, I was so afraid." Then she laid her head against his chest. "I didn't want to think that you could hate me. But sometimes, when I haven't seen it coming . . ." She heard his heart beating beneath his shirt. "It was never so important."

He took her in his arms. "I thought, America is safe. There, at least . . ." A long, dry laugh. "Macedonians. Jews. We are both problems for the world."

He let her go. Without a word he walked to the stream's edge and hunched over the water. She could see only his back, his arms moving, his hands busy with something.

Then he rose and walked to her side. "Anna, take this." In her palm he placed a small stone.

She felt its surface, polished smooth. "It's beautiful, Spiro. But what . . .?"

He clenching his right fist. "Are we not all like this stone?" His glance revealed some inner weariness. "You? Me? Max? Shaped by when and where we are, and everything that came before?"

She searched the fine lines in his face for clues.

"I cannot find the right words. *Prokleto!* The . . . the stone is beautiful, Anna. It should feel pride." He ran his fingers through his mass of hair.

Looking at him then, his eyes urgent, intense, she finally understood. "My God. I've disappointed you."

Sadness tinged his smile as he shook his head. "America. All of your intelligence. And still . . ." He reached out for the hand that held the stone. Clasped it in his.

Her free hand slid along his cheek.

"There is another thing. My *kum*—godfather—my mother's tutor . . ."

She felt his breath warm her face. "Don't the Orthodox consider that a formal bond?"

"Yes, but not our family. My *kum*, David, was a Jew—unfit, according to the priests, to play that role. But he and my father were communists; they cared nothing for such nonsense. The father of David's friend, Trifon, was a priest—the Reds killed him after the war. He said some words in private. At least that is what they told me. David suffered during the war; they interned him in Haskovo. But I grew up with his stories. I know things others do not." He gestured at the wild landscape. "You are right, Anna. Some here hate Jews. But you see how we live. Poor schools, propaganda, power-hungry leaders. Communists say things. Priests too." He shook his head, "Most of them are only tools of the system." He pursed his lips together in a bitter smile. "The Jew is a reason, an excuse. And in Pirin . . ." His hand massaged his bottom lip. ". . . the Macedonian is a Jew."

He pushed his hair back with his hand, his eyes glistening almost as if they held tears. "Sometimes, Anna, vision seems a curse."

"For God's sake, Spiro. It's what you do. How you live. Helping others see better." His response to her news had elated her. But where had this come from?

"It is . . . too hard." A groan, like a sick animal. "So many truths. About the world. About ourselves." The grooves along his mouth deepened. "And I can teach only what I see. How can I know if it is right?"

She saw the sadness in his eyes and longed to take him in her arms. "But isn't that where Socrates began? Sure only that he wasn't?"

"You understand so much, Anna, except about yourself. Kosta? Jordan? What do they know of the world? Even if they have traveled a bit. Of Jews?"

"They listen to you, Spiro." She took his hand in hers, held it up to kiss a shiny blister. "And you've changed them." She thought back to her first meeting with Kosta. The Mercedes on the street outside the Grand Balkan. To Jordan in the *kafeana* the night before Max left.

A smile cracked Spiro's face. "You know Ivan Šišman?"

"I don't."

"The Turks killed him in 1396."

"And why should I know him?"

"Ivan was . . ." He buried his face in her hair. ". . . the last native Bulgarian king." He kissed her eyelid, then moved down to her chin. "His mother was a Jew, Sarah, the second wife of Ivan Aleksandar." He kissed her neck. "Ivan's first wife went into a nunnery. And Sarah became Bulgarian Orthodox to be his queen." His hand slid underneath the neckline of her blouse. "But still, by Jewish law, I think, the last truly Bulgarian king was Jewish."

She touched her finger to his cheek. His smile dispelled the grooves around his mouth. Despite the early evening cool, he set her down on the grass blanket beside the stream, under an eggplant melon sky . . .

THE EVE OF *ILINDEN*

Anna's head hung over the dark hole. Eyes closed, she tried to fight the stink of vomit and the shit below. To keep from sliding in, she clutched the wooden sides with all her waning power. Her stomach was completely empty now. But dry heaves racked her body and she spat out bitter fluid.

For the fourth straight day she'd crept into the pre-dawn calm, doubled over, clutching at her abdomen. She couldn't risk the chamber pot. He'd find it. Her fear of snakes had let her check the vomit long enough to slip on the boots she'd hidden beneath the bed. Then she'd raced to the outhouse in the garden. So far Spiro had slept through peacefully, rising only with the sun, and—

Two strong arms grabbed her around the waist. Whatever it might mean, she let him take her weight. "*O, Bože,* Anna! What do you do here?"

Her body, then preoccupied, prevented her reply. He seemed to understand.

Once the spasms ended, he pulled her up and wiped her mouth and forehead with his shirttail. "God, Anna." His hands pushed back her hair so she could take a breath of clean air. "You must be cold."

But she was sweating from the energy she'd spent, while he stood chilled and nearly naked, his shirt unbuttoned, loose over bare trunk and thighs.

He carried her back to the house. By the time he laid her on the bed, the sun's first rays had crowned the mountain peaks. With care he lifted off the caftan-like garment she wore—this she'd also stuck under the bed after that first morning of sickness. He moved her body until she rested comfortably beneath the quilt. Then he left, returning with a damp cloth that he pressed against her face. Each touch of its cool weight soothed her hot skin.

At last he lay back on the pillow next to her and asked in his low voice, "What is this, Anna?"

Her insides raw, her mouth fetid and dry, she said at last, "Ljuba's *ajvar* last night."

Smiling, his dark eyes on her, he shook his head. "I do not think so."

"Why not?"

"It is now the fourth day, and before there was no *ajvar.*"

So he had seen her leave the other times. Why had he waited till today for this?

"What should I say?"

"Maybe . . . the truth?"

"Then . . . my period was due six days ago. I missed the last one too." His eyebrows arched. His upturned lips opened to show those straight white teeth. "I'm always right on time. Twenty-six days. I never miss. And this makes twice."

Propped on his right elbow, he was scrutinizing her with tender eyes.

"So, anyway," she went on, since he hadn't spoken yet, "I wasn't giving it much thought."

A budding joy softened his face.

"Well, maybe . . . yes, I was." She'd done the record-keeping in her head. With Peter there'd been no slips. She hadn't slept with Max. That left only Spiro. Was it justice or blind luck that the first time she allowed herself to love, a child was made? "But then, I've been so tired, and the morning sickness seemed an omen, not that I know anything about this stuff. I mean . . . it had to have been that first night . . . and—"

His arms enfolded her. "*Glupavo malo pilence.* Silly little chicken. You said you were okay, so I assumed . . . I would have used—"

"My period was due the next day. All the signs were there. And I wanted . . ." She inhaled more of this good air. ". . . to be free. To do it naturally, without thinking. And if this happened, then—"

"Quiet, *mala majko.*" He brushed her forehead with his lips. "So, little mother." His hands cupped her face. "The egg of my grandmother had great power. First it brought you. Now you are the mother of my son."

"Son? You know already?" She loved how his eyes glowed now.

"Am I not Macedonian? Then, boy or girl. But let it be a boy!" He grinned. In the soft rose light, his smile filled her with peace.

Where were her second thoughts, the dreads that prompted several friends to risk back-street abortions? Sari had nearly bled to death in a Baltimore motel room. From DC to Mihajlov was a quantum leap. Yet she felt no doubts, no question as to whether she would have this child. And Spiro had become a doting father. In the strange logic of life, the child was now a reality.

As Spiro began to dress, prepared to set off for his garden plot, she felt her senses dimming gradually. Somewhere in her head a word repeated. *Love.* And then another. *Home.* And finally a whisper. *Child. Love, Home, Child.* The words became a chorus that repeated and repeated till she . . .

* * *

The afternoon was warm. His errands done, Spiro came home to check on her. He squeezed her some apricot juice, then insisted that she nap.

But when he tiptoed in, she wasn't sleeping. He undressed quietly and slid in next to her. "Can we . . . is it all right?"

His tender, almost timid tone made her grab his mouth and press her lips hard against his.

"I am serious, Anna."

"It takes nine months, Spiro. Could people go so long without—"

He gave a hearty laugh and shook his head. "But it seems strange to me. The tiny thing and I . . . in you together."

"Your saying it that way . . ." She stopped briefly, recalled the ardent rhetoric of her more radical girlfriends. ". . . it makes me glad . . . to hold you both."

He was nibbling on her ear and neck. He'd started moving farther down, when suddenly he raised his head and sought her eyes. "These breasts, Anna, these nipples." He held them in his hands, studying them, as if he'd never seen a breast before. "They will feed my son." His tone was filled with wonder. Then he kissed them with what seemed like reverence, so that pleasure was the smallest part of what she felt.

As his mouth traversed her flesh, Anna lay beneath him in a kind of trance. Her skin tingled; her body came alive. But what ignited her still more was the deeply serious joy with which he touched each part of her. As if this were some holy rite, an act of consecration.

At last, swallowing hard, he sought her eyes.

She whispered, "Yes."

His hands parted her thighs gently, to make sure she was ready. His thick black hair mixed with her own, he kissed her there, then lifted himself up and entered cautiously. "I am not hurting you?"

"No, my love." Those words seemed right, as his gentle rhythm turned their love into a sacred dance.

* * *

Anna lay back on the pillow, Spiro's head cradled between her breasts. She felt tears on her chest. They were not hers. Bathed in sweat and semen, she sensed how far they'd journeyed together. That loss of self—was that nirvana, transcendence into cosmos? Her fingers stroked his scarred back. "Are you sleeping?"

"*Ne, srce moe,*" came his low whisper.

My heart. She loved how these words sounded in his mouth.

They lay together, sated, until they heard a knock. A frantic rapping. Loud. Repeated. Then a hoarse young voice, "*Ajde!*"

Spiro flung himself from the bed, pulled on his pants, grabbed the same shirt he'd worn since dawn, and left the room. But Anna huddled beneath the quilt, not wanting to get up now, still basking in his warmth and all the new sensations she'd felt.

Seconds later Spiro came back, knelt beside the bed, and whispered, "Kole, Ljuba's son. I have to go." His lips on hers were rough, nervous. "I will be home by dark."

Nearly to the door, he stopped short, wheeled around, and walked to the armoire. From the bottom drawer he extracted something long and narrow, wrapped in a white cloth. A silver circle stuck out from one end.

"Spiro?"

"Anna, I must go."

His right index finger against his lips, the long white bundle underneath his arm, he turned his face toward her. On both sides of his mouth she saw those lines. And though he tried to smile, to hide his worry, she recognized the darkness in his eyes.

"Sleep, *ljubov moja,*" he said. "Tomorrow will be busy. *Ilinden.*" Then he left, shutting the door behind him.

* * *

It was nearly midnight, pitch-black, and Spiro still hadn't returned. She threw herself into the bed, unable to wait longer. She'd had a full day. Tended the herbs and poppies, cleaned, done laundry and dishes, fixed *tarator*—a cold cucumber salad she loved—and stuffed eggplants—*imam bajaldi,* a Turkish name from the five-hundred-year-long Ottoman occupation of Bulgaria. She'd tasted it in Washington, but never dreamt that one day she would make it in a place close to its origin. The food, uneaten, ready in the icebox.

Ilinden. The name reverberated in her head. The women had been cooking since Monday. Yesterday she'd helped Ljuba prepare *ajvar* and bottle her *rakija.* Everyone was baking special breads and cakes. To her surprise, the people here in some way still revered St. Ilija, linking him to the harvest and the pagan thunder god, Perun. Last night Ljuba had flashed her dimpled smile while kneading dough and said, "If Ilija not like, he make beeg noise. Bring storm. Hurt garden. House. Maybe—fameely."

The men were getting ready for *kurban,* the sacrifice. In Pirin they killed sheep. Spiro had told her his grandmother's people in Vardar more commonly killed roosters, though he'd added, his low voice full of irony, "Before that, it was bulls. And first, humans." A tasty meal, the slain creature appeased Christian and pagan powers alike. She loved how the old remained alive within the new, despite official Party lines.

Once she'd known *Ilinden* from a distance, as a name in history books. But Spiro had mentioned it on the square and his stories had brought it closer. Now she knew that on the second day of August, 1903, VMRO had attacked the Turks at Kruševo, in Vardar, Macedonia, using some of the ransom money Sandanski had received for Ellen Stone. After their initial victory, they'd proclaimed the Kruševo Republic.

Last night, as she and Spiro were washing dinner dishes, he'd reflected on the end of *Ilinden.* "After ten days, Turkish troops crushed the rebels. Made them pay a heavy price. Mutilation. Rape. Two months more of terror throughout Vardar." Setting down a dish, he'd sighed. "This century gave *Ilinden* a new purpose: to honor, with St. Ilija, the martyrs of VMRO."

Then he'd repeated something he'd raised that first day—the rebels' multi-ethnic ideal. "Imagine, they asked even Turks to join their Republic. They wanted Kruševo to be a model. A haven for all who lived in Macedonia. A lovely dream, yes, Anna?" His lips had curled into a bitter smile. "And like all dreams, it ended. St. Ilija must have been displeased."

She knew that on the square tomorrow, in the absence of the old *guslars*, the singing bards, Spiro and his men would read from epic poems and lead the village in some hero songs. In the empty bedroom, the memory of his melancholy laugh set free a rush of images she'd chosen to ignore, not wanting to admit that more than *rakija* was brewing. He'd tried to keep it from her, like she had tried to hide her morning sickness. But there were signs, though she'd declined to read them. Those times when, as he spoke to her, his eyes would wander into space or he would stop in mid-sentence. Or when, as he sat silent, his brows would knit and lines would form near the corners of his mouth.

There had been meetings, too. Many more than usual. And he had been so long away at several. Then, three days earlier, after cycling home from Ljuba's cottage, she'd found two bikes on the walkway. The house had been empty, but loud voices were coming from the rear. Through the kitchen door she saw three men standing, their arms making large gestures.

Spiro's broad back blocked her view of the others. She recognized only a tall head of black curls. Jordan. Then Spiro moved. Revealed a shorter man with cropped brown hair. Blagoj? Spiro, Kosta, Jordan, and Hristo were roughly the same age. Childhood friends, they shared more than their politics. They also helped the village families, including Hristo's ailing wife, who needed more support than he could give.

The younger men she knew less well. Blagoj was one of those. The few times she had seen him, his eyes had made her nervous. They held a kind of restlessness that, coupled with their keen intelligence, seemed somehow menacing. More than once she'd caught him studying her, but she hadn't told Spiro . . . she might have only imagined it.

Blagoj had acknowledged her politely and excused himself. Jordan had flashed a look she couldn't read, but stayed to have a glass of *rakija* with them. The drink and quiet chat had seemed to relax him. He had dark, pitted skin, the legacy of bad acne or a dreadful case of chicken pox. But his open face, with its generous mouth and light-brown eyes, conveyed solidity. She wanted to like him, to trust him.

The three of them had spoken of Kole, a rising soccer star among the village lads. "Like his father," Jordan said. "Sveto."

As she burrowed into the covers now, the thought of Sveto's name transported her to Ljuba's kitchen last week. Kole had burst in from soccer, filthy but excited. He'd scored the winning goal. Ljuba was chopping onions. Suddenly her face blanched. She bowed her head and said, "Kole same like Sveto." Then she wiped her eyes on her apron hem. "When Kole seek, we need . . . *medeetseena.*"

"Medicine?" In Ljuba's voice Anna heard a hidden world of grief.

"*Da.* Yes. Medicine," she said, pronouncing each syllable with reverence. "But too much money. So he take how much Kole need. Then . . ." She made staccato sounds.

"They shot him?"

"*Da.*" Ljuba's eyes narrowed. "Shot." She concentrated on the word, as if it held great power. An onion in her left hand, a small knife in her right, she stood with both hands still, weeping.

Anna found the ways of memory strange. Associations had moved her from *Ilinden* to the men's meeting and finally to Ljuba and Sveto, to their brief life together. In the photo on Ljuba's armoire, Sveto stood stiff in a dark suit that ill fit his athlete's frame, a coarse-featured but handsome man. Ljuba's face still reddened at the mention of his name. Her smile would grow wistful, her eyes hungry.

Anna began to squirm beneath the covers. Where was Spiro? Most of all, she hadn't wanted to face what she'd seen last night. Returning from the outhouse before bed, she'd stumbled over something at the far edge of the yard—Spiro's old boots, caked with damp, foul-smelling mud. But that morning he'd worn his walking shoes when he'd set out for Mihajlov. And when he'd come to meet her at Ljuba's toward sunset, those shoes were on his feet.

She and Spiro often hiked together; the exercise and fresh air did her good. And they would store wet footwear on the kitchen mat to dry. Why hadn't he asked her this time? Had he gone to *Sina gora?*

He'd urged her to trust him but hadn't shared a thing about his group. This tension wasn't good for her or the baby. Could she keep living like this—always on edge, seeking signs for something dark she couldn't name? Unable to dismiss the thoughts that drifted through her head, she didn't find the sleep her body craved.

* * *

The door creaked open. Light footsteps. Underneath the quilt she waited, silent.

Spiro shed his clothes and shoes without a sound and eased himself into the bed facing away from her. In the dark she could hear him breathe. His hard back was a wall that made her colder than before. A clotted silence held until his low voice murmured, "*Srce moe.*" Then he turned to her and burrowed deep into her breasts.

Picking up the sounds he made, the strange grunts of an animal in pain, she clasped him fiercely to her.

"It is . . ." A low moan. Strangled sounds.

"Spiro?"

His grasp tightened around her.

The sudden pressure hurt her breasts, but she felt him working to shield her from what he couldn't speak.

"Kosta . . ." A long pause. "Kosta is dead."

"What . . .?" A scream lodged in her throat. "Ljuba and the children . . .?"

He stroked her face. "They are with the Stojanovs. Dina will look after them."

Kosta is dead. How could she process those words? An oxymoron. She saw him again that first time, on the square with Max outside the Grand Balkan. Gold chain. Lusty stare. That beery voice. All hairy chest and confidence.

Wanting to know more, to understand, she tried to ask. But only "How?" came out.

"Not now, my love." He kissed her chin. "I cannot . . ."

She'd never heard his voice so low, so cracked.

They lay like that a long time, holding one another, silent, until, blowing hair from her eyes, he said, "I want . . ."

The darkness hid his face from her, but she could hear his urgency.

". . . for us to be . . . married."

"Married," she repeated to herself. In her world, among her friends, that word was highly suspect—the end of life, of freedom. But in his mouth it sounded like a blessing.

He moved his face near hers, brushed his lips against her cheek. "You heard me, Anna?"

"Yes."

"All day I kept thinking." A heavy sigh. "You have not spoken much about your family." He kissed the soft place in her neck below her chin. "But my parents had a bond that only death could break."

"My mother and father fight too much. Still, they are each other's worlds."

"I want us to have that."

"We do. What difference does a word make?"

"It is not the word, Anna, but what it means." He curved his long body around her trembling legs. "I want us written in my mother's Bible. All these years she hid it from the communists. It came from her great-grandmother. My birth. The dates my brother and my father died. The date I entered for her death. Our names should be inscribed with those entries."

"Your brother?"

"Živko. He lived only two years. After, I came." Suddenly he lifted himself off her, lay back on the pillow, and lowered her on top of him. His hands caressed her back and thighs, the rough skin gently touching hers. "My father called himself an atheist, but he cursed God for the hell He made of this world. In spite of him, and of his death, my mother kept her faith. She would have wanted us married 'before God.'"

Anna let herself melt into him. She felt his chest move up and down with each breath.

"Sometimes on the mountain, or today with you, I feel . . ." He stopped, filled up his lungs, exhaled, then kissed the crown of her head. ". . . I cannot . . . I do not know how to name it. But I want us to be part of it."

Her tears were filling up the cleft between his chest muscles. For Kosta. Ljuba. Spiro's lonely quest, still so mysterious to her, which she now shared. And for herself.

"Then, you can write your parents you are married and with child. We will have entered history." His fingers brushed away her tears. He raised his head to kiss her eyes. "I want to hold you like this when we are old, our bodies bent, our bones creaking, our children's children sleeping in the next room."

"Yes." She curled her face into the soft flesh under his hard shoulder. "But how?"

He ran his hands lightly along her arms. "Of course, no civil marriage. We cannot risk the official registry. The visa . . . it was only for a few days, I imagine."

"Mm-hmm." His hands, stroking her buttocks, gave her comfort.

"A Westerner with an expired visa? They would feel compelled to track you down, arrest, deport you. And priests, they cannot marry the unbaptized. Besides, they are not trustworthy. To do their work, they must support the government."

"Then how—"

"I will write David, my *kum* near Melnik. He is a learned man. Perhaps he knows a Jewish ritual. And Trifon, son of the priest the communists killed."

"Yes. I remember."

"He has no use for the Church. But he has still some faith. Together they could find something to say for us, and for our child."

Hearing his need, his certainty, she said, "That would be beautiful."

He brushed her left breast with his hand. "Tomorrow we must celebrate *Ilinden*. The village will demand it. And pay respect to Kosta. Then we will bury him."

She let him press her eyelids shut and smooth their flesh.

He kissed her chin. "Let us try to rest, *srce moe*."

My heart. The perfect words for what she felt.

They shifted their positions. In the dark they lay like spoons, their left hands joined, waiting . . .

ILINDEN

Early that morning he'd helped her stave off queasiness. Had brought a mug of cool water and wafer-thin patties of salty baked dough. Wiped her forehead with a rag. She'd felt better. So now, mid-afternoon, he led her to the square.

As they drew near, she heard fat crackling over open fires. A swirl of scents. Lamb roasting on a spit. Sweet fennel. Mint and basil, mountain thyme, rosemary and laurel. The acrid odor of tobacco, the heavy sweetness of *rakija*. What she saw there made her empty stomach growl, her mouth water. Vats on tripods, full of stew. Tables bearing platters of sliced meat, lamb bones and shanks. Cabbage and potatoes. Lemons, peppers, onions, garlic. Cucumber. Tomatoes. Fresh breads, honey, *banitsa*—those cheese pastries with many different fillings. Cheeses, *bakrdan*—a corn-based side dish like polenta—and *ajvar*. So good, and she so hungry.

Then her stomach lurched. Too much. Too rich. As she doubled over, Spiro caught her. Rushed her to an open spot just off the square. Held her shoulders while she vomited again. Afterwards, they sat still on the grass. She closed her eyes and waited for her breathing to grow steady. At last she told him she was ready to return.

The day was clear, the sky bright. Already just a hint of something crisp, fall-like, hung in the air. The sun made whitewashed walls gleam. The village sparkled. Many older men wore traditional dress—white leggings, shirts with vests, sashes and *opintsi,* Macedonia's name for that ubiquitous Balkan footwear, toe- and heel-covered flat leather sandals, often with fancy straps. A few among the younger men and boys mimicked their elders, but most had on dark pants, homespun shirts, and, like Spiro, a plain black vest.

Over their white shifts, the *babas* sported richly patterned vests and aprons cinched with woven belts and giant gold or silver paisley buckles. Intricate designs edged sleeves, hems, high stockings. Some younger women chose traditional finery. Others draped their often ample bodies in modern dresses with floral prints.

Anna wore the white shift Spiro had found in his mother's carved pine chest that morning. The mauve and crimson flowers of her teal vest—the one she'd bought in Sofia with Max's *leva*, buried in the bottom of her satchel till today—hid the single vomit stain. Spiro had said she needed something to bring some color back into her face. She was grateful the clothing fit loosely, in case her queasiness returned.

A local band was playing on the square. The *zurna* and the *gajda* pierced the air. The *tapan* added its deep booms. The *tambura* and *gadulka* plucked and fiddled their melodic lines. Above them floated the *kaval's* breathy, wistful tones.

At first only a few men danced something slow and heavy with high lifts and big leaps, and sharp shakes of the shoulder to the drumbeat. Before long more joined in, including Hristo and Spiro. She loved to see him like this, lost inside the music. The leader, older, pot-bellied, did squatting steps. Spiro, toward the end of this small line, moved with economy, his feet making clean motions.

Then the music changed, gentled. A *lesno*. Everyone joined the open circle, even small children and haughty teens. Spiro came for her, smiling, and led her to the line. Soon the tempo shifted once again, sped up. Spiro held her right hand. Nasto pumped her left arm up and down, exuberant. He was another of the young men in the group. She guessed that he was close to her in age. Lanky, short, he had a pleasant smile and fine blue eyes. But his face seemed somehow unfinished. She could never quite identify what was missing. Nasto did odd jobs around the village, mostly carpentry, and spoke only a guttural Macedonian. As he flashed her a wide grin, his slightly crooked front teeth made it childlike and endearing.

The whole village was on its feet. She shut her eyes. Her body moved to the deep throb of the *tapan*. She flowed along with the snaking line.

Spiro whispered, "You are okay, Anna?"

"Yes. I'm feeling much better." Her hand squeezed his, Nasto's sweaty palm holding her other one.

Time and place receded. The village was alive, rhythm embodied. Within the steady throb she felt weightless, suspended by the dancers in the music. Spiro's tall body beside her floated on the wave as well. Barely moving, yet in constant motion, they wound and curled and wove concentric circles round the square until the band needed to catch its breath, to eat something and take a drink.

Once they reassembled, Spiro left her briefly and walked to the *tambura* player. She watched him hold out *leva,* then scatter the bills on the ground near the musicians. Responding to his praise, the band began to play a *ručenica* like the one when they'd first danced. The music had a vibrant sensuality. It forced her feet and shoulders to respond. Lines and couples formed. Spiro stood across from her, straight-backed, his arms and chest thrust out, his eyes gleaming. She began that little three-step, lifted her arms up, rotated her hands. But as she circled slowly, flouncing her skirt, sending her most enchanting smile, she detected in the darkening of his eyes, his furrowed brow, the lines around his mouth, the fact of Kosta's death.

The ground began to spin, the square to blur. She couldn't breathe . . .

* * *

The air had grown colder. The sun had set. The cooking fires were dying down. A small dais with crude wood planks for stairs now stood at one end of the square where they had earlier danced. Spiro walked her to its edge and climbed up with the men. They began reciting from the ancient hero tales, rooted in that long ago battle, *Kosovo Polje—Krali Marko*, the Kosovo cycle, the mythic poems and songs that linked so many in the Balkans to their common history of victimhood. Each man took a section. Even the smallest children stood attentive, listening.

After the recitation, everyone began to sing. The old folks knew most of the words. The children sang the refrains. Voices raised together, the village mourned its fallen heroes. Such pain-filled songs, their dark beauty enhanced by untaught voices in raw dissonances. Haunting, fragile melodies in half steps, like the Gaelic and Yiddish ballads she had learned when she was young. Embodying the legacy of those whose cultures have been trampled and denied . . . the ache of suffering, loss, and death. From Ljuba, Anna knew that Kosta had planned to share the makeshift stage with his compatriots. She felt a sudden sharp pain. The plangent tones, the elegiac words, had woven an homage to their most recent martyr.

When the singing ended, all the men but Spiro left the stage and mingled with the villagers. Moving among the crowd, they passed out one-page flyers. A collective whisper arose from the square. Blagoj gave Anna a sheet. She tracked him as he roamed. Caught the glance he threw at Spiro from the corner of the square. Something in that look made her shiver. Envy? Distrust? Hostility? She wasn't sure. She'd have to ask Spiro about him later.

Beneath the leaflet's black border ran large red headlines—"Kosta Stojkov: 1933-1968." Anna lacked the energy to struggle with the block of text below. The little words, the alien script, the waning light—they made her feel depleted.

The square was hushed. Alone above the crowd, Spiro began to speak. His low voice filled the cool night air, his tone almost a plea. She grasped little of what he said, but made out some words and phrases. From the crowd's response, its somber affirmation, she knew she'd understood the essence of his brief oration. They would honor Kosta, their newest hero, and maintain their culture despite the demands of the State.

Quiet now, Spiro bowed his head. Some older women wiped tears from their cheeks with handkerchiefs in gnarled hands. Some younger ones stared at the sky. The men, their eyes cast down, puffed stoically on cigarettes and pipes. For an instant the world seemed to stop. No wind. No breath. No sound. Then he left the stage.

"That's done," he whispered, reaching for her hand. His jaw was set, pain locked deep in his eyes.

Silently the villagers dispersed. The women packed away the food and doused the dying embers. The men removed the folded tables, empty vats, tripods, the remaining wood and ash. A grim resolve replaced the spontaneity of earlier. The band had gone. But sounds of *tambura* and *kaval* drifted through the square, making a slow, sad music that began to lull . . .

MELNIK

So here they were at last, with Spiro's *kum*. Anna watched as David Isakov brought the tray to the terrace. He was a tall man, not yet stooped, though he had to be well past sixty. His blue eyes and compact body conveyed a latent force. In him she saw a glimmer of her mother's grandfather, Avram, who'd lived and died in Bessarabia. Anna had known him only from old family pictures.

The sun blazed down on them. A lone pear tree cast shade upon the chairs and table on the terra cotta tiles, the terrace nestled up against the sandstone cliff.

She rose to help David.

"No, Anna. You rest. The trip must have been hard for you."

While he prepared the coffee, Anna closed her eyes and traced their journey here, especially the descent from the mountains. These tawny sandstone pyramids recalled the red bluffs and arches of Monument Valley, which had stunned her on the trip west last summer. Primal forms filled both landscapes, natural icons of earth's distant past.

Yesterday, as the borrowed Renault had lurched along the cobbled streets of Melnik, she'd felt more southwestern echoes. The town, Spiro had told her, was built by Greeks and Serbs fleeing the Turks. His mother's father had come from a long line of Greek winemakers. The tall, narrow homes built onto ledges framed by rugged cliffs were Ottoman with hints of Greek. Yet the washed earth tones and bright wild flowers that protruded from the soil reminded her of the valley towns in New Mexico.

Dusk had fallen by the time the car pulled up in front of David's cottage outside Melnik. Exhausted from the bumpy ride on poor back roads, Anna had eaten the meal David offered and gone to sleep soon after.

Alone with him this morning, she watched his small, neat movements.

He caught her glance. "Unfortunate that Spiro had to leave, Anna. But Trifon needs his help. Let us get to know each other while we wait. Were you about to say something inside?"

"I was."

"Please, go ahead." He filled a demitasse and handed it to her.

"Thank you." She savored the thick coffee. "So good. Well, I was going to ask . . . if you could explain how Spiro came to America."

"He hasn't told you this?"

"Only bits and pieces. He's been very evasive."

"No doubt he feels ashamed." His voice had lowered, as though he were talking to himself.

"Ashamed?"

"He was so young. He couldn't grasp what they would want from him. He thought it was a chance to see the world, to learn what he could not get here."

"I'm lost."

David reached for her hand. "In those years, no one here went to America."

She felt the strength that flowed from him. The touch was warm and reassuring, powerful. Not like an old man's hand at all. "That's what I thought. Were there even diplomatic ties?"

"No. Your country broke them off."

"*We* did?"

"Yes. Some diplomatic tangle angered Truman. Spiro left in 1952." David's glance moved to the peaks above the shelf on which he lived. Pillars carved by nature, capped by broadleaf trees and giant rocks.

Anna saw him staring at those strange shapes that made Melnik seem improbable. How had the town arisen from such hostile soil? But there it was in the distance, tiny and beautiful.

At last David began to speak. "Spiro said you had questions. He wanted me to answer them. Perhaps this is why he left us here alone. And you should know, since you will marry him and bear his child. But Anna, it is not a pretty story." With a smile that seemed to take in all suffering through time, he gave her arm a pat. "The DS wanted him to learn math, science, engineering, and, of course, language and culture. So he could spy for them in the US."

The DS? Spy? She flinched.

From the table he picked up a small wood box. Studied the lacquered flowers in red and green. "Like most young people, Spiro was a member of the Youth Committee. He . . ."

She tried to picture Spiro as a communist, a spy. She could feel her eyebrows knit, her jaw harden. And she saw that David noticed.

"You find it strange, Anna? But even now he has some ties. I, too. Without them, we could not survive. You know something about us here. It cannot be such a shock. Spiro was a star pupil." He searched his pockets. Found a pipe. "Will this bother you?"

"Oh no. I love the smell. My father smokes one sometimes."

He filled its lovely carved wood bowl with tobacco from the box and tamped it down. "His father's background made things easier. In Strumica, when he was young, Dimko joined the communists. He thought they would bring progress and unite Macedonia. In Vardar and Pirin, he helped to organize. Then, as Spiro likely told you, the Party smiled on Macedonian separatists."

She nodded. This, at least, she knew.

"He helped disrupt the occupation forces in Vardar. A People's Hero, so to say. That gave his family some protection after . . ." He drew a puff in deep. Exhaled. ". . . after he began to change."

She cared nothing for military history. In all those World War II movies, the ones with John Garfield and Dana Andrews, she could never tell the Allies from the Germans. And the campaign in the Balkans had been so very layered—so many different groups, opposing goals. She remembered her confusion that first day on the square in Mihajlov. Even now she didn't fully understand.

"I see that he has told you this."

"Yes. Fragments. But I've never seen it whole." His smile told her he realized how hard it was to penetrate that maze.

"For a while, at least, communists from Bulgaria, Yugoslavia, and Macedonia joined against the fascists in Vardar. And they supported Macedonian nationalism. Dimko's early ties, and his ability to recruit and lead men, made him a fine resource. But by 1953, after Stalin's death, Dimko had fallen out of favor with the new gods. They linked him to the old ones."

His pipe smelled dark and mellow, so different from a cigarette.

"Since Dimko was from Strumica, now Vardar, Yugoslavia, the DS could give Spiro a new identity, make him, perhaps, a Yugoslav refugee. After Tito broke with Stalin, America had begun to admit a few. And likely help came from inside America. So he had false papers, a background that would bear close scrutiny. Once he finished his degree, provided he performed as they demanded, they could spirit him away. He was fluent in Serbo-Croat, so they could plant him in Strumica to perfect his role before they brought him back to America."

"But if his father had criticized the Party, why would he want to work for them?"

"A good question. But think. Spiro was only seventeen. Yes, he loved his father, but he lacked Dimko's experience and his wisdom. Like Dimko in his youth, Spiro saw the Party as a force for good, for progress. And by this time, Mihajlov had become a jail for him. If he followed the Party's plan, he thought he could escape Bulgaria and help his people at the same time."

This was a lot to process. But yes, she could see how a gifted teen would ache to leave his backward village and his isolated country. Nor would he, lacking maturity, compute the cost. "Was no one in America suspicious?"

"The KGB works with our DS. His papers were likely impeccable. And Spiro's youth, his intelligence, protected him. An eighteen-year-old student from a nation the US hoped to recruit as an ally apparently set off no alarms."

"And then?" The DS again. She felt a sense of dread as David started inching closer to the truth Spiro had never shared with her.

"After graduation, they flew him back to Sofia to prepare him for his first mission."

"They who?"

"His handler in the DS, I imagine. The one who trained him, followed him. Spiro was to be an engineer at a plant in Strumica. His record pleased them. He spoke Serbo-Croat. He'd done well, worked hard, stayed away from trouble."

She wondered what they might consider trouble.

"Even as a trainee, he could help them learn what Yugoslavia was planning, at least in Vardar. But Spiro refused to go."

"He told me that but left out why."

"Marija was dying. He had had some time to think about his father's death—the Party meant for it to look like Serb revenge for actions Dimko took in Vardar after 1944 that could be made to look as if they'd tried to undermine the KPJ, Yugoslavia's communist party. But Spiro sensed the truth. His father's disillusionment with the Party and ultimate embrace of Macedonian self-rule had grown increasingly hard to hide. That made him a risk, especially given his special skills."

"So when Spiro left Bulgaria, he hadn't yet become a . . . a separatist?"

"Exactly." David took a deep breath. "In America, he met other Macedonians. From Canada and the US, Yugoslavia and Greece, even Australia. Together they found common ground, shared histories. An ugly picture emerged. Spiro came to realize that the Party had used his father and the idea of a greater Macedonia to further its own ends. He did not want to take his father's place, to betray either his father or his people. But he had made a deal with the DS, and they expected him to honor it."

David stood and started pacing up and down the terrace, puffing on his pipe. "By then he was twenty-two. He had lived four years in a different world. Perhaps what looked . . . romantic . . . at eighteen had come to seem a kind of servitude. He worried that they might groom him to be someone's assassin."

She moved stiff legs, cracked aching knees. "So they sent him to Belene."

His glance took in the mountains once again. "He told you about that?"

"Enough to explain . . . his scars."

"Ah, yes." He stared straight at her now, compassion in his eyes. "They pushed him hard, but he refused to break. When he came home, he was not in good shape."

Anna's hands tightened around the chair arms.

"You know, Anna, guards did not only beat and whip men there. They used electric shock, humiliation."

She sensed that he was pointing her toward something he would not disclose.

"I should stop now."

"No. Please, go on." She worked to make her face loosen, her hands relax.

He cleared his throat and shook his head. "After all, he was only a stupid boy who thought he could refuse to be . . . their pawn. As if he ever had a choice."

She felt the blood drain from her face.

"You need some water, Anna?"

"I'm okay."

"He said the end was worst of all. They bound him to a post inside his cell. Left him for . . . he could not tell how long. And all that time he heard the screams of others. His mother, Marija, told me, when I visited before she died . . ." A funny little sound broke from his throat. Not quite a sigh or cough. Not quite a moan. ". . . sometimes at night she heard him weep. She would lie awake in pain, so close to her own end, imagining what caused the sobs that came from his dark room. Praying he would find some peace. Wondering if he would survive."

Anna shut her eyes against the bright light of late morning.

"It must hurt you to hear this. But Spiro wanted you to know and lacked the words to tell you. Please forgive me that I've left you with such images."

She heard his voice from far away, so gentle in the dark behind her lids. "So then, why did they let him go?" Her eyes clamped tight, she heard his sigh and felt his hand patting her arm.

"Anna, it is business. They invested in him. They did not want to sacrifice so promising a player. So they changed their plan. Created a new game."

"What game?"

"They brought him back to Sofia. When he refused again, they exiled him to Mihajlov. To teach in the school he'd left as a boy. Far up in the mountains. Alone among the peasants. You see how it is there. After Sofia and his American adventure, they bet this isolation from the world would drive him back to them."

She studied David's still handsome, weathered face, those lines that were a book on suffering. "Who won the game?"

"Up to now it is—how do you say—a draw. They check on him from time to time. Not closely. 'Keep him in their sights,' I think the phrase is. No doubt they think he will soon outgrow his patriotic phase."

"But isn't this game risky?" The Party. The army. The damned DS. Živkov's house held all the strongest cards. Spiro must have known the game was rigged. She remembered the Easter Rebellion, that prelude to the Irish Civil War. The vastly outnumbered Jewish fighters of the Warsaw Uprising, doomed but steadfast against the Nazis. And ancient Masada, where fewer than a thousand Jews held off a mighty Roman force for several months. In the end, refusing to forsake their identities, they'd chosen suicide over submission.

"Exactly what his father came to understand. But that is life here now for most of us, Anna." His smile was dark. "In any case, the last year of Marija's life, he worked, and cursed, and . . . felt himself dying. She had reason to worry. Until a student came to him whose uncle had been taken. The family did not know where to or why."

Anna recalled Spiro's answer when she'd asked how he'd survived his prison trauma.

"Spiro met with them. After, others came. He tried to help them all. Teach them their history. He began to have a purpose."

She had to ask the most important question. "But, David, who will win this game? And how will we know the winners?"

"Alas, Anna, we recognize who has the power." He spoke without emotion, his eyes steady. "And we know Spiro will not stop. He will not be a tool for them."

"So it's going to be like this until they change the game again, or . . .?"

"Do you want for me to say the truth, Anna?"

As his eyes bore into her, she felt her stomach churn. But she said, "I need to know."

His face dropped. Suddenly he looked very old. "You are so young, so full of life and hope. It pains me to say so, but if I am honest, the answer is 'yes.'"

She saw it now—a life of constant tension. David was right. Spiro would never stop fighting for his people. But he faced a power that would crush the smallest insult it perceived. The end seemed preordained.

Unless . . . there was a chance. What if she convinced him to return with her to America? Once they married, couldn't he? Political asylum? Why not Spiro, if so many others? His background would make him useful to the government. And Max could help them flee. Of course, they wouldn't be a legal couple yet. But some Belgrade official could marry them.

Then she realized that this would make Spiro another kind of pawn.

She looked into David's eyes. "You've helped Spiro so much. I'm grateful Spiro's had you in his life."

"You are too kind. But I gave him love, at least, and some advice, even if he seldom chose to take it." He paused, set down the pipe. "The way we are here, Anna, you will not find life easy. Though now America has come apart in some way, too. Like a fancy shirt, its sleeve unraveling."

Images flashed before her. The faces of those little girls the bomb had killed in Birmingham. The marchers beaten near the Selma bridge on Bloody Sunday. And last fall's demonstration that had ended at the Pentagon. She'd been there, seen the angry kids smear pig's blood on its steps, the signs—"Johnson, pull out like your father should've!" Remembering, she said, "Such violence and hate. It must have lain beneath the surface, waiting to explode. Everything we didn't want to face."

"Your country is still young. No longer an infant, but not yet quite mature. Here we are old and weary. All that you yourself escaped this summer—the crushing of dissent, the stifling of a culture, the war nobody wants—we have lived for centuries."

Even in his gentle tone, the words made her feel spoiled and weak.

"Anna." His voice lowered. He leaned toward her, his eyes earnest.

He was about to let himself be seen. It moved her that he gave his trust so simply, so spontaneously.

"In March of 1943, I traveled to Plovdiv. When I came back, the Jews of Sofia were gone, sent east. Later they interned me, too. But the Jews in Macedonia . . . our government, still fascist then, sent them to die in western camps. In Serbia, Croatia, Buchenwald, Auschwitz. While I was building roads in Haskovo. Conditions were not good, but we survived. Afterwards, I thought we had all learned enough of horror . . ."

Spiro might have called her eyes "haunted," but David's really were. In them she saw the ghosts of Jews unfortunate enough to live just to the west, across the border, in what was now Yugoslavia's Macedonian Republic. All caught in the great net.

". . . until people began to disappear again for no reason. Until I saw my sweet Marija's son nearly destroyed for power-lust. Fascism. Communism. What difference? Each suppresses to maintain itself."

His sweet Marija? Spiro's voice came back to her. His words about his mother. She watched David and listened carefully.

"And it goes on. So many enemies to choose from—Macedonian separatists, like Spiro; *pomak,* Bulgaria's converts to Islam; Roma, always likely scapegoats; Turks who live here still, eternal villains; teenagers who crave the freedoms of the West. Eliminating those it names as dissidents, a government can keep its power."

As he gave a long, slow sigh of utter weariness, Anna thought again of Spiro on the square when they'd first met. He'd tried hard to explain, but it had been too much for her to sort out then. Now, at last, she had a clearer picture.

David's face and eyes reflected loneliness mingled with empathy and pain. Spiro had said he was David's only family. Yet David had spoken of Spiro's mother, Marija, with palpable devotion. As if, almost . . . but best to leave it there. She wondered what had filled his life before and what sustained him now.

At last she asked, "Have you warned him to quit the game?" She hadn't planned to plead but couldn't stop herself.

"No. And I will not." His eyes bored into hers. "Spiro has his reasons. And so, too, do the rest. Even the Party."

"Then where does that leave us?"

"Where we have always been, Anna. In chaos. Each one out for what he thinks is right."

His words echoed those of Mahmoud at Mama Ayesha's last year in DC. And David's care-worn face evoked the old man in the Sofia synagogue. She said, "I was told most Bulgarian Jews went to Israel. Did you consider it?"

His laugh cut like the sharp edge of a paper. "It is true, most of our Jews went there. But look at Israel. She is another kind of mess. Right on all sides. Everyone a martyr. No, Anna. I was, and remain, the only Jew I know of here, in this part of Bulgaria. But even back in 1948, I was too old for Israel. This is what I know. It is my mess."

BEGINNINGS

Mid-afternoon. The sun no longer lit the sky like a great fire.

"Some think . . ." David gazed at her with those eyes that seemed to have witnessed everything, "this is a Greek town stolen first by Turks, then by Bulgarians."

Footsteps on the terrace. Spiro, followed by a balding man with bushy eyebrows and a thick gray beard. Heavy, wrapped in dark clothing, he resembled an Orthodox priest.

"Anna, my dear friend, Trifon."

She and Trifon cheek-kissed three times.

"Anna, Spiro. Why don't you get ready now? You want to change, I think. Yes?"

She and Spiro smiled and went inside, she to the room David had given them, Spiro to David's bedroom.

Anna washed her body and her hair in the large clay bowl. She wanted to be absolutely clean. From the bag Spiro had packed for her, she removed the wedding outfit and arranged it on the bed. Another treasure from his mother's chest—a white shift embroidered in red at the sleeves and neckline; a gold-paisley blue vest and matching apron; long blue stockings and *opintsi*. Anna dressed with care. The clothes fit well. Marija must have been about her size when she was young.

On the dresser stood a cup of rosemary water. With this she rinsed her face. Then she daubed some rose extract at her temples and behind her ears, from the vial Spiro had given her before the trip. And though she rarely wore make-up in Mihajlov, she'd brought her lipstick here. It was her wedding, after all. Its pale mauve understated, it matched the flowers on her vest. She towel-dried her hair and brushed it out until it fell heavy and full.

She'd planned to wear no ornaments but found a sprig of sweet basil, white-flowered, on the bed, a pin attached. A local custom—David must have put it there. She fastened it to her vest.

At the bottom of the bag lay a small red-papered box. Inside she found two pearl and garnet earrings set in gold. She put them on and inspected herself in David's antique mirror. What she saw there evoked the picture on the wall in Spiro's bedroom—his parents on their wedding day in 1930. She'd often studied that old photo, to see if she could find Spiro in them. Marija doll-like, lovely, in these very clothes and earrings. Dimko, tall and striking in his peasant garb, his strong features and cheekbones Spiro's legacy.

Anna felt a rush of tears. How much she missed her own parents and Miriam. They didn't care for empty ritual. But this wedding meant everything to her. They would feel that, too, and share her joy. It hurt so much that they weren't here.

She'd written a long letter. Told them everything. To mail it had required a plan, since Spiro had reminded her that correspondence from Mihajlov to America would invite the censors' scrutiny and register her existence in the village. Jordan had transported the letter to Razlog—to Slavko, Max's cousin. Slavko would pass it to Max, who would mail it somewhere in the West. The return address for now was the Majestic, in Belgrade. Max would bring the mail to Slavko or to them. Their own pony express, slightly up-dated. But it was far too soon for any answer.

Her *opintsi* fell softly on the bright, embroidered rug in the main room. Looking up, David turned white. "You wear her dress and earrings well," he said.

She noted how he'd worked to keep his tone even, but from his face and eyes she sensed that what he'd felt for Marija had been more than paternal.

"How radiant you are, Anna."

"Thank you." She wished Spiro had spoken more of David and Marija, the teacher and his pupil. Could that relationship alone have shaped so tight a bond? Maybe Spiro didn't know the truth. Maybe only David knew. "What's taking them so long?"

"Trifon had to get something. And Spiro must make himself worthy of you."

Then Spiro entered in his father's wedding clothes—baggy white leggings, red sash, full-sleeved white shirt, red and black embroidery around the neck, the black vest with its handsome red geometries. He shared his father's build and oval face. But Marija had given him her slanted eyes and olive skin. His hair combed long and wavy, he might have been an icon.

They were staring at each other.

"So this is what it takes, children," David said, "to quiet you."

Spiro's mouth cracked into a slow grin. He moved toward her, shaking his head. "You are . . ." he swallowed hard, "so lovely, Anna." He was leaning down to kiss her when David cautioned, "Shall we wait?"

"Oh, yes. Of course." He pulled himself away. "Then hurry. Where is our 'priest'?"

"Trifon will return soon." David gave Anna his arm. "Let us go outside, before the old gods. It is a lovely day."

* * *

On the table lay a fluted silver tray that held goblets of ruby wine. The three of them were sitting, chatting, when a clatter from the house told them that Trifon had returned.

"*Ajde,* Trifone," David said, as his friend came through the door onto the terrace.

"*Zdravo,*" Trifon answered. He held a camera in his hands. "Pictures. For your children."

Spiro looked at David, who shrugged, his blue eyes shining.

Trifon and David motioned for Anna and Spiro to rise and stand before them where the terrace tiles met the scrub-dotted earth. The men had fashioned Orthodox, Jewish, and pagan rites into a ceremony just for them. When the time came to exchange vows, David asked in his strong voice, "Will you, Anna Rebecca Rossi, accept Spiridon Dimitrovski Svetkov as your husband, under the law of the force that drives the cosmos?"

"I will." Just then a ray of sun pierced her. Its warmth made her feel like a rose unfolding to the sky.

She glanced at Spiro. His face was rapt, as if he felt, like her, that they had stumbled into a new world and found themselves together in a skiff on an uncharted sea. But ready for the challenge. Buoyed by love.

Trifon's deep voice boomed, "And you, Spiridon Dimitrovski Svetkov, you will accept Anna Rebecca Rossi for your wife, before the one God that unites us all?"

Spiro seized Anna's hand. "*Da. Jas—*" He cleared his throat. "I will."

"Then, Anna, please, your pledge to Spiridon."

Since last week she had turned this over in her mind. David's letter had asked that they create their own vows separately and not share them until the day itself. She looked into Spiro's face. "I've always been so selfish. I justified it in the name of seeking truth. But loving you, Spiro . . ." She had to stop. Her eyes were filling up with tears. ". . . has made me see better. You matter to me so much . . ." How frustrating to feel all this and find no way to tell it. "I vow . . ."

She glanced briefly at the two older men, grown soft-eyed with young smiles. Then her gaze rose to the cliff. The plane trees at the top shimmered within a sphere of light. She saw that Spiro, too, was staring at the halo on the mountain. He squeezed her hand as she continued speaking. "I vow to keep myself open to you and to this world, whatever problems we may face. I may always be selfish, but I'll fight it with the power of what I feel for you."

Spiro stared at her with parted lips and wondering eyes. She'd seen that look before. One morning in the meadow, they'd stumbled on a downed nest where a mother fed her still wet-feathered young. At their approach the bird had spread her wings to shield the tiny creatures. Spellbound, Spiro had made sure they stood still and kept silent. The scene had felt like an elemental drama, unveiling an essential truth about the universe.

Trifon said, "Now, Spiridon, you make your promise for Anna."

"It was the same for me. Selfish. So selfish."

The men's eyes grew wide. Then they shook their heads in affirmation. As if it made clear sense that she and Spiro would share even this admission.

"Until my village needed me. Pushed me from myself. Still, I thought that I would never know the love my parents shared. That I would end . . ." He made a little movement with his mouth, a sort of helpless smile. Taking her hand, raising it to his eyes, he studied it.

"With you I have seen, have felt . . . how beautiful this world is. These mountains, trees, flowers . . . and all the people, trying just to live, to find meaning somehow, to . . . I do not know. All of this." He gulped and made a broad circular gesture with his hand.

In his eyes she glimpsed the two of them, old, a little stooped, white-haired, but light with joy, their love still vital, though calmer now.

"I promise to keep nothing of myself from you . . ." A shadow crossed his face. His eyelids fluttered as he swallowed audibly and whispered, ". . . unless it can hurt you."

A shared silence.

"Anna Svetkova, my love, you have returned to me the sense that life is more than what reason tells us. And that more is worth . . ." He threw his head back, filled his lungs with air, and turned his eyes to her again. ". . . everything."

His eyes were dark pools. Bottomless. His smile made Anna brush back tears. David and Trifon blinked hard.

Then she and Spiro sipped wine from the same crystal goblet, and Spiro placed his grandmother's gold ring, entrusted to him by his mother for some future daughter-in-law, on the fourth finger of Anna's right hand, according to the Orthodox tradition. The tiny circle glittered in the sun.

"Children," Trifon said, "now before God you are one."

"And the child you have created . . ." David added, "will be the blessed fruit of this union."

As Spiro cupped her face between his hands and gave her a soft kiss, she felt his body shaking.

"Patience, children. Not much more," David said. He lay something in a white napkin on the ground. "Stamp on it, Spiro." Knitting his eyebrows at David, Spiro lifted his foot high and brought it down, smashing the glass—the only ritual she recalled from her aunt's wedding so many years before.

"With this," David said, "Jews remember when their temple was destroyed. The broken glass reminds us that though buildings die, people live on . . ." Spiro took her hand and laced his fingers into hers. "And they can keep the spirit that an army cannot kill. Anna, Spiro, if you cherish what you love most, you will secure your temples."

Then Trifon pointed to a thick black book on the table beneath the pear tree. He opened it and said, "I write your names, Spiro, Anna, on the 21st day of August, 1968." As he bent over the old leather-bound volume, Anna watched his beefy hand flourish the fountain pen and add them to the others on the page. Spiro's hand was resting on her shoulder.

"Before we go inside, pictures," David said.

They laughed and posed—Anna with Spiro, then with David, then Trifon; Trifon and David there beside the table with the Bible. Trifon set the camera to take a picture by itself. All of them together. Likely it would fail, he said, but why not try?

"Now," David said, "inside! Let us celebrate this marriage."

ENDINGS

The men had assembled a feast. They must have kept some village women busy with their list. *Tarator, kevapćinja, banica,* goat cheese. A braided bread in which Anna found two silver wine goblets. Even fish from a stream high in the cliffs.

After, they had taken turns at chess. Anna managed a good game with Trifon, but he beat her in the end. She never had the patience for a strong finish. They talked and laughed and drank good Melnik wine, though she took only a token sip.

It was now quite late. The sun had set. The air had grown cooler. Reclining in their chairs, the old men smoked their pipes. Anna and Spiro shared the banquette by the window. Spiro puffed a Marica.

"Shall we try Radio Sofia?" David asked, looking across at them.

Spiro frowned, then nodded. "Some *rakija,* Anna?"

"Thank you, no, I really can't drink lately. But I could use some water."

He headed for the kitchen.

The radio crackled. David turned the knob slowly, hoping to coax a stronger signal from the old brown box. Melnik lay in Pirin's southern foothills. The mountains must have made reception hard. She hadn't heard a radio in weeks and hadn't missed it. Now she felt so calm and full. She paid little attention. The quality of sound was poor, the static heavy, the language not her own.

Halfway to the couch with her water glass, Spiro stopped short. His face darkened. David and Trifon leaned forward, their pipes unsmoked in still hands.

"What's happening?" she heard herself ask, like a schoolgirl.

"Not now, Anna," Spiro snapped. She began to chew her thumbnail.

After several minutes he came to the couch, sat down beside her, and put his arm around her. The men sat motionless, their faces grave. "Forgive me, *ljubov moja*. I was short."

She felt the darkness in the air, but still she asked, "What was it?"

"News about the Czechs. I wanted to hear everything."

"What everything?" Hadn't Dubček opened up the country since the spring? She recalled her professor friend Renata from the *Aurelia*, whose address was still somewhere in her satchel. Had planned, before her life had changed, to visit her in Prague, now free and open.

"This week the Czechs sealed off their borders."

"Why?"

"The Russians moved their tanks up. Started circling them."

"Tell me, Spiro. I'll be okay."

He bent his head and whispered, "Last night the Russians went in."

"You mean . . ." So he had screened the world from her. ". . . invaded?"

"Yes."

"You knew about this earlier?"

"I did."

"Since when? How?"

"From the first." He lowered his head. "Papers, from Blagoevgrad and Sofia. Jordan's radio."

Of course, they had their news sources. She was an idiot. "Well?"

"Early reports from Party organs. The usual. Rants about the Jewish threat of counterrevolution."

Her eyebrows arched.

"No open opposition to Dubček till mid-July. At a Warsaw Pact conference, Živkov urged action against 'the assault on socialism.'"

"Živkov? Why?"

"He rose to power like Novotny." His hand was playing gently with her ear lobe. "Maybe he got scared that some Bulgarian Dubček would topple him. Anyway, from then Russia began to push the Czechs hard."

She remembered Renata's silver-blond hair, her intense brown eyes behind glasses with tortoise-shell frames. "I planned to visit Prague before I sailed back to DC." She felt him stroke her shoulder. "I met a woman on the ship to England. She gave me her address. She had such hope."

"Like us."

Those words, the flat tone, spoke the end of more than dreams about the Czechs.

"The real blow is the number of Bulgarian troops . . ." A bitterness had crept into his voice. "Bulgarian kids destroying freedom for their 'brothers.'"

His face was a kaleidoscope of feelings. Love for her. Guilt for keeping all this to himself. Hatred for the communists. Compassion for the victims and the young men forced to carry out a tyrant's whim. She could barely hear his next words. "They say some Russian soldiers killed themselves. Couldn't bear to carry out the orders. Of course, they call them cowards here."

"Spiro, please." A vein above her left eye had begun to pulse. "It's our wedding night. Can we put this away?"

"That bastard Živkov. He thinks the Kremlin owes him for his help. This year's celebration of the Patriotic Front may be the biggest we have seen for quite a while."

She ran her hand slowly along his back. Silent, he sat up and took her in his arms. Her head against his chest, holding his hand, she thought about her friend, her friend's husband, the son Renata had said was her age. Intellectuals were always vulnerable at times like these. Perhaps someday she'd find out how they'd fared. But these mountains were now her home.

Nestled against her husband in the darkening room, Anna felt a sudden chill. She knew their love was great. But something else claimed him as well, a dream born of a different love.

Spiro's grip on her tightened. He must have sensed her tears. She couldn't help imagining what lay ahead for all who held such hopes—Renata and her family, Spiro and herself.

He whispered, "Anna," through her hair, tickling her ear. "Think of *Ilinden,* of joy and pain together. That . . ." His body straightened. "is . . . well, just life, yes?"

She lifted up his rough-skinned hand and kissed it.

"Come, *srce moe.*" He pulled away from her and drew himself up slowly. "Let us say goodnight to David and Trifon, and celebrate our marriage."

* * *

Spiro slept with his left arm on her hip. She touched his hand. His breathing didn't change.

Some dark shadow had wakened her, its bleak images breaking up the deep sleep that had crowned their feast of love. A clearing in the forest, a ring of black, the boom of a *tapan*—fragments from Kosta's funeral. She saw again the village cemetery, surrounded by tall trees, serene yet ominous. Something fearful in the faces, underneath the women's kerchiefs, in the hard eyes of the men.

Ljuba held her hand tight in her own, refusing tears. As if she'd locked them all inside. Only two years earlier she'd buried Sveto here. This time Kosta would enter the cold earth beside their parents' grave. Father. Husband. Brother. All her men gone now, except Kole. Her face was a tight mask.

The priest finished the ritual. Poured oil mixed with red wine over the coffin. Sprinkled sand inside it, to signify the body's joining with the earth. Said what was his to say in a flat voice. His watery blue eyes were cold, without affect. Nothing in his face or body had shown the inner truth of what had happened here—the sense of private loss, the pain of a community, the latent anger, building into what?

Rain clouds hung above them like a promise. The clearing darkened. Dropping Anna's hand, Ljuba moved toward the fresh hole in the soil. Kole and Jana, his older sister, followed her. Leaning on his shovel, Spiro stood with Jordan and Hristo, waiting for the sign to seal their comrade in his earthen bed.

Finally it was over. Silence drifted from the clearing as the group dispersed. The mourners came to Ljuba's. Working in the kitchen, Anna recalled Matt's funeral ten years earlier—the fancy glass suburban home, the manicured front lawn, the elegant attire. But on the faces that same hint of unease.

In the tiny room where she'd slept her first nights in Mihajlov, Spiro and his men were gathered, sitting on the Turkish-style banquette that lined the walls—Jordan, Hristo, Branko, Zoran, Nasto, Blagoj, Stevo. When she entered with their *rakija,* they stopped speaking to thank her. But she could sense their eagerness for her to leave.

Later that night, after she and Spiro had thrown themselves exhausted into bed, wanting only comfort from each other, he cursed under his breath. "*Sranje.*"

"Spiro?"

"Shit."

"What?"

"Kosta." He pulled the quilt around them. "How he died."

"Ljuba said police in Goce Delčev killed him."

"Yes." He sat upright. "Said they caught him stealing guns, that he had threatened them. A good excuse to shoot him where they found him."

"Could what they said be true?"

"It's possible." He gave a heavy sigh and shrugged. "You know, he had a record here. Also in Germany. But we did not send him for guns."

She heard it in his voice, had seen it in his eyes since the day before *Ilinden*. "You don't believe it, do you?"

"No." His hand reached out for hers. "Not now. He had no reason."

She sensed him in the dark, his mind searching, sifting the facts, trying to solve the puzzle.

"He was going to meet a contact there . . . about a man who had to escape Bulgaria. Someone must have alerted them." His finger traced her cheekbone. "They would have followed him. Killed Kosta and the contact."

She shivered in the circle of his arms, those muscled bones that sheltered her from the vast darkness outside.

"Who?"

"I am not sure."

"I don't like how Blagoj looks at you." She felt his chest contract.

"You must stay out of this, Anna."

"I want to keep you, Spiro." His tone had allowed no room for debate.

"Things are complicated."

"You always say that. Can you at least tell me where you went with Kole?"

"We had to find money to ship Kosta home." He moved closer to her. "Ljuba has no pension from the State. The Party can ignore the families of these 'criminals.'"

"You came back very late that night." She huddled against his chest. "And took something with you."

"We had to share what we knew. To see. To form a plan." He pulled the cover tighter, warmed her legs with his. "We went up on the mountain. We were not sure that would be safe, that someone had not compromised the group."

"*Sina gora?*"

"Yes."

"I don't—" His hand covered her mouth.

"Enough, *srce moe.*" His hands began to knead her lower back, the place he knew was always sorest now. "The ruins, Anna . . . they are only a marker."

She'd grown used to the rough skin; their gentle motion soothed her weariness. "Nearby . . ." he moved his head to kiss the spot, ". . . there is a cave."

"A cave?"

"There are many in these mountains. The *ajduks* used them. VMRO. Partisans. Now it is our turn."

She remembered Goran's tale. Those bodies tossed down pits inside Slovenian caves.

"I took my grandfather's knife."

The words might have been Sanskrit. "Knife?" Despite herself, her voice had come out shrill. "But why, Spiro?"

He paused. Took a deep breath. "A knife, Anna, is silent. Sometimes, maybe, that is what you need. In case . . ."

The edge to his voice, like an echo from the past, brought back their first day, on the couch, before they'd gone to bed. His mention of the bond he shared with Max.

"My God, you are shivering." He pulled her closer to him.

"You should have warned me, Spiro." She kissed the soft flesh on the inside of his arm, near the armpit. "Suppose you hadn't come back then?"

"I wanted just . . ." He pressed his lips against her lids. ". . . to keep you safe."

"It isn't in the armoire."

"What?"

"I looked."

"Let us stop this now. Some things, my love, you must not know."

Then rain began to fall, and with it came loud thunder. A sudden flash of lightning lit his face, a study of despair—

As she tried to repel these images that took her far from David's bed on this most special of all nights with her new husband, her beloved, Anna felt her terrors coalesce into a dense cloud of foreboding.

CHECKMATE

"They are still sore, *srce moe?*"

"Not the way they were." His fingers were tracing circles on her nipples. Her breasts tingled with pleasure. She was grateful for this sign of normalcy, and for his body in the bed. Though he'd been late, as usual.

August 28th. Almost September. Two months pregnant. Seven days a wife. The weather had grown damp and dreary, cooler. She could feel an early autumn in the air. The first hints of a long winter. The baby would help keep her warm. Strange the way things worked.

"School will start soon," Spiro said. "September 16th."

"It will be almost three months then," she whispered, mostly to herself, still thinking of the child.

"I must go to Blagoevgrad to arrange for supplies, textbooks."

"They let you do that?"

"Yes."

He rubbed the flesh below her shoulder blades. How good it felt. "Even though . . ."

"They think, you know, that one day I will change. And maybe they are right." His voice had frayed edges.

"Bad news today?"

"More of the same. Živkov . . ." His hands began to fondle her breasts. "He is planning his big show. And in America—"

A gust of wind surged through the window she had not quite closed. Spiro rose, rushed to the wall, pulled the glass shut. His long, lean body rested for a moment against the pane, silhouetted in the dim light of a few cold suns. He was staring out at something. What? His past? The winding route by which he'd come to this place in his life? Or did he see only the mountains etched against the sky under the scattered stars?

He hurried back into the bed. "Cold," he said, curling himself into her body. "What was I saying? Ah, yes . . . Chicago."

"God, Spiro. Your legs are ice." She had to fight the urge to jerk her own away. "What about Chicago?"

"The Democratic National Convention. They are reporting riots there. Kids protesting Vietnam and civil rights. The police could not control it. The mayor called in the National Guard. A mess."

She shook her head. "It never seems to end."

His body was beginning to warm up. As she moved her hands along his hips and flanks, touching his welts softly, she felt his penis hard against her belly.

"Stop, Anna. When you do that, I . . . I cannot think."

"Good." Though it was late and she was tired, she wanted to make love, needed the peace it brought. "Why think? You've earned your pleasure." She tried for a light tone, but somehow couldn't get the pitch quite right.

"Anna, I . . ." He patted her head and pulled away. "Not now, please. I cannot."

His fist was clenched against her side. Her fingers pried it open and smoothed the rough skin flat.

He said, "I keep thinking. What have we done, really? And Kosta's death. Useless."

"Maybe there's another way."

"Not one that I can see."

This gave her the opening she'd been hoping for. "Come back to America with me. You could write, tell your story—like Ellen Stone did after Jane Sandanski. To reach people. To help them understand what's going on here." Even as his fingers drifted down her spine, kneading out the tightness and the aches, his dry laugh unnerved her.

His body stiffened. "Cigarette?"

"No thanks. They make me sick lately."

"It is okay if I smoke?"

"Of course."

Stretching out his arm, he searched the table. Found the pack. The matches. Lit one. "You think it would be easy? The DS would just say good-bye and wish me well?" He lay back on the pillow, arranging her in the crook of his right arm.

"I—"

"No, *srce moe.* Too much at stake." His left hand fluffed her hair.

"Then we could flee. Can't Max help us?" In the cigarette's dull glow she saw those lines around his mouth.

"You're serious. But this is fantasy."

"No more than when a bourgeois American girl marries a Macedonian freedom-fighter, is it? I love you!" She kissed his chest below the left nipple. "And our . . . son will need his father."

"I have worked too hard. I cannot leave it like this." He sucked in smoke, then blew it out and bent his head to kiss the top of hers.

"Leave what, Spiro?"

The cigarette between his lips, he stared up at the ceiling. In the pause, she saw that he was tethered, like the Gypsy's bear in Belgrade, his pole the men in Sofia.

"Even in America," he said, expelling the words slowly with his smoke, "Bulgaria has eyes. You think they would applaud my new identity? Enjoy my book?"

His body warmed her, but his words were cold. The truth. He couldn't leave the game.

❊ ❊ ❊

A week later she woke from a bad dream to find herself alone in bed. Three days remained until the big national observance. September 9th, 1944. The Patriotic Front—or the Socialist Revolution—the date on which the Russian army, with the anti-fascist coalition, had freed Bulgaria from her fascist-royalist yoke. Each year the State made sure its citizens honored its founding fathers.

The room was dark. But muffled sounds came from under the house. The storage area. She recalled Spiro's warning that morning in early July. "The cellar is a mess, Anna, and full of dust. Until I can take care of it, if you need something, I will get it for you." She drew the quilt around her as the noise continued. No longer could she play the innocent. Her ears had made her an accessory.

After Spiro left for Hristo's later that morning, she decided to go down. A stair on the outside wall near the back led underground. The heavy door was cumbersome but unlocked. She pushed it open, sickened by her violation of his trust. The dark, musty space smelled of onions and potatoes. A low ceiling hung over a dirt floor. Men would have to stoop here, especially Spiro and Jordan. Some sacks dangled from hooks. Others lay along the ground. But over in the far corner she spotted several boxes, long and narrow. Wisps of straw littered the earth around them.

She crossed the room and pulled the cover off the closest one. Her nervous fingers pushed aside pale strands. Disclosed a long, thin object whose identity she recognized from movies. Some kind of machine gun. Given where they were, it was likely a Kalašnikov. The guns lay sardine-like inside the case. She wasn't going to count the number in it.

Tentative, she lifted one. She'd never held a gun before, never imagined its weight, so heavy she could raise it only a few inches above the box. A symbol of the power she'd believed his group opposed, the gun canceled the quest for truth, or what Spiro had called essence.

Relief came as she set the weapon back in its resting place. Then she ran her fingers along the wood and metal. It was strangely beautiful—neat proportions, sleek lines, like a sculpture. Each part precision-made, a work of art become a killing tool, it revealed to her, as nothing had before, the underside of Spiro's dream. Touching it, she smelled death.

Her body so heavy she couldn't move, she collapsed into the dirt beside the box. Paralyzed by the force cradled within it, she stared into the darkness of the cellar and tried to fathom what this meant and why he'd kept it from her.

After some time she rose and grabbed a large sack of potatoes. This she carried upstairs to their bedroom.

Though it was nearly noon and she was ravenous, she couldn't eat, or cook, or clean, or teach herself Macedonian from Spiro's little book. Reality had shifted.

* * *

It was deep night by the time she heard his heavy steps, the thud as he removed his boots. Another evening on the mountain. Getting set for what?

She had to be prepared for him, so she rose quickly, slipped on her caftan, and lit the kerosene lamp on the bedside table. Then she placed the potato sack in the very center of their bed.

At last he pushed the door open. "Anna?"

"Yes?" It came out in a squeak.

"I thought you would be sleeping." He stood still, watching her with wary eyes.

"Did you?"

"What is that look? You are angry?" Then he saw the bed. "Fucking hell!"

"We needed some potatoes."

He stepped toward her, his eyes sharp slits, his cheekbones angry slashes in a face that threatened to explode. His hands reached out.

Was he about to strike her? She flashed back to her parents' fights—the objects thrown, the shouts, curses, yet never physical violence. She began a soundless weeping.

But his arms clasped her with tenderness, as if he meant to start a waltz.

"Calm down, my love." He kissed her hair and wiped away her tears. "Anna, Anna. Quiet, *srce moe.*"

Her strength had ebbed. Her legs gave out. She was falling—

He caught her, led her to the bed, and helped her to lie down. Then he moved the sack to the armoire. Watching him, she wondered for a moment if she'd merely served the needs of a desperate man.

He sat beside her on the bed and took her hand. "We will move them tomorrow night."

"It's not so much their being here. It's that . . . you said . . . you had no use for guns."

As he handed her a white cloth from his pocket, his lips began to move. His mouth opened, but no sound came out.

"You have nothing to say?" She wiped her face.

He sat still for a moment, swallowed hard, then plunged his head into his open palms. The chafed fingers amid the black tangles imaged dejection.

"First the knife. Now this." She edged closer to him. "No violence, you said. Help me, Spiro. I don't understand." She touched his hands. Kissed them.

He raised his head. His red and swollen eyes pleaded, as if she could somehow save him. But seeing them, she lost all hope. They held too much. Guilt. Frustration. Anger. Fear. Uncertainty. Yet always, love.

"Anna, I—"

"After all those meetings . . . this is your great plan?"

"Please—"

"Ever since this morning, I've tried to figure out—"

"Stop, Anna. I . . . I cannot . . ." His voice dropped. "The group . . . it is divided."

"Really? Just like VMRO, then. So here we are again. History just keeps cycling back. Was this what you wanted your students to learn?" She couldn't help her sarcasm.

His head snapped to the side as if she'd struck him.

"You said someone informed on Kosta. How can you be sure it wasn't one of them?" She remembered Blagoj on the square, his envious glance at Spiro.

"You shield them. Your love blinds you." She saw him clench his teeth.

He raised his chin to swallow but something seemed to stick there, choking him, back behind his throat. "I've known Blagoj since he was twelve. He was so bright, so angry. I . . ." His eyes drifted away.

She could see it now. The teacher encouraging the smart young village boy, affirming his identity. Likely he had seen himself in Blagoj, whose eyes, like his, held passion and intelligence. But he'd missed that hint of restlessness. Or maybe not. Maybe he'd hoped that Blagoj would begin to understand the knot that was his history. To care about his people. It must have hurt to watch his protégé elect a different path. But hadn't he, too, chosen it when he was young?

Strange about Kosta. He'd been no great thinker. She could hardly picture him in a classroom, sitting quiet at a desk, even as a young child. But he'd reached, perhaps with age, a certain clarity that seemed beyond Blagoj.

"I need a drink." Spiro heaved himself up and headed out the door. Several minutes later he returned bearing a tray with some of Ljuba's *rakija* and their two wedding goblets. Red blossoms lay scattered around them.

"What are those?" she asked.

"The wind blew some of your poppies down in front. So lovely. Delicate. Even in their deaths they give us pleasure." He filled both glasses, handed one to her, and downed the other in a single gulp. Then he poured a second for himself and began to pace. "I do not know, Anna . . ." His tone was flat, stripped bare. ". . . what is . . . what I should . . .?" Silent, motionless, he squinted. Searched the dark for words.

She blinked. He seemed so naked. She could almost see his heart pumping within its cave of bones. She remembered that day long ago when she'd told him she was a Jew—when he'd first revealed his doubts about the group, about himself.

"Kosta trusted me with his life. It killed him."

"But—"

"Hristo cannot do much now. His wife's sickness is worse."

She wished his eyes looked less forlorn.

"So there is only Jordan. And I do not know how he feels."

"Because of me?"

"Why do you say that?"

"It's in his face . . . the blame for taking you away."

He stopped pacing and turned to her, his arms limp at his sides. "At first, maybe. Now I am the one he does not trust."

"Ridiculous. Where's your confidence?" But something in his words made her afraid.

"Ah, but here you show that even you doubt me."

She saw his lips make a grimace that shared little with a smile. She took a sip of brandy. Its hot sweetness suffused her body. Its warmth pumped through her veins, returning her some courage. "Not you. The others. The guns were never your idea, were they?"

He shook his head and made a wretched noise, half groan, half snigger. She thought how far "laugh" had to stretch to name a sound like that.

She studied the structure of his face—its sharp planes, skin taut over bones, brows arched above tapered sockets—until beneath the smooth olive surface she saw the bones themselves. Like the skulls at *Ćele kula*. "Let me guess," she said. "Blagoj?"

He nodded. "Yes. Blagoj, and . . . and . . ." His mouth had trouble keeping still, shaping the words. ". . . Nasto."

"Nasto? But he always seemed so innocent, so . . ."

Spiro's legs folded; his body followed. Now he was sitting on the floor, leaning against the bed frame. She came to him, knelt next to him, buried her hands in his hair. "Spiro, I'm afraid. Don't go with them."

"I must. To make sure they do not . . ." Turning to her, opening his right palm, he pressed it to her skin, dragged it along the planes and curves of her face. "I cannot tell you more. If something happens, Anna . . ." His fingers smoothed her brandied lips. ". . . the DS will come for you. They will try to make you swear that black is white, that—"

She stopped his lips with hers. Kissed his face, mouth, hands. Undid the top button of his shirt. Tasted the flesh and dark hair at his throat. "I'll go with you," she said at last.

How often she'd dreamt of this while she'd washed and scrubbed and made their food. She and Spiro hiding in the mountains, living off the land, thwarting the enemy. Too many folk tales and spy novels, maybe. "You want me safe . . ." She touched her right hand to his cheek. ". . . but I only feel safe with you."

"I have tried so hard." He turned his face away and addressed the air. "The younger men have no patience. They tell us we have lost our vision, and our nerve." His head was still, his eyes fixed on the wall, mesmerized by the shadows in the weak light of the ancient lamp. "Then Kosta. And while we were with David, Branko's father. He would not say he was Bulgarian. They sealed him in a coffin till he gave them what they wanted. Now he cannot work. His spirit left him there."

His words struck her like a blast of frigid air. As if a monstrous storm had hit their skiff, and even though they'd bailed and bailed, the boat was filling up.

"You're still their leader. Can't you buy some time?"

His silent stare was the one answer she didn't want.

"So when is it? The 9th? With rifles? A serious confrontation, then?"

"A protest in the town. The guns are for insurance."

That low, cracked voice. Trying to convince them both. "Insurance? What does that mean? And for what?" A bitterness was working in her stomach. Would she have to vomit? "You'll need support. I guess you'll print more fliers. More dead heroes."

"*Sranje.*"

A *shit* for everything gone wrong. His growing impotence laid bare. She locked her teeth together to keep herself from screaming out the pain.

"Anna, what can I do, really? What do you want from me?"

She grabbed his hands and fought to keep herself steady. "What you promised on our wedding day."

His shoulders sagged. His eyes had glazed over. He stared out into nothing, the muscles of his face moving, wrestling phantom images he seemed to see. She inched toward him until her body rested against his, put her arms around him, and began to sway.

"Don't leave me here, my love." She'd begun to rock them both, forward and back, her movements slight, cradling his head and chest within her arms. "Take me with you."

He let her rock him. Let her fingers stroke his cheek. Let her push his hair back in a steady rhythm. The way her mother had soothed her so many years ago, when she had almost died of whooping cough. "I know. Here women don't go on the mountain." Her chin rested atop his head. "But what about the women in your songs? Your stories?"

"What—"

"Mirka. Jordana. Jana." She bent her lips to kiss his hair. "The others."

His body twisted toward her, on his face a bitter smile. "Everything was always fine, Anna, until the Turks, Nazis, or Ustaši caught them. Then . . ." He drew two fingers straight across his arched neck. "Just like all the other *junaci.*"

She touched the smooth skin of his cheek, so different from his hands and back. She loved that olive darkness, its supple warmth beneath her fingertips. "But, Spiro, they were women, those heroes."

His hands took hers and moved them from his body to her sides. "So," he said, inching away from her. He took a deep breath, then exhaled. "You would die with me. For us. Our bodies joined in death on *Sina gora.*"

His eyes burned her.

"So romantic. Maybe, even, they will put us in a song."

His dry, self-deprecating laugh numbed her. As he began to stroke her eyelid with his thumb, she felt a surge of heat and cold.

He jerked his head, then stared straight at her out of reddened slits. "But you would risk our—"

"Stop, Spiro." The right side of her face began to twitch. "I understand." Her mouth moved, then her nose, in ugly spasms. She sniffed but couldn't get control.

"When I think of you, *srce moe*..." Turning just a bit, he placed his hand over her lower belly. Rubbed the little mound beneath the cotton of the caftan. "I feel . . . I . . ." He bowed his head.

A heavy silence followed.

She rose, slipped off her caftan, and climbed beneath the quilt. Spiro extinguished the lamp. Took off his clothes. Joined her in the bed. They made sad, tender love. Before they let go consciousness, he kissed her neck and whispered, "I would take you with me, *ljubov moja*. You are my heart; you feel what I feel. And you have the spirit of a warrior woman. But those women, Jana, Mirka, they were not pregnant. Can you understand, forgive . . .?"

THE LAST NIGHT

Blindfolded and bound, she feels them there beside her on the stairs. One on each side, they grip her arms hard, lurching her along with them. A door opens. She's shoved inside. They snarl something she doesn't catch. Untie her. Slam the door shut. A key turns in the lock. Footsteps retreat.

She tears the cloth from her eyes with aching arms. Sees only a blur, then gradually distinguishes white walls lit by a bulb hung from a ceiling wire.

On a gurney lies his naked body. Livid purple blotches cover chest, arms, groin, legs. Torn patches of skin trail red. A bloody circle underneath the left shoulder. Gunshot? Stab wound? Jordan hadn't been certain. Too much had happened all at once.

His head moves. He is still alive. She bites her lip. Sees again the guardsmen at his cottage, rifling through its contents while she looked on, unable to move. Realizes what her fate will be since she refused to flee with Jordan.

She draws closer to view his face. Prepares herself, determined not to lose control.

The left cheek open to the bone. The left eye blackened. Swollen shut. His good eye follows her. Careful not to jar him, she positions herself on the gurney's edge.

"I—I . . ." He cannot find the breath to finish.

"Shh. Don't talk, Spiro." To watch him strain for wisps of sound is hard. Her fingers tremble as she smooths his blood-streaked black hair, loose and matted now.

"Jordan said . . ." He manages a hoarse whisper. ". . . he would get you out."

"He had it all arranged."

"Then why—"

"You thought I'd leave like that?"

His head moves upward. "But now . . . you are in danger."

"I'll deal with it." Her confidence is an act she fears he'll recognize. Her hand takes his and presses it gently. Her eyes move down his torso to his penis, lying limp in reddened hair. They must have kicked his groin repeatedly. Taking care to place no weight, she eases her head down along the bloodied softness of his testicles. Gives them a light kiss. Feels a tiny stir that instantly subsides.

"An—na," he stammers, as if his earlier words had used up all his energy. His listless fingers touch her hair. Despite her hand that now rests lightly on his lips, he tries to talk. "I—I . . ." He bubbles scarlet foam.

She stands, moves to the metal table near them. Wipes his mouth with the stained cloth she finds there, which smells much cleaner than it looks. Spoons him water from a metal cup, then puts her ear next to his mouth and waits for him to finish.

"*Greshki* . . . mistakes. I made . . ." He stops to take a slow breath. ". . . so many."

The good eye scares her. In it she sees pain beyond the physical.

"Now Hristo is dead. And . . ." A spasm interrupts, contorts his face.

In the white silence she hears the drip of water. A leaky faucet? The rain that threatened in the afternoon? The single high window reveals nothing.

His right eye shines with unshed tears. "I wanted," he swallows, "to teach my son soccer."

"Son? You must be Macedonian." She tries to find a smile for their old joke. A gurgling in his throat. His Adam's apple pushes in and out. She helps him lift his head to clear the passage. Then she places hers near his right nipple. The hairs beneath her smell of blood. His chest rises and falls weakly; she monitors each breath. Her hands press in against his sides, as if their force could push his body back into one seamless piece.

The room is still. Between each breath she hears the steady drip-drip of the water. When she looks up at his face, he seems elsewhere. Far off. But his fingers stroke her hair. Listening to him breathe, she knows he wants to speak again.

"A—an—na."

She has to work to hear the broken whisper.

"I have loved you so much."

"Shh . . ." She kisses his chest. "Rest, Spiro."

"*Sranje. Prokleto.*" His eye wanders. "I fucked everything up . . . no time."

"Please, Spiro." Her fingers stroke his cheek.

"Go back." He hushes her. His hand is a light weight against her lips. "Your home. Your people." He winces, coughs, his face flushed from the effort. "Live your life and raise our s—"

A low rattle she recognizes as a laugh.

"Our child."

He shuts his eyes. Another cough. A tremor. "But if you . . ." His limbs spasm. ". . . have this child . . ." His left hand moves with difficulty to his throat.

She reaches for the water cup, her eyes burning.

". . . you will be alone. The world . . ." He takes more water from the spoon. ". . . is hard, not only beautiful."

The water won't go down. He spits up phlegm. Again she wipes his mouth, her teeth clenching against the sobs that rise into her own. Does he want her to abort his child? Fruit of their love, their bodies' joy in one another? She might as well cut out her heart.

Resting her head lightly on his chest, she clings to him, drowning, until her cheek picks up a change. Frenetic beating of the heart beneath its covering.

"Your tears, Anna, *moja dušo.*"

His hand patting her hair is like the flutter of a butterfly. She hasn't even realized she is crying.

"They soothe . . ." A rapid drawing in, a wheeze. ". . . my . . ." A low gurgle.

He struggles now for every breath. But his nipple shows no sign of suffering. She longs to touch it. Make him feel desire. Stop this. Enter her now.

He gags. She swabs his mottled face. Rests her cheek once more against his chest. So thin the walls dividing them. His life ebbing away beneath her skin while she does nothing. If only she could breathe for him as she breathes now for their child. How has this happened? How has death entered him? Right there, beneath the wounded flesh, a heart, two lungs. So powerful this morning, making love, laughing with her over breakfast, singing that old *ajduk* song while he dressed himself for his funeral.

May her passion pierce these membranes, bleed her into him and give him life. But she knows her prayer is futile.

Shallow breaths now, slow, uneven. Then a gurgling in her ear. A fluttering beneath his ribs and chest. She presses harder at his sides, her own heart pumping fast. His hand lets go her hair. Settles flat against the cold metal. His chest no longer swells or falls.

She feels the blood pulse in her neck. Is this the end? Can this really be all? So still a passage out after a life so full of movement?

She hears loud breathing. Lets herself imagine he is still alive. But she knows it is her own. She cannot lift her head. The nipple near her eye appears unchanged, as if, once coaxed, it would respond. How cruel to tease the living with these vestiges of life. Better if he'd melted into nothing. No shell to taunt her with the finality of death—the form emptied of content.

At last she makes herself stand up and look at him. Despite its wounds, his face in death is strong and proud. Almost as it was when first they danced. As if he has completed something serious, important.

The one good eye is glassy as she reaches down to close it. His parted lips bear drops of mucous. She wipes them for the last time. But kissing them, she finds the flesh neither warm nor pliant. These are not the lips that could arouse her with a touch.

Her hands become a comb to separate and smooth his tangled hair. She wants to cleanse his cold skin. The cloth has grown sticky with phlegm and blood.

The body is inert. How different from this morning in the bath. The arms that grabbed her playfully around the waist and nearly pulled her into the washtub. The lye-roughened hands, suds-softened, stroking her neck while she soaped him. The sensitive skin of his chest that made him beg for mercy as she tickled him. The penis rising toward her, even though they'd just made love.

She uses all her strength to turn him on his side, to reach his back and buttocks, that field of scars from Belene. Such pain to touch this still body, its fire snuffed out.

Somehow she must cover him. Allow him dignity before the ones who've tried to take it from him all these years. The party hacks, police, the secret service. But there is only what she wears . . . the way she was dressed when they took her from Spiro's cottage. A blouse, a sweater, a skirt over a slip.

* * *

They've taken him away. Without a word. As if she were invisible. And after, when she tried to leave, she found herself locked in.

Time has stopped.

She cannot bring herself even to stand, as if that act would rearrange the molecules in the room and somehow alter what she's trying to preserve in memory.

The wait, the stench, the flies that somehow found their way into this closed-off space, the constant drip of water that punctuates the air. She feels a creeping numbness. As if the sun has died and she is ice. Yet she embraces it. Longs to find oblivion, to lapse beyond—

But as she feels herself descending into nothingness, she finds their child. It melts her core. To nurture this seed, this piece of him and her, and so defy his death, she vows to live. He'd called her *moja dušo.* My soul. Now she must fight to preserve his.

And just when she is sure that death has killed the music in her, she hears his favorite song—the one he'd sung that morning, his low voice full of hope. She starts to speak the words, just in her head. But now she sings, remembering as best she can.

"*Subrali mi se pribali, dor sedemdeset i sedem/ na irin Pirin planina.*"

She lingers on the slow notes, sliding up the half tones, caressing them as he would, imagining this meeting of seventy-seven heroes. Spiro and his men had used the mountains too.

"*Na ajdushkata ravnina.*" They had met on Pirin, too, the *ajduk* plateau. *Sina gora.*

At the final line, she shifts the words. "*Spiro im beshe voivoda.*" Not Dakoj, but Spiro, had been leader of these *ajduks.*

As she sings the words, the dark chromatic tones become a lullaby, for her and for her child. And now, her face tear-washed, she feels a link to all those widows down the centuries who keened for their dead heroes.

INTERLUDE

A MOUNTAIN VILLA

Late October, 1968
Somewhere in southern Pirin

The air had grown much colder, heavier. She was grateful for the extra coverlet the guard had brought before she slept.

Images were flickering at the edges of her consciousness. She shut her eyes to pull the scattered pictures into focus. Maybe catch something she'd missed. Always hoping to discover what had happened there, in Mihajlov, to Spiro and to her. Concentrating, digging slowly through the recent past—

The meadow behind their cottage. Spiro with a polished stone he'd gathered from the nearby stream, smoothed, he'd said, by water over centuries. His face so somber, eyes blazing, adamant that she embrace her family's disparate strands and appreciate their beauty.

Jordan in their cottage doorway, wild-haired, panting, begging her to flee with him while she still could. He gave so few details. Said only, "Security police. Ambush. Too much at once. But Spiro makes plan for you before, in case." And when she asked about Spiro, he whispered, "He they beat hard—what else I am not sure, maybe shoot or stab. He make red trail in dirt. They follow him." At last he said, "He gone. Police. You come with me now, Anna."

The guards who came soon after Jordan left. They burst in, held her down, bound her, ransacked their things—the armoire, the bookshelf, the study in his old bedroom. She looked on, helpless, as they took his papers, some books, her satchel, and the Indian bag. She longed to scream, felt tears, but she refused to weep at this desecration of their home and lives.

The gurney. Spiro's battered body lying still. The steady drip of water.

Her swollen face, raw thighs, sore pelvis, wrists and ankles throbbing where their ropes had tied her down. Yet thankful that the blood had stopped, relieved to find her lower abdomen still slightly distended. She could only hope that even though she'd barely slept or eaten, despite the beatings and the rape, their child had lived, safe in its watery world.

Buoyed by this thought, she allowed her mind to float . . .

* * *

The door flew open. In the dim light she could see two guards. They entered, silent. One she recognized. He set down a basin in the far corner. The other she had never seen. A towel over his left arm, the left hand carried something flat, rectangular. A bar of soap? A fabric sack hung from his right. He placed the towel and sack beside the basin.

They left without speaking, though she only heard one set of footsteps move away. Disconcerted, unsure what this meant, she wondered if the guard outside her door would enter now, as she undressed. But she dismissed those fears . . . as if they mattered anyway, given where she was and what had already occurred. Instead, she moved toward the basin, from which she saw steam rising.

A bath? That would be a first. A few times they had brought her to a cold, windowless room and hosed her down like an animal. What could explain this change?

The soap and cold air stung her bruised body, but still she scrubbed. Then she dried herself as well as the flimsy towel would allow. Fingers worked through tangled wet hair, longer now but clean at last, an icy weight against her neck and back.

In the sack she found a bra, a pair of nylon panties, a plain white blouse, and a light blue cotton skirt. As she put them on, she recognized them. They had been hers once, long ago. Now the skirt and blouse hung loose. The lingerie squeezed her belly and tender breasts. The blanket tight around her, she waited for whatever would come next.

A knock—an unexpected act that seemed absurd in its civility. She whispered to whatever waited outside, "I am ready," though she didn't know for what. In case this was to be the end, she hoped she could stay strong.

The new guard stepped inside. Thickset, fortyish, his thinning hair the color of a pigeon's coat, he held a pair of low boots and some heavy socks she'd never seen. A Timex, too, like the one she used to have. "Put," he told her, pointing to the watch. "We go." After she had followed his directions, he tied a black cloth around her head, seemed to make a loose knot, and helped her up the stairs, his hand gentle in the small of her back to steady her. Other guards had shoved her all the way to the room where she'd been grilled. Why this act of kindness?

He led her down a hall, opened a door, and walked her inside. Then he removed her blindfold. Her eyes blinked from the gray glare that streamed through the bay window. But as the blur subsided, details began to form. Whitened pines and snowy peaks announced a late-fall storm. Or was it winter now? The room itself, quite beautiful and warm, contained a crystal chandelier hung from a recessed ceiling, a carved mahogany desk, and three plush leather chairs. The guard pulled one out and motioned her to take it. He stood nearby, next to a man in uniform.

Behind the desk sat a fleshy man whose sensual mouth and cold eyes made her wary. "We are done with you, *kučko.*"

Bitch did not sound friendly. But why would they have had her wash and dress if . . .? Or was this a tease? He gestured to the second man, who placed a canvas satchel on the desk in front of her. The one she'd brought from Trieste.

"Open it."

She did. Discovered there the simple clothes she'd chosen for the trip with Peter, the rest sent on to Athens in her suitcase. Had they claimed the Samsonite? Searched it, looking for leads? Discovered the contacts from her job and university—bankers, cabinet ministers, academics, journalists? Perhaps they had tracked them down. Found them, like her, only dead-ends.

Beneath the top layer of clothes she felt the sequins of her Indian bag, inside it the lipstick, wallet, and Christos' earrings. Next, her fingers touched the thick embroidery of the vest she'd bought with the money Max had given her. She blinked away an image of its mauve flowers floating on a crowded square. *Ilinden* in Mihajlov. So distant now, almost a dream. And the addresses she'd gathered on the ship? Renata in Prague? The Skertić children in Rijeka? Dušan in Dubrovnik? The Eurail Pass? The money that remained from her parents' check, which she hadn't yet exchanged for local currency?

"Looking for your documents?" His smile hid knives. "We took your dollars. To pay for your visit with us."

Her restless fingers, probing farther, felt the envelope with Max's *leva*. Why were they still there?

The man pushed something toward her. A slim booklet, light green. On its front, in gold letters, "*The United States of America.*" Someone else's passport. He signaled her to open it. Inside, a name like hers. The picture of a girl she used to know, used to resemble. According to the stamps, this girl had spent four months in Serbia. Had first come to Bulgaria on the 18th of October, scheduled to depart the 22nd.

"Is it," her voice, unused to speaking, cracked, "today . . . really the 22nd?" The man shook his head from side to side to signal yes. October 22nd. Six weeks since her world had shattered. Nearly four months with their child, whom she had struggled to protect through all that time—the deprivations, rounds of questioning, bouts of brutality.

The man's cold eyes examined her. She was grateful for her weight loss. The outer garments, falling loose, concealed the tiny belly bulge that pushed against the panties grown too small.

Observing this man, smug in his well-tailored suit, bright tie, and gold cuff links, she wondered if he knew that she was pregnant, or at least had been. How could she be sure that she'd concealed it from their prying? Perhaps they had done tests after the rape. Perhaps they knew whether the child still lived. Would that explain . . .? No more. To think of this would keep her from the most important thing—preparing for whatever this portended.

"In back of the passport," the man said, "you will find a bus ticket. To a town along the Greek border near Serres. You will enter Greece from there. You will walk across." His steely eyes checked the watch on his thick wrist. "Today at two. Take it. Leave this country. After, you will not be safe here."

She stared down at the ticket. The border near Serres? Aegean Macedonia.

"Enough." He gestured to the guard that he was done. "They will take you into town. If you do not board the bus, your visa will expire. Police . . ." His eyes finished the sentence as he motioned her to stand.

PART V: TO ISTANBUL

A BLUE FIAT

The new guard guided her into a darkened room and shut the door.

They were alone. No windows here. She felt a surge of acid in her stomach. He moved toward a square table with something on it. Something small and black.

Was this the end? The plan from the beginning? To make her think that she could leave, until they fired the bullet through her brain?

He picked it up, and then she saw that it was not a gun. Only a small black book. The man said, "Take."

She did. Fingered the threadbare binding. Opened it. Recognized the strange letters inside. Ran her index finger over them. Recalled the old man in the Sofia synagogue and felt again a sudden longing for that culture, alien but somehow also hers. She stared up at the guard, his face stony, unreadable. Watched him push his hand into a bulging pocket in his pants.

So this was it. She backed away. Willed herself to hold the scream that rose into her throat.

He grabbed her free hand. Pushed it open gently. Covered it with his. Her mouth gaped at the touch. Her palm now held a wooden egg. It sent a shock of sensuality, then pain.

"Put." The guard bent to open the satchel on the floor. She knelt and pushed the book and egg inside, beneath some summer blouses. Then she stood, her arms loose, waiting. For the end? For what?

Again the guard, expressionless, searched a pocket, this time in his shirt. Removed something. Proffered his outstretched palm, in it a thin circle of gold. "Take." In disbelief she touched the ring. The contact with its surface sent a shock that made her tremble.

Her eyes examined his hard face but found nothing to help her understand. The book and egg had lain there on the table at her first interrogation. That much she remembered. She was positive she had it right. And the ring . . . they'd pulled it from her finger before they'd dragged her from the room where Spiro died. How had this man, only a guard, come by these things? Why had he kept them? The ring, at least, would bring hard cash on the black market. Was this an act of kindness . . . or a trap?

"Queek, Mees." In his voice she heard Kosta. While he watched, she stuck the ring inside the satchel, in the envelope with Max's *leva*. Then he blindfolded her again. She knew this would be the last time, however it concluded.

He led her from the room and moved her down the stairs with care, making sure she didn't fall. Then others came, their movements rough, and pushed her out into the cold. The bracing air, grown dense after the snowfall, penetrated her light blouse. She heard a car motor rev up. Strong arms shoved her inside, onto a seat. She shivered until a heavy warmth fell around her shoulders.

No sense of time. Vibrating wheels. The reek of garlic. A beefy thigh beside hers. At first new noises, voices, motors. Then just muffled sounds and, finally, silence.

Ruts. Her body registered each one. A poorly paved road? Then smaller bumps. A town? Cobbled streets? The vehicle came to a stop. The door beside her opened. Arms thrust her from the seat.

She fell. Her side and hip struck stone. A nearby thud. Then whirrs. A motor gunned once more. The car driving away. She lay, pain-frozen, waiting for silence.

After several soundless minutes, she tore the blindfold from her eyes and blinked out at the cold gray clouds. This time she adjusted faster to the light. She glimpsed, beneath a light blanket of snow, a narrow street that opened on an isolated square. Run-down. No movement anywhere. To the far right, in the distance, hung the station sign. Beside her lay the canvas bag.

A bench stood nearby, its surface dusted with snow. She pulled herself up, each movement an effort, and forced her aching legs to take her weight. At last, hunched from the painful fall, new bruises added to the old, she stood, lowered her arm to grasp the bag, and limped toward the bench, grateful for the boots, though they were heavy and too big. A streak of red ran down her shin.

She scraped off a space on the bench and sat down on the cold wood, burrowing inside the DS's last gift—the source of warmth she'd felt inside that car, apparently an ancient military cloak. Grateful for fresh air despite the cold, she inhaled deeply as she gazed out at the ridge circling the town. Then she searched her bag until she found Marija's ring. When she slipped it on the fourth finger of her right hand, heat flooded her body.

* * *

She must have dozed off. One o'clock, the Timex read. As if she'd never been without it.

Freezing despite the cloak, she rummaged in her bag. At the very bottom lay the cable-knit sweater from Marks and Spencer, bought in early June, when London clouds had banished summer sun. She steeled herself, removed the cloak, buttoned the cardigan over her blouse as fast as her cold-stiffened fingers were able, and wrapped herself in the moth-eaten mantle once again. A bead of light attracted her attention. The golden circle on her right hand glittered in the clouds' gray glare.

A sharp pain in her stomach. A loud rumble. Maybe the station had food.

The streets that edged the square looked like the one near where they'd left her. Steep and narrow. Rising toward the mountains. Little color in the vista. Browns. Grays. Wintry whites. Except the tips of green along the lower slopes, and the frosted gray of the sky. Somehow they were all empty.

But what was that—there, on the right? Across the square. Along a street that rose up toward the peaks. Near the ground. Something. A flash of red. The barest hint of yellow. She shook her head and looked again. No more color. Nothing. Was she dreaming?

She focused on the empty square. Was someone watching now? Tracking her until she took her seat inside the bus? Ready to arrest her if she didn't? She saw no one. The shops fronting the square were closed, some boarded up, the only sound the drip of melting snow from overhanging eaves. The whole place seemed deserted.

She let her eyes return to where . . . nothing. Of course, nothing.

Wait—there it was again. Red close to the street, yellow above it, reminding her of something—what? Where had she seen this before? Low red. High yellow. Was it, could it be? Red heels? Bottle-blond hair? Impossible. That dream had ended. Jordan. Donka. Part of a dead world.

But her eyes fixed on the colors, weaving in and out, now here, now gone, will-o'-the-wisp. She rose. Lifted her bag. Limped off toward the mirage. If they were watching, they would come in their own time. According to their plan. Until then, she would follow this apparition. Why not? Once she had felt safe. But what did safety mean here, in these mountains?

She dragged the heavy boots along snow-slicked cobbles. As she crossed to the left side of the square, heading away from the station, the colors began to move up the narrow street bordered with stone walls, arched doorways, and entrances to old courtyards. She kept on, exited the square, then headed toward the mountains, the distance narrowing between the red, yellow, and her—

But now, again, nothing.

She stood still. Waited for the colors to return. But they did not. Whatever she had thought she'd seen had melted into air. Even so, she moved along the steep street rising from the square. Maybe, after all, captivity had left her mad. She should head back to the station. Take the border bus. Why go chasing phantoms?

The silent emptiness enveloped her. Ahead, the whitened peaks. Along the sides, gray stone and snowy eaves. Yet she trudged onward, her feet ice blocks inside the boots.

But—what was that? Just over there?

A flash of motion on the left. An arched doorway, slightly ajar. She turned. Inched her way toward the entrance. Her fingers eased its heaviness. Pushed it open. Inside, a large room, chairs and tables scattered without pattern. Not a home. More likely a *kafeana.* No light except a window that looked out on a bare courtyard.

She saw another door, ajar. It yielded to her touch. She found herself in a dark hall, at its end another door. Heavy. Shut. She had to work to turn the tarnished brass knob. Had to press her whole body against the door . . . until it thrust open and sent her reeling out into an empty alley. A dead-end on the left. To the right, a narrow lane.

She took it. Reached the point at which it flowed into a slightly wider road, on each corner a dark stone house with windows boarded up. Looking left, she saw more cobbled street and stone façades. But a small blue car was parked around the right corner. She thought it might be a Fiat.

Its front door opened. A man got out, bearded, in a heavy coat and hat. He walked slowly toward her.

She froze on the narrow sidewalk.

She should run. But where? And if this were the DS?

The man stopped near her, bent his head, and whispered, "Spiro."

A code word from a dead world. She felt herself breathe faster.

He made no move. Allowed her to reflect. Her watch read 2:30. The bus was gone by now. Or maybe this was Balkan time and it had not yet come. Then she could go back, board it.

Or she could leave with this stranger. If he were an agent, he might take her to the mountains. Rape her. Kill her. Bury her in some distant, thickly-wooded spot where no one would ever find her. Was that how they had rid themselves of Spiro? Would she be closer to him now?

But . . . the DS could have seized her on the square if they had wanted to. They wouldn't need this ploy. Why waste their energies?

The stranger gestured toward the car and whispered, "*Az sŭm Mladen.*" The man who called himself Mladen examined her. His thin lips made a straight line, not a smile. But his eyes, a chocolate-brown with amber flecks, were curious, not cold.

Someone who knew of Spiro had devised this plan. She would go with Mladen.

She let him take her bag and throw it in the back. Then she climbed in next to him.

He fed her coarse brown bread and spicy sausage. Let her swig the water from his bottle. Covered her with a quilt from the back seat. They didn't speak. He'd introduced himself using Bulgarian, not Macedonian. And she was far too tired to make an effort to communicate.

As the Fiat snaked through the mountains, the smells from Mladen's quilt and the DS cloak evoked the cedar chest of Spiro's mother, and her own grandmother's ancient steamer trunk, inside the vintage dress-up clothes with which she'd loved to play. Warmed by the heavy layers and comforting scents, she fell into a stupor, a kind of waking dream churning with images—

When they came for Spiro, silent. Leaving her on that cold stool, alone.

When they returned for her. Transported her, blindfolded, bound, from the police station in Mihajlov to wherever she had been confined. That long ride in the dark. With each bump on the road, she'd bounced, untethered, from side to side in the back seat.

A blur of unmarked time. Six weeks measured only by occasional trays of hard cheese, moldy bread, thin soup. And, always, interrogations. Gentle at first but ever more intense. She'd tried to buy time, meted out her facts slowly, certain they already knew that much.

Her decision to keep silent once she knew she could withstand the pain they gave. She wouldn't make up answers; didn't want to hurt people she loved in case her fictions held some germ of truth. Funny, after all. However much she'd resented Spiro's secrets, they'd achieved his goal. Since she couldn't tell what she didn't know, she'd stayed alive.

The agents' growing anger and frustration. Their escalating force. That final act—the rape. Afterwards, the brief moment of triumph in their faces, until they realized that she had nothing more to give them.

Blood, pain, loss of consciousness. Waking fearful for the child. Finding her body washed and wrapped in a robe whose softness soothed. Recalling Spiro's scars, she'd wondered how she'd wear her own.

That first yogurt, a sign that they intended her to heal, though why she couldn't fathom. The memory of that good taste soothed her, made her head feel heavy . . .

MOUNT FALAKRON

A wintery sun streamed through lace-paneled curtains. Its harsh glare off the white-tiled floor and stucco walls made Anna shield her eyes. Sipping thick Greek coffee, she'd begun scribbling words on paper from the front desk of this inn, somewhere between Serres and Drama. Falakron, the stationery read. Outside, snow-covered peaks and a gray sky threaded with cloud tufts.

Thankful for the warm down quilt, the bed her first since Spiro's death, she'd slept well. Now she hoped to find some order in yesterday's mysterious jumble of events. There were no guards here. No police. And once Mladen had led her to her room, he'd disappeared. There was no record of his staying at the inn.

She set the pen down and took a spoonful of her yogurt. Her body needed calcium. Until that first yogurt after the rape, she'd had no milk for weeks. Now she hoped to help the child grow strong. The cool tang made a pleasant contrast to her hot coffee.

A waiter, round-faced, pot-bellied, brought bread slices and honey. "*Oriste.*" He smiled as he set down the plate. Her ears were unprepared for his soft Greek. Though she shook her head to show she hadn't ordered it, he didn't take it away.

"*Blagodaram.*" Intending to thank him in Greek, she'd spoken Macedonian. His eyebrows knit. "*Efkharisto,*" she said at last, acknowledging his kindness with a word he understood.

He grinned. "*Parakalo.*"

She spread some honey on the bread. Tasting it, she missed Ljuba.

She tried to recall, to write about, the border crossing. Mladen had awakened her not long before they'd reached it. Night had come. She must have slept for hours. He'd stopped the car on the shoulder, turned to her, and said, "*Pasport, molja.*"

She handed him her passport, which he returned immediately. But he kept the bus ticket. Then he left the car, walked off the road into the trees, and came back empty-handed.

Twenty minutes later, the uniformed Bulgarians, curt but not unpleasant, surveyed their papers and waved them on. But the Greek guards snarled at Mladen and ogled her. Both were young and dark, one muscular, with short black curls, the other soft, his lank hair falling straight from a side part. They strutted as they forced Mladen from the car, as if under the Colonels, Greece had become Eden for Bulgarians.

Mladen's face showed nothing as they checked the tiny Fiat for the goods, human or other, that might be hidden there. At last they verified that she and Mladen were alone, they matched their papers, and the contents of her satchel didn't implicate her in nefarious deeds or offer them a chance for gain. Only then did they wave the Fiat through.

In Greece she'd slept again. By the time a bump awoke her, they'd already passed Serres. She saw a sign that read, "Drama—20 kilometers."

Mladen took no chances as he steered along the poorly paved and rising road. Mountains surrounded them. The southernmost extension of Bulgaria's Rhodopes? She wasn't sure and couldn't ask. Then Mladen said, "*Gledi.*" Looking where he pointed, she glimpsed a building through a stand of snow-hung beech. Backlit by a slice of moon, its white stone walls stood out against a black sky strung with stars.

Mladen signed the ledger, deposited her bag in the small room with its two singles. Before closing the door, he whispered, "*Doviždanje.*"

She'd finished for the moment. As she sipped more coffee and chewed another bite of honeyed bread, a low rasp startled her.

"Anna, is that you?"

The voice was so familiar. The hairs on her neck began to rise as she smelled a trace of musk.

She looked up. A man stood beside her, his eyes tapered blue ovals, the skin around them crinkling as he smiled. Handsome. Not too tall. Long, shaggy hair, a well-trimmed beard and mustache—all dark blond. He wore thick boots, a brown leather jacket, and a blue sweater over Western jeans. Could it be—"Max?"

"Ernst," he replied. "Ernst Gruber."

"Ernst." A new name for blue eyes and dark blond hair. She had to figure out the script. "I can't seem to remember where we met. My schedule has been hectic these last months."

"Belgrade. A *kafana* in *Skadarlija*." His lips curved slightly. But his gaze was hard and serious. "The name, I think, is *Kosovo Polje*."

"Oh, yes. Now I recall." She tried to check her shivering. "Could you remind me where you're from?"

"Magdeburg. East Germany." His blue eyes probed her face. "You will, perhaps, invite me to sit down?"

She nodded, though her mind was too exhausted for more plots.

He pulled over a wooden chair and slid his body into it, then let his eyes explore her. "My God, Anna," he whispered, very low.

She felt her face flush as he stared at her, focused, intense. But she did not respond.

"You look like someone from a . . . a camp." He edged closer. "They make things hard for you?"

"I'm here. It could have been worse."

His mouth fell open, but he didn't speak.

She searched this stranger for the man she thought she'd known those few months, which seemed like years, ago. Those eyes, or what passed for them. She'd read about cosmetic lenses, plastic covers for the tinted portion of the eye. Actors sometimes wore them, to intensify the color of their irises. Which were real? The blue? The brown? Both almond-shaped. That much he hadn't changed. Who was he, after all? This rugged-looking fellow? The elegant one, who had brought her to the mountains? Or someone else entirely?

"Those words, what you just say . . ." His eyes seemed to look inward.

"Yes?" She wanted Max again, not someone new. Needed solid ground, not this sand that shifted under her.

"When I . . . ask Spiro—it is now more than ten years . . . he tells me these same words."

To hear his name aloud silenced them both. Max flinched. She began to weep. She couldn't stop the tears. Max let her grieve.

She scrutinized the blue key pattern bordering her demitasse. Time weighed heavily until she dared to raise her head. "And what about your jail? The one in Munich, after you met Ko—" Suddenly she saw an earthy smile, a hairy chest. A man so much alive. She forced herself to say, "Kosta."

His eyes darkened, as if caught by surprise. But didn't he imagine she would learn about his past from his two friends? That she would seek pieces of him that didn't change to fit his needs?

"Not like Turkie jails." He gave a wilted smile. His shoulders drooped. "There, it is at least still Germany."

The wry curve of his lips. The light, self-deprecating tone. Every Max tale she had heard from Spiro was branded in her memory. As she studied him now, appraised his well-constructed mask, she felt the depth of his self-hate. As if he were the ghost, and Spiro suddenly alive in some strange way.

While she was recalling a polished stone in a distant Balkan meadow, this man, this Ernst or Max, took her right hand. His finger touched her wedding band. Looking up, she saw his dark face whiten.

"I . . . I . . . Anna . . ." He squirmed in the chair. "You are so thin. Is the—" He brought his lips together, began to shape a *b*, but stopped himself.

"No, Max." She wouldn't call him Ernst. She'd just regained herself. "I didn't lose the baby."

He shut his eyes for an instant, sighed, and swallowed. "That is a good thing, Anna." He paused, his eyebrows knit. "Isn't it?"

"It is."

"So." He cleared his throat. Leaning on his elbows, he peered through lace panels into the glare of sun-lit snow.

She saw him adding up the evidence, computing what it meant. Concluding something, storing it away.

"This is what I . . . we all hope."

"We?" Here, perhaps, a clue.

"Slavko tells me first what happens. After, Donka—"

The image of an empty square, a snow mirage. "It was Donka."

"Yes."

"But . . ." She pinched the handle of her demitasse. ". . . she was like an apparition. Bits of red and yellow. No body."

He nodded, lips curved upward. "So. After all, it works."

What *it*? Another swirling sign she couldn't read.

"From Munich I bring Donka a white coat. Nice. Long. A fur collar. For winter. If the mountains have an early snow—we get reports—then if she wears it, white against white, maybe, we think, you will notice more. Flashes. Like a signal. Maybe, also, where they take you, no one else will see."

"A town, a bus station, but no people? How is that possible?"

"Some places for the ski close mostly down till winter. A villa, above, in the mountains, the State runs it—a good place to store people. A bus maybe comes through the town below sometimes. To bring supplies."

So simple. She began to see it now—the blond beehive above a long, white body lost against white snow, and underneath, red heels. A ski resort off-season, controlled by the DS. Hearing this affirmed her sanity. Maybe, after all, her memories were real, not shaped by madness. Yet this implied more questions, questions she could not yet frame.

The waiter brought them both a second coffee. Max thanked him and took a sip. Then he set his cup down, turned to her, and leaned in close, his head nearly touching hers. "Anna, I drive now to Istanbul. Today I put you on a train for Athens. Or," his eyes studied her for some sign, "you can come with me."

His right hand, warm, clasped hers. Its smooth skin felt so strange, so unlike Spiro's.

In Athens she could find the embassy, contact her parents. Say good-bye to stratagems and plots.

But what she'd lived since she and Max first met—the beauty and passion, the tension and pain, Spiro's death, this unborn child that seemed to hold the promise of a future—all of that had changed her. Leaving now would violate the choices she had made, the person she'd become. She had to stay within this world to unravel the mystery at its center. She said, "I'll go with you."

A PACKAGE

Max met her at the hotel desk with three brown paper bags. He gestured toward the ladies' bathroom beyond the marble counter. Leaving Max her satchel, she grabbed the parcels and entered through the ornate wooden door. Found a stall enclosing two brass indentations for the feet and a marbled hole for squatting. Brass fixtures at the back—to flush. Luxury and basic plumbing all at once.

Max's bundles held a new wardrobe. A blue dress in homespun. A black wool skirt. Two thick sweaters, one rose, one blue with flecks of green. Two cotton turtlenecks, both black. Cotton panties larger than her own. Sleek black boots, tall but not too heavy. Several pairs of thick beige socks. A long blue woolen coat with matching scarf. Simple but tasteful. When had he bought these?

How . . . but she stopped thinking. Wriggled into the dress. Traded her old panties for a new pair. And thrust the old and new clothes and the boots from the DS into the paper bags. These she gathered up and, with the coat over her shoulders, rejoined Max. He was standing in the lobby by a long buffet table atop which rested her satchel. As she neared, he nodded his approval. "Blue is nice for you, Anna."

She thanked Max, removed the contents of the bags, sorted them, and began to fill the satchel with what she'd chosen to retain. Last was the Bulgarian army cloak, so large she couldn't make it fit the small space left. As she tried to fold it, Max asked, "Why keep that?" He pointed to the handsome brass receptacle against the wall that held her other discards. "You can put it there."

"Oh, no. I want it, Max."

"But Anna, it is ugly. Old. So many holes." He mimicked comic horror.

"Max," she said, her tone tender, as if he were a child who required patience, "I need it, to remember . . ." She didn't say that even now touching its heavy cloth brought back cold fear, the surreal square, the mad dash up the cobbled street into the unknown.

With a shrug he pulled the cloak from her, rolled it tight, and forced it into the satchel. Then he closed the bag, grabbed its handle, circled her waist with his free arm, and squired her out the door.

* * *

Was time looping around? This strange arc made her think of theories she had read and little understood, of multiple dimensions in mathematics, of strange twists in the physical universe. Was this some parallel world, a mirror of the one from which she'd come? For here she was again. Another black Mercedes. Max behind the wheel, she riding shotgun. But he was blond and she was pregnant. He was silent. She was numb. They were headed toward Xanthi, traveling southeast via Kavala. The northeast route wound through mountains. Max had feared that way would prove too treacherous.

Out the window spread an unexpected winterscape. A white plateau. White hillocks on the left. Behind them white mountains, like mounds of whipped cream on a graying sky. She guessed that as the land sloped toward the Aegean, the white would yield to dry earth, dead brown grass, and the cold blue of a mid-fall sea. This land had given birth to Orpheus. To Dionysus and his revelers. From here had come the forms that led to comedy and tragedy, the twin masks of Greek theater. How strangely fitting, after all, that she should journey through it now. Though she desired to move beyond these masks.

The new Max said nothing. The other never played the radio, but this one let it fill the heavy silence. Some twangy voice. Electric drum and bouzouki. A dismal bit of Greek folk rock. Working to screen out the hybrid noise, she wondered what had happened to that other Max, the one who'd brought her into Mihajlov. Then they'd played at verbal sparring. Now there were no words and too much space.

The outside monochrome soothed her. But then she felt her eyes close. She tried to make the lids open but they would not. Against their black screen scrawled a trail of blood. Tracking it, she reached a place of brush and dirt. Of chill winds and dank odors. The stench of open flesh, of dead bullets, like old matches, corrupted the crisp air. The edge of a tall cliff. His arms drag his torn body. His fingers tear at earth, pull with some internal force that almost takes him back to her . . . until, their flashlights harsh beneath the black curtain of night, the uniformed men, tracking his red line, find him and let his body take their long-nursed rage.

Her hands flew to her mouth and eyes. Jordan had told her only of the trail Spiro had left on *Sina gora.* But she'd experienced this scene as if she'd lived it with him.

Tires grating against pavement. The Mercedes slowing, gliding to the shoulder, rolling to a stop. Her head rested inside her hands. She felt arms hold her, fingers stroke her hair. "It's okay, Anna," Max whispered, his low rasp somehow soothing. "It's okay." Her shoulders heaved. She couldn't stop the avalanche of tears, the sobs. She was glad to let him comfort her.

After some time, Max asked, "Shall we go on, Anna? You are ready?"

"Yes." She wiped her cheeks with the white cloth he had given her. They lapsed into silence.

On the highway once again, she mulled over the journey from Bulgaria. "Max," she asked at last, "who was Mladen?"

He stared ahead at the boxy landmasses that lifted flat against the sky. "A man we trust."

"He barely spoke to me."

"It is," he cocked his head but didn't turn toward her, "safer. He is a, a . . . driver."

"So he knew nothing? But you had to pay him, didn't you?" How simple could a transporter of such cargo afford to be?

"No. He owes this, from before."

She had a sudden glimpse of a broad net, cast wide, within it more than Macedonians. Max's group could help in quite specific ways. Perhaps Spiro's *četa,* his shrunken band grown even smaller after Kosta's death, had been one of many that reached out to those who lived diminished lives.

"If only I'd had a note or something." She turned her head to take in every movement of his face. "For reassurance." Nothing changed. His eyes held steady on the road ahead. The land, no longer white, declined. In the distance she could see a thin gray watery ribbon edge the sky.

"Anna, look. We keep it simple. For the border. In case there is . . . some problem."

She considered this. What if the guards on either side had held them? Questioned them? Better to know nothing, to be clean. The only tie, Mladen's contact. Probably not Donka. At least two or three steps removed. And if Mladen did 'owe' them, then he would want to hide that name. It made sense. She could see that Max was right.

She remembered Mladen's face when he'd first approached. His eyes had darted past her, nervous, to the streets in back and front. Like her, he must have feared, uncertain whether she were his contact or a DS agent.

"But what if I," she concentrated on the distant sea beneath the lowering sky, her fingers twisting his white handkerchief, "had not entered the car?" She saw his cheek muscle twitch.

"We know this can happen. But we count on you, Anna. We think that you will . . . somehow . . . understand."

"A gamble, then. A risk for both of us." She felt a sudden wave of anger. "So pleasant, too—wondering for so long if we were going to make it past the next turn."

He sighed but didn't move the hand that steered. "What matters more? The way you feel? Or your safety—and ours? The postman, when he brings a package, does not ask from where it comes. Who sends it. Who will open it. He only must deliver it."

The words silenced her. Made her think. She pictured a web of dissidents like the Underground Railroad, working to resist the government. And then she understood. If a link were revealed, those still active would pay . . . and those they sought to help. Suddenly the names of Spiro's men, their families, rose into her mouth. She spat them out, hoping for relief. "I know Hristo died, but what about Jordan?"

Max flinched. His knuckles whitened as he gripped the wheel.

"Ljuba? Vesna, Hristo's wife?"

"Jordan." He squinted at the sky before scanning the road again. "No word from him. Perhaps he is dead or in a camp." A long pause. "Though someone tells Donka he comes to Yugoslavia. More we do not know."

He pulled the wheel sharply to miss the body of a large dog, barely visible against the gray paved surface of the road. "We hear nothing of Ljuba and her children. Or Vesna. Only Slavko, who stays with family in Štip. Vardar."

"David? Trifon?"

"Anna . . ." His voice dropped as he looked left, where a dirt road seemed to wander into nowhere, merging with the sky. "The old men, they are gone. If not already dead, then in prison. The police come for them after you and Spiro . . ." He couldn't hide the wince. "Maybe they do not kill them. But there are camps for prisoners, and camp is death when you are old. You cannot do such kind of work, like Spiro does in Belene. It is too hard. In such places even the young can die."

She was staring at his well-kept nails, a fact that matched the old Max.

Her mind could barely process what he'd said. David and Trifon had risked so much for her. For Spiro. Would have named their baby in the spring. Despite their personal losses and the suffering they had witnessed, they'd rejoiced in and honored their world. Had nourished Spiro from their trough of love. Her friend, Ljuba, to whom she had drawn close. And Hristo's Vesna. Everyone respected how he'd tended to her care. Was any of them still alive?

"Max," she said, under her breath, afraid to ask yet unable to hold back, "who?"

He turned his head toward her. "What—"

"Who told . . .?"

His lip straightened. His eye blinked. "Nasto? Blagoj? Hristo's cousin? Branko's younger brother? Maybe, even, someone we completely trust. I do not know." He sighed. "Someone who envies Spiro, or has a problem in his family." He pushed back his long blond hair. "Someone with a need the powers can fill or just who wants power."

"And those other men . . ." she couldn't bring herself to speak their names, "the younger ones?"

"Like Jordan. They are gone. No word if they are dead, in camps, or living well in some new place." He shrugged.

She looked into his eyes, or contact lenses, wishing she could see the truth. "And what about me?"

His head straight, focused on the road, he said nothing.

"How could you know where they took me? If I were alive? When they would let me go? That it would snow so early?" Inside the warm coat she shivered, thinking of that last day, its progression of apparent ends, the bitter taste of fear. "There must have been someone."

Another shrug. "Not my business."

At last she glimpsed the role Max played. Vital to the group, he was always on the edge, at the periphery. Itinerant, as those inside could never be.

"Who?" She couldn't let it go.

"Maybe someone like Donka." He gave a little laugh. "The way she collects people. So now she knows this one, who knows that one, and . . . you see?"

She saw.

Another silence gathered them within it. Until she said, "That's all you have for me? Spiro is dead, and you have no idea who compromised him. Yet you still work for this group."

"Yes. But I must change my route, and who I am. I cannot go back to Mihajlov."

She had to push him, needed to know more. "Why do you still take this risk?"

He sat immobile, staring out the windshield. "No point to say more, Anna." He shook his head. "Better just you think about the baby. And the future."

STORKS AND TURKISH GENERALS

Past Kavala the highway wound along the coast. Anna was growing queasy. "God," she moaned.

"Anna?"

She clutched her stomach. "I think . . . I should eat something."

He took the next side road, slowed to a crawl, skirting potholes till they reached a small village. Faded shacks lined its single street. Behind the low buildings, a church stood on a mound ringed by dead grass.

"Look." She pointed to a shaggy oval mass atop its steeple. "Up there. What's that?"

"A nest," he said, parking the car before a small *taverna*.

"Weird shape. What kind?"

"It is—how do you say—'storks'?" He helped her from the car.

The air was heavy, brooding. Storm clouds hid the sun. Suddenly a long white shape flew toward the nest. Childhood stories filled her head. Of large birds holding diapered infants in their beaks. She'd never seen a real one.

They entered a small room that smelled of marinated chicken. A few old men nursed coffees and ouzos. Max chose a table far from their smoke rings. Anna ordered *rizogalo*. She'd always loved the texture of Greek rice pudding. So rich with milk and egg yolk. Currants in the rice, a hint of fresh vanilla, and cinnamon on top. She forced herself to take small bites, to make sure she could keep it down.

Sipping mineral water, Max kept his eyes on her. Between bites she stared into them. "So are they blue or brown? Your eyes, I mean."

Max took a sudden interest in the street outside the window. Observed an old woman passing by, all dressed in black. He breathed in deep, then exhaled. "At the border, Anna, call me Ernst."

She bit her lip. Winced. Muttered, "Not to worry, Max. My acting is much better now."

He gave a guarded smile.

She kept eating slow mouthfuls and hoped he didn't spot her unease. His hand moved suddenly toward his cheek, as if to brush something away. She didn't understand till he repeated it. Then she rubbed her lips with her napkin. "Okay?"

"Almost." His finger touched a spot above his mouth. She wiped again. A gentle grin crinkled his eyes. "Glad you enjoy your pudding."

Finished, drinking water to counteract the heavy aftertaste, Anna shaped a question she had vowed to keep for later. Their earlier mention of David and Trifon had rekindled her interest in David and Spiro's mother. "Do you know how David felt about Marija?"

A muscle in his cheek twitched.

"Max?"

He inched his body forward. Rested his elbows on the table. "Only what Spiro tells me."

"And?"

"David is Marija's tutor. He loves her, but she is too young." His eyes studied a thin crack in the whitewashed wall. "Also, he is a Jew. Marija's father . . ." With a finger Max traced his glass rim. "He is Greek Macedonian and Orthodox. He is okay with David for a tutor. But for a husband, well . . ." His right hand brushed imaginary cobwebs from his face. "Then Dimko comes to Melnik, doing something secret for the Reds. Marija meets him. He is young, handsome, and Macedonian. Like Spiro. You know. Their wedding picture."

"Yes."

"Marija loves David always, like a . . . a big brother. But she wants Dimko. He is a teacher too. And also Red, in those days not always so good." Max stared down at his hands. "But he, at least, is young. And not a Jew. Her father cannot be so cruel two times."

"So, Dimko asked David to be their *kum*?"

"Dimko, yes. He has respect for David. He is not . . . uh . . ." He hunted for the word.

She offered, "Threatened?"

"Yes." A sheepish smile. "Threatened."

"And did David ever marry?"

Max didn't seem to see her. His eyes had clouded. He was far away. "Spiro tells me," he said at last, "David never loves again."

The story weighed on Anna. But it was Max, lost in some sadness of his own, who really burdened her. She asked to sleep in the back seat.

* * *

A thunderclap awoke her. Wind was pelting trees. Rain slicked the road. The sky was dark as night, though her watch read only 3:00. They were winding along through hills. Ahead she saw a river. "The Nestos," Max said. "After, Thrace. Sleep well, Anna?"

"I guess so."

Near Xanthi she saw mountains, likely the Rhodopes. The rain became wet snow that melted on the road. The towns they glimpsed recalled the ones in southern Serbia and Bulgaria. Whitewashed houses. Red-tiled roofs. Tall minarets against the sky. Already more Turkish than Greek. In Thrace, she knew, lived many Turks left over from the Ottoman Empire.

"North of here, near the border with Bulgaria," Max said, concentrating on the rain-obscured road, "it is a military zone. You need a permit to go in."

"Why?"

"Greeks say, Bulgars make trouble. Turkies say, this way Greeks keep Macedonians quiet. Keep people from seeing what happens to them."

"And what do you think?"

"Greece . . ." His smile twisted. ". . . is like Bulgaria. You know, in the US, Spiro meets Greek refugees. Mostly Macedonian Slav. From Solun. Kukuš. Other places where they cannot keep their ways or speak their language. Greeks call them Red spies. Maybe now is worse. Since the Junta last year, the Colonels run the country. Fascists, like before."

Solun. Kukuš. With these names Max showed his loyalty to Spiro's cause. She'd read that Thessaloniki, Solun to Spiro and his men, had once contained the largest Jewish community in Europe, nearly eighty thousand in 1900. But of the fifty thousand living there in 1941, only a handful had survived the Holocaust.

And once, after Kosta had mentioned Kukuš, she'd asked Spiro, "What's that?"

"Until the Second Balkan War it was a Slav Macedonian town. In 1913 the Greeks attacked. The people fled. The Greeks burned it. Left nothing. Today . . ." Spiro's voice had become a whisper. "It is Kilkis, a Greek village."

She wondered what had made her draw Max back to this topic. Suddenly her brain was full of Spiro. Voices buzzed inside her head. Spiro's. Kosta's. David's. She was so tired.

The highway veered southeast again. The land flattened, though she still saw cliffs. Not far beyond the small port town of Porto Lagos, Max stopped at a taverna by the road. The bag-bellied host led them to a dark kitchen that smelled of herbs and garlic. He had them check the oven and each pot on the stove. Max chose *stifado,* brown beef chunks with pearl onions and string beans in tomato sauce. She picked a slice of spanakopita. Craved its creamy feta cheese, spinach, and onion center.

"We go soon," Max said as he sipped his red *domestika.* "The border is still far and it is nearly dark already. We must make Istanbul tonight."

The urgency in his last words made her wary. But she concentrated on the finely flaked filo and sipped the bottled water the waiter poured for her. Nodding first toward Max, then toward the window, where the rain beat a staccato rhythm on the glass, he said, "Romantic, yes?" His broad wink made her cringe. She saw Max blanch.

Picking at the last bits of filo, she watched Max eat, so proper, always so controlled. "Max," she said in a low voice, "do you do it for you or for them?"

His fork hung in midair. Head cocked, he studied her. "Why do you ask this, Anna?"

She shrugged.

He rubbed his jaw with his left hand, then gave a nod. "I start for me. When I go West, I know to mine, to steal. I have no schooling more than just to read and write . . ." He stopped. Lifted an onion with his fork. "How can I find work? Get money? To live?"

"And now?"

The fork entered his mouth. His jaw worked the food until it must have been reduced to liquid. At last he swallowed. "Still it is for me, but sometimes . . . it helps them."

Now she couldn't stop, had to ask about his former love. "And Eva?" His head jerked like a knee does when the doctor's mallet hits it. The rain was coming down hard, beating against the windows. "Max?"

"Spiro tells about her?"

"Yes." His piercing blue-eyed gaze made her feel naked.

"What do you want to know?"

"Would you have married her?"

He sat silent a moment. Kept his eyes on her. Then his lips pulled into a strange smile. He stood. Walked to the window nearest their table. His back to her, he watched the rain.

Soon he returned. Slid his lithe body into his chair. "She cannot marry with someone like me. A smuggler. A, a . . ."

"What do you mean, Max?"

"She . . . knows things. Wants to . . . understand things." He refilled his glass. "What can I give her?"

"Max . . ." She tried to calm her voice. "You asked her, didn't you?"

"There is . . ." he swigged the wine, ". . . a boy. In England. Someone she grows up with. A student at the university. Like her. Also a Jew."

"Did she say she loved him?"

"When she speaks of him, I know that for her I am not—"

The naked pain as he wrestled with his identity made her wince. If only she could help him see what he could give, who he might be, what he already was. And everything he'd done for others, even as he'd put himself at risk. "You never asked, did you?" she heard herself whisper.

He dropped his glance. Lowered his head. Murmured "No" into his empty plate.

They sat without speaking until he said, "We must go now." The host brought them a large carton that Max held over them like an umbrella. But the dash to the Mercedes soaked them anyway.

Inside the car she shivered. "Don't worry," Max said, shivering too. "The heater will warm us." Slowed by the rain, they traveled northeast, past a sign that read "Komotini." The steady squish-squish of the windshield wipers marked their journey.

"More mountains," she observed.

"The Rhodopes again," Max said, holding the wheel with both hands.

"Am I mad, or do we just keep making loops?"

"Maybe someday . . ." he chuckled softly, "they will build a straighter road."

As if she hadn't figured out by now that he was taking care to hide their tracks, to shake off anyone who might be watching them.

Staring through the windshield, he said, "Anna, look. Down there."

Following his eyes, she saw nothing but night. Rain and the busy wipers blocked her vision. "What?"

"Look harder."

She stared and stared, until from the liquid dark emerged a twinkle in the distance far below. "I see it. Yes." It glimmered like a star against the black that was now everywhere. "What is it, Max?"

"The lighthouse in the bay. Off Alexandroupoli."

Alexandroupoli. An Aegean port from which tourists embarked for Samothraki. She'd loved that island since eighth grade, after she'd researched the Winged Victory. At the Louvre, in another life only four months ago, she'd stumbled on the statue. Atop a wide marble staircase, its surfaces alive, its splendid curves like a ship's prow against the rectangular base, it seemed poised to take flight.

By the time they'd descended the mountains, drawn near the port and veered away again, the rain had stopped. Deep black surrounded them. Max watched the road as if he thought it might vanish. Past Feres he pulled over. Turned himself to face her. "We cross the border at Kipi. Greeks also make trouble now. Not just Turkies." His lips curled up slightly.

An image flashed, of Mladen and the arrogant Greek border guards.

"Remember when we cross into Bulgaria? You play the hitchhiker? This time, too, you will ride in back." He fumbled underneath the seat for something. Handed her a pouch. "Turkish liras. If they take me, you will need them." As always, he was ready with the local currency.

"Are you expecting problems, then?"

"This place is not like the border between Serbia and Bulgaria. More people. More police. And soon the Turkies celebrate Republic Day. Maybe there will be the army, too. So . . ." he smoothed his right thumb with his middle finger, "remember who I am. Okay?"

"Yes, Ernst."

Soon they came to a bridge that spanned the Evros River. Halfway across stood sentries. Max whispered, "The middle of the bridge—that is the border. If we get through the Greeks, the Turkie frontier is on the other side."

The Greek guard took some time with their passports. Made a cursory check of the Mercedes. Smiled at Anna in the back, where she had no trouble acting exhausted. Then he passed them through.

As Max had predicted, a knot of people clustered on the Turkish side. Ahead stood four soldiers. On the left, two armed border guards. To the right, what looked like several high-ranking officers, huge men with close-cropped hair and medaled chests. The tallest one, his eyebrows dark and bushy, recalled photos she'd seen of Atatürk, among Greek Macedonia's most influential exports.

The guards flagged down the Mercedes. As Max rolled to a stop between the two groups, closer to the guards, Anna willed her breaths to slow and tried to project calm. Max sat still as the men traded loud words.

"How's your Turkish?" she whispered from the back.

He shook his head. "Keep calm. They will not hurt you."

Given the stories she'd heard, she wasn't sure. Turkey was especially tough on smugglers. She and Max would make a fine display to showcase Western decadence.

The guards signaled them through, but an officer waved them to the right. He ambled toward the Mercedes and signaled for Max to open the window. "You go there," he ordered, pointing to the crowd of uniforms. She could barely breathe. The only weapon in the car was Max's charm.

Max inched the Mercedes forward toward the officers and stopped. Another giant leaned his head inside the open window. "Nice car." He tapped the shiny black fender. "You go Istanbul?"

"Yes. Lovely city." Max's tone, obliging, made her smile.

"General Eroglu . . ." The man pointed to his taller colleague. "He need ride. Keşan."

"Of course," Max said. "Plenty room." He wasted no time unlocking the front door.

The generals spoke in rapid Turkish, ending their barrage with "*Inşallah*," God willing. Entering the Mercedes, their newest passenger barked, "Keşan." His tight smile let them know how grateful he thought they should be.

And so they drove along the road to Istanbul. The General occupied his own space, sitting ramrod straight, silent, ignoring them. He asked no names, as if they were too lowly for such gestures. Max might have been his chauffeur, she some concubine of whom he'd grown weary. But the border had been crossed, and they were safe.

She rolled herself into a loose ball in the back and began to reflect. She'd come into Bulgaria with Max, with Mladen into Greece, and now, as they appeared set to make Istanbul at last, it was Ernst and General Eroglu. With each passage she'd changed. She'd left Serbia for adventure, Bulgaria for safety and the chance to heal, but as Greece receded, she felt strong and determined. Ready for the chance to probe the mystery of Spiro.

So be it. Max, cat-like, had many lives. She didn't think he'd used up all nine yet.

EINE KLEINE NACHTMUSIK

Max had stopped to change money at the airport, or so he'd said. Even in the dim light of the parking lot, she'd seen something at work beneath the surface of his smooth features and guessed that all had not gone well. But she'd climbed inside the Mercedes and let her head fall back against the seat. It had been another long day.

A bump jostled her face against the window, waking her.

Deep night. Rainy. Cold. An old section, its houses low, a narrow cobbled street. Few lights. The only noise the car's engine. A briny smell. Salt tang. She glanced over at Max, who seemed lost in his own world. They wound along until the road came to an end on a narrow outcropping of rock. Far below, black water slapped against a shore she couldn't see. The Golden Horn? The Bosphorus? Marmara? A few glimmers of light made fuzzy circles in the wet dark.

Max drove onto an oval ringed with boulders. Small cars lined the space. "Come," he whispered, once he'd parked the Mercedes. He took her hand and led her down stone steps embedded into the incline. At the bottom stood a line of two-story stone houses. He guided her to one whose front window was streaming light. The sound of lapping water came from nearby. Max pulled her gently to his side, put his arm around her waist, and pushed open the door.

She saw a narrow room. To the right, a bar and a door. Against the left wall, simple wooden tables. At the back, an upright piano and a second door. Her ears picked up the scratchy strains of some chamber ensemble. She couldn't see the radio. It had to be behind the bar.

A heavy man, his flannel shirt hugging his thick torso, poured amber ale into the stein of a fellow on a bar stool, whose gray-blond, thinning hair hung in his eyes. Max let go a burst of rapid German. Emerging from behind the counter, the bartender embraced him and shook Anna's hand. "Welcome. I am Hugo." His fat-lipped smile puffed out his cheeks.

After they had greeted one another, Max sat her at a table near the bar. "Anna," he said, leaning over, whispering, "Hugo will take care of you until I am back." She sighed. More business to conduct.

Glancing around the room, she saw no women. Four men sat at a table drinking beer, chatting, their voices low. Six, including Hugo and the blond man on the bar stool. All middle-aged, tired, thick-jowled, wearing heavy jackets over flannel shirts. The music on the radio, spare but lush—was it Schubert?—didn't match the scene.

Though she'd asked for nothing, Hugo brought a steaming cup of tea and a small biscuit. "Here," he said. "You must eat. You are a skinny little bird." He winked. "But pretty."

She trembled at those words, so like the ones Spiro had spoken that first day in Mihajlov. But she managed a smile and thanked him.

As she sipped the tea, under the dim light in the room, her eyes found the piano. She felt a sudden wave of intense longing. Her fingers stirred. She rose. Walked to the battered instrument, its keys yellowed, its surface marred by cigarette burns. A stool, a tattered leather seat. She eased herself down. Faced the keyboard. Pushed back the old panic—from when her father would insist that she perform for visitors. Let her eyes adjust to the weak light in the dark corner. Then her hands reached out, became wings spread above the ivories. Though her mind said, "No," her fingers made contact. Found the tone surprisingly good, the action firm.

First a Bach prelude. Slow. Full of intricate tonalities. Fingers. Wrists. Forearms. All working. Shaping lines. Rising. Cresting. Ebbing. Like the act of love itself. Then its fugue. Notes dancing, playful. Fluid short tones over the sustaining base. Then it, too, dances, flirting with the treble. A heavy chord makes an uneasy space, withholding resolution till, when all seems lost, it falls away into a soothing peace.

The keys light up somehow. She sees clearly. The first chord of a Chopin prelude. Number Four. In the instant of its life she steels herself against what follows, those slow, repeated harmonies that sing the pain of love and loss. Then her fingers reach into her core, pull out her deepest knowledge. Add it to the tonal elegy Chopin created as he loved George Sand and began to die on Majorca. Her foot pedals the last chord till it fades away to nothing.

Hot tears cascade down her cheeks. A nocturne. Soft, melodious. A hymn to the velvet night. Then restless fingers move to a mazurka. Its staggered rhythm, alternating light and dark, brings her back to Mihajlov. The circle that pulsated on *Ilinden*.

She breathes deeply. Her work-calloused fingertips have power. They animate the keys.

Her hands are ready now for Beethoven. What should she pick? The *Tempest*? The *Appassionata*? No. The *Pathétique*. Those first stern, brooding chords. Then release of passion, energy. Notes tumble, surge. Her fingers fly. The keys lay bare her heart, speak all her grief and hope, conjuring the life she lived with Spiro. And from these tones Spiro rises. The space around her fills with the scent of apricot and garlic. With the texture of lost love.

Beneath her fingers notes whirl, toppling over one another. The melancholy builds into a storm, rampages, carrying her into herself so far that—

A loud clatter. Her hands in mid-descent, she stops. Remembers where she is. Turns on the stool.

Utter silence. People have formed a half-circle around the piano. One man holds a candelabra. Another reaches to the floor for his. Its flames have gone out. Candle wax is everywhere. The man stops. Cradles his right hand. Hugo stands beside a smock-clad woman who wipes her face on her apron. The beer-drinker. Two others. Against the wall, his eyes staring, his mouth open, stands Max.

"I'm so sorry," she said, having understood at last what happened here. She saw that they had brought light. The candles had burned down too far, singeing the man's fingers, and he'd let go. She gestured toward him as he raised the fallen holder.

"No stop," Hugo said. "Please, Miss. You play more."

"*Ya*," the beer-drinker agreed, a wet track on his cheek. "*Mehr*."

Hands moved together. Clapping filled the room. But Anna could play no more. With the final note she'd lost Spiro again.

Her arms ached and her head hurt. It was so late.

Max came to her. Let his arm support her. He said, "This I . . . I do not know . . ." His eyes were moist. He shook his head. "So beautiful." He pulled her to her feet and steadied her. "Come with me. Hugo has something for us in the back."

She followed him through the door near the piano, past a kitchen, to a room that held a sofa and a low table. He helped her sit, then handed her an envelope. His face drawn from exhaustion, his lips making the semblance of a grin, he said, "Hugo—he is another mailbox."

The large manila envelope lay in her lap. On the front was written, Anna Svetkova, in Latin letters formed with care. She turned it over, saw the red wax seal, and looked at Max. "How did it come?"

"To me from Yugoslavia. It goes by Slavko first, in Štip. He sends it to Hugo. Safer that way now."

"And . . ." she hardly dared to ask, "nothing from my family?"

His head shook. "Bulgars find my mailbox in the Majestic."

Her hand flew to her mouth. Was that because of something she'd revealed to her inquisitors?

"The next day after Spiro dies . . . a Belgrade contact comes to the hotel. To leave something for me. He sees the concierge give two men what is in my box."

"So if a letter came, the DS would have taken it?"

"Let's see." He calculated. "Your letter, how we send it, takes time to reach America. To send back takes more time. The second week of September . . . yes, they maybe take it."

She pictured some DS agent reading her parents' response. Then she realized they would have heard nothing from her since early August. How much she'd made them suffer, though she'd never intended it. But she would make it right soon. Would tell them everything. For a moment she imagined their joy to learn they would be grandparents, Mimi an aunt.

Then, with trembling fingers, she broke the heavy seal on the envelope. Inside she found a thick book bound in black leather. Her heart raced as she freed it from its paper covering. Placing her palms over it, she could see an old man writing on a white page. She looked for the inscriptions— *Živko, Dimko, Marija*. Then: *August 21, 1968 Spiridon Dimitrovski Svetkov y Anna*

Rebecca Svetkova. Her fingers tingled as she traced the sharp Cyrillic letters, as if they contained the spirits of those they invoked.

Resting the book on her lap, she sat still, dazed, until Max said, "Look. Something is there, in back." She opened the book to the back cover. Inside were two photos in black and white. She and Spiro in their wedding outfits, underneath a branch of David's pear tree. Another, blurred, of two old men and a young couple. Lifting the first photograph, she stared down at Spiro, his hand entwined in hers, his hair framing his face, his intense eyes gentled by love. She willed herself into the scene, that hot, dry afternoon, the stark sandstone formations . . .

She must have sat for some time before Max patted her shoulder. He handed her a sheet of white paper and whispered, "This comes out when you pick up the pictures."

It was hard to read the letters, written in a shaky hand not easy with the Latin shapes. As if the author had copied them, then written them again to get them right. Even this last draft contained a few words exed out with black pen, and she could not decipher what replaced them.

My dear Anna,

*If you read this, you * * * alive. I keep Marija's Bible and these * * * for your * * * visit. This morning they take David. I think they come soon for me. I send these by * * * so you and the child have some * * * of Spiro."*

Anna shut her eyes. Recalled the old men toasting her at dinner, dancing with her, first one, then the other, to the muffled music on the radio. To think of them now, dead, or suffering somewhere . . . She forced herself to finish.

*That you go to Spiro shows * * * strength. Live well, Anna. Know how he loved you and why. Because you are strong and you are yourself.*

*My * * * for you and the child*

The signature was freer, in Cyrillic. Trifon's name.

Was she strong? Was she herself? What had he meant? She could not check the tears. Max eased himself down next to her, clasped her to his chest, and let her weep into his blue sweater.

At three a.m. they entered a hotel in Beyoğlu, near Taksim Square. Max signed the ledger, ordered two rooms, carried up their bags, and kissed her on the right cheek as they stood before her door. "Istanbul, Anna," he said. And though his eyes could hardly stay open, he found a smile for her. "Sleep well. Tomorrow will be busy too."

LEANDER'S TOWER

A knock. A pause. Some shuffling at the door. Then, "Time to wake up, Anna." She heard him try to make his voice sound light. "Meet me in the dining room. You need breakfast." A pause. "And dress warm. It is cool outside."

It didn't take her long to bathe and get ready. She chose the black skirt Max had bought, the matching turtleneck, and the rose sweater. Looking in the mirror almost made her cry. A haggard face stared back, with pasty skin and red-veined eyes. At least her bruises were now barely visible.

From her Indian bag she pulled the tube of mauve lipstick, untouched since her wedding day. Her hand shook as she traced her lips. Though she had always wished them fuller, Spiro had loved their shape. "Small," he used to say, "but delicate and sweet, like ripe plums from our tree." A rosy mouth now smiled into the mirror. The simple act had armed her for the day ahead.

Was this how one got through the pain of living? With ordinary acts transformed by loss to magic rituals that brought past into present?

The hotel served good pastries and coffee. But Max made her nervous. His dark-circled eyes wandered the room. Between bites of her croissant, she said, "I want to wire my parents. Let them know I'm okay." Last night she had decided this. The time difference, the cost. Too much to say, to feel. She didn't trust the telephone. She needed to prepare herself, and them.

Max said, "As soon as we leave the hotel."

While he retrieved the Mercedes, she waited inside the front door. Several minutes later, a small, tan, bug-like car pulled up and honked. She ignored it till she heard, "Anna." Then she turned her head and saw Max leave the driver's seat. He walked her to the car, a Peugeot with French license plates. Once settled in, she asked, "Where's the Mercedes?"

"Gone," he muttered, his cheek muscles tensing.

Something must have happened; she'd sensed it even last night, at the airport. If, like Spiro, he chose to keep it from her, she wouldn't press him further.

A few blocks later, Max pulled over. "Here, Anna. A PTT." He waited while she ran inside the post office to send the wire. It said only, "I love you. Everything is fine," and gave the hotel address. At least she'd written them from Mihajlov, so they knew that she'd been happy. But if they'd answered, and she was sure they had, how much they must have suffered at her silence.

After she had paid the few *kuruş*, she felt relief, then pain. As if the act of sending word had reopened a barely healed abrasion.

"Mees, you okay?" the blondish man behind the desk asked her.

"Yes, thank you. Do you say . . . *Teşekkür?*"

"We do, yes." He gave a broad smile. "*Allah'a ismarladik.*"

Did that mean, "Go with God?" If so, it seemed a charming way to say good-bye.

From the door she saw Max waiting in the car. What prompted his devotion? Spiro? Eva? Some code he'd taken for himself? As she reached the curb, picturing her parents' relief to know she lived, remembering Spiro's marriage vow, tallying the debt she owed to Max for all his kindness, a wave of love seared her.

The sky hung low over Beyoğlu. Gray clouds touched the rooftops. A breeze blew from the northeast, from the Black Sea. Anna absorbed Istanbul. It was all she had imagined, a marvelous hybrid of old and new, of East and West. Except that in her fantasies the sun had lit a clear, blue sky and she had been exuberant.

Cars and humans clogged these narrow streets. Down the block, a blond woman in European finery lunged past a tattered urchin whose brass tray held a silver urn and one small cup. A man dressed like a peasant from a century ago shined shoes for someone in a tailored suit whose leather attaché case rested on a faded Turkish rug. As traffic stopped the Peugeot, a pair of legs staggered along the sidewalk; a huge sack hid the body's head and back.

She'd read that Beyoğlu was where the Europeans lived and where the fancy hotels were. Taksim Square, its center, was noted for its elegance. A suburb of the Old City, this section had sprung up in the last century. But its Western traces seemed only a facade, like the iron grillwork on the shops that lined the cobbled streets. Some Eastern idea of the West that didn't fit the sights and smells, the bodies and the faces that crowded these sidewalks.

Suddenly the city pushed in on itself. They must have entered Karaköy, the section by the water, near Galata Bridge. Old buildings abutted one another on steep streets that shrank until their tiny car could barely fit. Scents mingled in the cold air. The sharp, sweet smell of coffee houses, pungent odors from food stands, the stink of rotting produce, the salt tang of the Bosphorus and Marmara.

Even on this day that threatened rain, clothes hung over streets on lines that ran from roof to roof, window to window. Carcasses of fish, old vegetables, and coffee grounds cluttered the cobbles. Waifs with dark curls and enormous eyes ran wild. Men slouched on corners, smoke rings rising from below their mustaches, or sat in tearoom windows, smoking water pipes and moving tiles on boards. "*Tavla.* Tric-trac," Max said. He must have read her mind. "Backgammon. Turkies love it, like they love their *narghile.*"

"So many men." She remembered when she used to take the train into New York. Of how, nearing the city, she would see dark men in tee-shirts hanging out tenement windows, or silhouetted in their lonely rooms, nursing bottles and smoking cigarettes. "Are there no jobs?"

Max shrugged. "Many come from the country. What do they know? Like me, when I come from the East. So hard . . ."

She tried to picture him among these unkempt men in winter rags.

At last Max parked the car in front of an imposing stone building. He said, "Wait here, Anna. I will be quick." Then he climbed the steps and disappeared inside the large black door.

She watched gray billows rolling fast along the sky until she heard the door open again. Beside Max on the landing stood a man with the body of a boxer gone to seed. He beckoned her. "Come, Madame. I have nice room. All special, only for you and my friend Max."

His accent sounded French. She waited for a cue from Max, who said, "Kind of you, Henri. But we have an appointment."

The men shook hands. Then Henri went back inside and Max came down the steps. He drove off, silent, his face a mask.

She wasn't going to ask him questions now. Instead, she tried to take in their surroundings. Soon they left constricted streets for broader, tree-lined boulevards that ran past grand homes and mosques. They followed a café-lined street north along the Bosphorus. To the right, ahead, she saw a sprawling, two-tiered marble wedding cake she recognized from photos. "It's that Palace, Dolma . . . Max, are we doing a tour?"

"We are, yes. It is the Dolmabahçe. You like it?"

"It's . . . gaudy." She paused. "Oh, Max. I have no heart for sightseeing."

"It helps to forget some troubles, yes?"

Maybe Max was right. Distraction might be good. To focus on her surroundings would keep her from the buzzing in her brain. "You win. Today I'll be a tourist."

"Good." He chuckled. "Gaudy? Even more, inside. Everything too much. Still, it impresses. The guy who does the Paris Opera designs it."

"When?"

"The eighteen-fifties. A German does the Gardens, and the harem-room." He winked at her. "All European tile. From Italy, I think."

The irony made sense for this fantastic bridge between Europe and Asia.

The sky had lightened briefly while the sun fought to break through. Across the water she could see the Asian side, where charming, several-story wooden houses lined the shore. Soon they passed a lovely park.

"Rumelihisari," Max said. "Byzantines, they make it to guard the Bosphorus. The Turkies take it right after they finish." His laugh was not warm.

They pulled into a nearly empty parking lot. "What day is it?" she asked.

"October 24th."

"No, Max." His knit brows told her his thoughts had been elsewhere. "I mean, what day of the week?"

"Ah, sorry. Thursday."

A nasty weekday, off-season. No wonder so few were here.

On each of two adjoining hills stood a tower; a third rose at the water's edge. A thick, ridged wall connected them. Inside she glimpsed the stone staircase that ran its length, like that Escher where the stairs went in impossible directions. She'd never seen so vast a fortress so intact. "Shall we climb it, Anna? To the top?"

"Yes." She let him help her, take her hand. They entered by the lowest tower. The climb was hard but beautiful. The wall smelled of its centuries, as if it had stored time. Once they reached the tallest point, she studied the large expanse within the fortress. A bit like Kalemegdan. A stadium. A maze of stone walkways. A mosque and minaret. Below them lay the Bosphorus, a cold gray under this bleak sky. Boats of all kinds filled it, from tiny fishing skiffs to ferries and barges. And across the water stood another tower. "Max, what's that?"

"The Andaluhisari. Poor, crazy Byzantines. They build one for the Asian side and one for the European. The Turkies take both. Just here is the shortest way across the Bosphorus. The towers guard . . ." he pointed north ". . . the opening to the Black Sea."

Then, like a child, she stepped into the space between the top ridges and leaned herself out, careful of her footing. She let the wind blow through her hair. Spread her arms out like an eagle. It felt so liberating—as if she could cast off her old selves and become a new person.

Two hands grabbed her. "You are crazy, Anna." She fell against him. Instantly they recoiled from one another.

"Before, how you are standing," Max said, his poise regained, "you look like that statue . . ."

Still tingling from his touch, she moved away from him. "What—?"

"In the Louvre. Is it the . . . *Victory with Wings?*"

Her mouth fell open. How had he seen so far into her?

"Come, Anna. We will sit. Rest. Watch the water."

He walked her from the wall down to the stadium. They found a stone bench. Lost in swirling thoughts, she felt his hand take hers. She let it stay, but the gesture made her nervous. "Max, you don't seem quite yourself today."

His eyebrows arched. "Myself?"

That laugh again. Self-mocking. Wry. She searched his face. His almond eyes, beneath those knit brows, drooped. "What's wrong? Can't you tell me?" She yearned to touch those creases near his eyes, around his mouth. To show how much she cared. But that would only . . . what?

"I . . . well . . ." He tried to smile but swallowed hard instead. "I must leave soon." He looked away from her, out at the water.

"Leave?" A flutter in her stomach.

"Even, maybe, tomorrow. Before—"

"Max?" Her voice rose sharply.

"Do not be afraid." He sighed. Lifted up her hand. Gave it a light kiss.

Where his lips had touched, the skin prickled. A dangerous sensation from a world she thought she'd left far behind. She went rigid. So many feelings all at once.

"Forgive me, Anna." Head bowed, he dropped her hand and inched away from her. They sat silent a while, not touching. Then he rose, brushed off his jeans, and helped her stand. "Let's go," he said with forced enthusiasm. "A bit more to distract you."

* * *

The clouds had wandered off and left a sky of blue-gray patchwork. They crossed Galata Bridge into Beyazit, the Old City. Looking toward the far side, Anna spotted the great domed mosques whose minarets impaled the sky.

Max took her first to Topkapi, but she had no patience for endless rooms of jewels and eastern finery. Then to Ayasofya. Despite Ottoman ownership, its Christian source was present in the massive nave and artwork filled with Christ and his disciples—those haunted Eastern faces like the ones she'd seen in Sofia, in the Alexander Nevski.

Only the Blue Mosque made her feel peaceful. The intricate carvings in walls and ceilings, the endless variations of blue tile, the myriad windows. Even without sun, the light shown through with such beauty. She reveled in the vast calm of the empty vault above her. No Christ, Mary, or Emperors. Just pure geometries in tints of blue, ivory, and gold.

It seemed a sacrilege to leave the mosques for the bazaar. But Max wanted to make sure she ate something. Munching *şiš kebap,* they watched the throngs pass by as she purchased presents for her family: a shawl for her mother, a pipe for her father, and beautiful earrings for Mimi. As they left, Max bargained for a small, light suitcase. Once he'd settled on the price with the shop-owner, he said, "Your things will fit better now."

She was tired, but Max hadn't finished his tour. He headed west along the Golden Horn, a narrow channel separating Beyoğlu from the Old City, to Eyup, whose sacred mosque was among the holiest in Islam, or so she'd read. Beneath an arched walkway, vendors displayed their wares. Pigeons filled the walled courtyard and an empty stork's nest lay atop a minaret. The mosque itself was white, except for blue prayer rugs and a blue mosaic border on the inner walls. Edging it were ancient graveyards strewn with tombstones like the ones she'd seen in Serbia. Max pointed to a broken rose carved on one slim pillar. "Look, Anna. For a young girl."

Though Max was a good guide, he seemed distracted. Now and then he made some quip or offered some background. But mostly he was subdued. Amid the wonder of this place, his distance troubled her.

As night fell, it grew colder. She had to will her legs to move. Her lower belly ached. "Enough," Max said. "We eat in Pyer Loti."

"Where?"

"A teahouse close by. Some French writer spends time there once."

"Do you mean . . . Pierre Loti?"

He shrugged. "You know these things, Anna."

The look he gave was soft, gentle . . . loving. She felt her cheeks flush suddenly.

They ate pilaf and drank tea at the café. From there they had an enchanting view of the Old City, the Golden Horn, Karaköy, and Beyoğlu. Her head swam from exhaustion and the splendor of this multi-faceted jewel.

At last Max stood. "So late. Sorry."

The drive back was another kind of magic. Floating clouds hid a pale moon whose ghostly light made minarets and domes shimmer like phantasms. As they recrossed Galata Bridge, she noticed a beam on the water off the Asian side. "What's that?"

"Leander's Tower. You know the story?"

"I thought it was the Dardanelles."

A shrug. "About this I am not sure."

Hero and Leander. Each night they shared their secret love when he swam the Hellespont. Until the day when Hero found Leander's drowned body washed up against her island tower. Her heart broken, she threw herself into the sea. Anna thought of Byron's line—"Leander swam for Love, and I for Glory." Why had he mocked those poor lovers, or used their tragedy to mock himself? She glanced at Max, and then, exhausted, began to weep again. The world had lost so many lovers, unnoticed, unmourned. Leander had his tower. But what of Spiro?

She stopped her tears. For, after all, she'd chosen life. The child would be his tower.

* * *

It was late when they reached the hotel. Max walked them past the desk to check for mail. The clerk on duty said, "The young lady has something in her box." Having withdrawn it, he handed her a telegram.

"You will read it now?" Max said.

"I'd rather wait a bit." He nodded as she stuffed it into her bag.

Max left her at her door, kissed her cheek, and stroked her hair. "Tomorrow," he said, "I wake you for breakfast."

She undressed, took a long, hot shower, and climbed beneath the covers. Only then did she reach for the telegram on the bedside table. Holding it, she shook. It read—"*We love you very much, Annie. Come home.*"

A HERO OF OUR TIME

The radiator hissed and gurgled, but the room was cold. Restless, Anna pulled the covers tighter. The day had brought too much. The city was so palpable a feast, and darkness had ambushed her with a torrent of emotions. She worried for her parents, imagined their feelings now, what questions they must have. And Max. How would their winding journey end? She prayed for sleep. Tomorrow would come quickly . . .

She spirals downward in the swirling current. They follow just behind. The ones she does not know. The faceless ones, forever in pursuit.

A log. She grabs hold. Lets it carry her to shore.

A bloodied foot protrudes from under a large bush. She stumbles toward it. Kneels beside a mound covered in brush. A falcon shrieks, "Spiro." Something, someone, whispers, "Anna." She hears gunshots and slips behind a boulder. Lying face down in the sand, a body.

She knows about bodies. About the good eye and the bloodied one that does not see. The holes pierced in soft flesh. The flies. The stench. But this new one, torn, twisted, wearing baggy pants and purple sash. She knows it from another dream. How did it find its way here? Is this a dream if she can ask that question?

Before, he spoke German. Directed men with guns. She hid behind a rock like this. Longed to touch his face.

The shore recedes. She finds herself in a mountain glen, a body in the dirt, streaked red.

She inches toward it. Turns it over, shocked at her own strength. No face. A red hole filled with shreds of ivory and gray tissue. One eye, blue-brown, dangles from its socket. The child speaks from her belly. "Daddy—?"

A knock. She strains to hear. Another knock. She claws through layers of consciousness toward waking. Finds herself sweat-bathed despite the cold, the smell of rotting flesh still in her nostrils. Forcing back the bile that rises in her throat, she tries to remain calm. Tells herself that this is only a bad dream . . .

"Anna." Then where was she? "Anna." The low voice lingered like an organ point. Was that Mikis behind the door?

The dream vanished. Her head cleared. This was Istanbul. Mikis was a memory from Washington. Spiro was almost two months dead. The man chanting her name had to be Max. Shivering, she dragged herself from the bed, grabbed the still-damp towel off the floor, and wrapped it around her, fashioning a makeshift knot between her breasts. Then she tiptoed to the door. From somewhere came the scent of musk.

After she had pulled the chain from its round hole and pushed the lock above it to the right, she turned the handle and opened the door. The words she'd been practicing froze on her lips. Hunched against the right side of the doorjamb, his arm supporting him against the other, his head drooping from his bent neck, Max filled up her doorway. Had the bullet from her dream caught him? His eyes, dark in the dim light of the hall, begged for admission. She stepped aside. He entered, circumspect, as if danger lurked in the silent hotel corridor. She pulled the towel tighter.

"Anna." He took a step toward her. Held out his arm. Let it fall, as if uncertain what he wanted it to do. The draped window let in a crack of moonlight. Its pale beam struck his face. His hair was still dark blond, but his irises were brown. For an instant she saw him as on that first day. Those high cheekbones that made her think him Slavic, the dark eyes, barely slanted, the strong but narrow jaw. His stories flooded back to her. The war, the missing father, the dirt-poor mining town near the Czech border, the flight, jail, Kosta, Spiro . . . Eva. Somewhere in the depths of those dark eyes was the real Max.

He raised his right arm once more. Stroked her cheek, the smooth skin of his hand so unlike Spiro's. His fingers played with her long hair. She felt tears push into her eyes. Had she not wept enough?

"Sorry, Anna, I . . ." His voice cracked.

"It's okay, Max." They'd been heading toward this moment from the first. A force had joined them, then pushed them apart. What she felt for him now, wasn't it a kind of love? "I understand."

Like a cripple, he dragged himself to the bed. Took off his clothes with slow movements, as if in pain. At first she bowed her head. This was too close, too intimate. Then she forced herself to look. Fine muscles marked his narrow frame. Beneath his moon-paled skin, she could see each rib outlined. He looked so vulnerable. This time she did reach out her hand to trace the lines around his mouth. But catching her fingers, he brought them to his lips.

She sat beside him on the bed, still wearing the towel. As he undid its casual knot, she flinched.

"Anna." He hesitated. "Is it—"

"Oh, Max. I . . ." The towel had fallen to the bed. He buried his face in her breasts, tasted her skin. When she touched his shoulder, his whole body shook. He pulled away and took a few slow breaths.

She told herself that this was Max—her friend, her confidant, her benefactor. And he needed her now. But didn't she need him as well? And was it right or wrong? She didn't know. Somewhere in a shallow grave lay Spiro, his flesh rotting. By now the DS agents were interrogating someone else, and . . .

His smooth hand wiped the tears that wet her cheeks. "Anna, please. I'm sorry." He bowed his head.

She heard him swallow, saw his eyes shut tight. Then she stretched out on the bed, under the sheet.

Seated on the edge, he took her hand and whispered, "Please. Forgive me . . ."

Who was he asking? Her? Spiro? Eva?

She watched the slim curve of his back, the way his head set on his neck beneath its shock of hair. He made no sound or movement for some time. Then he sighed and slid in next to her. He took her in his arms. Gave her hard kisses. His lips on hers were hot. Against her will, she felt pleasure. But in the dark she found those men who'd hurt her. And there was Spiro, too. That she, pregnant, her husband dead, her body raped, could feel desire— what had she become? Or was this what living meant? Her body still alive. Her feeling for this man, here, now, a vital force.

Max laid his hands on her belly. "Spiro's baby," he said, his voice awe-filled. His eyebrows knit. Her fingers on his lips stopped him from saying more. He moved away from her.

Reaching for his hand, she said, "I understand. You loved him too. It's hard . . ."

He drew closer, pulled her to him, touched her belly, buttocks, thighs. More kisses.

Then she began to kiss him back. Soon she felt him hard against her thigh, his chest pounding on hers. But when he kissed her there, below the belly, something inside her broke, like the string of a viola in the middle of a piece. After all, her body belonged to Spiro and their child.

Max didn't seem to notice her withdrawal. And since she longed to show him that she cared for him, she kept her eyelids shut. Her hand explored the smooth skin of his back. She returned his kisses.

Soon he started moaning. "Anna." Little kisses. Harder ones. His breaths came faster. He was panting now. "Anna," he moaned again, raising himself above her.

Memories engulfed her. Swept her far from him to arms holding her down. A massive engorged member. Searing pain. But then . . . the soft touch on her body of rough skin. The pebbled feel of Spiro's back. The joy—

"Ev—Anna?"

She heard it as a wrenching groan. "Max?" He'd stopped his motion. "What . . .?" She hadn't meant to ask, to force something from him.

For a moment more he held his body over her, supported on his arms. Then he arched back with a muffled sound, and lowered himself next to her. The room grew hushed. His low sobs filled the dark. After all, the bed had been too crowded.

* * *

His back to her, he faced the window far too long. The girl she once had been would have enjoyed seeing the powerful reduced to impotence. But she was not that girl, and this was Max, whose pain now humbled her. Reaching out to him, she gathered him to her as if he were a sick bird, careful not to jar hurt wings.

Their bodies lay still, heavy. She monitored his breathing, wanting to be sure he had not somehow died of sorrow or of shame. The silence suffocated her.

At last she felt his hands stroking her hair.

"So, Anna."

Where she touched his face, the skin was wet.

"You see me, what I am." A hollow laugh. "Nothing."

What could she say? What words could soothe? The truth? "How else could it have ended, with Spiro and Eva both here?" She felt no need to mention her captors.

As he ran his fingers down her cheek, he nodded. "You are changed, Anna."

"Maybe we shouldn't talk now," she said, stopping his hand.

"No, I am sorry. I must say something."

She watched as he stared at the ceiling, tried to find himself again.

"Before, you are a . . . a girl. Charming, yes. Maybe, fascinating. Also, too proud." He patted her arm. "But now you are a woman. And somehow . . . wise."

Her turn to laugh. "Wise? I don't think that word fits me. Maybe . . . lost?"

He shook his head. "You think so, but it is not true. You are different."

"How?"

"It's like you are . . . somewhere. Before, you want to get there. Now . . ." Another of his wry laughs. "You see how I am poor at words."

"It's Spiro," she said. Strange for him to think that she had gotten anywhere, when she had no idea where she was going. How could he have missed this, when he so often got her right?

"Maybe. Or maybe it is in you already . . ."

She waited. He'd seemed about to say more. But when no words came, she asked, "What about Eva?"

He nodded as if he'd understood her question. "She dies before she has herself."

"And us?"

"What do you mean?" He propped himself up on the pillow, stared into her face, then repositioned her so that her head lay on his shoulder.

"I couldn't tell, that first day . . ." she traced his mouth with her fingers, "what you wanted from me. Did you know?"

"Yes." He stroked her hair. "I know, but I do not think it works. You are like Eva, but you want . . . more." He craned his neck toward the window. "So I take you with me to Mihajlov. The town, the people. Something special. Kosta. Ljuba." A long pause. "Spiro."

And for his kindness he had lost her to his best friend. "Did you hate us?"

His face was still as he considered this. "At first, yes. But even then, I see it." He breathed in, let the air out as if it burned his insides. "Spiro is honest, straight. He . . . how do you say . . . makes peace with himself, the different bits. You know?"

She saw that he had understood.

"You were so close to him," she said. "Why didn't you learn—"

Another dry snigger at his own expense. "Spiro is a good teacher."

He'd pulled the words right from her mind.

"But I am no student. I am . . . nothing."

"Damn it." She pinched his arm, not quite in jest. "Why do you keep repeating that?"

"Because it is true." He rubbed where she had hurt him, then laughed again, shaking his head. "Besides to play these crazy games, Anna, what can I do? I know nothing, like these Turkies—"

"Max, you know life, people, places, how to give—"

"Someday, Anna . . ." he found her eyes and held them with his own, "you will see me in the newspapers. Big shooting. Dead. What else can be for me?" He rose. Paced to the window, his graceful body glowing in the thin sliver of moonlight. "For this, tonight, I am sorry." He seemed to labor for his words. "I know before I come here, I am wrong to push you. But I . . ." Opening the drapes still more, he stared into the night.

"Wrong?" She pulled herself up in the bed. "No, Max. It had to be. We were unfinished."

He came back. Sat against the headboard next to her. "So Anna . . ." She let him take her hand. "I never trust Frenchie." He looked down into her face. "But now, after this morning, I am sure. He works with the police." His body grew tense as he spoke. "I leave tomorrow morning. On the train . . ."

"Max." This time the truth hit hard. She nestled into him. If only she could keep him with her, in this bed, forever. He made her feel secure.

"You cannot stay here. Frenchie sees you with me. If they come for questions—"

"Please, Max. Can we stop now? No more talking?" She needed to absorb his news. This once she wished he smoked. She longed to have a cigarette, a prop to occupy her hand. They were so naked here. "Could we lie here together, maybe sleep? I'm so tired."

"If it pleases you, Anna." He gave her eyebrows a light kiss, then dropped onto the pillow, took a deep breath, and squeezed her arm as she lay in the crook of his. The silence was no longer tense. She kissed his wrist. He patted her shoulder.

* * *

She was close to sleep when she remembered Spiro that first night. Sitting on the couch, speaking of Max. Beside her now, Max lay quiet. But though he seemed asleep, his chest rising and falling in an even rhythm, he was staring at the ceiling. "Max," she whispered.

"Yes."

"You're still awake?"

"As you see, Anna."

"There is this thing I meant to ask."

"I am listening."

"Spiro once mentioned . . . you two shared something. He never got to tell me what. Will you?"

He bent his chin down, turned to her, and kissed her cheek. "Sleep. You dig too deep, Anna."

"It's one piece I don't have. Please help me now."

He sighed and rubbed his chin with his forefinger. "Alright, if it means so much to you."

Was she prepared for what he might reveal?

"But you must see. Anna, we are younger then. Without patience. Like the young men in Spiro's group." His hand played with her hair. "It is so easy when you think . . . that guns and knives can change things."

"Can't they?"

"Yes." He nodded. "But not the way you want."

"Then tell me how, Max. Please."

"It happens in 1959, after Marija dies." He shook his head. "Nearly ten years already. Life goes fast."

"Yes."

"It is a bad time for Spiro and his . . . our . . . people."

She'd never heard Max own that shared background before.

He filled his lungs. Exhaled. "Does Spiro ever mention the *Goryani?*"

"Not to me."

"This is what their enemies call them—it means, the forest people. The group starts when the Reds win, in '44. They go to the forest, the mountains—like the *četas* in the old days—small bands fighting power. They make contacts in towns and cities, too, many in the south who want the same end. The government destroys them. Some, like Spiro, remember. They try to . . . to help people in danger."

Lying still, he paused, she guessed to let her take this in. She saw that it made sense. Once an organization had existed, and some still chose to keep its aims alive. Like Spiro and his men, with Kosta, Donka, and Max as liaisons, linked to others elsewhere . . . the guard inside her prison, and Mladen.

"Spiro makes his little group. To teach their history. To help the village people. Police take some old man away, the grandfather of a student. Spiro tries to find what happens. But he learns nothing."

The muscles in Max's face—his mouth, his eyes—made small movements. Watching him, she knew that he was focusing, evaluating, searching for the words to tell the story. "And then?"

"The father of another student disappears. Police take him to jail for stealing—like Ljuba's husband, isn't it? He dies. A young man, only thirty. They say . . . he has a heart attack. But he is one big bruise."

His words carried her back to Mihajlov. Those faces. All the mournful songs. Kosta's funeral. Spiro's body on the metal table.

"Just this time Spiro asks me . . . can I get guns? In case something will happen."

She saw Spiro that last night. The darkness in his eyes.

"I am young. Stupid. So I say yes. Why not? I bring, somehow, a box of rifles through customs."

"You didn't worry that you might get caught?"

"No. I think only how to do it, like a game. Anyway, the guns are old and lousy. Something just to shoot. We climb to *Sina gora.*" He straightened his legs.

"To store them?"

"Yes."

Another iteration of the same dark history.

"We hear something. Behind us, then in front. Two men with guns. Police. They catch us—how do you say—red-handed." He chuckled at his youthful arrogance. "Spiro signals me. I take the closest. He is big, but I am quick. My hands go around his neck, then in his eyes. He screams. Then I hear shots. I wonder, am I dead? Is Spiro? But I feel nothing. Maybe, I think, in the dark they miss their target." He cleared his throat. Stayed silent for a while. "We are still on the ground. Four arms, four legs. Like one body. Then his arms go loose. They slide away." He sighed. "I look up. Spiro holds a knife. It drips blood on my shirt."

She saw the scene as if it were unfolding there, in the hotel room. Recalled the gleaming metal in the white cloth Spiro took from the armoire. The only thing she couldn't guess was what Spiro had felt when he had used it. To cut the thread of those men's lives. To kill that way. Close. Intimate. But the opposite of making love.

Max ended his tale without her asking. "Now to hide the bodies. We find another cave and take them there. Spiro throws a rock down a big opening. We wait long till it makes a sound. We know, then, it is safe."

"You threw them down a shaft?" Like the old stories.

"We did."

"And nothing more happened?"

"The next morning I leave. But Spiro says later it is in all the papers. Blagoevgrad. Sofia. About the men who disappear. Police come. Then Security. Ask questions. Bring in Spiro many times. Others, too. But in the end they find nothing."

"Were they suspicious all these years? Was that why they beat him so terribly?" She felt Max wince. Of course, he'd never known the full details of Spiro's death.

"Maybe, Anna." He shrugged. "But these men beat who they want, how they want. They do not need suspicions."

She wondered where the silver-handled knife had gone. He'd never put it back in the armoire. Had he carried it on that last trek? She felt compelled to ask, "Did it hurt him?"

"You mean, to kill?"

"Yes, Max."

He seemed to crawl inward, to find the reel of memory that offered up an answer. "We say nothing the whole way down the mountain. Then Spiro tells me, 'Now we have guns. But we must think hard before we use them. The cost is great.' After, he is different."

He swallowed and kissed her hair. "It is almost morning. Can you sleep now, Anna? Or does this make it harder?"

"No, Max. You've helped me see."

They pulled the covers over them and huddled underneath. Lying on his back, awake, he nestled her on his chest. Her right hand held his left, and with his right he touched her hair with even strokes until she found her eyes heavy, her lids drooping . . .

CHOICES

A beam of weak light entered through the open drapes. Anna rubbed her eyes, reached out her arm to Max. But she was by herself in bed.

Seconds later Max emerged from the bathroom. Already dressed in jacket and jeans, he was toweling his face dry. She saw that he had brought his case into her room and placed it by the dresser. Unaware that she no longer slept, he hung the towel on the doorknob and stood before the mirror. From the bed she saw his elbows, high, moving, his hands working at something there. "What are you doing, Max?"

He turned around. "At last you are awake," he said, his voice tender. He pointed to the window with a smile. "Look. The sun tries to find us." Taking something from the dresser top, he went back to his task before the mirror.

"What is it? Are you hurt?" She felt her heart pump faster.

"Not to worry, Anna. It is just . . . I have to match my papers, yes?"

"Yes, Ma—Ernst." She heard him chuckle.

When he turned again, she found no traces of the anguish he had shown last night. He stood smiling, blond, blue-eyed, strong jawed, lean in his scruffy jeans and weathered jacket, smelling of musk and almond. The lenses in. The mask secure.

He came to the bed. Bent his head to kiss her cheek. "It is time, Anna. I will pack and pay the bill. Can you be ready in an hour?"

"Yes." And so the end had come. The last morning.

From the open door, he said, "Maybe you will wear the blue dress? It is lovely with your eyes."

His glance stung her. If only she could take him in her arms again and comfort him. "You really have to leave?"

"Yes."

"Will you be safe?" She couldn't bear to think of him as she had seen him in her dream or in the visions his words last night had conjured.

He shrugged. "Who knows? But . . ."

There it was again, the light smile she knew well.

"I am good at these games, Anna."

He left, shutting the door without a sound.

⁕ ⁕ ⁕

After she had bathed and dressed, she transferred her belongings from the canvas bag to the suitcase Max had purchased in the Grand Bazaar. The military cloak went first, cushioning the bottom. Then the old Hebrew prayer book. Beside it Trifon's package, with Marija's Bible, the photos, and the letter. The winter clothes from Max hid those sacred papers.

Only the red Easter egg remained. She planned to wedge it in among the heavy garments near the top. As she picked it up, her palm tingled. A strange vibration heightened all her senses. She smelled the barest trace of apricot and garlic. While the feeling lasted, she stood still. Then she pushed the egg into the folds of the rose sweater.

During breakfast they said little. Max made no attempt to find his customary smile, and despite the Viennese coffee, she couldn't quite wake up. Her croissant nearly finished, Max produced a guidebook of the city. "Here. In Munich I have more. You take it now."

She wanted no more sightseeing, but to please Max she put it in her bag.

Then he lay a packet on the table. "This, too." As she reached to take it, his hand covered hers. "Enough *lira* to stay a week. To eat. To buy a ticket where you want."

"But—"

"When you finish, we will go again to Beyazit."

She gazed into his face, wanting to memorize it.

Lost in thought, Max sat oblivious. He didn't notice the older woman at a nearby table, blond, stunning in an elegant suit and chic high heels, whom Anna caught staring at him. Did she simply find him attractive or was she some sort of spy?

Soon he paid the waiter and walked her to the Peugeot with their suitcases.

As they crossed Galata Bridge, the spikes and circles of the great mosques loomed against the eastern sky. But this time Max drove toward the university. On a bustling street he pulled over before a low gray building, apparently the girls' hostel he'd found. The large, warm lobby held a few tables and well-stuffed chairs. A sign on the front desk announced in Turkish, French, and English—"No men past this point." Setting down her suitcase, Max paid the blushing clerk too well. Then, glancing at his watch, knitting his brows, he beckoned Anna outside.

Another cold, gray day. Clouds had banished the weak sun and a wind blew from the north. His head cocked, Max examined her as she stood on the sidewalk. "Here are only girls," he said. "You will be safe from Turkies."

His mouth curved upward in that little smile, making those creases she loved.

"In the envelope, I write where I live. Also Slavko. Hugo. You can find me, if you need." He took her hand. Pressed it against his cheek. "If you . . ." His jaw hardened. His lids fluttered.

She grasped his left hand. Her fingers entwined in his, she prayed that he would have the confidence to speak the missing words.

"I . . . I will keep you and the child, if you will want," he said at last, bowing his head.

He had asked. He had found the courage. Her arms circled his neck. She couldn't help her tears. It didn't matter that the passersby were staring. She whispered in his ear, "I'll miss you, Max."

Even through his thick jacket, she felt his body shaking. He replaced her arms at her sides. With his hands he cupped her chin. Then he kissed her one last time. She tasted love, hope, pain.

"You will be okay, Anna. You are now strong."

The wind lifted his words and swirled them down the sidewalk like dead leaves. He swallowed hard and stuffed his hands into his jean pockets. Stepping back from her, he stood quiet and let his eyes stay on her face. Then he turned away and with bowed head began to walk toward the corner.

Halfway down the block, he spun around. She hadn't stirred from the spot. His mouth opened. Then he shook his head, blew her a kiss, and took off once again. Her eyes burned as she watched him vanish in the crowd, absorbed into the dream of Istanbul.

* * *

As she lay on her narrow bed, she recalled that this was Friday, in the last week of October. Four months since Spiro and she had conceived the child.

She began to retrace her path here. She'd been glad to flee America's chaos—the outpourings of hatred and the violence they provoked. Then Trieste, and Claudia's note. Alone in southern Europe, she'd feared obliteration of the fragile self she'd brought with her, unmoored, aimless, about to self-destruct. Like Kit in that Bowles novel.

But even then she'd found herself yearning for something more, something she had only glimpsed, could not yet name. So she'd gone with Peter, the seasoned drifter sealed off from the world through which he traveled. But that had led her to Max, who'd grasped her need, become her guide, and sacrificed his own feelings for her, and for Spiro, his friend.

Oh, Spiro. Your love unlocked my frozen heart. You opened me—to myself and to the world, in all its joys and suffering. So beautiful. And so . . .

She had to stop. Couldn't risk revisiting Mihajlov, Spiro, her prison days. She needed all her strength.

And so at last she'd gone with Max to Istanbul, where not even four-star hotels in the European enclave could protect her from the fierce heart of the city. Its soul, heaving with raw life, seeped through every crack, refiguring the myths of East and West. And in himself Max fused and countered both.

She'd hoped to nap. Decisions loomed. But her mind couldn't relax. Too many thoughts swirling inside. She might as well get up and face the day. Max's guidebook sat on the bureau, a paper in one of its pages. Opening it there, she saw an entry circled in red ink. She brought the book to the bedside chair and started skimming it. "The Ahrida. The oldest functioning synagogue in Istanbul. Built by Jews from Ohrid, in 1460." Reading on, she learned that Ohrid, Macedonia, once the center of the Eastern Church, belonged first to Bulgaria, then to the Ottoman Turks.

1460. She calculated. These Jews had come after the Serbs lost *Kosovo Polje* in 1389 but before the Sephardim left Spain en masse in 1492. Defeated Christians. Displaced Jews. Empire. Exile. Her mind buzzing with all the strange connections, she rose, splashed water on her face, and grabbed her coat and bag.

On the front desk in the lobby stood a large phone book. She found the listing. Asked the clerk, the one who'd blushed speaking to Max, where Vodina Cadessi was.

"Balat, near the water," the cheerful, pudding-faced young woman said. "A big walk. You take *dolmuş*, Miss. Near Eyup. You know?"

"Yes. I've been there. Lovely."

"But you must be careful. Too many mans." The way she looked at Anna, her eyes patient but curious, suggested that because she knew this place so well, she would do her best to look after the charming fellow's American friend.

"Thank you," Anna said.

She dashed outside and stopped a *dolmuş*, a sort of communal taxi. Adding hers to the bodies wedged close together, she told the driver, "Balat, *lutfen*. Ahrida." She didn't know the Turkish word for synagogue.

"Ah," he said. "Ahrida. Temple."

"*Evet, teşekkür.*" She moved her head from side to side, but the driver's eyes remained on the street ahead.

The clerk had been right; she was alone among men. In shabby clothes, unshaven, they recalled the ones she'd glimpsed on the train to Grand Central and around the station when she rode to Central Park East for her piano lessons.

All those drawn, dark faces. Once she would have viewed these men as predators. Now she felt no fear. Each seemed a wondrous mystery, his own rich world, with singular insights and blind spots, hates and loves, sorrows and joys, desires—

"Mees, temple. See?" The driver pointed out a well-kept building on the opposite side of the street. She paid him. With veiled eyes and quick nods, the men made way for her.

KADDISH

Anna crossed the street lined with low buildings and ancient walls, some bearing Stars of David. A plaque in Hebrew hung above the entrance to the synagogue. She opened its elaborate door and entered. The hall was empty. Sabbath wouldn't come till dusk.

At either end, a staircase led to the women's galleries. She knew the sanctuary was a space reserved for men. But since it was too early for a service, she thought that it would do no harm to enter.

How beautiful and quiet was the place, its high-domed ceiling lit by a chandelier suspended from the center like a huge crystal teardrop. Above, the women's gallery, its wooden banister a gleaming fence to keep them from distracting men at prayer. She once scorned that Orthodox tradition. But in this vaulted room she tried to picture all the women, sitting with their heads covered, praying, swapping recipes and good, or bad, advice. A vision came of Ljuba with her bees, feeding chickens, baking bread. Doling out a few coins for the children. Scolding Kosta for misplacing a scissors or a knife. All with dimpled smiles despite her widow's pain.

For months Anna had traveled in a world of men. The coffee and tea houses, the buses, cars, and taxis. But she'd been with women too. Had become a Balkan wife. She knew that in the home they held the power. Within that precious space, the men deferred to them. Below the empty gallery, she felt one with the women who'd once filled it and those who might come later that evening.

She lowered her gaze. Took in the sanctuary. On three sides were the wooden pews for men. But in the center what looked like a ship's prow extended out into the room. Long and curved, higher in front, graceful. The guidebook referred to *bima*, a word she didn't know. She guessed it meant pulpit. According to the text, the boat-like shape invoked both Noah's Ark and the ships sent by Sultan Beyazid II to gather Spanish Jews in 1492 and bring them to their new home, where Muslim Turks would guard them from the hate of Europe's Christians. She stared at this unusual but fitting sign for sanctuary, imagining the stream of Jews who'd prayed here through the centuries. By what ties was a people bound to its culture? How had she lost hers? Or had she cut the link herself? And if so, why?

Her belly seemed leaden. She felt unsteady. But she wasn't yet ready to leave. She sat in one of the men's pews and absorbed the beauty of the space. Her head played back the chants at Yom Kippur, among the most vivid memories from her childhood in their small Jewish community.

Resting there, almost entranced, listening to internal melodies, she thought somehow of Schoenberg, whose music she'd never liked—too cerebral for her taste. But she'd come to love the man in his letters— especially one written after he'd fled to France in 1933, when his German world was collapsing. To whom was it addressed? Webern or Berg? No matter. It had moved her when she'd read it last year. Severed from his Jewish roots, born from generations of converts, Schoenberg had finally seen that being a Jew wasn't merely a matter of religion. Witnessing, experiencing, his people's fate, he'd understood that he was Jewish, too, even without practicing that faith. She couldn't recall exactly what he'd written. Something like*, And so last Saturday, in a small Parisian synagogue, I made official what has been true all along.* Not only had he named himself the Jew he'd always been. By writing to his friend, he'd made it public.

She shivered in the empty space. All her years of self-loathing, of shrinking from the gaze of those whose eyes perceived as they'd been taught, of yearning to cast off this painful, conflicted identity—rooted not in land but in culture. Like Schoenberg, she would name herself what she'd always been—a Jew. With pride. As Spiro had wanted. To reconcile the paradoxes, the cruel ambivalences imposed from outside and within. To embrace the long history of suffering. Not to celebrate, or glorify, or feel superior. But to link herself to those who had accepted their identities and lived them, or died because of them, aware. Like Spiro and that piece of Max that still linked him to Spiro's group.

And the child in her belly? How rich its legacies. Its parents mirror images, oleos of suffering ethnicities. Irish Catholics, Ukrainian and Romanian Jews, Orthodox Macedonians, Serbs, and Greeks.

She heard internal music. Plaintive Irish ballads. Tragic lullabies of long-dead Eastern European Jews, in the Yiddish that was dying out as they had. Those hero songs in minor keys the villagers had sung on *Ilinden*.

The coldness of the sanctuary ate into her bones.

As the haunting strains began to coalesce, she thought, *oppression breeds oppression*. This was hardest to digest. Israel, the IRA, VMRO. Serbs, Greeks, and Bulgarians in the Balkan Wars and after. "An eye for an eye." "Fight for freedom." "Might makes right." The old sword story. Spiro had faced it head-on when he and Max first killed. Had understood its full meaning the night before his death. He'd paid with his life for the lives he once took. But what of the rest?

In that welcoming space, she thought of the victims everywhere who answered with the sword. For whom love sanctioned violence. Yet one couldn't be other than what one was. That seemed the greatest paradox. Family. Tribe. Religion. Culture. Nation. Even to renounce those ties asserted their great power. They marked and molded one . . . like the forces that shaped Spiro's stone.

The light from the chandelier began to glare, or were her eyes tearing? Would Max someday embrace with love his German and his Serbo-Macedonian selves? Until he could accept them, with their weaknesses and strengths, their muddled histories and all the stereotypes applied to them, he would wear his mask and hate himself.

Beneath shut lids her eyes felt hot and scratchy, ready for the cleansing power of tears—the release Spiro had bequeathed her. As she tried to calm herself, to let the soft power of the place flow into her, she saw a parade of faces. All the men and women she'd encountered. Limited by circumstance. Living in pain. Waking each day to dead ends. Yet trying to give and take joy, to be kind. Could she somehow help them? There would be so much to learn.

A rush of warmth, the sense of an embrace, stopped her from shivering. She half expected to look up and see a falcon flying in a meadow red with poppies. A wave of sweet grief surged through her as she recalled the passion Spiro brought to all he did, despite the weight he carried every day. He'd wagered his life to ease his people's pain. She would love their child and work to help repair their world. In this way she would honor him. Each dawn would bring another chance to share his legacy—the love that filled her now.

Music and dance would always bring her pleasure. Her fingers itched to feel the keys again, to shape beauty from grief. Her body would move again to twisting rhythms. But she, like Spiro, needed work that filled her life with meaning, to lead her from herself into the world. She wanted to act, to help make real change.

Her eyes still shut, she pictured an open book and pages dense with words. A tool . . . for what? Civil rights? Refugees? No need now for clarity. A single mother with a child, she would face setbacks. But she would manage somehow.

A sudden image came from the Wisconsin years when she was young. Men in fringed shawls bobbed their heads, chanting the Kaddish, the Mourner's Prayer. Her father, who knew something of the culture and religion—even if he cared little for what he called those 'stiff necks'—had said that since the dead could no longer sing this praise to God, their mourners had to do it for them.

So it was with Spiro. Could she . . .?

She strained. Tore at her memory. At last she found "*Yit-gadal v'yit-kadash s'mey raba.*" As the words faded away, she felt a pang of guilt. She didn't even understand their meaning. She trembled in her wool coat.

Then she heard a distant melody from long ago, and with it ancient, alien words. She saw the visiting cantor pull each note from the deepest part of him, the dark ladder of tones baring the truth of what he was, sinner and man. Even at nine, she'd felt the naked power of that hymn. The *Avinu malkeinu*—"Our Father, Our King."

The empty sanctuary wouldn't care if she, untutored in her people's ways, should stumble through the fragments she recalled. So she began to hum, to find a register that she could hold. Settling on a note mid-range, she stood up straight and raised her head—

Avinu malkeinu / sh'ma kolenu. Avinu malkeinu / chatanu l'faneycha.

Her small, shaky contralto rose, then fell. The minor thirds resounded in the chamber. "Our Father, our King. Hear our Prayer. Our Father, our King. We have sinned before Thee." The words seemed just, begging God to hear the prayer of sinners. For everyone, everywhere, had sinned. Imperfect, only human, beings. She and her rapists. The guard who kept the egg for her. Ljuba. Kosta. Blagoj. Max. Even Spiro. But most of them with passion-filled hearts and a hunger, even if latent, for something larger than themselves.

Next came two identical musical phrases. Then a climb to the apex, dissolving to the first note of the chant—*Avinu malkeinu alkenu chamol aleynu/ V'al olaleynu v'tapenu.* "Our Father, Our King. Have mercy on us, and on our children."

Yes. Grant us your mercy. And for our children. Our child . . . Her mind wandered to her parents. Hurt children, they'd hurt their own. To fight was safer than to love without a shield. Yet she'd sensed their passion, fierce despite the pain and fear they bore inside. Reflecting now, she saw how love, in this form, too, could hurt.

What unintended wounds would she inflict upon her child?

She pondered the refrain—Our Father, our King. Her father had said it proved Freud right. The Jews were just a primitive tribe, yearning for a strong Father to govern them. But as she'd sung its lines aloud here, making those little tremolos so natural to chant, she'd felt a female presence in the Sanctuary. As if her tiny voice had called into this place an essence from the world beyond. As if God's mercy came not from a Father but a Mother spirit.

A fine Jew she was, making the religion fit her own ideal. But she could only think that any God worth singing to would fuse both male and female, and from that wholeness birth mercy and love—as she and Spiro had joined to conceive their child.

She glanced around the Sanctuary. Through her tears the space seemed draped in mist. So be it. Let Spiro, washed clean, enter the cosmos. Let his love live on in hers, and in their child, its fruit. Once again she heard her Uncle Matt repeat, "Life is a gift."

Her arms spread wide to embrace the anima. And Spiro, if he could come.

Now—

What was that?

A twinge. A sharp sensation beneath her ribs. She couldn't breathe. Her legs began to shake.

Was something wrong with the child? That heaviness she'd felt all day. What if . . .?

A thought began to take shape. But—

In her belly something fluttered. Undulated. Like a tiny fish moving through water. She gasped.

Another rippling movement. Slowly she unbuttoned her wool coat. Moved her hands inside, over her dress. Placed them on her belly. Barely breathing, she willed her legs, gone weak, to hold her weight. Then—

There. And there. And now . . . here! Beneath layers of wool and skin, the tiny creature wriggled in its watery ark. Though Spiro hadn't entered her embrace, she felt him close. And love was all around her suddenly. Through tears of joy, she hailed the pregnant emptiness:

Did you hear the words I sang for you, Spiro? You are atoned.
And our child is safe within my womb.
I pledge to wrap it in our love and raise it as wisely as I know how.
Forgive me for the errors I will make,
And bless our child, who has today begun the dance of life.

POSTLUDE

MUNICH

May 19, 1969

Frau Bauer separates her tenant's mail into two piles. She likes things organized. Herr Heidl is on the road again. A traveling salesman's life is hard, though he seems to make a good living.

She does this service gladly, since he is a fine tenant. In his three years here with her, he has rarely asked for anything, has kept his flat in order, and has paid the rent on time despite his frequent trips. She has noticed, though, a change since fall. When he is here, he does not bring back all those, well, those young women. He listens to nice music now. Chopin, Bach, Beethoven. But he looks quite sad, poor boy, though he always manages a smile for her, and never fails to comment on the beauty of her garden.

Many bills. Some advertising flyers for the trash. A large postcard, on the front a Greek building. She picks it up, looks at the back. Dated April 22nd, it bears a Washington DC postmark. America? How does Herr Heidl know Americans?

She prides herself on maintaining her tenants' privacy. But this is just a postcard. What harm will it do? She brings it closer, so she can make out the English words—

Dear Max,

I will write soon. These days I'm busy. But I wanted you to know. On March 30th, Rachel Rossi Svetkova entered this world, with dark eyes and a head of jet-black hair. She only weighed six pounds, but she is healthy, thriving on her mother's milk. I want to ask, will you be Rachel's kum? And

maybe you could come to DC some time to visit your goddaughter and me.
Say you will.

Love,
Anna

A mystery. Frau Bauer has no idea what *kum* means and cannot think who this Anna might be. But maybe this will cheer the lad. With a shrug she lays the postcard on the stack she keeps for him.

AUTHOR'S NOTE

Winding through this novel are two issues that have been with us since long before 1968 and are still with us today: anti-Semitism and its corollary, the Holocaust, and the Macedonian Question. I'm confident readers are familiar with the former. Many, however, may be less familiar with – or even unaware of – the latter, though it has dominated Balkan politics since the late 19th century and played a significant role in the pan-European policy landscape as well.

Remember Philip of Macedon and his son, Alexander the Great? That was the heyday of Macedonian identity, power, and influence. Since then, the land and people that were once part of the Kingdom of Macedon have been overrun, subjugated, subdivided, and suppressed. First the Romans, then came the Ottoman Turks (1299-1922). The lands that were formerly Macedonia came to exist within parts of three more powerful entities: Serbia, Greece, and Bulgaria.

More recently, the nineteenth-century European idea of nationalism as an ethnically homogenous political entity rooted in a common history and culture spurred the unification of Germany and Italy but also fueled the suppressed desire for such identity in the Balkans. For the Macedonians, this took the form of an anti-Turkish movement called the Internal Macedonian Revolutionary Organization (IMRO – VMRO in the Macedonian language). But even within the IMRO, there was debate about what really defined a Macedonian; some linked their roots to the ancient kingdom, others identified with Bulgaria.

Things got worse in the early 20th century. *Ilinden*, the IMRO's major push against the Turks, established the Kruševo Republic, which was soon brutally quashed by the Turks, resulting in a Macedonian diaspora to Bulgaria and other parts of Europe. The First and Second Balkan wars each ended with a treaty that divided Macedonian territory to no one's satisfaction. Serbia's part was called Vardar, Bulgaria's Pirin, and Greece's Aegean, and each of those countries set about "re-educating" its ethnic Macedonians. Max's uncle Ljuben left Vardar to escape its program of Serbianisation and keep his Macedonian identity.

The Western powers, meanwhile, hovered behind the scenes, trying to preserve a political balance that would benefit them. Spiro held them responsible for accepting the partition of Macedonia, and many today in the Balkans blame the West for using them as pawns.

Post-World War I, IMRO-instigated violence continued in all three countries, even as the internal IMRO factions (fascist and communist-leaning) quarreled among themselves. Eventually, the organization came under the control of Ivan Mihajlov, a pro-Bulgarian fascist whose goal was to wrest Macedonian lands from Serbia and Greece. Mihajlov collaborated with fascist leaders in Italy, Hungary, and Croatia and directed the murders of many left-wing IMRO leaders and some important public figures, including the King of Yugoslavia. Mihajlov finally had to flee the Balkans for Italy, where he played an important role for the Macedonian nationalists in diaspora.

The end of World War II saw the creation of the Republic of Yugoslavia, which amalgamated many Balkan nation-states into what at first became a client republic of the Soviet Union. Vardar Macedonia was once again subsumed into a large entity. During the Cold War, Greece – which, with US aid, had avoided a Communist takeover – expelled all ethnic Macedonians and began a forced-assimilation campaign aimed at those who remained. The Communist leadership in Bulgaria at first declared everyone in Pirin to be part of an official Macedonian minority, no matter their actual heritage, but when Yugoslavia split with Moscow, Bulgaria reversed course and declared everyone living within its borders to be Bulgarian. From the early 1960's, those who identified as Macedonian, like Spiro and his village, were surveilled and sometimes persecuted. So while Mihajlov is an imagined village, such places may well have existed.

When the Soviet Union collapsed, Yugoslavia broke apart. Vardar initially became the independent state of Macedonia. But the regional dispute over who can claim to be Macedonian still festers. Greece, insisting that Macedonia is Greek, forced the new republic to rename itself. The eventual compromise of "North Macedonia," intended to facilitate admission to the EU and NATO, angered nationalists in both countries.

Even today, neither Greece nor Bulgaria recognizes the Macedonian identity or language. Both assure the world that all their citizens are happy Bulgarians or Greeks. Despite criticism from international human rights groups, Bulgaria has banned a political party formed to ensure Macedonian rights and has prohibited public meetings of Macedonians, while in Greece, Macedonians fear using their language in public.

Recently, North Macedonia again felt the power of the West when France denied its bid for EU membership. Having failed to persuade Macron to change his position, Prime Minister Zoran Zaev declared, "Nationalism and radicalism can rise again. There is a risk to open conflicts inside of the countries again. Also to open conflicts between countries again."

For those who would like a more detailed account of Macedonian history and culture, I recommend Hugh Poulton's *Who Are the Macedonians?* (Indiana University Press, 1995), a relatively neutral analysis the non-scholar may find useful. While unbiased books and websites on this issue are tough to find, for the modern situation I would check out online articles by Human Rights Watch and Minority Rights Group International, as well as reportage from the BBC and the *New York Times*.

NOTE FROM THE AUTHOR

Dear Reader,

Given the reality of publishing today, a book's survival depends upon word-of-mouth and reviews. If you enjoyed *Anna's Dance*, please leave an online review, wherever you are able. Even a few lines can make a huge difference in the life of this book and will be greatly appreciated.

Thank you so much,

Michele Levy

ABOUT THE AUTHOR

Like Anna, Michele Levy was bewitched by Balkan dance in her early twenties and has been captivated by the Balkans ever since. She has traveled there several times and published on their literature, history, and culture. In this debut novel, Michele portrays the special beauty, vibrancy, and complexities of the land and its peoples. And she still delights in dancing to a sinuous rhythm and a strong drumbeat.

Thank you so much for reading one of our **Women's Fiction** novels.
If you enjoyed the experience, please check out our recommended
for your next great read!

City in a Forest by Ginger Pinholster

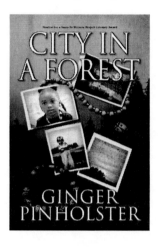

Finalist for a *Santa Fe Writers Project Literary Award*

"Ginger Pinholster, a master of significant detail, weaves her struggling
characters' pasts, present, and futures into a breathtaking,
beautiful novel in *City in a Forest*.
—IndieReader Approved

Made in United States
North Haven, CT
07 January 2022

14319057R00186